Revenge of Jesus

Release 1.2

by

Alexander Francis

Revenge of Jesus

Other Novels by Alexander Francis

Memory Gap

Are We A Band Yet

Mick Grundy…Spy Hunt

Mick Grundy…The Russian Connection

Mick Grundy…Elapid

Geminknot

Beware The Exit

The Green Scarf

The Copy Candidate

Since Antonius

Please visit afnovels.com for more information

"HERE, TOO, THE HONORABLE FINDS ITS DUE

AND THERE ARE TEARS FOR PASSING THINGS;

HERE, TOO, THINGS MORTAL TOUCH THE MIND."

— Virgil

"THIS NOW IS PLAIN ENOUGH, THAT ALL THESE CHIEF GODS WHICH I
HAVE MENTIONED HAVE A CHIEF EVIL CORRESPONDING TO THEM,
WHICH IS THEIR EXACT OPPOSITE. I NOW PUT IT TO YOU, WHOM
SHALL I FOLLOW? ONLY DO NOT LET ANYONE MAKE ME SO
IGNORANT AND ABSURD A REPLY AS, ANY ONE, PROVIDED ONLY
THAT YOU FOLLOW SOME ONE OR OTHER. NOTHING MORE
INCONSIDERATE CAN BE SAID."

— Marcus Tullius Cicero

Preface

The moment I opened my tenth grade Latin book and began to look at the photos of ancient Rome, I was hooked. Julius Caesar's elegant, succinct Latin was so different from English and I suddenly realized why so many of our public buildings as well as our money are embellished with latin phrases.

After much of my life was spent pursuing other pursuits, I sat down one morning wondering what it would be like to actually visit the past. The idea grew into this book and the subsequent sequel, written several years later.

Any book, even fictional ones, about this era have to take into account the religions prevalent at that time or any realism is lost. I endeavored to keep to the facts as much as recorded history allows and I realize that some will not feel I did justice to their faith or their beliefs and so I apologize humbly to them. But to me, this book is not about religion, but love, faithfulness and responsibility and I hope a reader will see it that way and not be offended where offense is not intended.

As necessary, this book liberally uses words from other languages. For the most part, the meaning will be obvious, but other times a translation is provided. But all languages have a beauty of their own and at times translation looses some grace as well as meaning. I learned a lot during the process of creating this novel and I hope you will gain something by reading it as well.

Alexander Francis

Table of Contents

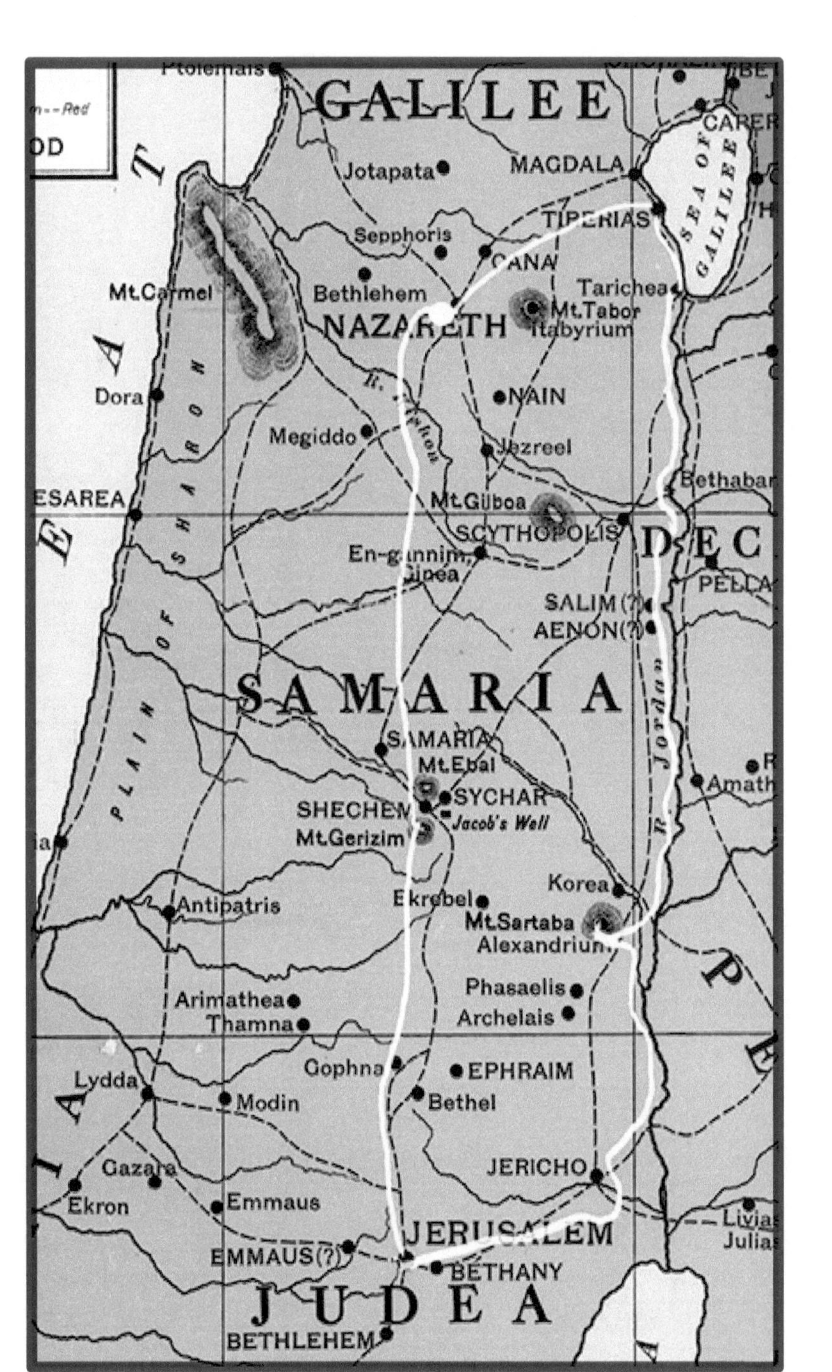

GALILEE
SAMARIA
JUDEA
SEA OF GALILEE
R. Jordan
PLAIN OF SHARON
Ptolemais
Jotapata
MAGDALA
TIPERIAS
CANA
Sepphoris
Tarichea
Bethlehem
NAZARETH
Mt.Tabor
Itabyrium
Mt.Carmel
NAIN
Dora
Jezreel
Megiddo
Bethabar
ESAREA
Mt.Gilboa
SCYTHOPOLIS
DEC
En-gannim
Gibea
PELLA
SALIM(?)
AENON(?)
SAMARIA
Mt.Ebal
SYCHAR
SHECHEM
Jacob's Well
Mt.Gerizim
Amath
Korea
Antipatris
Ekrebel
Mt.Sartaba
Alexandrium
Arimathea
Thamna
Phasaelis
Archelais
Gophna
EPHRAIM
Lydda
Modin
Bethel
PE
JERICHO
Gazara
Livias
Julias
Ekron
Emmaus
JERUSALEM
EMMAUS(?)
BETHANY
BETHLEHEM
CARER
m--Red
OD

Chapter 1

Riot In The Streets

Chicago Loop

A rain of rocks against the windows and repetitive chants from the street crowd made it difficult to conduct a normal conversation. The noise came in waves, as did the fear that crept into the room. Was the angry mob about to storm into the building or even set fire to it? No way to know until it happened. Captain McMurphy looked out of the window again, shaking his head at the sight, then pulling back quickly as a large stone just missed the glass, impacting the aluminum frame with startling violence. An immense weight of responsibility hung on him, pressing him downward and smothering his ability to think clearly. McMurphy was a man used to decisions---he could think in a linear fashion, as he was taught so many years ago, and that usually helped solve problems---but not this time. This was mass insanity. There was no reason, no logic, behind the actions of the crowd. Something was acting as an infection, passed by thoughts alone, and the result was beyond anything he had previously encountered.

"Must be over a hundred thousand down there, all of them insanely angry. How does he do it? How does one man have that kind of control?" He was speaking to no one in particular, but all present also nodded their wonder about those particular and pertinent questions. He looked again, this time farther away. "Looks like we'll get some rain shortly. Maybe that'll cool them down."

"Not likely," Rollins answered thoughtfully. "Not that bunch of fanatics. Want me to call the Governor again?" he asked.

"He's hiding from us. No way the State wants responsibility. You might have better luck calling China for help," McMurphy said and then returned to the table. Across from him was the pitiable wretch who was the source for the mob's anger. The multitude outside desperately wanted him and wanted him dead or alive. They all knew what would happen if the mob got their hands on this little insect, and it wasn't going to be pretty. Tony was wearing a dirty white undershirt, jeans and sneakers and smelled as though he had been sleeping in an outdoor toilet. The bald spot on the back of his head faced McMurphy, his face hidden in his hands in an act of despair, or was it prayer?

"Sit up straight, Tony, and tell me why Jesus and his adoring cult outside are about to tear our walls down and take you to your ultimate, and likely well-deserved, fate?"

"I tried to kill him."

"What? Who did you try to kill?"

"Jesus."

"Why?"

"I was paid to do it. Fifty thou, in advance. Only problem is that you can't kill him. No one bothered to tell me that. Now he's chasing me, him and his devotees. I can't get away from them, and coming in here was my last choice but only remaining hope." Tony started to cry, distorting his face and showing most of his dirty teeth, repelling the small team by his stark ugliness. All of his life he had thoughtlessly inflicted pain and suffering on others, and now, by some fate, it was his turn, and Tony was clearly not man enough to take it. Somewhere below was the sound of breaking glass, the yelling spiking louder, sending a shiver along the spine of the police officers and causing Tony to emit another of his self-pitying moans.

"Sounds like they are going to come in. Any orders, sir?" Rollins asked, his brow deeply furrowed. Rollins had advanced to the level of his incompetence, which was now shining through his perspiration. He started nervously tapping his ever-present pencil on the desk.

The Captain looked up sadly and wiped the top of his bald head with his hand. "Tell downstairs to shoot anyone entering by force and to keep shooting until they run out of ammo."

"It won't be enough," Rollings injected, his voice a full pitch higher. "When the same thing happened on the North Side, they just kept pouring in over the fallen bodies. If you want my advice, Captain, we should send Tony outside. It would save a lot of lives, perhaps even our own." He looked around as if to submit this suggestion for approval to the others present.

"Not until I understand what is going on. This may be our last chance to know. When Tony dies, what caused this dies with him." McMurphy turned his big frame toward their uninvited guest. " Now, Tony, talk and talk quickly and tell us why we should protect you."

"Captain?" Officer Schmidt said as he raised his hand like a first-year college student. "Could we conference before Tony tells his story? I have his file now, and it's a big one." The Captain reluctantly rose and motioned all to follow him.

"Sit tight, Tony. We'll be right back," Rollins said as he closed and locked the door behind him. Tony resumed his face in his hands posture and shrunk lower in his chair.

Schmidt arranged the papers in front of him and cleared his throat. "Tony Cardo is well-known to the Chicago Police Force, and his rap sheet is six pages worth. He was even an inmate at Joliet before it closed. Few convictions, but lots of charges over the years. He is a genuine bad boy. We won't lose anything of value if the mob outside tears him apart." He glanced furtively at Rollins to enlist his support.

"Why and how could he try and kill Jesus, and who is this Jesus anyhow?" Captain McMurphy demanded, slapping his hand on the surface of the table. His mind still carried the image of himself as a young, tough and fearsome officer, but the years of desk work, and, admittedly, too many doughnuts, made him something less than formidable. After his wife of twenty years called it quits and left for Florida, he had rapidly gone soft, existing mostly on fast food and beer. Retirement was starting to sound appealing and now this.

Rollins spoke first. "The man who calls himself Jesus appeared out of nowhere roughly two months ago and right away started collecting converts. He says that he is the actual Jesus come once again to "liberate" his people. At first, everyone laughed, but look down at the street right now, and you don't want to laugh any longer."

"I've heard all that before. Where did this guy come from? I was told that he couldn't speak English at first. What about that?" McMurphy asked.

"That seems to be true, but he learns very quickly. He has everyone intimidated because of his fanatic believers. It's like a wave of army ants, relentless and mindless. No matter what we might do, there is always more of them, and the flock grows daily. Where did he come from? Nothing that I have heard makes any sense. Several newsmen are referring to him as being *Levantine* in origin." Rollins said.

"What the hell is '*Levantine*'?" McMurphy snapped.

"It means from the Levant, a word which has come to mean the Holy Lands, all are now Arab except for Israel." Rollins said.

"May I interject something, Captain?" asked Schmidt.

"Speak."

"I interviewed Rabbi Steinberg and Bishop Malveccio last week, and I asked them for an opinion about this Jesus problem. They both had exactly the same response. This Jesus is not the real Jesus Christ, as he claims, but a pretender. They both said the same thing; he is smart and dangerous and has a hypnotic, messianic hold on nearly everyone who hears him. When he first arrived, he was speaking an archaic form of Arabic called Aramaic, also some Latin. Now he speaks excellent English. Neither one had any suggestions of how to stop him or even a guess as to what he actually wants. Their biggest fear is that he will be proclaimed as the second coming of Christ, and if that happens, we can expect exponential growth of his influence. Rabbi Steinberg said that the Synoptic Gospels would call the Chicago Jesus a *Pseudochristos*."

The chant of the crowd penetrated the concrete walls which seemed to vibrate with energy from the throng of angry people out in the street. "Gee-sus, Gee-sus, Gee-sus," over and over and over they shouted until a wave of nausea and fear gripped the insides of those in the building.

"We have to extract from Tony Cardo what he knows, and he doesn't have much time left," McMurphy said, and as he finished his sentence, they heard a collective shriek from somewhere distant along with more breaking glass. The building shuddered, and for a brief moment, there was silence. "It's coming," McMurphy needlessly said.

McMurphy's cell phone rang as they returned to the holding room containing Tony Cardo. He answered and held up his hand in a halt command, and the group stopped abruptly, waiting as he listened to his phone. "Thanks, I'll do that," he said and hung up.

"A large, private helicopter is landing on the roof, and they want to pick up Tony and anyone else who might want to go. Sounds like a plan to me. Round up your staff, and I'll get Tony and head for the pad," he commanded.

"What about all the others in this building. Do they just die?" Rollins asked.

"You can stay and be torn apart with them if it makes you happy, Rollins. Remember the proverb that says, 'Live to fight another day'? Your choice. Mine is to leave," McMurphy said.

The group crouched low as they approached the throbbing machine, its double rotors still spinning. It was large, dressed in flat, dark, nearly military grey. Before the group made it to the side door, it opened and a short man was tossed out, followed by a uniformed paramilitary soldier holding a short automatic weapon, who nimbly jumped into a crouch. The man curled up on the deck was remarkably similar in appearance and dress to Tony, who stood watching with gaped mouth. Wordlessly, the soldier picked the man to his feet and pressed the muzzle of his weapon into the man's neck for emphasis, herding him along toward the edge of the roof. Through the beats of the helicopter and the swell from the streets below, they could just make out the pleading sounds of the captive begging for mercy. Like a robot controlled by a computer, the soldier pushed and prodded the man closer and closer to the edge with jerky, remorseless pokes. As the man stepped up on the wide edge, he was spotted by the crowd below, and the roar intensified. He held his hands in the air to keep his balance against the coming storm and looked to the dark sky above in a last plead with a higher authority. With one tap of his gun barrel, the soldier pushed his captive backwards into the void and into the amoebic maw of the angry throng far below.

"That'll slow them down for a while, better get on board while you can," said a voice from over the helicopter's loudspeaker. A young woman was beckoning them from the open door while the soldier threateningly stood nearby, gun at the ready.

Chapter 2

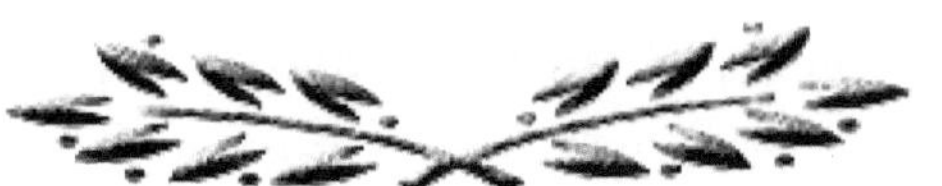

The Commission

Somewhere Over Lake Michigan

The chopping sound increased in intensity as their helicopter sat down lightly on the ferryboat deck which was bobbing on the low swells of the lake, out of sight of any shore. The helicopter rotors slowly spun down with a whining noise, with whump whump echoing from the steel deck as the long blades passed over and around. During the short flight, the group of twenty-five had been crammed into tight quarters. All of them thankful to have boarded the chopper while yet regretting leaving so many others stranded to face the expected surge of fanatics. When the helicopter door slid open, fresh cool air from the lake poured over the passengers as they emerged and rapidly were led below. They were expecting the usual rough, chipped painted metal and industrial decor common to car ferries but instead were surprised at the lushness and opulence of the interior. Congregating on the thick red carpet, the little group surveyed the main waiting room, talking in hushed tones. Double walnut doors swung open on the other side of the room, admitting a small but distinguished man who headed toward them. He carried with him a smug, overbearing quality, as if he could always be found on the winning side of things, an attitude complemented by his fine clothing, his groomed Van Dyke, and to complete *l'image parfaite*…a scarlet boutonniere.

"Ah, Captain, and of course your highly qualified staff, welcome to our new quarters. We are just getting it in shape, because, as you must know, our previous facility was burned and lost recently," the man said, speaking in heavily accented but smoothly delivered tones, as if he was taking them into his confidence.

"And who might you be?" Captain McMurphy inquired, his brow wrinkled.

"I am Raymone Chauncy Servierlo, chief consul for The Commission. You may call me Ray as does everyone here. Welcome to each, and you may all relax and be seated. Your quarters are below this deck, and I'm sure you will find that they exceed any expectations. Our waitstaff will assist each of you momentarily. Captain, if you and your senior staff will accompany me, we will get down to business." He shook hands with Captain McMurphy and his three deputy chiefs in turn as they made their way past the ornately carved walnut doors. In some distant recess, a powerful diesel motor started, lurching the ship into motion just as the first sheets of rain started hitting the sides of the ship and the circular portholes.

The room they entered was in the Baroque style with heavy carvings and lavish use of gold leaf. A long, massive, and ornate table, inlayed with exotic cuts of figured wood, stood in the center of the room. The surrounding chairs were similar and padded with thick red cushions. Recessed lighting illuminated pastel partitions of the ceiling, giving the room a rich, warm glow. Visible through the portholes, the grey water of Lake Michigan was being pushed into confusing white-tipped waves by the sudden wind gusts as had happened for endless time before men dared to venture out on the inland sea.

Ray motioned toward the head of the table, and the Captain and his team moved to stand behind their chairs, following the example of Ray on the other side. When they were motionless, waiting with forced humility, Ray nodded subtly and the other door opened. An elderly man emerged, assisted by the same young woman from the helicopter. The group watched with rapt attention as their host was seated, looking around expectantly and rather mechanically. There was an odor of history emanating from him, as if he were already part of it. He wore a plush wool suit, overstuffed in the shoulders, leaving the impression of a frail man wearing the clothing from a younger, more vibrant era of his life. Ray pulled his chair back, as did the others, and they all sat down at the same time.

"My name is Professor Gargan. I am acting head of The Commission, and I have been looking forward to meeting you." He spoke in Italian-accented English and appeared physically frail but mentally quick. As he spoke, a blue tortuous blood vessel, visible through the thin, transparent skin of his temporal area, pulsed with his heartbeat. "We are happy to have assisted your escape from certain death today," he said, smiling…or was it gloating…with satisfaction.

"Fine, and thanks, except you made us all witness to a murder. Do you think a policeman can ignore and forgive murder?" McMurphy asked, loudly emphasizing the last word.

"Oh, that," Gargan waved off the thought with a slight flick of his hand. "A necessary evil. A trade-off. Your lives for a hardened and convicted criminal. Worth it to you?"

"See here, Professor, we were glad to get away, but we are sworn to protect lives, even those who are on the bottom."

"I am told that, at this moment, the crowd bought the ruse and is dissipating. Our little stage play saved the lives of those in the station and those who would have attacked the station. All that in exchange for the life of one despicable criminal. There will be no further discussion on this. You are here at my discretion to discuss Jesus, and I'm afraid that when you hear how this started you may have a real reason to be angry. What we need to discuss is how to fix a problem which grows exponentially by the minute."

"Are we to infer that you know this Jesus and where he came from?"

"I'm afraid that I know the answer to only part of the question. Where he came from is easy. Who he is is not. Clearly he is not the Son Of God that he proclaims that he is, which is what excites his flock. What he actually is may be something that we don't understand, because we have no prior experience or not enough imagination. He is powerful, seemingly all knowing, and treacherous beyond anything we could have imagined. No human in history quite lives up to this man in ability. We have unleashed something on the world that cannot be easily undone."

"You said 'We'. Do you mean that your institution had a hand in this?" McMurphy asked gruffly.

"The answer is, unfortunately, yes."

"And are you ready to tell us the story?"

Gargan drew himself up straight and took a long drink of white wine, then carefully patted his lips with his linen napkin. "We have been working on a solution for the problems of mankind for over fifty years. There have been thousands consulted, and they were the best and brightest among us. The Commission is an assembly of eminent historians as well as others who study the past as well as the present. You can't study history without coming to the conclusion that sometimes things go the wrong way. Small events correct themselves over time but big, really big things, never do." He sighed and took another long draught of wine. "The question that has been posed is: can errors of the past be corrected…can an event which has happened be undone? Our study shows that, on occasion, a single individual is the spear point of change. Recall Adolph Hitler. How would history be different if he were never a powerful player? Some say better, some say worse. We thought bigger than Hitler. Much bigger. European and Western history is linked with religion. Intertwined and infected is a better descriptor. We studied and pondered what would have been the course of human events if religion was never there. Recall how advanced was the knowledge of the Greeks and Romans. Much of it lost for nearly two millennia. For fifty years, thousands of minds worked on the problem, and finally, this year, we reached a consensus. Keep in mind what it could mean. No collapse of the Roman Empire. No Spanish Inquisition. No quest to find gold in the New World to decorate churches and no Holy Crusade. How could all this come about? The answer seemed so simple. Jesus Christ could not be allowed to set things in motion. He would have to die and die young. The result? Stability, prosperity, and a chance for democracy to flow over the world from Rome and a continued advance of civilization from discoveries in science and industry. Galileo would not have been threatened with torture and imprisonment for simply rediscovering what the Romans and Greeks already knew." He paused to sip his wine and look around at the new faces with his watery eyes.

"Just a moment," Rollins interjected. "I'm no historian but religion has also been a force for good. We have a code of conduct and good behavior, thanks to our faith, and most churches work for the benefit of the poor. In the last two centuries, Western countries have not battled over religion but for land, trade and honor. That would still happen without religion. In my view, religion has soothed some rhetoric which could have led to war. Catholics helped bring down Poland and with it the Soviet Union. Where would we be without our faith?"

"Of course we would be changed, and change is unpredictable, and you would have to balance the good of such a thing against the bad. That is why it took so long to think it through. There is no question or point that you can raise that we haven't considered in depth. After a long, deep breath, we acted. Things didn't go as planned, to put it mildly, and your Chicago Jesus is the result. It's a very bad result," Gargan said, sagging visibly.

"Another question, Professor, before you collapse. Assuming that Jesus Christ...the real Jesus Christ...was the Son Of God, what made you think that you could kill him?" McMurphy asked.

"Simple. The Romans did. Easily, in fact. If they could do it, we could do it. Just earlier."

"This is ridiculous," Officer Schmidt said loudly. "Did it occur to anyone that Jesus Christ lived over two thousand years ago? Have you people been watching some really bad movies lately? To kill him, you would have to be able to go back in time." The room became silent as each person studied the face of the others. It dawned on the newcomers that time travel would have to be used and was used. Time travel was possible, and it had been done. They were collectively aware, nearly at the same moment of comprehension, everyone suppressing all other thoughts but that one. Time travel. It was not just for bad movies and bad fiction. Someone had done it.

Gargan cleared his throat and slowly rose to his feet. "Yes. We can do time travel. And we did time travel. The very unpleasant person in the next room did it and came back. Tony was sent back to the time of Christ and returned. He is the only person to have ever done it and to have survived. We know of four others who never returned. That is when you acquired your problematic Chicago Jesus. He is from the past and traveled forward into our time, and now we are unable to do anything about it."

They all looked at each other trying to take in and process what Gargan said. He implied that the Chicago Jesus was more than just a man from the past and was certainly not a holy man and especially was not the

Son Of God. Something deeply evil has come out of the past, and it has certain gifts which make it able to command and intoxicate large numbers of followers to its own ends. What does this Chicago Jesus want, and what are our choices of dealing with him was on everyone's mind at the same instant.

"What went wrong with your plans, Professor. How did you miscalculate after all your research?" McMurphy asked.

"There is another group who opposed us. Spies informed them of our ideas, and they disagreed, rejecting our clever calculations, and sent a team back before we did, changing everything. Their plans didn't go as expected either, but taken together, ours and theirs, it has ended in disaster. They call themselves Our Faith and are connected with a wide range of religious interests and are well-funded. Their mission is to prevent any tampering with religion, and they don't give a fig for history. They don't understand history, but they don't want it altered. The result...history has been altered, and it's our present history."

"So, I assume that you know what happened back in history, what happened to the teams and what they did while they were there?"

"No. Only fragments from what the perpetually unreliable Tony tells us. At least, he came back. The other two we sent never did, and we don't know enough to even guess what happened. The team from Our Faith, both of them, were presumed captured by the Roman Army, possibly executed. Tony might know more, if you can get it out of him."

"How did you choose your team? I'm appalled that such a prestigious group would pick a common criminal for a world-changing mission," McMurphy asserted.

"Your assessment is correct. He was a bad choice. However, do you think you can easily find an individual who would take on the task of murdering the most famous person in human history for cash? Who could you find to do such a deed? I'll tell you, because I made the effort to find him. First, he had to be expendable, but also able and willing to kill an innocent person, and lastly, dumb enough to be the first time traveler in history. You can only find a thug like Tony who fits all the requirements. He has a history of murder for hire and readily agreed, partly because he didn't fully understand what he was getting into. We were as dumb as he is to trust him. The two accompanying him were different and well-chosen."

"Did you consider sending another group back to correct what went wrong or to find out what happened to the other members of your team?" Rollins asked, not hiding his sarcasm.

Gargan looked as though he didn't want to answer at first but eventually looked at Rollings and answered, "It was the first thing I thought we should do. The Commission had no more stomach for it by then, and there was the question of qualified people to send."

"What do you mean by qualified?" Rollins asked.

"To go back is one thing, but you should realize this isn't a trip to the dinosaur times. People of the ancient world were intelligent, perceptive, alert to their surroundings, perhaps more than we are. Several different languages were spoken around Jerusalem, and you would have to communicate with people if you went back in time. That means you have to at least speak Latin, Hebrew and Aramaic fluently, and I mean fluently. Not many people are around who know the ancient dialects, even if they have a passable knowledge of the language. They have to be young and fit as well. The list is short, and if they are told the truth, that the mission is very dangerous, even shorter."

"How did Tony get back?" McMurphy asked.

"Tony is a survivor. He has eluded Jesus and his ever-expanding tribe for the past weeks in Chicago. Of course, he had to live like an animal to do it, but it shows what he is capable of. After his team left him, he was on his own, and he claims to have attempted to complete his mission. After narrowly escaping retribution, he made it back to the Portal. He was being closely followed by a revengeful Jesus who came back into our time while hunting him."

Captain McMurphy stood and looked around at the others, leaning forward on the table, bracing on his clenched fists. "Sounds like the simple solution would be to have this pretend Jesus killed. You hired Tony, Gargan, just hire more exactly like him. You people created this monster, and you should be the ones to do the housekeeping."

"Not so easy, Captain. You will find that the Chicago Jesus is not easily killed. There is something other than his followers protecting him. Based on what Tony says, we don't even think he can be killed. Then there is the aftermath. If you try, succeed or not, his people will erupt like you've never experienced previously. They absolutely believe that their Chicago Jesus is the Son Of God, and everything he utters is both true and a command from God's own mouth. You may have to kill them also, and they grow in number by the minute. Our society isn't prepared for that kind of mass murder. It will tear the fabric of society, and this country might cease to exist as an entity."

"Is our only choice to do nothing? If he is hard to stop now, think of the situation in three more months. We must have a solution."

"The politicians won't get involved because of the massive number of voters he already controls. The U.S. military will not be called on to help, you can count on that. The solution is, I'm afraid, up to the Chicago Police Department. We created this mess, but only you can solve it."

"Suggestions then?" McMurphy asked.

"None that I can think of. Sorry." Gargan answered.

"One more question, Gargan. How did you do it? How does the Portal into another time work?"

"The answer is complicated, and no one really understands fully what I'm about to tell you, and the story, at least in part, involves politics. There was, and is, a circular particle accelerator at Fermilab called the Tevatron. It was operative for a few years but was shut down in 2011 because lack of adequate government funding made it obsolete. Similar research has largely moved on to Switzerland. We found out that during some operations, a Portal ---a window into the past--- was established while the machine was running. Very few people knew about this, and those that did were sworn to secrecy by the Department of Defense. Via this temporary Portal, samples of soil taken for carbon dating and variation in the 14C/12C ratio in the atmosphere, both geographically and over time, lets us accurately date any samples from ancient soils, but we also found that measurements of air give even more detail. Experimentation showed that the date and location of the Portal was changeable, depending on the energy cycles of the Tevatron. In short, you can focus the opening to any time and place in the past. There was an absolute directive put forth preventing anyone going through the Portal because of a fear of contamination in both directions. The fear was not only of bacteria and virus particles but of technology and influence as well as the well-known worry about changing the past and its effects on the future, our present. For our own ends, we put up enough funds to keep the machine running and kept secret why. The spies of Our Faith were ahead of us and used our own experiment to send their people through a week before we were ready. They were waiting for us on the other side."

"I'm afraid that I don't understand the U.S. Government knowing about the Portal and letting some group like yours get control of it," Rollins said.

"Don't you see that knowledge concerning the Portal was so secret that they couldn't tell anyone about it. Very few knew, and they were ordered not to say anything. They surely couldn't tell the legislators about it without the world finding out. If we could go back in time, other countries would also, and the consequences could be disastrous. It had to stay secret forever. Fortunately, or unfortunately, someone working there wanted money, and he found us. It may be that he or she also sold out to Our Faith."

"No one knows except The Commission and Our Faith, you mean. You both found out and used it. Now we also know. Just like an infection, it spreads until everyone knows. Your failure was more complete than anyone could imagine. First, a stupid scheme to rid the world of religion and then allowing a demon to follow your man back. You could not have done worse, and doesn't that prove that the Government was right all along?" When McMurphy finished he could see his team nodding agreement.

"Right on both counts, Captain. We have all earned the right to be executed for our mistakes, but don't worry, eventually Jesus will catch up to us and do it for you. They are hunting down anyone who knows what actually happened. All of us have narrowly escaped several attempts to capture or kill us, and it's only a question of time. Our fate is sealed, but yours? You must come up with a solution before it's too late. Get rid of Jesus as soon as you can or lose the chance."

The room grew silent as everyone withdrew into their private thoughts. At last, Gargan signaled his young aide, and she came over and again helped him to his feet. He stood with effort and looked over those at the table. "My task is complete, my friends, and my life is soon drawing to a close either way. I would like to ask if anyone has any idea of how we should proceed?"

Captain McMurphy looked around but saw no raised hands. "I want more information before I give any suggestions," he said. "Someone go and get Tony Cardo and bring him in here. We are going to find out what he knows, and this time we need to know everything."

Chapter 3

Tony Cardo Talks

Tony had resumed his swagger now that he was both clean and safe. He entered, leading with his chin, and gave the other guests a flippant salute with the back of his hand. He seemed to feel that he was, or should be, a celebrity and had earned everyone's respect for being the first human to travel in time successfully. He sat apart from the others and put his feet up on the polished wood table.

"Gents, Dames. Salutations. What can Tony do for you?" he asked with a smirk. Tony was fresh from his shower and wore a new pair of jeans and, of course, a white undershirt.

Captain McMurphy quickly rose, sweeping Tony's feet off the table. "Listen up, Tony. Cooperate completely, or we'll let the mob tear your limbs and head off at the first stop of this boat. To us, you are still gang trash, and now we have a witness stating you told him that you had done murder for hire, so you can wipe the smirk off of your face. Help us understand what happened to you, or you have no use at all, and you will be treated like excess baggage and discarded."

Tony sat up and looked at the others, taking in the general contempt hanging in the room. "Whoa, people. Tony is going to tell you everything he knows. Alls you got to do is ask. As for the murder thing, your man's word against mine, and I'm sayin it taint true."

"Fill us in, Tony, and start at the start. Don't leave any detail out, however small," Captain McMurphy said and sat back down.

"I was there for, I think, a month. This is going to take more time than you got. What about a summary?" Tony asked. He was answered by a palpable silence.

"First time I was involved, two big dudes snatched me off the street and stuffed me in a trunk, and I got let out at the swanky headquarters of The Commission. The old man offered me a fat wallet to do somebody. Easy, he says. The guy is unarmed and not expecting trouble. In and out, he says. So, I needed the dough, I says yes. Then he tells me the rest. I have to go through a tunnel over in Batavia with two other people. The tunnel leads to a foreign place by some hocus-pocus which I didn't get at the time. Then he drops the bombshell. The dude I have to off is...hold your breath...Jesus Christ! Not just somebody from some Latin country. The real deal. Well, I'm stunned. How the hell, I think. Then he tells me the rest of the story. The two going with me are translators. They know the area and will help me find Jesus of Nazareth but...guess what...they don't know that I plan to bump Jesus of Nazareth off, and I can't tell them! Know what I do? I demand more money, lots more. I mean, who else they going to get to do a hit like this? I got them over a barrel. Cash in advance, like that. Know what they do? They pull out the cash and put it in my hand. Just like that. Catch is, they won't let me leave until I come back out of the tunnel. Another catch. If I don't do it, they bump me off. Imagine the nerve! Bump off the bumper. They got me over the barrel. I got to do it or else. So here I am." He started to put his feet back on the table and then saw Captain McMurphy's glare and hesitated. "Anything else you want to know?" Tony asked.

"You little worm," Captain McMurphy hissed and clenched his jaw and fist. "You know that's not enough. You're going to tell us the rest or else, so help me."

Ray had been sitting quietly since Professor Gargan left but now spoke up. "If I may, Captain, I have a timeline and some other facts for you while Mr. Cardo is recalling his story. There are some relevant facts which would be helpful to know."

"Please."

Ray cleared his throat and snapped open a briefcase. "Some things about the Portal first. As Professor Gargan said, we can focus in on the date accurately, and we can reproduce the spot with precision. If any parameters are changed, we can't control exactly where the Portal is located within a five kilometer radius, nor can we hide the opening from view. We don't yet feel certain exactly where the present Portal is located, but cursory sightings taken of local elevations and comparison with modern maps, and most importantly, star sightings, give us a certainty of within fifty square kilometers. Judging by our side, the opening is easily visible. There is a large energy expenditure to keep the Portal open so we elect to have it exist twice a day for only five minutes each time. Since Jesus came through, we have not opened it again, fearful of what else could come through. The original team members carried timepieces and were carefully instructed in regard to opening times so that they could be retrieved."

"To us, this sounds like you have abandoned the other two members of your team for the past two months. No wonder you don't know what happened to them. For all you know, they are standing there and waiting for the Portal to open," Captain McMurphy observed.

"True, Captain. Jesus was not expected through and look what he has done in two months. What else is back there to fear? We don't want to find out."

"Here is what we are going to do, Ray. I'm going to Batavia on your helicopter. Call out there and have them get the machine going. I want to see the Portal for myself. The rest will stay here and let Tony finish his story." Captain McMurphy turned to Tony and wagged his thick finger at him, "If you don't tell everything you know, every detail, my men are instructed to throw you off the boat. You hear me?"

"Sure, chief. Whatever you say," Tony muttered.

Ray spoke again, "First, Captain, I want to tell you about those two who didn't make it back. We did an extensive search and found the ideal pair. Our Latin scholar is an Italian named Cosimo Petronie. Cos, for short. He is 28, handsome and very fit. Cos speaks both Latin and Greek fluently and has a passion for Roman history, and, of course, also speaks Italian and English. He and his friends are well-known for their staging of Roman life in authentic costume so he was enthusiastic beyond description for the chance to return to the past. Our bet was that the Romans would never guess that he was anything but a cultured Roman citizen. The other one was located in Israel. She is nearly the same age as Cos, born in Jerusalem, and knows Hebrew and English but also has extensively studied the ancient Aramaic language. Our research indicated that the Aramaic language was predominant in Judea and Galilee and is almost certainly the language spoken by Jesus Christ. Mary has participated in historical digs in Israel and Jordan and has an impressive knowledge of the history of that area. She is, by the way, very attractive."

"What is her last name? Or should I ask, what was her last name?" Captain McMurphy asked.

"Point well taken, Captain. Her last name is Solomon. Mary Solomon. Perfect, don't you think?"

Captain McMurphy patiently waited for the rest of the story and finally broke silence by asking, "So, did they just walk in? How were they dressed, and what did they bring with them?"

"They were all in traditional garb suitable for the time and place. Cos chose to wear a simple Roman tunic, and Mary was in a black hooded robe fashioned of coarse wool. We employed a firm to create reproduction coin money, duplicating Herod's coinage, and they each were given a small leather bag full. Tony was armed with his favorite handgun, which he wore under a loose fitting tunic. Cos and Mary also carried small electronic devices, and several additional memory chips, which could record visual images and sound. The plan called for rapid execution, forgive the word, and rapid withdrawal. We guessed three days max. The Portal was opened twice a day just before dawn and right after dusk."

"And neither Cos nor Mary knew why they were there?"

Ray laughed, "Of course not. They are both devoutly religious and would have never agreed to go. We figured that after the shooting, it wouldn't matter because the mission would have been accomplished. All they were told was to find Jesus of Nazareth, photograph him and talk to him if they could. Tony was there to make the kill when they found him. Our carefully worked out plans abruptly changed when Cosimo decided to enter the Portal by himself and a couple of days later brought back a Roman officer with him. They, all four of them, left together, and we don't know what happened to anyone other than the miserable Tony."

McMurphy shook his head and looked at the others briefly before asking, "Have you ever read science fiction, Ray?" Captain McMurphy asked.

"Some. I'm not a fan, I must admit."

"You told me that The Commission was trying to change history. Do you think it was possible that the world would have changed so much that there would be no Portal for the team to return through?"

"My personal opinion is that we likely wouldn't recognize the world at all. I am sure that the Portal would vanish, and they would be stranded in the past or nonexistent if the mission were successful."

"Did anyone think that it was fair not to tell Cos and Mary the truth and let them decide?"

"Think about it, Captain. If the mission were successful, then none of them would have existed at all, and the mission would not have happened."

"That's my next point, Ray. How could the mission have happened? You think about it. If it were successful, then it could not have happened and therefore didn't happen. Jesus Christ could not be killed by Tony, don't you see? The past cannot be changed for that reason."

"A highly theoretical hypothesis. And interesting. There is something wrong with the logic, though. We have seen five people go back in time and nothing happened to our present. Surely they did something back in the past that could have led to a slight change. Why did nothing happen? It means that your theory is false. Jesus Christ can be killed, and if he is, it will alter the present. I believe in our theory. Too bad it wasn't tested."

"Thank God it wasn't tested," Captain McMurphy said softly.

The helicopter pilot appeared in the door and said, "Going to Batavia, anyone?"

Captain McMurphy pointed to Tony and said, "Talk and keep talking. If your story isn't complete by the time I return, you better sprout fins." Then he waved to the pilot and left the room.

Rollins stood and glared at Tony. "Cardo, get up and come with me." Rollins opened the door and signaled to one of his staff waiting in the lounge, then pointed to a small side room.

Chapter 4

Object out of the Past

After lifting off with a jerk, the big grey machine twisted around violently then leaned uncomfortably forward, aggressively accelerating, accompanied by loud drumming and vibration of the aluminum shell around its human cargo. McMurphy had no idea that this type of machine could move so quickly. He looked through the glass and saw the hazy image of Chicago grow larger and more distinct by the second. The tilt softened as the helicopter rose in altitude then tilted even more forward. Downtown Chicago, with its congested streets of colorful cars, slid directly below as the ship tumbled toward the west side of the big city. The distant, pale green landscape grew richer and darker as the helicopter slowed and descended. McMurphy recognized the large circles of the Fermilab facility below in the distance, and the thought struck him that they were like some vast modern version of Mound Builders' effigies. As he looked absently out over the big lake to the north, he thought about the responsibility he had accepted. No, he clarified, not accepted, been thrust into unwillingly and without preparation. It dawned on him that this might be the most important human event since the birth of Jesus Christ, and he was caught in the middle of it. How can any man rise to such an occasion? Abruptly, the machine changed from forward motion to vertical descent and, with a soft, cushioned stop, came to a rest. Outside, he could see two uniformed officers from the CPD crouched down and holding their hats, waiting on the large rotors to stop.

McMurphy was the first out when the door opened, and he quickly moved toward the waiting policemen. "You men briefed?" he yelled over the helicopter noise.

One of them spoke, yelling above the diminishing rotor sounds, "All we were told is to get here and assist you, Captain. There is someone waiting for us by the Tevatron, whatever that is." He pointed to an odd-shaped building nearby, and McMurphy could see a woman in the doorway wearing a lab coat and watching them.

"You men grab your shotguns from your car and follow me inside," he barked. He watched his men run toward the nearby patrol car as he walked toward the waiting scientist.

"Captain McMurphy," he introduced himself as he went up the stairs. "You waiting for me?" he asked breathlessly.

"I'm Dr. Susan Harmes, Captain. I was instructed to help you in any way that I can. You are here regarding the experiment of The Commission, I gather?"

"Yes, Doctor. You know about the Portal?" he asked, and they both noticed his men sprinting toward him holding their weapons.

"Surely your men don't expect to go in there with those guns?" she asked with more of a command than a question in her voice.

"No. No one is going in. We want to make sure nothing comes out. You know why, I'm sure."

"I certainly do know. Jesus came right by me on the way out. I saw those eyes for just a second, and I knew that we were in trouble. Just an instant of proximity and I felt something compelling come over me. It was like standing on the edge of a cliff, some part of your body seems to want to fall. Sort of pulls you into the air. I still have nightmares, and I don't look forward to starting the machine again."

"Did you meet Cos and Mary before they went in?" McMurphy asked.

"Oh yes. I briefed them on the times we would open the Portal. They both are wonderful people. So full of energy and enthusiasm for the trip and so well-prepared."

"Tony Cardo. Meet him also?"

"Unfortunately. I still don't understand why he was allowed to go on the trip. I can say that he went in cocky and came out terrified, like an animal fleeing a large predator. Why was clear when Jesus came through after him. Did he ever get caught?"

"Not yet, but Jesus is still trying."

"I am told that you want our Tevatron to spin up. Can you tell me why,

Captain?"

"Don't you think we should try to get Mary and Cos back? Is it right to strand them back in time?"

"Those two can take care of themselves there. They might even like it. What else might come through, if we open the Portal, frightens me."

"My men will stop anything like that. Come on, start it up, and let's have a look. We have no choice, Doctor." Susan Harmes visibly sagged.

She considered herself a scientist first and foremost and had spent virtually all of her youth and energy on achieving a PhD in physics from the University of Chicago. After a short couple of years of blissful research, she was appointed to a management position and her personal involvement in research stopped. Now this. There wasn't anything about it, especially the secrecy about the actual mission, that she liked. She suspected foul play mostly because of the hush-hush, to her an indication of conspiracy, and the slickness of Raymone Servierlo, the smooth-talking Spanish lawyer who supplied all the money. Susan also suspected that many people knew that something was going on. Fermilab was full of intelligent, perceptive people, and it was a small community of equals. No matter what the government agents instructed, people talk. One particular physics grad student named Stridor seemed to be all ears. There was always something about him Susan didn't like, and her intuition told her that Stridor knew more than he should. Stridor always seemed to be in the vicinity of the target tubes every time a project was running. This is exactly what Susan hated about her present position, dealing with Raymone Chauncy Servierlo and being in charge of something she didn't understand while shadowed by opportunistic rabbits like Stridor.

She sighed to herself and decided not to think about what she couldn't control. "The site you are seeking occurs in one of the tunnels off the Tevatron ring. We discovered it by accident. Actually a female physics grad student from NIU found it." She pointed to a door, and they descended a long metal staircase. The hum of the gigantic machine and the sudden clanking sounds reminded McMurphy of his recent trip to an MRI unit. But this was no simple medical unit, and some of the most profound discoveries in physics were made at this site.

Dr. Harmes started describing the machine to the policemen as they descended. "Luminosity in excess of 1×1032 cm-2sec-1 is enough to open the Portal. We tune the opening by adjustment of the stacking rate of antiprotons. You understand?"

"No, I never took physics in school. Too sissy for me," McMurphy laughed but garnered a hard look from Susan Harmes, who obviously took it personally.

"The energy is created in three phases," she continued. "First, the LINAC starts the particles moving and forces them into the Main Injector. After suitable acceleration, they are fed into the large ring of the Tevatron and eventually out to the Switchyard. The Portal occurs in the tunnel of the Switchyard, and that's just up ahead," she summarized, pointing down a dark horizontal shaft the size of a New York subway tunnel. The hum grew louder, and the hair on the back of his neck started to tingle.

"Is it safe in here with this thing running?" McMurphy asked.

"No, we don't think so. Feels funny, doesn't it?" she shouted above the hum. Susan took her out watch, noting the hands approaching twelve. "Soon now. Watch over there, and you'll see it come into focus." She pointed to a vacant area on the concrete floor, and the officers checked their weapons.

A dim glow started just where she was pointing. At first it was faintly yellow and flickered, but as suddenly as a camera autofocuses, the opening was right in front of them. It seemed to be a stunningly clear oval photograph of rock and gravel with larger boulders in the background obscuring any distant views. The image was crisp right to the edges and was at least four feet in height. It looked as though you could just stroll up, reach in and touch the rocks.

"What time is it in there?" McMurphy asked.

"It's early afternoon. This isn't when they were told it would open so don't expect to see anyone standing there."

McMurphy walked closer and squatted down right in front of the opening and looked closely. He twisted his head back and forth looking at something on the ground just in front of him. "I see something. Can I reach in and touch it?" he asked without turning around.

"We don't allow that. Try this," she said and handed him a long metal pickup with claws that opened and closed, a small handle on the other end. She passed it over his shoulder and watched as he stuck it into the opening, digging in the soft sand. In a moment, he pulled the pickup back and looked at his prize.

"This is a memory chip. Funny, isn't it, to find that back in the first century?" McMurphy plucked it from the jaws of the tool and blew off the dust. "A message?" he speculated and then stood erect.

"Is it acceptable if I close the Portal for now, Captain?" she asked. He could see the worry on her face, and he nodded agreement that it could be closed. She walked over to a waiting terminal and clicked some keys rapidly. There was a loud sound, like a metal door closing, and the hum diminished slowly. The image of the past flickered out and returned to a view of painted concrete.

"Got a lab where we can view the contents of this?" McMurphy asked, holding up the chip.

"Sure do. My office. Please follow me," she said and led the way. With the pressure off, McMurphy let himself look Susan Harmes over more carefully. She was middled-aged but trim and very sure of herself. She wore half-glasses which mostly hung against her chest from straps tethered to the ear pieces. He noticed the soft glow of an orange-colored silk blouse under her starched white lab coat. Her brown hair was obviously long but was braided and wound up carefully on her head in the French style. A most attractive woman, he thought wistfully. The footsteps of the other policemen kept pace behind them. After what seemed to be a long walk, they turned several corners and were shown into a brightly lit white room, humming with computers stacked along one wall. An antique English desk was by itself near the center of the room, and Dr. Harmes name was imprinted on a small brass sign displayed near the end of the desktop. After she sat down and adjusted her chair, she pulled a small laptop computer from a drawer and held her hand out for the memory chip. McMurphy handed it over, and she deftly plugged it into the side of the small machine. She pointed to a large digital screen on the distant wall as the first image popped into view.

"That's Mary. Pretty, isn't she?" Susan remarked. The girl in the image was dark-haired with full dark eyes and eyebrows. She was smiling into the camera, her face isolated by her dark hood. A classic photograph, making her seem to be both from the present and the past at the same time. The way the photo was framed and backlit, it was obvious that Cos had an artistic touch and previous experience behind a camera. The next photo was of Cos, beaming his big perfect teeth at the camera. His brown curly hair fit his head like an artificial cap and flowed over his hand-stitched collar. He wore a simple off-white tunic adorned with a bright metal circular pin on the shoulder, typical of Roman statues McMurphy had seen at the Art Institute. With his prominent Italian nose, he was the very image of a Roman patrician and radiated striking confidence. The next several were of small inhabitable huts with partially clothed brown-skinned children standing around watching. Stray goats seemed to be everywhere, and the absence of any pavement or electric wires was striking. The next image seemed to be taken furtively and had partial obstruction of the lens by Cos' sleeve. Two mounted Romans were pictured riding past in resplendent armor. One carried a very long spear, and both were intently looking back at Cos and his camera lens. Even in a still photograph, it was a frightening moment. There was a photo of Tony, who didn't look very happy, the bulge of a pistol under his simple garment plainly visible. In the background, an occasional tuft of grass pushed out between the rocks, but the scenes were mostly of dirt, yellow to brown rock and low slung formless hills framing the distant background.

"There are several audio files here. Want to hear them as we watch the photographs?" Susan asked.

"Please," McMurphy said, and he pulled up a chair and sat down.

Chapter 5

Voices From The Past

reetings from the past. I am Cosimo Petronie, and I am from the twenty-first century. Unless the Portal to our time opens again, this story will not be heard for two thousand years. My fellow traveler, Mary Solomon, is here beside me, and she will speak to you later. If this memory chip is found before we have to leave this area, we want to tell you that we have been at this spot every morning and evening for the past three days hoping to be allowed to come back, and we will continue to do that for as much time as we have left. Our path led us far away from the Portal for a long time, and when we finally returned, it seemed to be gone. We parted from Tony some time ago, and we don't know where he is or what he is doing, and we don't care. Both of us were horrified when we learned the truth about our mission, and we didn't want any part of it. Before that happened, we did manage to find a man who called himself Jesus of Nazareth. Actually, he found us, but that's another story. Now, we are very sure that we made contact with the wrong man, because Jesus Christ is alive and is a different person. We have both seen Jesus Christ, and there is no doubt that he is what history says he was. Also, we found two men from our time here, and it was a moving moment when they realized what was about to happen to them. You can tell whoever sent them that they aren't coming back, because the Romans crucified them. We are under the protection of a young Roman officer named Antonius with whom I first connected soon after my first foray. Without his help, we could not have survived for as long as we have. Mary has had some interesting contacts among the Jewish people. We can both state with frankness that this is a hard place and time to live and is much worse in some ways than we expected, but its people are just like people back in your time. Some are good and some are not, but it always seems that the bad rise to the top as has happened for as long as there have been humans. Unfortunately for us, Antonius is being recalled to Rome, and unless we go with him or find the Portal open, we will try to live the best we can in this ancient time. If you find this message, please, please open the Portal on its original schedule." The recording ended at the same time a photograph of Cos with his arm around Mary was being shown on the monitors.

"Have you heard enough, or should I play another?" Susan asked as they both studied the last photograph.

"Try another one. I would like to hear Mary's voice," McMurphy said softly, overcome by emotion.

"Hello out there! Is anyone listening?" a soft female voice asked. "My name is Mary Solomon, and I am a traveler into the past. I am standing beside Cos, and his arm is around me, but still I am feeling very small and helpless. We are in Judea around the year 28 AD, as far as we can tell. Here, the years are not counted the same and real information is scant. I thought I would feel at home in the land of my people, but I was wrong. This is a hostile place, full of ignorance, poverty, and a constant threat of violence hanging in the air. One of the two men I can always count on is Cos. He has been there for me, no matter the risk to himself, and I feel the same loyalty toward him. We both feel empathy for the people here, but there is little we can do to change their circumstances or their viewpoint. Never before have I been so stricken with the stark difference between haves and have-nots. There is no real middle class, and the masses of poor people are used and treated no better than animals by the rich and powerful. In some ways, the ancient past and the twenty-first century are similar in this regard. Religion, tribes and wealth still divide humans, and it will ever be so. It is depressing for the truth to be so obvious. Both of us are ready to come home. Please open the Portal so we can return."

"Still wonder if we should try and bring them back?" McMurphy asked.

Susan wiped her eyes and was unable to respond other than to choke with tears. Yes, they should come back, she told herself.

McMurphy glanced at his watch. Two more hours until they could open the Portal. Looking up at the monitor one more time, he saw Herod the Great's temple hovering above the small city of Jerusalem. It was a massive structure, inspiring awe and wonder. The photo was taken from a small elevation outside the city and also showed the surrounding stone walls, cast in shadows by the yellow evening sun. "How many people would love to see that image?" he wondered aloud. "Doctor Harmes," he said. "We need to think ahead on this. Should Mary and Cos come through this evening, they should be cleansed and dressed as well as have a medical exam. Are there people here who can manage this?"

Susan stopped crying and thought for a moment. "I see what you mean. You are right, we should have thought about this previously. No, I don't believe we are equipped for that kind of support."

"Just as I thought," he said. He opened the office door and motioned to the waiting policemen. "Contact the Sheriff's office and have them send a HAZMAT team over here. Make sure they bring a portable shower. Another thing, round up a set of clothes for a man about your height and a small woman and make it quick. And before you leave there is one last thing." McMurphy glowered at the men to be sure he had their attention. "Don't dare ever say a word about anything you saw and heard today. Not a word to anyone, and that means anyone. Got it?"

"Yes, sir," the men said in unison, then hustled off to accomplish their tasks.

McMurphy turned back to Susan Harmes. "I need to make some calls. Why don't you listen to the rest of the recordings before they return so we can be up to speed. Would you have time for that?"

"Yes. I'll take time. It's my fault that they were stuck there. I was simply afraid. That's a poor excuse given what they have gone through, but it's the truth," she said and blew her nose again. As McMurphy left, Susan turned her attention back to her computer and pulled on a set of earphones. She recalled clearly the night that Tony Cardo burst through the opening screaming, "Close it, close it!" and headed as fast as his short legs could go for the exit staircase. Just as the upstairs metal door to the outside was closing behind him, another figure entered from the past, and this one was different, she remembered. He was a tall, scruffily bearded man with penetrating eyes, his head covered by a dirty cloak. His intellect seemed to bore right into her soul. He stood erect for a moment, looking at the surroundings, taking everything in before scrutinizing the steel staircase for a few seconds. Seemingly divining that his prey had gone that direction, he suddenly started to sprint up the stairs, without apparent effort. After the upstairs door closed, Susan summoned enough presence of mind to first close the Portal and then fearfully ascend the stairs, drawn to follow and discover what was about to happen. After she emerged into the sunlight, she saw the strange man standing in a large grassy clearing facing the distant skyline of downtown Chicago, hovering on the horizon. He lifted his hands and arms up as if to pray or to summon the city to him. She understood immediately that she was looking at an epochal event, something powerful and compelling about it making her tremble. As she watched, the figure started a slow purposeful run toward the city, never looking back.

Once alone in the endless hallways, the Captain punched in a number on his cellphone. "Rollins," he commanded into the small phone. "McMurphy here. What have you learned from Tony?"

"Very interesting, Captain, once he settled down to talk. A couple of high points you should hear. The translators, Cosimo and Mary, who went in with Tony were told that he was their bodyguard and didn't find out differently until he pulled his gun and shot at the man he took to be Jesus. The translators must have watched as Tony fled, pursued by Jesus and two of his men. Tony said that he managed to get off three rounds, and he claims that he ordinarily never misses, except this time, and the pursuit started in earnest. He doesn't know what happened to the interpreters, but he presumes that they managed to get away. The other interesting thing is that Tony insists that the man claiming to be Jesus was aware of them all along and seemed to be luring them in from the start. Various people would come out of nowhere and direct the group along, as if they had no control or freedom to choose. The directed path led straight to Jesus. Since Tony doesn't speak any languages other than English and some street Italian, he was unable to get any help from locals while he was fleeing. He quickly ran out of money and had to cross a lot of terrain on foot and under cover of darkness. It's an amazing story of survival by hook and by crook. He stole food, water, and even a donkey, changing clothing three times but never shook his pursuers. It sounded to us like they didn't want to catch him. I think they wanted to see where he was going, almost as if herding him instead of following. Tony is completely ignorant of history, even biblical history, and he didn't really look around at his surroundings very closely. Being cast back in time and able to see with his own eyes the events and people who changed the world was all lost on him. After he got back, though, he had the significant advantage of knowing Chicago and all its dark corners like a cockroach. Even here, Jesus and his growing flock got closer and closer over time and this time meant it."

"Are you done with his interrogation?"

"He actually knows so little I have to say yes. We seem to know what he knows, or at least what he is capable of telling us. What did you find in Batavia?"

"First, regarding Tony. Put him under lock and key for his and your protection until I return. Good news on this end. I really feel that we are going to see the two translators in person tonight, and I'll let you know when and if we do. What's next is to listen to their story and see what they know and what they suggest. They will be a great help if we can get them back."

"Well, good luck on that Captain. Anything else I can do for you?" Rollins asked.

"Yes. Have Schmidt contact Bishop Malveccio and ask him to call me right away."

"Will do, Boss."

McMurphy put his phone away and started back toward Susan's lab when it rang unexpectedly.

"McMurphy here," he said. "Forget something, Rollins?"

"Captain McMurphy, this is Bishop Malveccio. I understand that you want to talk, and I'm sure I know why."

"Thanks, Bishop, for calling so quickly. We should have talked previously, and I apologize for taking so long. I need to know what you know about the so-called Chicago Jesus."

"As I expected. This conversation would best be done eye to eye, Captain, for it is a troubling and difficult subject."

"We will meet, I promise, but right now, I need to pull in all the pieces I can to get a handle on this thing. The main police station was nearly stormed earlier today by an immense mob who were chanting "Jesus" over and over. I understand that they eventually dispersed, but we had a close call. I don't understand what is going on, and I want your insight."

"Clearly, to all the Christian leaders, this man who calls himself Jesus is a pretender. I don't know where he came from, and I admit that at first, we ignored warning signs when he seemed to be attracting larger and larger crowds each time he spoke. A few days ago, I watched a video of him in action. He comes right out and states that he is God. Even Jesus Christ didn't say that. The problem is that people are believing him, large numbers of them, I regret to say. There is something hypnotic about his eyes and his body movements, and I had to force myself to turn off the video. He is the most dangerous man alive right now, and his power grows larger with every tick of the clock. I have to say that my conclusion, or at least my speculation, is that he triggers some built-in response in human beings, but by what mechanism, I don't know. You recall from our recent national elections that there is frequently a cult that forms around certain political leaders, members of the cult throwing away reason, believing in their candidate no matter what lies they are told. I am ashamed to admit it, but religion does the same thing to people. We ask that they suspend reason and logic and only follow their beliefs. They do so willingly and fervently. The same hold on people is seen in politics as in religion, and a bad leader will lead them to their deaths just as a bad minister will lead them to Hell. He leads, they follow. It's an old human story, and we are seeing it here right before us on a large, dramatic scale. The Chicago Jesus is a master at hooking his crowd, and there is something evil in his intentions. I am at a loss to advise how to stop him, and I am not certain that he can be stopped. We may be facing the end of our civilization as we knew it. There are dark times ahead, Captain."

"Thank you, Bishop Malveccio, for your thoughts. I'll let you know if I find out anything we can use to stop this madness, and I hope to see you in person soon."

"Before you hang up, Captain. Did you find out where the Chicago Jesus came from?"

"Sure did, Bishop. From just outside of Nazareth. But how and why can't be discussed over the phone. You already have a lot to think about, Bishop, just as I do. We'll talk again."

McMurphy walked up behind Susan, stunned by the current images displayed on the monitor. There was a long row of heavy crosses along a ridge top, on each one a limp man hung from his hands. Two Roman soldiers stood defiantly in the foreground looking intently at the photographer, their large shields and spears nearby. The next image was a close up of one of the crucified men, and the following image was of a different man on a similar cross. McMurphy assumed that these two were from Our Faith and were the ones mentioned by Cos earlier. A bad way to end, McMurphy thought.

"Anything new, Doctor?" he asked, causing her to jump a little before taking off her headphones.

"Oh, hi. Made your calls already?" she asked limply. Listening to Cos and Mary had taken the fight out of her, and he could see her red, puffy eyes.

"That bad?"

"Some of it. The one bright spot is the friendship they made with the young Roman Centurion named Antonius. There is a photo of Antonius with his arms around both Cos and Mary at the same time, and all three were smiling broadly. No mention of who took the picture. I should tell you that I met Antonius when he came back with Cos. He was only here for a couple of hours, speaking only in Latin, but his honor and courage were obvious. It was also apparent that he can be very dangerous, and Tony nearly met his premature death that day. I wish that that had happened, I really do." She blotted at her eyes, trying to regain her composure, causing Fred to lay a comforting hand on her shoulder as if to tell her that he understood. After a pause, she was ready to continue, "Most of the recordings sound like a travelogue, but they do give life to how it felt being there. I couldn't finish the one which describes meeting Jasper Cruze and Tom Simon. They both were in a prison cell at the time and were awaiting execution by torture and crucifixion for being spies. There are photos of them being nailed to the cross in case you are interested. Oh…I couldn't bear looking at them. It makes you realize how dangerous it was and is for Mary and Cos. I am holding my breath that they are there when the Portal opens."

"I talked with Bishop Malveccio just now. He has no idea how to stop our Chicago Jesus, and he is in despair about the future because of this man. It seems that everything is riding on these two coming back from the past. I just hope that they have a solution for us."

"We have a little less than an hour to wait, Captain. Want to take a break with me and just walk outside for a bit?"

"It would be an honor, Doctor, and especially if you could call me Fred instead of Captain."

"Thank you, Fred. I'll do that. It feels very comforting to have you here right now. You make me think that everything will somehow turn out all right. By the way, you should get used to calling me Susan, if you please."

McMurphy paused for a moment, then asked, "One more technical question, Susan, if you don't mind."

"I don't mind technical questions, Fred. They don't trouble the soul. Ask."

"Why can't you just set the time for the Portal opening back a couple of months? We could get them back for sure that way."

"Not that easily done. It's true that we can adjust the time and place of the Portal but only after extensive experimentation. We don't know exactly where it is going to open within a fifty kilometer square area. Allowing the settings to stay the same, we advance in time just as they do on the other end, but that way we always know exactly where the Portal is going to be. They would never find it if we started playing with the settings."

Chapter 6

An Epic Begins

osimo, I would like you to meet your new partner," Raymone Chauncy Servierlo said, and with a flourish of his arm, the side door opened and admitted a small, but very beautiful woman. Cos looked her up and down quickly, like the accomplished Italian lover that he thought he was, then slowly moved his gaze over her long, lustrous dark hair which was matched with her large, dark, expressive eyes. Her obvious poise told him that she not only knew how attractive she was but had intelligence to match her looks. Cos stepped back and smiled at her, waiting for his introduction.

She quickly advanced toward him and offered her hand, "I am Mary Solomon. I understand that you also are a linguist." Standing this close, Cos felt the powerful presence that some especially beautiful women radiate. Her long hair hung loosely over one shoulder and was pinned with a gleaming metal ornament that Cos noticed had been crafted from an ancient Roman gold coin. She was wearing an exotic perfume, one that he had never previously encountered. The scent came to him softly, arousing something like a pleasant memory, or the hope of one.

"When you ask me that, I can't recall knowing any language but the one you are speaking."

"Oh, and also a flirt!" she said and smiled back at him.

"No, Miss Solomon, I meant it."

Ray pushed between them and said, "On to business, children. You are brought here for a unique mission, and your skills will be challenged. We searched the globe to find the exact pair we wanted, and you two are the so-called pick of the litter. Let me pose a question to both of you, and you may take this question very seriously and give me a sincere answer." He returned behind his formidable desk, sat down, then motioned for them to also sit. Interlacing his hands, he moved them to a prayer position just under his bearded chin. There was a moment of anticipatory silence, then he spoke again. "If you could travel back in time to say… twenty-seven AD, do you think your language skills would allow easy communication with people you meet?"

"You mean in China or in Central America, sir," Cos said with a straight face. Mary giggled softly.

"Well, for you, Cosimo, I mean Rome, Italy or Greece."

"In that case, I say yes, but with a caveat. I know the language and how it was used. There is no way to know what my accent would sound like to people from that era, and we are not sure about the use of common words or substitutions."

"I see," Ray said solemnly. "And you, Mary, if I specified the same time period but in Judea?"

"My answer is the same. We cannot know dialects or references to current events. Impossible to know what they would think."

"However, don't you both think that you could be understood and comprehend any response?"

"There is no way to answer you, sir. We just don't know. May I inquire how this is a reasonable question?" Cos asked.

Ray shook his head, "Not yet. I have another question. Also hypothetical. If it could be done, would you be willing to try?" For a brief moment, Cos and Mary looked at each other to be sure they had heard correctly.

Mary sat up and held on to the arms of her chair. "Are you asking us to travel back in time? It's impossible, isn't it?"

"No one has actually done it, but yes, it seems to be possible," Ray admitted.

"To be able to see Rome in its glory! Who wouldn't want to do that?" Cos exclaimed, beaming his teeth around the room.

"Every Jewish person would like to see the Temple before the Romans destroyed it," Mary said in a matter-of-fact way.

"If it can be done, I'm afraid that neither one of you will likely see those things. What we have in mind is to go to Galilee and hunt for Jesus of Nazareth. It's more a religious undertaking and, hopefully, will be a quick trip. There and back in perhaps three days."

"How do you know it is safe to go if no one has done it?" Cos asked.

"Yes, and how do you know where and when?" Mary inquired.

"We have made every effort to insure the answer to both your questions. There is another problem you might not think about at first. Assuming for the moment the trip there and back is safe and puts you down in the correct place and time, you would find yourselves in a land of turmoil and violence. In other words, there are inherent dangers of all kinds in going and just trying to survive. That's why I was wondering about your verbal skills. You wouldn't want to stand out in any way, you see."

"I speak Latin and Greek," Cos said. "I would likely only be able to talk with Romans."

"And I speak only Aramaic and Hebrew," I could not communicate with the Romans," Mary offered.

"And that is why you are paired together," Ray said, lifting his palms up and smiling.

"The places that I would fit in wouldn't accept him and also vice versa," Mary stated the obvious.

"The things I have read about that time tells us that Judea and Galilee were basically occupied by Roman armies and the population resisted, sometimes with violence," Cos added.

Ray nodded agreement. "The threat of revolt was building at that time but didn't actually fully erupt for another thirty or so years. It will be as safe as that region ever gets."

"What, actually, do you want us to do if we agree to go?" Cos asked.

"Simple. Find Jesus of Nazareth by asking around, then photograph him. Record his voice if you can. Talk with him if you have the nerve," Ray said, grinning broadly at the simplicity of it.

"You want us to prove that he existed? We already know that he did. How is this going to change anything if we have photographic proof?" Mary asked, her voice rising with the tension in the room.

"And who would believe us anyhow? We would be labeled as the biggest fraud artists of all time," Cos said, looking at Mary for agreement.

"All of that is our problem, The Commission's problem. You will be paid handsomely, and you will visit the place that both of you have spent your young lives dreaming about. Isn't that enough? If this works, there may be more trips ahead. You may yet see Rome or the Temple. Interested?"

"All right, one more question. How do we protect ourselves from harm? And, isn't there a theory that you shouldn't tamper with the past? If we change something, even a little thing, the effects could be widespread. Doesn't that worry you?" Cos asked.

"I guess that we will never know until we try. Look, all you are going to do is to walk around and take photographs. How could that matter?" Ray said with some irritation. He admitted to himself that these two were smart and had quickly focused on key questions, but he had to put them at ease. "About your safety. We are sending a man...call him your bodyguard...who should be able to protect you if things go wrong. His name is Tony, and you will meet him the day you leave."

"This Tony will have a gun?" Mary guessed.

"Yes."

She sat silently, staring at Ray for a moment, thinking things through. "Twenty- seven AD?" she repeated. I seem to recall that Jesus Christ was crucified in roughly thirty- three or four. If we are going, shouldn't we go and watch him perform his miracles or even witness his famous incident at the Temple? We may not be able to find an unknown person. Why choose that specific date?" She pursed her lips, giving her face a hint of confrontation.

"The Commission has thought this through many times. If you go after Jesus of Nazareth becomes well-known, he will be surrounded by followers and believers. The chance of getting close is slim and pulling out a camera could be interpreted as a threat by the people around him. He will be unprotected and approachable in the year twenty- seven."

Cos spoke up, "If you are looking at proof that Jesus Christ was the true Prophet, as the New Testament claims, then Mary is right. All we are likely to find is a humble carpenter dressed in rags. It won't prove anything, because he could be anyone. We might as well not go."

Ray could see that these two were not easily misled, and both had a deep knowledge of history. In all ways, they were the perfect pair to make this journey. He knew that he had to convince them to go, and he quickly decided on a different tack by withdrawing his offer. "I can see that all our research and efforts mean nothing to either one of you. The Commission begs your forgiveness and, of course, will pay all your expenses for your return to your homes. You must promise me not to mention this discussion to anyone. We are protecting the past, because it is our mission. Others, should it become evident that time travel is possible, will not be so careful. Regrettably, we will expand our search for other interpreters to replace you. Surely, there are others out there." He rose from his chair and extended his hand for a farewell shake.

Cos stood quickly. "Not so fast, *Señor* Servierlo. We didn't refuse, but we reserve the right to go as intelligent humans preserving our ability to think things through. Your failure to clearly explain our mission is the problem. I'm sure that I want to go and see the ancient world, and I believe that Miss Solomon feels the same. We have plenty of reservations, that's all."

"Let's do this, my young friends," Ray said. "Think about it overnight, then meet me at Fermilab sharply at nine in the morning, and we will give you a look at the mechanisms of time travel. Acceptable?"

Mary was the first to speak, "I'm comfortable with that suggestion. Cosimo and I will talk this through tonight, but I desire to know a lot more about the whole process before I am willing to do something so rash as time travel."

"I feel the same as Mary. We will agree, at least, to meet you in the morning, *Señor* Servierlo. I'm looking forward to it," Cos added.

Renaldo's Restaurant, Chicago Loop 8:00 P.M.

Mary raised her wine glass and extended her arm toward Cos. The candlelight shimmered from the moving surface and caught on the cut sides of the glass, bouncing playfully along her long dark hair. "A toast to us, Cosimo. We already acted as a team while talking to Servierlo, and we held our ground with him."

Cos beamed across the linen-covered table and raised his glass to gently tap hers. "Well said, Miss Solomon. You and I seem to be thinking alike already." They both took a sip and then each took a long look at their new partner. Cos was dressed in a fitted, Italian tuxedo over a radiantly white pleated shirt. His bow tie was of crimson silk, matching his pocket square. The full head of curly hair and his arm and hand motions during conversation were so distinctively Italian. He had an intimate way of looking across the table at her with his head slightly lowered which matched his quiet appassionato voce. Mary felt herself realizing how attractive he could be, and Cos, on the other side of the table, was feeling the same toward her. She chose to wear a simple black shift with a deep open neck. The only jewelry visible was a silver disk swaying on a slender chain around her neck. Cos could see the appreciative glances toward her from passing males, and he was the first to agree that she was darkly beautiful. The more he looked at her, the more he wanted to. They were dining at the expense of The Commission and had selected one of Chicago's best restaurants, the kind that had dark vaulted ceilings, was lit sparsely, and carpeted in thick, sculptured wool. The other diners ate and talked in hushed tones which allowed the elegance of the surroundings to impress even more. Each table was assigned its own waiter who stood rigidly in the shadows waiting to be of instant service.

"May I call you Mary?" he asked, suppressing a smile.

"Yes, Cos, I would like that."

"I keep looking at your piece of jewelry. It's so simple but mesmerizing. What is it?" he asked.

"My father gave it to me. He had it made from a small fragment of Roman glass we found on a dig. It has a silver surround and isn't really worth much except for sentimental value."

"On you, it seems invaluable. Stunning."

"Thank you, Cos," she smiled back.

The waiter interrupted the long look they were taking of each other and started placing the dishes of food. He looked at his patrons furtively but understood what was happening. He had seen it many times before.

"More wine, Signore, Signorina?"

Without looking away from Mary, Cos answered, *"Naturalmente, e tenerlo a venire."*

She looked slightly puzzled, and Cos explained, "I just said yes. Forgive me, but I could tell that he knew Italian."

"Can you switch to Latin so easily?"

"Turus sum retinebit Italus accentus."

"Yes, you will speak with an accent. And so will I. Servierlo was correct to be concerned. Remember the old saying, 'The proud nail gets the hammer'? That could be us. I admit that I am afraid and that doesn't even take into account my concerns about the time travel part. At this point, I am not willing to go, are you?" she asked in a coarse whisper, leaning forward toward him.

"We don't know enough to make a decision yet. One step at a time, and we must wait and see what tomorrow brings. I have a feeling that we are not being told the truth or, at least, not all of it. I agree with you that this mission makes no sense. Some facts are missing. Still, I would love to see the past, since I have spent so much of my life thinking about it," Cos said and raised his glass to her again.

"Cos. You were born in Rome, is that not true?" Mary asked.

"Yes, and I am already reading your mind. You were born in Jerusalem. We are just like the people of ancient Judea. How is it possible that we can get along? Is that what you are thinking?"

"Historic and natural enemies, something like that," she said and smiled playfully.

"We have our love of history to bind us together. If we make this journey, we will only have each other to depend on. I pledge to you, Mary Solomon, that I will do my best to see that nothing happens to you, even at the cost of my life. You will be more important to me than our mission or the history of mankind. I swear it." Cos spoke in a level, low but sincere, voice, and his little speech quickly brought a rim of moisture to Mary's eyes.

"That's a lot to offer to a stranger, Cos. Thank you for saying it."

"That's what it will take to succeed. I will only have you, and you will only have me. In addition, I want to also add that they could not have chosen a more lovely companion for me to travel with."

"You Italians have a gift for romance. I am so flattered. I'm beginning to like you Cos."

"It's really this fine Italian wine forming and shaping your emotions. An old continental trick we use." He beamed his magnificent teeth at her, and she rewarded him with a smile.

"Tell me about yourself, Cos. You know, the little personal things."

"You can't be serious! The personal things are...well personal!" he laughed.

"Come clean, Cos. You know what I mean."

"I was very much what you would call an Italian street urchin. I ran freely through Rome with fellows like me, and that's where I picked up my love for the ancient city. In some places, if you stand and look at the columns and the old paved streets, you can almost feel voices talking to you. You hear the old Latin being shouted across the street and hear the march of feet and the orders of the *decanus* keeping his men in order. Often I would obtain, by theft if not otherwise possible, a fresh brick oven-baked loaf of bread and sit on a fallen column, imagining Rome in the first century. The feel of ancient Rome wrapped around me was always a part of who I was and who I would become. And here I am looking across the table at a most excellent companion and about to go and visit the past in person!"

"Thanks for that too short bio, Cos," Mary said. "You are likely to see Judea and Galilee through the eyes of a Roman, and that's different from what I will see. We know a lot about the Roman history thanks to their many historians. Sometimes they wrote about my people, but it usually involved some type of conflict with the Jewish population in the Levant. I am interested in the common people who paid their taxes, worked hard every day and raised their children. We know almost nothing about them and how they lived, especially the women. My people were dominated by males who frequently fought each other as much as anyone else. So far, my life has been spent trying to learn the story of the rest of them, the common man and woman." Mary's eyes glistened with emotion, and she stopped for a moment. "I wasn't brought up in a wealthy family, and we all worked and lived together in a small, crowded apartment. That kind of life makes you struggle to better yourself, whereas a soft comfortable life is apt to invite sloth. I served my time in the Defense Force, and I take care of my aging parents as they took care of me. I have never had the luxury of frivolity or the leisure of luxury. That about sums me up, Cos. A hard-working girl who never had much."

"You have obvious strength of character, burning intelligence, and consummate beauty. There isn't anything that you don't have. One more thing that you do have, Mary, is my unabated interest in such a charming and eloquent colleague."

The candlelight glinted in her eyes, and she was silent for a moment. "Cosimo, where have you been?"

Chapter 7

First Glimpse

Fermilab, Batavia Illinois

P lease follow me," the guard instructed. Cos smiled, shrugged, then fell into step behind Mary and the armed guard. They headed across a well-kept grassy area toward a massive, oddly-shaped structure which looked like an inverted Y. After a few minutes, a metal door near one end of the building came into view, making them realize the large scale of this structure. Cos could see movement at the side door entrance, and as they closed the distance, it was obvious that Ray Servierlo was waiting beside a woman wearing a white lab coat. The pair waved, and Cos and Mary waved back.

"Good morning, my young friends! Glad you decided to visit us today," Servierlo called out, holding his hands like a megaphone. The woman standing with him made no comment and looked either serious or worried. Her half-glasses were set low on her nose, and she held a clipboard in one hand. "Allow me to introduce," Servierlo said, as they got close. "This lady to my left is one of the directors at Fermilab, Doctor Susan Harmes. Doctor Harmes, these are Doctors Solomon and Petronie from Israel and Italy, respectively. They prefer to be called Mary and Cos."

"Welcome to Fermilab, and please call me Susan. We are very informal at this place. If you will follow me, we can get started." Without waiting for their reply, she turned and started descending a dark metal staircase. While following in the rear, Cos and Mary went arm in arm for an unsettling trip down the long staircase which descended into the depths and darkness. When they arrived on level concrete, they realized that they were in a long tunnel, disappearing into darkness in both directions.

Overhead, and along the upper part of the tunnel, was a vast assortment of cables and tubes. The area was dead silent except for their footsteps and the chatter of Ray Servierlo ahead of them. An ordinary concrete floor was painted a color somewhere between orange and yellow, with periodic markings and numerals in blue, making it rather a scientific ruler, a vast measuring device on a dwarfing scale. Echoes of their footsteps made the place seem larger and more ominous, the cavern of the minotaur, resurrected from the distant past. Following Susan, they were led through several sets of double metal doors when at last she stopped and turned toward them.

"This is the place. Please find a chair, and we'll talk this through for a while." Cos and Mary looked around but saw nothing different from the rest of the tunnel they had just passed through. A set of folding chairs was along one wall, and the three of them sat, facing Susan who waited impassively. She sorted through her papers with a furrowed brow and passed Mary and Cos a stapled form.

"This facility is managed by the U.S. Department of Energy. There is sensitive research ongoing here, and we require a non-disclosure agreement to be signed by everyone who gets this far into the labs. Breach of the agreement is punishable by ten years in the Federal Penal System." She paused to look at their faces and waited in silence until the forms were signed.

"Now there are things you have to understand. We conduct particle research at Fermilab, among other things. 'Atom Smashing' in public jargon. To do this requires a lot of energy, which is brought in by the electric towers you see all around the grounds. It requires thousands of dollars in electricity costs to power up these enormous machines. The process starts far from here when a boost is given to electrically charged particles of atoms, eventually the beam passing near the spot I am standing, then continuing on toward the terminal areas, where the subatomic particles are separated and analyzed. That's what we are supposed to be doing. A side effect of our research has been the discovery of an opening…an aperture through time…just a few feet from where we are standing. It took several years of patient effort to understand what we had accidentally created and how to adjust the effect. After I give the signal, you will feel and hear the energy build, and suddenly a window into the past will open. The financial cost of achieving this effect is high, so we can't keep it open very long. We have taken soil and air samples and dated the matter visible in the opening with the most sophisticated methods known, and we are sure of the date and fairly sure of the location to within fifty square kilometers of error. We allowed animals through the opening on two occasions and brought them back in by their tether. To this date, they remain healthy. Should the experiment go forward and humans enter the opening for more than a brief moment, we will guarantee an opening that will last five minutes each twelve hour period. There are many unknowns involved in going through, not least of which is what is waiting on the other side. Frankly, speaking for myself only, I would not agree to venture into the opening." She stopped and waited for any response or question.

"Question, if I may," Mary said and raised her hand. Susan pointed to her with her index finger and nodded approval to speak. "How do you know where this opening is since you have not been through it?"

"One of the major problems has been that one. To give a simple answer is not easy, because it took us two years to discover the answer to the question you just asked. There are two separate scientific findings. The first is derived from our extensive experimentation with energy settings. At some locations, we could see through the opening to various well-known landmarks, and eventually we understood how to program for location. The other is ridiculously simple. We stuck an optical device through and took measurements and sightings of the stars, and our colleagues in astrophysics did the math for us. Those measurements and calculations also help confirm the date as well as the location. Any more questions?" She looked around at Ray who was indicating with a twirl of his index finger that she could start the machine. Susan walked over to a computer terminal, and after a short period, an ominous clanking sound rattled through the tubes, and what started as a low hum grew louder and louder and ever more shrill.

"I feel like my hair is standing on end. Is it?" Mary asked Cos.

"Not that I can see, but I feel the tingle also. A bit frightening, isn't it?" he said. Just as he spoke, there was another loud metallic clank like some huge metal door closing.

"There it is, folks. Your opening into the past," Susan said loudly above the background noise. As Cos and Mary strained their necks, an oval window magically appeared about three meters from where Susan was standing. Through the opening was a view of reddish soil and medium rocks but nothing else. Cos and Mary stood to get a better look.

"You can come close. There is nothing to fear," Susan assured them with a limp smile as if she didn't believe that it was truly safe. Cos and Mary held hands and came before the opening, squatting in front of it.

"Amazing!" Mary exclaimed. "It's like you could just reach out and touch the ground. Where, exactly, did you say this opening is located?"

"We are convinced that it is in Galilee, somewhere just south of Nazareth."

"Here goes!" Cos said and then slowly put his finger forward until part of it was on the other side. "I can't feel any difference!" Then he quickly reached out and grabbed a fist-sized stone, withdrew it and stood up. "Here it is, everyone, a living rock from the past!" He laughed and tossed the rock playfully to Ray who let it fall to the floor without touching it. "Are you afraid, Boss?" Cos mocked, then turned back to the opening.

"Mary, you hold on to my wrist. If anything goes wrong, pull me back in," Cos said.

"Hold on, Cosimo. You don't have permission to pass through yet," Susan said.

"You do realize that we have been recruited to go in there and try to find someone? I need to test it for myself, or you can forget about me letting Mary go in there." Cos looked defiantly first at Susan then Ray to see if they still had any objections. He could see Ray's shrug toward Susan which meant that he would not object to the test.

Cos offered Mary his wrist, and she took it, bracing her feet as if she were going to pull on a rope. He crouched down and slowly put his head and upper body through the opening, leaving only his hand and wrist inside. He slowly stood erect, extending his head above the opening and out of their sight. Suddenly he crouched and dove back through to the inside.

"Better shut it down, Doctor. I was seen by a group of armed men, and they are running this way," Cos said excitedly, then pulled Mary away from the Portal. Susan rapidly went to the terminal, and just as voices from the other side could be heard getting louder, the opening vanished.

"I'm convinced, most assuredly convinced, that I just went through a window into the past. That was a group of Roman foot soldiers out there. I think all of us just had a close call," Cos said, showing his teeth. "Look at my hand! It's trembling!" he laughed, holding out his hand.

"We just learned something, thanks to the bravery of Cos," Mary announced. "There seems to be no risk from going through the opening, but plenty after you are on the other side." She helped Cos dust off, while Ray and Susan watched in silence.

"I have a suggestion, Susan," Cos said. "I think the Portal should be opened only after it's dark on the other side. There is a primitive road only a few meters away, and it appears to be well-used."

"That's a good recommendation. We'll work out times for the opening to make sure that is the case. See anything else?" she asked.

"Not a lot of time to look, but I think I saw the edge of a large rock formation. With only a glimpse, we still can't tell exactly where the opening is located, and that brings up a point about the trip we are being asked to make. You do realize that we can't carry a GPS device? There is really no way to know exactly where we are. Finding our way back here might be very challenging."

Mary's eyebrows elevated as if she had just discovered something. "Say, there are maps which have been constructed of the ancient world, and the exact location of some cities are known from our excavations. You know the approximate location of the opening from your studies. If we combine the two, we will have at least something to go on. We must also be allowed to bring an accurate orienteering-style compass which will allow us to sight landmarks and plot our location after we get there."

"Does this mean that you two agree to make the trip?" Ray asked.

Cos stepped in front of Mary and turned to face Ray, "It means that we still have to talk it over first."

Mary looked around his arm with excited eyes, "May we return here again in the morning?"

Ray shrugged again, "If that is what it takes, then that is what it takes. I really want to get on with this project, but I can respect your caution in wanting to get it right. Tomorrow all right with you, Susan?"

"Sure, it's The Commission's money we are spending. It will be dark in Ancient Galilee at three in the afternoon, our time. See you then."

"Ray? One more thing," Cos asked. "Did you have appropriate clothing ready for us to wear if and when we do this mission for you?"

"Our researchers have already selected and created your attire. You will be dressed simply, but as a wealthy Roman who is not in the army would have dressed. That means a fine but simple tunic and shoes, not sandals. You will carry a small leather bag, and we also have a nice full purse of reproduction Roman coins for you. Mary will wear a robe of coarse dark wool and be shod in sandals. Tony will be in various rags. The cover story is that you are a Roman from the equestrian class, but who is on his way up the social and political ladder. You are in the area to act as an observer who will report back to a powerful but unnamed party in Rome. Mary is your interpreter, not your slave. Tony will be instructed to act as if he were your slave and will not be permitted to speak."

"Seems like you have been well prepared. Please have my clothing, at least, here tomorrow at three," Cos requested.

"Do you plan to go in tomorrow, Cos?" Ray asked.

"I thought it would be a good idea to go in and take bearings of the local geography to find out exactly where the Portal is positioned before all three of us go in. I would also like to get a longer look around. Is there a problem with that?"

"No. I have no issue, and I find that acceptable. I'll get our people on it right away."

La Polonaise Restaurant, Chicago

Once again, they looked at each other from the opposite sides of a dimly lit table, soft music floating in the air. The murmurs of other diners were occasionally punctuated with a clink of glass or a loud, brief laugh.

"Ever been to Italia?" Cos asked.

Mary's eyes sparkled as she smiled broadly at him, "Of course, I have! Many times, in fact. My father is an archeologist, you know, and he has a passion for Roman artifacts. We have many friends in Italy."

"Riesci a parlare Italiano?"

"Enough to tell your fellow rude Italian males to keep their hands away from my buttocks."

"No! You cannot accuse me of this. Haven't I been polite with you?" Cos asked, acting offended with cast down eyes.

"Yes, Cos. You have acted with perfect courtesy. However, I will continue to keep my eyes on you."

"And I have my eyes all over you. You are a magnificent beauty. Meeting you might change my life."

"That is exactly what I mean. You Italian men have it in your mind that women take one look at you and practically pass out because they find you so handsome. Get over it, Cos."

"Don't you find me at the least a *breve* amount attractive?" Cos said, holding up his pinched fingers.

"*Minuscolo*," she answered, holding up a pinched thumb and index finger.

"I will grow on you as you have for me," he laughed.

Mary did find him far more attractive than she would admit, but she wasn't ready for a personal relationship just yet. The mission was on her mind, and she now understood that they were being asked to take on enormous personal risk for a few snapshots of the past. When she thought about it with the logical part of her mind, it seemed preposterous and unwise. Her emotional part, the part that saw history as a giant shadow of the past, that part of her wanted ever so much to go. Just to go back in time and breathe the air and feel the soil from Judea, Samaria, and Galilee thrilled her. The chance of meeting Jesus Christ in person was the fondest wish of endless numbers of people from the present and the past, and she had the chance to actually do it. At this moment, she was nearly ready to agree to go through.

"Cos, are you going to go, or are you still making up your mind."

"I am going in alone tomorrow. Whether you go, depends on what I find. You realize that I spend nearly all of my life dwelling on the past, and that part of me is aching to go in there and see that world. Yet, we don't want to throw our lives away because of a poorly thought out scheme. We should be the ones who decide, based on facts. I know enough about Roman history to know that they were smart, well organized and efficient. The word "ruthless" doesn't even come close to describing what they were capable of. If someone odd shows up, making them feel suspicion or uncertainty, then that person's life will be quickly forfeit. I don't plan on it being us."

"It's not just the Romans we have to consider, Cos. You, for instance, will be a Roman pretending to be a Roman. The Jews of that time felt oppressed by Romans' control and hated what they saw as an occupation. The people in that area had a history of uprisings against the Greeks following Alexander's conquest. Romans tried to control the area by force but always sensed that trouble was not long ahead. Julius Caesar wisely appointed a Jewish leader we know as Herod the Great to rule the area. He did rule, but with brutality, and most people from Judea never accepted Herod as one of them. After his death, Augustus appointed Herod's three sons to divide and rule the area and govern according to Roman wishes, but they were hated by the people just as much or more than Herod the Great. We are going to be there in 27 AD, and during those years, there was rising tension among the Yehudi people. The big revolt against the Romans finally occurred in 66 AD or thereabouts. Roman retribution to quell the uprising is said to have cost the lives of over a million people in Palestine, totally destroying most of its cities. When Jerusalem finally fell, the Temple of Herod was taken down, block by block, stone by stone, and leveled to rubble. My point is that you personally are risking violence from the indigenous people, because you are so obviously Roman. Ray said that his boy, Tony, will be there to protect us, and that's a real laugh. If he does manage to shoot somebody, it will bring the house down on us. A few bullets won't stop the Roman Army or an angry mob. I personally want to go, but I really don't see any way that this is going to work."

"You're right to feel that way, Mary, and in my rational mind I think the same way. The only way it's going to work is for us to know exactly where we are coming from and where we are going and keep a low profile, moving in shadows and making no waves. Jesus of Nazareth should be close by, and we are going to find him and leave before anyone knows we are there. I think you would agree that we would be safer going into Rome itself rather than this conflicted area. Perhaps The Commission will have another trip for us if we return successfully from this one. Once we get used to being there, we will adapt and fit in. We may even like it."

Chapter 8

Antonius Severius Maximus

os stood in the middle of the floor, twirling around like a young girl, looking down at his billowing tunic and his new Roman shoes. He threw his head back and roared a long laugh. "Look at the Roman who finally is a Roman!" and laughed again. Mary laughed with him and was struck by the magnetic attractiveness of this combination of a well-muscled man possessed by the spirit of an adolescent boy.

"If you are finished showing off, Cosimo," Ray interrupted, "come over here and make sure this is the equipment you need." A folding table was laden with items which included a red cloak, fasteners, a sheathed knife, a professional folding compass and a goatskin bag of water. The map was rolled tightly and held with slender rawhide straps, and Cos picked it up and started untying it.

"Ah," he exclaimed as he unrolled the thin sheepskin. The printing was done by computer but appeared rough, as if hand drawn. The map had the familiar elevations and compass bearing markings. "This will do nicely. Thanks for the extra effort to disguise it."

"Everything you need there, Cos?" Ray asked.

"I'm only going far enough to take sightings of two or three elevations to exactly locate our position, then I'm coming right back in. Just in case, though, a little money wouldn't hurt." Ray tossed him a small leather bag which jingled in the air before Cos caught it. He hefted the bag a couple of times and seemed satisfied.

Standing by the computer terminal, Susan called out, "Ten more minutes." There was a sense of urgency in the room, nearly like they imagined a space launch would be anticipated. Cos shouldered his equipment and slung his robe over his shoulders and for the first time seemed subdued.

"You'll be careful in there, Cos, won't you?" Mary asked while clasping his hand in hers. She looked up at him as if she would never see him again. Her eyes said that this departure was as one of a would-be lover, and much too early.

"Last minute reminder, Cos," Susan said above the increasing whine of the apparatus. "The opening will last exactly five minutes, then open again just before dawn for another five minutes. If you don't show for either one, we will keep trying at those specific times for at least a month. No one is going to be allowed to follow you back in time, so understand that you will be on your own. Please tell us now if you still want to go in."

"Yes, I'm ready, Dr. Harmes. I have to get three bearings, and I may have to wait for the second opening if that takes some time. If I don't come right back in, please don't become alarmed." Without looking at Mary, he squeezed her hand, which was still in his. There was an increasing intensity of mechanical noise, and they all could feel the tingle, starting at the base of their neck.

A loud metallic clang preceded Susan's shout, "There it is!" This time the opening was dark, seeming to absorb light from the room. Susan clicked some keys, and the ambient light in the tunnel dimmed to a soft glow. "We don't want the opening lit like a bulb," she explained.

The opening sat there like a living presence, dark and mystifying, waiting to take Cos in, consuming him like a wolf gobbles a small rodent. Cos had a last look around, gave a short wave, leaned forward and disappeared into the night of long ago. For a few brief moments, they could hear his footsteps on the dry soil, then silence. Mary couldn't help putting her hands over her mouth to suppress her emotions when the last glimpse of Cos passed out of view of the opening. They all waited, listening for any telling sound that he was returning. They had a long wait ahead.

Cos crouched down low after going through and looked back into the Fermilab tunnel to reassure himself that there was still an exit should he need one. Listening, he stood slowly erect, looking around cautiously, letting his eyes adjust to the natural light of night in a world only lit by flames or nature. Nothing was moving, not even the wind, and the stars above him were more clear than he could ever remember. For as far as he could see, there was no light made by man, as if he had landed on the surface of the moon, surrounded by silence and rock. Distantly, toward the right, the dim blue outline of an upward swelling of the otherwise nearly flat landscape hovered on the faint horizon. He searched for another hill, but a small rise in front of his position obscured any remaining landmarks. He would have to find a small elevation to take bearings, and he readied his compass. Moving slowly forward, he focused on being alert to any threat from dark shadows. After a short walk due north, he slowly began to make out something ahead, but it was darker in that direction, and he couldn't tell if the shape was manmade or a rocky formation. There was a soft shuffling, scuffing sound, drifting on the wind from ahead, growing more distinct with each moment, clearly human in origin. Then he heard the voices.

"Custodi in gradu stare querentes," [Keep in step and stop complaining] a harsh voice said with malice. The clink of metal against metal sharply penetrated the night air as the column grew closer. Cos heard at least two horses blending with the growing cacophony of troops. The Roman column seemed close enough to see, but Cos still couldn't make out anything other than a dark squirming mass slightly to the east. He flattened himself behind a large stone hoping that they would pass quickly. The first close sound was a soft crunch of gravel just behind him, and he suddenly felt a sharp point in his back, causing him to groan and stiffen.

"Tardius surgere aut hic moriar," [Get up slowly or die here] a gruff voice growled behind him. The point dug farther into his back for emphasis. As directed, Cos got slowly to his feet, twisting to see his new adversary. In the dim light of the stars, he could make out a short but thick man, holding a very long spear which now was resting against his chest.

"Deponite hastam. Ego homo sum quidem ciuem Romanum, sanxit te ferat non sustinet," [Put down your spear. I am a Roman citizen and bear you no threat] Cos said, slowly while placing his hand on the spearpoint. The point pushed into his chest harder causing Cos to step back in pain.

"Attentus!" the soldier shouted, continuing to press his spear into Cos. A murmur of voices erupted and grew louder, the ground trembling as

others headed his way. Quickly, he was surrounded by similar soldiers all pointing spears at him, making him feel like an animal who had been brought to bay by hounds. Before Cos could again state his innocence, he felt vibrations from a mounted horse moving toward them, parting the circle of men. From his lofty position, a Roman officer surveyed his prisoner, the tuft of ornamentation from his crested helmet swaying with his motion,

"Quid quaeritis nomen tuum," [Give your name and why you are here] he demanded. The crowd of men stood silent, waiting for Cos to reply.

"Paulo Fabio Persico, ego filius sum, et vocavi Cosimus. Pereo." [I am the son of Paulus Fabius Persicus, and I am called Cosimus. I am lost.]

"Huc venturus Cosimus," [Come here, Cosimus] the officer ordered. Cos felt the spear pressure lessen, and he walked toward the horse and its rider. Two dozen spears remained pointed at him. He stopped, looking up at the dark shadow above him. A metal breast plate softly glinted in the starlight, but there wasn't enough light to see any detail. The officer shifted in his saddle and dropped to the earth just in front of Cos, enveloping him with the smell of sweat and leather.

"Tu nuper ab Roma uenerunt?" [You are recently arrived from Rome?] he asked.

"Utique," [Yes] Cos answered.

"Loqueris cum ignota accentus." [You speak with an unfamiliar accent.]

"Sum peregre fuit multis temporibus." [I have been away from home a long time.]

"Tu saltim lingua?" [Do you speak the language of the locals?]

"Non habeo interpres sed facti sumus separati." [No. I have a translator, but we became separated.]

Silence hung in the air like a living force as the fate of Cos hung by a slender thread. The night was still except for the exhalation of the horse and the occasional shift of some of the men. They all waited on the officer's word which could be either life or death. Cos was calm on the outside, but he was rapidly thinking of anything else he could say to convince this officer to spare his life.

"Vecordem juvenem es. Et venies nobiscum." [You are a foolish young man. You will come with us.] He quickly mounted and announced to the large group of assembled men, *"Ne respondeatis, aut mihi!"* [Do not harm him

or you will answer to me!]

Cos was pushed, roughly at first, into the group which headed back toward the waiting troop column. They fell into a rapid march step, boxing Cos into the middle between two large, well-armored soldiers, both ignoring him. As the moon rose, Cos could see ahead and behind a long line of marching troops. There was little talk, most of their energy consumed by the effort of walking while fully armored. On the horizon, he made out the irregular form of a settlement, outlined in silver by moonlight. According to his previous assumption, this would likely be Nazareth, and given the probable length of time and pace of the march, approximately seven miles from the Portal.

"Quod est ante Nazera?" [Is that Nazareth ahead?] Cos asked the man beside him. The man glanced briefly at him and shrugged. Either he didn't know or didn't understand Latin. Cos knew that there were several different languages mixed into this area, but he recalled that during this time period, Rome insisted that Latin was the official language of the military. But, this group may be an auxiliary unit formed in Galilee, he realized, remembering that although there were at least four Roman Legions permanently stationed in nearby Syria, Rome controlled this area largely by proxy. Cos assumed that a majority of the men in this group probably were *Auxilia*, recruited locally, most of the recruits natively speaking in either Aramaic or Greek, not Latin. The highly educated Roman officers were always schooled in both Latin and Greek. He decided to try again asking, *"Είναι ότι Nazera μπροστά,"* this time using Greek.

From somewhere ahead he heard a reply, *"Cognoscam te cito. Quiescite."* [You will find out soon. Be quiet.] Cos decided to be silent as ordered and so they marched with effort across the moonlit landscape toward an unknown fate awaiting Cos. He had plenty of time to think and look around. Was this what he wanted? To be back in time only felt like being in the present...the people, the soil, felt, smelled, as real as ever, his burning legs felt as tired. It was hard not to be impressed with these soldiers' willingness to bear physical hardship without complaint, not even a grunt. It was, after all, their lot, and they understood that they were better off than most. It dawned on Cos that he was here for real now, not from the future, and might never return to it. This era was now his to live or die in, and he resolved to force himself not to dwell on escape. He summoned his courage. After all, he thought, he really was a Roman. All he had to do is convince this officer that he had connections by birth, and therefore should be treated with respect. The army slowly made its way toward the village, looming as an irregular grey mass rising out of the dry soil. Cos recalled that this city was destroyed during the Jewish uprising of 63 because its Yehudim population dared fight against the might of the Roman Army. Everything in sight will be gone by the twenty-first century, the modern, mostly Arab city of Nazareth sprawling over the remains like a spider astride her nest.

They entered the southern edge of the city in darkness, traveling slowly north toward the other side. The smell of feces, animals and garbage greeted his nose and penetrated his sinus, and he had to fight back retching. Shadows moved and squirmed in the dark corners, but whoever or whatever they were, they wanted no encounter with this large armed force passing through the center of town, and the army continued to march in unimpeded silence toward the outer limit. There was no city wall and no gates. Fortifications will be created by Crusaders six hundred years in the future, but even they were gone by the twenty-first century. Cos was surprised, but at the same time relieved, that there was no stopping in this putrid place. About five miles--*quinque milia passuum*--of additional walking, the column abruptly halted. Off to the left were several long rows of what appeared to be conventional pup tents with two much larger octagonal tents in the center. Several fires were burning and shapes of men were moving near the firelights.

"Dimissa ad quietem cibum,"[Dismissed for rest and food,] a loud commanding voice said, and the men started moving toward the tents and fires. Cos was left standing without direction, unsure of what he should do. A heavy hand on his shoulder turned him around to face a very chiseled man covered in chain mail and holding a long threatening spear. *"Centurio vult. Veni isto modo,"*[Centurion wants you. Come this way,] he said, pointing the way with the sharp tip of his spear. As they walked past, the men were noisily shedding their armor and chatting freely in a language which was neither Latin or Greek. From the fires came the fragrant aroma of cooking food and freshly baked bread. Dawn was approaching and a pink border outlined the low slung hills to the east.

Cos had a close look at the tents on the way past and found them amazingly familiar and similar to tents he had used on camping outings in his youth. Most seemed to be at least eight man units made of glossy goatskin fabric and secured with line to iron stakes at the corners. In the center of the orderly camp were two much larger tents constructed of a lighter color fabric, decorated with tassels and colored cloth. Outside the main flap rose two gold staffs, each carrying a gilded crossbar and red textile cloth emblazoned with the number of the *Cohort* and the *Centuriae*...the *Textilis Anguis,* a sight which thrilled Cos to see as he faced the entry with increasing trepidation. This display of Roman authority humbled him as it had most of Europe for several centuries. As he pulled back the heavy cloth and leather tent flap to enter, he was stunned to see the dirt floor covered by wood planks and various cloths and carpets. A muscular man about his age, dressed in a simple linen tunic, sat behind a small wooden desk. The room was lit by scattered small bronze oil lamps, one flickering on the desk.

"Now you can tell me what you are really doing in Galilee, Cosimus," the man asked in Latin and looked up from his papers with a frown. There was a sheen to his arms, reflecting the dim yellow light in streaks and shadows, emphasizing his muscularity. He was handsome with dark, tousled and curly hair, very similar to Cos' own. Antonius was clearly a man used to living a hard life, accustomed to having unquestioned discipline from his troops and making judgments quickly and ruthlessly.

"The truth, Centurion, is that I am a historian, or trying to be. I am here to observe and write about history, for this is a historic land," Cos answered.

"What is your father's position in Rome?"

"He is a *Quaestor*, Centurion. Soon to be a Senator, he hopes." Adding, "and I also hope."

"To be sure, Cosimus. My name is Antonius Severius Maximus, and you may call me Antonius since you are not under my command."

"I am grateful to you for rescuing me from the desert, Antonius. My friends call me Cos, and I hope that you will consider me a friend."

"This place, Cos, is not safe for you to travel alone. There are bandits about and the local people hate Romans like us. Where are you going?"

"We were trying to get to a little village called Nazara. Is that the place we just passed through?"

"I am told that it is called Nazat. It is a place of no importance and filled with the Yehudim. Why would you want to go there?" Antonius asked with his penetrating stare.

"We were asked to talk to a man called Jesus who might live there."

"There are many called Jesus in this land. For what reason do you seek him?"

"A prophet said that Jesus is the Son of God."

Antonius laughed and sat back in his chair. "Cos, you may not live to see Rome again! You are on an errand of a fool. And your father seeks to be Senator!" He laughed again, then clapped his hands. A tall thin servant entered and stood waiting for instructions.

"Bring our food and wine, we are ready to fill our bellies," Antonius said loudly, and the servant bowed and quickly left. "Cos, you will stay and eat with me. I would like to know more about you. There is much that you are hiding, and I intend to find out what it is."

"I would enjoy knowing about you, Antonius. You seem destined to have a role in history, and I intend to discover what it will be."

"I am a simple warrior, Cosimus. Not much to know except that I have served the Roman Army for ten years and seen many campaigns in Gaul prior to being sent to this doomed place of rocks. It is my undeserved fate for having birth connection to a family which has moved out of favor. Emperor Tiberius was a good man at first, but now he retires to his island leaving the Roman people in the hands of Sejanus. No good can come of it, I feel, but there is little that any of us can do to change things from far away. The Roman Legions are kept abroad, and Rome itself is gripped by the fist of the Praetorians."

"You may have heard the rumors, Antonius, that Sejanus courted Livilla, the wife of Tiberius' son, Drusus, plotting with her to poison Drusus with the goal of succeeding Emperor Tiberius himself." Cos said.

"No! I have not heard that! It would explain Sejanus' rise to power. Where did you hear such talk?"

"I have my sources. I am friends with Gaius Velleius Paterculus, another historian, and he has access to those who know."

"Then Sejanus grows in power. Nothing can stop him."

"Don't despair, Antonius, things will change. In three years, Sejanus will be executed on the order of Tiberius, and afterward, Rome will enter a troubled period, where many now in power will fall."

"Cosimus, either you are lying to me or the Gods whisper in your ear. You know the future, then?"

"I know what citizens are saying. Hatred and fear build with time, and there is an end to all things."

"Then if you are correct, it was wise for me not to befriend any Julian. I may be able to avoid being cast down the Gemonian stairs with them." Antonius reached under his table and pulled out the possessions which had been removed from Cos when he was taken captive. "I need you to explain these items," he said, laying them out on the table. The map was untied and spread out, the compass and knife placed on top. "What are these, Cos?"

"This is a new way of finding your location, Antonius. The map is of Judea, Sumatra and Galilee. You can see the rise of the hills by these small lines and tell the grade by noticing how close they are to each other. The other item is called a compass." Cos opened it to demonstrate. "This moving arrow always points to the north. Rome is slightly north but mostly west of where we are now. Using the map and compass together, you can always find your way."

"Then my question to you, Cos, is why were you lost?"

"Simple. I had not had time to sight any hills and locate them on the map."

"If that is true, then you suddenly appeared behind that rock. Otherwise you would have had plenty of time. Another thing, Cos, this map is unsoiled and therefore never before used, just like your clothing or shoes or knife. It is unsettling to see that you have items that have never been seen or used before, and you also appear to know the future. Tell me, Cos, do you also know what is to happen to the lands we call Iudaea?"

"Will you believe what I say?"

"Uncertain. I do want to hear it though. Speak."

"There will be a great uprising in thirty years, and most of the cities and people will be destroyed. Afterward, Rome will attempt the extermination of the Yehudim people and destroy for all time the Temple of Herod."

"I believe what you say may come true, because I feel the looks of intense hatred coming out of their eyes. It is only a question of time before an uprising springs to life. Who or what are you Cosimus?"

"It is apparent that you and I have differences, Antonius, but I was born in Rome, just as you were, and I am a historian just as I have said. If I have knowledge that will serve you, then I will share it with you. Some facts will disturb you if I told you everything, and some of the things I know might prevent you from living a full life. Information is not always good, because it seems best that a person experience life as it comes. It is not meant for us to always know in advance what is to happen, because we would still be powerless to change it. One thing I want to clarify. I may know the general trend of history, but I don't know many day to day details. I never knew about you, for instance, before your men took me captive, and I know nothing about your fate. At this point, I don't even know my own. As for our relationship, Antonius, I would like to quote a noble and famous Roman who said, 'The rule of friendship means there should be mutual sympathy between them, each supplying what the other lacks and trying to benefit the other, always using friendly and sincere words.' "

"Ah, you know Cicero! Then here is my favorite quote of his, 'Friendship improves happiness and abates misery, by the doubling of our joy and the dividing of our grief'."

"We were destined to be friends, Antonius," Cos said and extended his hand to the hard shoulder of Antonius who did the same to him.

"Brothers, Cosimus, we will become brothers."

The aroma of roasted lamb preceded the servant who came in with a large tray of cooked meat and bread. He placed a flask of goat milk and one of wine on the table and sat the tray between them. They broke bread together and drank from the same flasks each carefully watching and thinking.

"Will there be a day that you will trust me with the truth, Cos?"

"I trust you enough now. The trust you should have in me is to believe me when I tell you that you are not yet ready. I would rather show you someday than to tell you now, because only then you will fully believe me."

"We will rest here today and tonight march on to Tiberias on Galilee.

You are welcome to come with us, if you wish, or you may go your way. Your things are yours to take with you. I will wish you good fortune if you leave on your own, because you are going to need it. You seem to have no weapon and no food and cannot talk the language of the Yehudim. Likely, you will not live to see another day, but your own life is yours to live or to throw away."

"I must try to fulfill my mission, Antonius. Please…I would like you to have my map and compass if you would accept them as a gift, and I will show you how to best use them today before I leave."

"The honor will be mine, Cosimus, and in return I will ask that you accept my sword. It may save your life someday. If you ever reach the city called Tiberias on the Sea of Galilee, search for me. It is only *viginti milium*, twenty miles, from here and you will find a Roman bath and abundant women there."

After night fell, the *centuriae* assembled to continue their march toward Tiberias, and Cos left alone, heading back in the opposite direction toward Nazara. He covered himself with his cloak trying to hide his new sword. Antonius told him that he would encounter few others at night, but if he did, he would need the sword. An uncomfortable thought. On this path, he was to pass directly back through the middle of the village, and there were bound to be some lurking in shadows who watched his passing. Assailants might shrink from a unit of eighty experienced and well-armed soldiers but not from a single man covered in a Roman cape who didn't speak any language they could understand. Antonius was right, this was to be a perilous night. The time had passed for the first Portal opening, and it was seven more hours until the next. Judging from the previous night's march he had at least five or more hours of travel time, more if he was diverted. Cos let out a deep sigh and plodded forward into the night.

Chapter 9

The Return Trip

On The Path 11:00 P.M.

The dark sky blended with the ink black landscape ahead of him as if he were entering a passage into the underworld. The absence of noise, even crickets, made the journey seem endless. There was no moon yet, and even the stars were dim. He regretted now that he had given Antonius his compass, but he remembered his delight as its usefulness dawned on him. Antonius had been like a child discovering a new toy and couldn't get enough of it. He begged Cos for more maps, which of course he couldn't provide. Over the course of a day, they became fast friends and had even discussed previous women in their lives. Antonius had both a primary and secondary education in Rome and had afterward been coached in philosophy, elocution and mathematics by private Greek tutors. He would make a fine Senator or perhaps a Praetor [General] some day. Cos was impressed with Antonius' depth of knowledge, not only regarding geography but also history and philosophy. So impressed that he feared discussing some subjects, because, at times, Antonius was the better informed.

Earlier at the Roman Camp 9:00 A.M.

"Cosimus," Antonius had abruptly said. "You appear to be fit. Are you skilled at arms?" The question was heavy with implication, and Cos was hesitant to answer.

"I have some knowledge, but compared to an experienced soldier such as you, I will not brag." He hoped that Antonius would forget the whole thing, but he was mistaken.

"In that case, let us see what I can teach you about using a sword."

Cos groaned. Some men were summoned, and they all walked together to the practice area, already in heavy use by several pairs of men. The assembly backed up and formed a circle, ready to watch their commander take on the newcomer. Cos could feel his upper lip running with sweat, as were the palms of his hands. Both shield and sword, borrowed from a nearby soldier, were heavy, the large rectangular shield seeming to weigh about twenty pounds. Even though Cos was very fit, as he watched Antonius warming up, he felt fear overtaking him. In his youth, he had studied karate and kendo, but there is no shield used in those sports, and the technique involved is more sporting than serious. This was the real thing with men who killed for a living.

"Lift up your *scutum* [shield] and *gladius* [sword] and defend yourself," Antonius commanded, advancing aggressively toward Cos. Cos readied himself and raised his large shield, obscuring his view of the oncoming Antonius. Quickly, the side of Antonius' gladius swept around his shield and slapped Cos on the thigh leaving a large welt. The men started to laugh at Cos and were pointing at him.

"Ready again, Cosimus. Defend if you can." This time the sword came around from the opposite side with the point aimed at his chest but stopped just short of penetrating skin. "You can do better, Cosimus. You are being killed." The men laughed again. Cos dropped his shield slightly to get a look at his experienced opponent, but as he did, the sword descended from above and rapped him on his head.

"Put down your scutum, Cosimus, you are hopeless. It's like fighting a woman," Antonius said with a laugh. "Have you ever fought before?" he asked.

"Boxing and karate. I did some work with a wooden sword for a couple of years." Cos answered, wiping away the sweat from his brow.

"What is boxing and karate?" Antonius asked loudly. The soldiers laughed again.

"Hand-to-hand combat. Should I show you?" Cos inquired, his eyebrows up. He felt that this time he finally had the upper hand and gladly laid aside his shield and sword.

"You should know, Cosimus, I am well trained in fighting, and I learn quickly." A warning that nearly made Cos have a sudden change of heart. Antonius laid his armor and sword aside and pulled off his tunic, exposing his very muscular chest and arms. Cos was a bit taller, but Antonius was clearly the more fit, and also superbly confidant. Cos went into a slight crouch as he was taught in his Dojo, bringing another laugh from the surrounding soldiers. "No, no, my brother. You have to stand up to fight," Antonius chuckled, and he started moving aggressively toward Cos. A foot shot up and caught Antonius squarely in the jaw, and he fell backwards into the sand.

Antonius sat up holding his face. "I had that coming, Cos, but it won't work a second time." He stood up quickly brushing off the dirt. There was a blush of anger in his face, and there was no more joking. Again he came forward with his hands nearly by his sides, and this time, Cos connected with a left punch to his nose. Getting up again, Antonius said, "I must admit, these are strange but effective tactics, but I'm not yet beaten." This time he ran right at Cos exploding with a loud yell. Cos sidestepped the rush and extended his leg to trip Antonius, who went down hard. Cos immediately jumped on his opponent's chest, holding him down with his knee and faking a strike to his face.

"At least I know something, Antonius, even though you are the better man," he said, then extended his hand to help Antonius up. The other men applauded and yelled their approval, and one picked Cos into the air in an embrace.

"You are victorious, Cos. This fallen warrior applauds you," Antonius said and held up Cos' arm for everyone to see. "Now, I have something I want you to do." He turned to a nearby soldier. "Bring the wooden practice swords," then turned back to Cos. "You are to learn to use a sword before this day is done. You will start with the smaller men and not be permitted to stop until each opponent is beaten. The larger and more experienced we save for last. I am going to get some needed rest. Take heart, this will save your life someday." With a small wave to the men, Antonius departed for his tent. Cos looked around at the grinning men. This was going to be a hard day.

North of Nazareth 1:00 A.M.

Cos stopped abruptly, peering into the darkness ahead. He could just make out the first structures above the rise. It was the village, and he felt his heart rate rising. The night was dead silent except for an occasional dog bark from far ahead. He didn't remember any barking when the column moved through, but he imagined that any dogs would have hidden from the Romans exactly like their masters did. A decision was needed about going into the town or around it, and quickly. The problem was that he didn't want to get lost while away from the path, since he no longer had a compass. A clear array of stars covered the sky, and Antonius would have no problem using them for guidance. So much for progress and technology, he thought. He was also stiff from being poked and thrashed by wooden swords all day, but he had to admit that he had learned an amazing amount in a very short time. Antonius had laughed at his bruises and his swollen face and had mercifully stopped his brutal training session for supper.

Earlier in the Command Tent 6:00 P.M.

"Tell me that you learned a lot from your injuries," Antonius asked with a smile. He patted Cos on the back and escorted him to a chair in his private tent.

"After my arms heal and my head stops hurting, I will certainly be better with a sword. Thank you, my brother, for seeing to my training," Cos said, falling heavily into the chair.

"My men tell me that you have a brave heart and would make a fine soldier. I have a proposal for you to consider. My appointment is Centurion of this Vexillatio, and I am under the command of the Legatus of Syria. I have need of a Tesserarius. I am permitted to appoint my own staff, and I would like you to accept this post."

"You do me a great honor, Centurion. I am humbled by what I have seen of your soldiers and the efficiency and organization of this group. Your men seem to hold you in high regard, not fear, and I believe that they would gladly die in battle rather than disappoint you. I am starting to feel like I belong here, and I hate to part from your company so soon. However, there are people waiting for me, and I must return to where you found me earlier. It is possible that we will come to Tiberias, and if we do, I will look for you there. If we never meet again, then I want to express my thankfulness for treating me with civility and respect. I'll never forget you."

"Since I have your respect, Cos, it is time for you to tell me the truth about yourself. We should have no secrets from each other, especially since we may not meet again."

"You would never believe me."

"You said that you could show me when I was ready. I am ready."

"When I tell you what you want to know, you will think that I am mad, and we will lose our connection to each other. I could only prove it to you one way, by taking you with me. You could see with your own eyes and even then you might not believe."

"All right, I will not ask again, and I will accept you as you are," Antonius said, disappointed.

Cos shifted in his seat, uncomfortable, because he had let his new friend down. He pondered how he could be more open, yet protect Antonius from knowing things he should not know but at length decided to tell the honest truth and see what would happen.

"Do I have your word that you will tell no other person what I am about to tell you?"

"My word as a Roman is my honor, and you have it."

"Hold on to your chair, Antonius. I was born in Rome, just as I have said, and I studied Latin and Greek just as you have. Most of my life has been spent learning everything I could about ancient Rome. Ancient, because I was born nearly two thousand years later than you. I traveled back in time to be here. I am from your future."

Antonius, at first just stared at him with a blank look and then started to smile and laugh. "I was not expecting you to say that! So funny!" He held his sides and rolled with laughter. "Never could I have guessed that you were from my future!" He laughed until his eyes teared, and as he wiped his face with the back of his hand, he noticed that Cos wasn't smiling. "Don't say that you are telling me the truth?"

Cos nodded, "yes," and then pulled up his sleeve and removed his wrist watch and threw it on the table. Antonius picked it up and studied it closely. "What is this?" he asked.

"It is called a watch. It tells time like your sundial does. The hours of the day are marked by the numbers of the decimal system. Each day has twenty-four hours, sixty minutes in each, and sixty seconds in each minute. The day of the month is visible in the little window. Ever seen anything like it?"

"No."

"I don't have much with me that will prove what I say. You already saw the compass and the map. My knife was copied after ones that were found in excavations, as was my clothing and my coins, and they look nearly the same as the ones from this time. You will either have to take my word for it or not. I told you that you wouldn't believe me."

"If you came from the future, how did you get here?"

"An opening was created, and I walked through it nearly where your man found me. It only opens twice a day for a brief time. The next will be just before dawn, and that is why I have to return. They are waiting for me."

"And when you reunite, you will attempt to find this Jesus you spoke of?"

"Yes. That is why I am here. We weren't sure exactly where the opening was located, and I came out to look around and was captured."

"Jesus must be an important person. Who is he?"

"We think he is just a woodworker. A nobody at the moment."

"Then, why do you want him?"

"I was asked to just find him, that's all."

"This doesn't make a good story, Cos."

"That's what I thought also. Do you believe what I have told you?"

"Of course I don't."

"I give you my word as a Roman that my story is true."

"I still cannot believe what I know is not true," Antonius said. They looked at each other for a time with nothing left to say.

"You may also keep the watch. It will work for two or three more years, then the battery will expire, and it will never work again."

"*Lorem ipsum*, Cos," he said, but a door seemed to close between them, and Cos could see a slight change in his new brother's eyes.

North of Nazareth 1:15 A.M.

Cos stood erect and decided to walk straight into the village, continuing on through, with as little noise as possible. He started forward with a determined stride, an inner calmness about his possible fate, just as he felt and heard the sounds of horses rapidly coming toward him from the rear. He quickly got off of the path, just as the horses crested the hill behind him.

"Cosimus!" Antonius called out. He pulled up to a stop, and the horse he had in tow did the same, raising a cloud of dust, visible even in the dark. "I decided to accompany you. You will need my protection a little longer. You ride, don't you?"

"Thank the gods, Antonius!" Cos said as he jumped back on the trail. "I thought I was about to use my new sword skills on someone."

"And I could not leave you alone in this evil place. Besides, you will show me proof of your fanciful story, won't you?"

"I will, Antonius. How long can you be away from your men?"

"By dawn, the main body should be nearing Tiberias. Several hand-picked men are waiting for my return back in camp, and we should be able to reach Tiberias after nightfall, if I return by morning."

After Cos mounted his horse, Antonius tossed him the reins saying, "Time is short, Cosimus, we go." They galloped toward the sleeping Nazara, chased by a cloud of red dust. "Keep your speed as we enter, Cosimus," Antonius shouted. A good plan, Cos realized. The village was small and asleep. By the time the residents heard the noise, they would be well past. The real problem would be crossing back through during the daytime, and Cos realized that Antonius had put himself at risk by his actions. The village looked different, even smaller, from the back of a galloping horse, and they quickly passed through without incident. The moon had risen, lighting the well-worn path in silver and grey, and they relaxed, slowing to a cantor. "Do you recall the place we seek?" Antonius asked after a couple of miles.

"I'm hoping that I can find it again. It will be on the left, just after a small hill," Cos answered. "Not too much farther, I think." Guessing at the time, he assumed that there were at least two more hours until sunrise. He felt apprehension that he would not be able to find the Portal and feared that Antonius would never believe him again. The terrain was dismally similar, mile after mile, with rocks and dirt and little else. The horses plodded along softly in the loose soil, making time seem suspended, as if this place had never, and could never, change. Cos realized that his saddle was remarkably comfortable. There were horns at the four corners, instead of one in front center, which resulted in a sensation of security. The night air was cool, and they both drew their long capes in tightly around them. Antonius was wearing his *galea* [metal helmet] which glinted in the moonlight. As a Centurion, he had the decorative top with long purple horsehair plumes hanging, swaying from side to side as his head rocked with his mount's step. Neither man carried a shield, but both had swords hanging from their left side.

"This may be it," Antonius said, abruptly halting his horse. Cos looked around but didn't see anything familiar. Antonius pointed to several piles of horse dung which were closely spaced. He was right, the column had stopped in this place. They both dismounted and led their horses off the path to the left side. "See anything you recognize, Cos?" he asked.

Cos started to sweat from stress. No, nothing looked familiar. He was lost as he feared he would be. Dismounting he started walking around, inspecting the rocks in the near dark. "Antonius, are you wearing the watch?" he asked. Antonius proudly held up his wrist and showed that he was indeed wearing it. Cos came over and looked at the time. Thirty more minutes until the Portal opened. Desperate to find the location, he stood up, looking back toward the horses as something familiar came to him. Right beside him was the rock he attempted to hide behind when he was captured. A close inspection of the area showed the footprints of the soldiers who had come from the path. A feeling of relief came over him, and he sat down.

"Something amiss, Cos?" Antonius asked.

"Not a thing. I found it," he said and pointed to where the opening was expected to appear. "We might as well sit and talk. We have thirty more minutes before anything happens."

They both sat on a nearby flat rock, passing the water flask back and forth. Other than the sound of the horses and footprints on the dust, there was no evidence that other humans existed or had ever existed in this place. The sky was unclouded, the stars and Milky Way brilliant and clear. Antonius took off his helmet and stretched out on the warm rock. "Do you know what stars are?" he asked.

"Sure," Cos said and laid down beside him, also looking at the stars. "They are just like the sun, except very far away."

"When I was studying in Greece, we were taught about Hipparchos and studied his trigonometry. He developed interesting theories which explained the eccentric orbits of the planets. Have you studied astronomy, Cos?"

"I studied trigonometry, but as I recall, they never mentioned Hipparchos. I never took lessons in astronomy."

"Hipparchos also invented the astrolabe. In my youth, I had one sent to me from Rhodes. It gives an exact time of day or night just by sighting stars, and I think that it could be used for navigation as well. It doesn't have a battery and lasts forever." The sarcasm was not lost on Cos.

"I take it that you excelled in mathematics?" Cos asked, trying to change the subject.

"It is a joy to be able to calculate the time and place of the next eclipse. You remember how the method was first discovered?"

"No, but I feel you are about to tell me," Cos said.

"Simple. There was a total eclipse of the sun where Hipparchos was staying in Rhodes. He learned of other eclipses from ancient Babylonian texts and discovered the exact dates and places they had occurred. It was simple math, because he had previously calculated the size of the moon and its distance from us."

"Antonius," Cos said, "Do you understand that the earth is round instead of flat?"

Antonius turned his head toward Cos and remarked, "No, Cos, the earth is not round. It is elliptical, more like an egg. You should know that."

"I do know that, but I'm surprised that you do," Cos said.

"Romans like me are expected to know geometry and other math skills. I simply took an interest in advanced Greek knowledge while I was there."

Cos propped himself up on one elbow and looked in the direction the Portal was expected to appear. "Soon, Antonius. You might want to see it when it happens." They both rolled to a sitting position, watching the area closely.

"You are the most interesting person I have ever met," Cos said. "The most capable and the most dependable by far." Before Antonius could respond, a flickering yellow light appeared, illuminating the rocks adjacent to the spot where they were looking, and a fraction of a second later, a crisp glowing oval materialized only a body length from where they sat, murmuring voices coming from inside.

"I hope he is there this time," Mary said.

"He said not to worry about him, Mary. We just have to keep trying to be patient and hopeful." It was Susan's voice.

Cos got up and leaned into the opening, smiling his radiant smile, "Hi! I'm back!"

"Thank God, Cos. You had me sick with worry," Mary said. Antonius saw a female head partially emerge from the opening and look around, then her head withdrew quickly. "Oh dear, there is another man out there with him," she said to Susan.

Cos beckoned Antonius to come with him, indicating that he should follow behind him into the opening. One at a time, with Cos leading, the two men entered the twenty-first century.

Chapter 10

The Newcomer

on't be alarmed," Cos said holding up his palms. "This is Centurion Antonius Severius Maximus. He is my close friend and protector. I wouldn't be here right now except for him." After entering the tunnel, Antonius Severius stood fully erect and looked steadily at the two women. He was an imposing and remarkable figure clad in chain mail overlaid with a gleaming anatomical breast plate. The purple horsehair from his helmet swayed softly in the moving air of the tunnel.

Susan looked angry, and she moved toward Cos with her finger wagging at him. "You have broken every rule we laid down about this. We cannot introduce our culture and technology into ancient times without consequences. You may also have put your friend at risk, because his immunity is different than ours. Remember what happened to native populations when the whites moved in for the first time. How dare you bring this Roman soldier into our time."

Antonius looked at the two women and smiled, then took off his elaborate helmet. He pointedly made a slight bow to each of them fixing their eyes in his, his armor rattling slightly as he moved. Antonius was an ominous presence, muscular and proud, yet somehow friendly. He watched as the women relaxed toward him. He could see the change in their eyes.

"Quid loquitur lingua sunt?" [What language are they speaking?] he asked without looking away from the women.

"Dicitur Anglis. Linguae Latinae hoc est enim corpus, et Saxonica Celt et aucta fuerit immutatus est," [It is called English. It is a mixture of Latin, Celt and Saxon, and it has been changing for twenty centuries,] Cos answered, and patted him on the shoulder.

Antonius continued to look at Mary with interest and said, *"Vidi mulierem pulcherrima es."*[You are the most beautiful woman I have seen.] She put her hand over her mouth, and her eyes widened as she tried not to laugh. Cos didn't need to translate what was obviously a compliment.

"Cos, what have you brought us?" she asked in a whisper. She continued to look at Antonius as he looked at her. He smiled with a twinkle in his eye, understanding that the centuries had not changed human behavior or the appeal between the sexes. Antonius began to glance around the tunnel taking in what was there. He became fascinated by the fluorescent lighting as well as the computer terminal with its large luminescent screen.

Cos took Susan's arm, pulling her aside, "Look, Susan, I know this was against the rules, but let me explain that in his world, rules are different, and in there, they don't care a thing about our rules. I owe this man a lot more than I can repay, but most of all, I owe him proof of my word. Relax. He already knew that I was from the future, because I told him. Trust me, Susan, this man is very, very smart and perceptive. He has a highly developed sense of honor and duty which is far beyond what I expected. Help me give him a feel for this new world before he has to go back into his. There isn't much time."

"Are you going back with him?" she asked.

"We all are. You better get Tony in here and get our equipment and clothing ready as quickly as you can. He saw to my safety tonight, and I owe him the same. One more thing. Get Ray to buy the best sword he can find in Chicago. It should be similar to a Roman gladius but very fancy. Tell him to make it fast."

"All right, Cos. I'll have to make some calls. Why don't you take him upstairs and show him the Chicago skyline at evening. That should convince him."

"Veni nobiscum, et ostendam tibi visus sit amet lectus," [Come with us, and I will show you a sight that will be hard to forget,] Cos said, pointing up the metal staircase. "Come with us, Mary," he asked.

Cos and Mary led the way up the long staircase, Antonius following closely, his sword occasionally clanking against the metal rails. "I can feel him looking at me, Cos. It's so uncomfortable," Mary whispered. Cos quickly turned and looked behind them.

"He sure is. Right at your butt. I'm afraid you have him hypnotized," Cos said laughing.

"*Tu loqueris: de me?*" [Are you talking about me?] a deep voice asked from behind them.

"*Mary sentit qui vos es truces eius.*" [Mary feels that you are staring at her.]

"*Inveni pulcherrimum eius plenum est et mihi date gloriam gestio.*" [I have discovered her most lovely part, and I am trying give it my full honor.]

"What did he just say?" Mary wondered.

"You don't want to know."

"I understood enough. Typical Italian," she said, as they both laughed, hearing Antonius chuckling to himself.

The door swung open and the three stepped into the Illinois evening, the big city on the lake lit up for show in front of them, reflecting the setting sun from thousands of metallic coated sheets of silver and gold glass. The nearby road still had considerable car traffic, and overhead, a big passenger jet was descending, jet engines screaming, heading for a landing at nearby Midway Airport. Mary and Cos tried to see the familiar sights through the eyes of Antonius, and in doing so, they discovered how awesome their world really is.

Antonius looked around taking it all in and took a deep breath, sighing, "*Tu veraces fuerunt, Cosimus. Nisi dormio, et futurum est deterret.* [You were truthful, Cosimus. Unless I am dreaming, this is the future, and it frightens me]

"*Ubi multa reperias quod vis.*" [You would find that there is much here that you would like.]

"*Non frater meus. Sicut Maria et omnes Lorem parva villa mulier et liberi. Sortem filiorum.*" [No, my brother. All I want is a woman like Mary, a small villa and children, lots of children.]

Mary moved between the two men and gently folded her arms into theirs as they all gazed out at the lights in the distance. Antonius smiled down at her in an affectionate way. He wanted to touch her hair or her shining, clean face, but he resisted. This was a woman out of his dreams, the ones he used to have in Rome as a young man. The years of war and the discipline of the Roman Army had made every stranger a potential threat, even women. He could see the softness in Mary, the way she held her head and the soothing tones of her voice, even though he understood none of it. Antonius sensed that there was already a bond between Cosimus and Mary, but he correctly guessed that they were not lovers. Not yet.

"Et reversus est hoc, Cos?" [Is this one coming back also, Cos?] he asked.

"Valde."

"Et venient ei nocere non potest." [Then we can't let any harm come to her.]

"Non," Cos said and nodded to the skyline.

"What did he say, Cosimo?" Mary asked.

"He asked if you were going back with us, and I said that you were." Mary looked between the men on either side of her, and for the first time, her apprehension of time travel fell away. These two would protect her, she was sure of it. Both were so capable and so gentle toward her that it made her feel safe just being close to them. She took a deep breath and felt relaxed for the first time in days. She started to laugh, suppressing it with her hand, her head down.

"Quid rides tu pulchra creatura. Rides me?" [Why are you laughing, you lovely creature. Are you laughing at me?] Antonius asked.

Mary understood what he meant, even if she didn't know more than two words of what he said. She squeezed his arm affectionately and looked up and shook her head no. "I could not laugh at someone so magnificent as you. But you two are so alike and were born in such different times that I felt it was funny." Antonius looked to Cos for a translation, but he pretended to ignore them rather than give voice to Mary's attraction for his new brother. A small bee of jealousy buzzed around in Cosimo's head looking for a landing. This Roman was obviously a superior package by any standard, but Cos already had developed some affection for Mary and, yes, some longing for her. He sighed. This trip could get interesting in ways nobody could have ever predicted.

As they stood there holding on to each other, leaning against the metal railing, a car sped toward them from the parking lot, pulling up sharply on the grass nearly at the foot of the stairs. A young man got out and looked at them in a strange way.

"You folks look strange for a bunch of scientists. Costume party going on in there?"

"Something like that," Cos said. "You want someone in particular?"

"I was told to deliver this package. Someone is in a hurry for it. Is there a Cosimo inside?"

"I am Cosimo. You found me." The young man shrugged and opened the back door and retrieved a long narrow package from the back seat.

"Then this is yours. I don't know what it is but it's heavy," he said and handed it to Cos who had come down the stairs. Cos opened his small leather sack of coins and retrieved one.

"This is a tip. Don't discard it; it's probably worth a fortune. Your lucky day, my friend, and thanks for the quick service." The young man held his shiny Roman denarius up to the light and shrugged. Cos went back up to the waiting Mary and Antonius. *"Haec tibi, Antoni, te et reuerentiam exhiberet. Nos tibi proderit olim meminisse, spero."* [This is for you, Antonius, and I present it to you with deep respect. I hope that it will help you to remember us someday.]

Antonius looked surprised and took the package with a dip of his head. He carefully pulled the paper away, and a polished sword in a black scabbard emerged. He withdrew it far enough to see the gleam of the handmade folded metal blade and the etched engraving extending down toward the tip. The black metal pommel was elaborately carved into a lions head and the grip was wrapped in black sharkskin.

"Munus apti centurio, princeps populorum et humilis sum. Gratias tibi Cosimus." [A gift fit for a ruler of nations and I am only a humble Centurion. Thank you Cosimus.]

Behind them, the back door opened a crack and Susan put her head through and called to them. "You should come back down, now. We are almost ready."

The three stood in front of the opening, impatiently waiting for Tony to change his clothes. He was unhappy about going, and when he saw Antonius, he took a step backwards. "Is that what they look like?" he asked. "You think I am a bad dude, but this one surely is. I'll bet he's chopped off his share of heads!" he laughed and walked in a small circle looking over the motionless Antonius. "And I see we have a little tight-assed Jewess to drag along with us. At least I have something in mind that she can do for me." Suddenly the statue moved, and moved very quickly, snatching Tony up by his shirt until his feet were dangling. Antonius slowly withdrew the hefty dagger from his waist and put it to Tony's neck.

"Non sicut hic homo. Possumus facere sine eo." [I don't like this one. We can do without him.] The knife left no doubt about his sincerity or willingness to kill. Tony tried to pull the muscular and hardened hand from his neck without success.

"Help! He's going to cut my throat!" he bellowed. Cos stood by, watching and smiling at Tony's discomfort. Frankly, he agreed with Antonius, and he decided not to intervene to at least teach Tony some respect. In a few brief moments, Tony had managed to alienate everybody in the room and earlier had made a big show of strapping on his large handgun under his arm. Flirting openly and insulting Mary had insured that, either or both, Cos or Antonius would become enraged.

Mary was slow to gather her thoughts, because the whole incident had only taken seconds, and Antonius had been so stunningly quick to act. She spoke firmly to Antonius, "Please put him down, Antonius. What he said shouldn't cost him his life. I'm sure that he won't make the same mistake again." Antonius looked at her while she spoke, then glanced at Cos who indicated by pushing his palm toward the floor that Tony should be put down. Antonius opened his hand, and Tony dropped onto the hard concrete floor.

Tony reddened, and with narrowed eyes and flared nostrils he clumsily struggled to his feet. He wasn't used to humiliation or being helpless, and he squared off facing Antonius with his gun dangling in full view. Cos could sense that he was thinking about using it on Antonius and so could Antonius, who unhurriedly withdrew his new glinting sword. In any test of speed, Tony was not likely to win.

"Go ahead and try, Tony," Cos said. "I wanted to see how sharp that new sword is. Don't worry, you'll never feel a thing." There was a moment when there was no movement, with time frozen as in a photograph, as the potential combatants sized each other up. If the explosive instant happened, it would occur in a fraction of a second, and Cos was certain who was going to emerge as victor.

Mary stepped between them and said, "Back off Tony, while you can. We have a mission to complete. By the way, you were about to die, so I want you to remember that the woman you insulted just saved your life." Tony stood erect, never shifting his eyes from Antonius who had not moved since he drew his sword. Mary turned toward him and said, *"Gratias tibi,"* and put her hand on his breast plate. Wordlessly, he put away the sword and then covered her hand with his.

"Despectum sui posceret actionem meam," he said. Mary acknowledged that she understood by smiling at him.

Approaching footsteps made everyone turn to see Ray emerging from the darkened tunnel. "Well, we have the team plus one, I see. He is everything you said, Susan, and more. Wow!"

"Ave Centurione. Raymone est nomen meum, et ego ex Hispania." [Hail Centurion. My name is Raymone, and I am from Spain.] Antonius turned slightly but didn't visibly acknowledge Ray. Not losing a moment, Ray continued, "I came by to wish you luck and good hunting and to see if there was anything else you need."

"We have all we need Ray but one thing," Cos said.

"And what is that, my friend?"

"Your promise that you will keep this opening in time happening until we return."

"I don't know what time period you have in mind, Cosimo. Everything has limits. For years, no. For days, yes. For months? I'll try for as long as the money holds out. Best I can do."

"Promise at least six months, Ray. That's what it will take for us to feel safe. We have no idea about what's going to happen or where we will end up. Promise us at least that."

"You have my word," Ray said and looked at each in turn. "Six months...no longer."

At a signal from Cos, they all lined up behind Antonius, and with one last look back at Susan and Ray, the small group entered into history.

Chapter 11

The Home of Jesus

The horses were still waiting, and both turned with ears forward, watching the group come toward them. Dawn was breaking, and the East took on a pink tint which rapidly changed to purple and yellow as the sun penetrated the sky just above the distant hills.

"Mount up, Cosimus. I will take Mary behind me, and you can either do the same for this carrion who came with you, or instead, I will gladly slay him right here," Antonius said as he nimbly sprang into his saddle. He reached down for Mary's arm and pulled her up behind him with an effortless motion. She looked at Cos and shrugged as if to say that she was powerless to resist the invitation. They settled in, waiting for Cos, who couldn't help but uncomfortably notice her arms around Antonius' waist.

"You have to ride behind me or walk, Tony. It's a few miles to Nazara if you'd rather walk," Cos said.

"Yeah, and you would like to have that crazy Roman kill me here, wouldn't you?" Tony sneered.

"That's up to you. Going or not?"

"I'm going," he grumbled and scrabbled his way onto the back of the horse.

"We are going to try to find this Jesus for you," Antonius said, turning back to look at Cos.

"You are going to miss getting back to your troops if you help us," Cos said.

"My Optio will see to the men. They will wait for me in Tiberias until my return." He turned back forward and urged his horse into a canter. The early morning appeared suddenly with the warm sun streaming in over the hills. The terrain spread before them consisted of low rises, scrub trees and brown to red rocks. In the distance could be seen small flocks of sheep grouped tightly together, and farther away were irregular groups of low mountains. Ahead, the trail wound slowly back and forth but steadily progressed north toward Nazara, which finally loomed before them as they made it up a last rise in the earth. Antonius slowed his mount, and Cos drew beside him.

"Neither one of them speaks Latin?" Antonius asked.

"Mary is not fluent but knows some words. This one behind me understands nothing."

"Tell me again why he is here?"

"I don't know. It's because Ray wants him to be. There is something that we have not been told. I am keeping an eye on him."

"He is dangerous, Cos. Don't give him any opportunity."

"Will there be danger in Nazara for us?" Cos asked.

"Not so much during the light of day and especially since there are three men in this group. I expect no problem, but there may be no cooperation either. They don't like Romans, and they are told that they have good reason to feel that way. The people pay two taxes. One is collected by Rome, and the other by the priests in the Temple. They resent both but are accustomed to paying the Temple tax. The tax collectors are Yehudim but work for both Rome and themselves. There is a great deal of corruption, and people are often taxed excessively. They don't understand that the money they pay to Rome is used to build roads and cities and to keep them safe from other armies. They are better off with our occupation than the Greek one, and still they resent us. Pompeius Magnus took this land for Rome ninety years ago and treated these people with respect, freeing them from the Sadducees. They forget that they have lived under *Pax Romanum* since."

"Would it be better that Mary ask about Jesus, since you and I will engender so much antagonism?"

"She can converse with them more freely than we can, but since you or I are not her husband or brother, and she travels with us, she will be called a harlot. For her own protection, she cannot be allowed to leave our side."

"Is that what you are afraid of, Cos?" Mary asked from behind

Antonius. "I heard the word harlot used. Was that about me?"

"Yes. Antonius is afraid that you will be seen as accompanying men who are not related to you. They may assume the worst. What have you learned about how they are likely to react?"

"We know very little of how women were treated. These people were, I mean are, capable of stoning a woman that is identified as a prostitute. An account of one episode is in the New Testament. I am not afraid because I have done nothing wrong and therefore have nothing to fear."

The village of Nazara was small. A central path led between structures built of rough stone and straw-reinforced mud. Typically, over the door openings hung a long, tattered piece of cloth. A few added a small courtyard, defined by a low wall in front, and most had goats and donkeys. A stray dog here and there bared his teeth, yapping at the horses. A few men were about at this early hour, and all had long beards and were uniformly dressed in long dirty grey robes. The colored banding on most of the robes had long since faded or been obscured by eons of grime making them all appear similar. The men of Nazara avoided direct eye contact, but their eyes could be felt on the back of the strangers' necks as they slowly rode past. Two large older men were seated against a building watching their progress when Antonius stopped his horse in front of them. Both had hard faces, weathered from a lifetime in the sun, and both had long beards streaked with grey. Their narrowed eyes did not look away.

"Καταλαβαίνετε είτε Λατινικά ή Ελληνικά," Antonius asked in Greek. They shook their heads indicating that they did not understand. "The devils do understand Greek. I can see it in their eyes. Being hung by their heels in the sun would change their answer to yes," he said under his breath.

"We are looking for the man called Jesus. His father is Joseph," Mary said in Aramaic. The two men looked at each other, and one of them spat on the dirt in front of him, wiping his beard with his sleeve. "We mean him no harm. Please tell us if you know about Jesus," Mary pleaded from behind Antonius.

"And if we don't tell, will you have your Roman soldier slay us?" one asked.

"I won't allow any harm to come to you. I am one of you, and these are my friends," she said.

"What would a woman born of the tribes of Israel be doing with three Romans?" he asked.

"I speak your language, and they do not. They needed my help to find Jesus. Do you know of him?"

The two men leaned closer to talk privately among themselves. After a pause one said, "We see no harm in telling you that Jesus is no longer here. His home lies empty, and his family has gone."

"I see. Can you tell me where his home was?"

"Just there," he said, pointing with his walking stick at a small place on the other side of the street. "You can see for yourself."

"Do you know where he has gone?" Mary persisted.

"If we did, we would never tell you. When you leave this place, you are not to return, because you are unclean," he said and thumped his stick into the soft dirt, raising a small cloud.

Antonius had been listening intently giving no indication that he understood anything being said. He leaned forward toward the two old men and glaring with fierceness said in Greek, *'Σε περίπτωση που κάποια βλάβη έρθει ποτέ αυτή τη γυναίκα, θα επιστρέψω και να σκοτώσουν όλους τους άνδρες και να υποδουλώσουν τις γυναίκες και τα παιδιά. Θα κάψει Nazat και να μετατρέψει το χώμα. Ξέρω ότι με καταλαβαίνεις."* [Should any harm ever come to this woman, I will return and kill every man here and enslave the women and children. I will burn Nazat and turn the soil. I know you understand me.] The two men glared back and were silent.

"What did he say to them?" Mary asked Cos.

"I'll tell you later," he answered.

Antonius backed his horse into the street, keeping his eyes on the two seated men. Gradually, he turned his head and his horse and moved to the small structure they had pointed out. He dismounted quickly and reached for Mary who leaned into him gracefully. He put her down lightly as if he had carried a fragile expensive object which might break.

Before them was the home of the family of Jesus, where legend states that he worked or helped his father work in wood. There was a small courtyard with a low wall made of loose stones on three sides. Over time, the dry gravel and dirt had accumulated a large overlay of wood shavings, giving a springy feel as they walked over it. There was a lingering odor of cedar making the place feel fresh. The structure before them was made from stone on the lower portion of the wall with smooth hard clay extending to the thatched roof. There was a single but wide entry formed by two stout upright logs which also supported the roof. Mary entered first, followed by Antonius and Cos. On instructions from Cos, Tony waited beside the horses. Inside was a hard-packed clay floor, smooth from years of sweeping. Through various cracks could be seen wooden beams which lay directly on the ground. The interior walls were of light tan hardened mud. One corner was occupied by a small hearth, shaped much like a gourd. It had a small opening for tending fire, efficiently heating the clay dome above it. An upstairs loft was accessible by a ladder in the corner. The high ceiling was supported by rafters of timber with thatch above. The little house made a very livable and neat home for Joseph, Mary and their children. Cos noticed that the ladder had been made by an experienced craftsman and to him it confirmed that this was the home of a woodworker.

"I don't know about you, Mary, but this place has a magic about it. It's like I know the people who lived and worked here."

"Yes. I know what you mean. Remember that Jesus was one of us. I claim him also."

"Seen enough?" Antonius gently asked Mary in Latin, offering her his arm. When she took it, he gave a sidelong glance toward Cos and winked. Cos waited until Mary looked at him, then narrowed his eyes causing her to laugh. They left the house together, emerging to find Tony facing two men. He had backed up against a horse and was vigorously shaking his head. The men turned just as Antonius came through the door and upon seeing an armored Roman soldier, the strangers took a step backward.

"What do you men want?" Antonius said in Aramaic. Mary's eyes went wide hearing him speak a language that she knew so well. He advanced aggressively toward the men who continued to back away. Both put their hands up, palms out, using a submissive gesture.

"We have information, Centurion. We offer to help you find whom you seek," the thin one said. He was covered by a soiled garment, hanging by threads in spots. His beard was closely cropped, his eyes hard.

There was something about him which made them feel that he was pretending to show fear but had none. The other one was dressed like the first, but had a muscular neck and legs. The second did not speak but seemed alert, tense and ready. Antonius saw the threat in their eyes but made no sign that he noticed.

"Tell us this information or be gone," Antonius commanded.

"You seek Jesus. For a coin, we will help you find him," the thin one offered.

"Or I could kill one of you, and the other will tell me."

"That would not release our information to you, Centurion. It is only a coin we seek."

"Cos, give both men each a coin, please," Mary said. "Quickly," she added after looking at Antonius. Cos withdrew two shiny, duplicated Roman coins and tossed each man one. They held their coins up, looking them over carefully before speaking.

"Jesus is south of the sea near the Jordan river. He is with the fishermen there," the thin man said. They backed slowly away, eyes fixed on the Roman in front of them.

"All right, tell me what happened?" Cos asked in Latin.

"We only know where they say Jesus is. The talkative one claims that he is near Tiberias, but those men were not what they seemed. They may want to lead us into a trap, and you made a mistake showing your purse of money."

"And you speak the language of the Yehudim?" Mary asked in Aramaic.

"As do you. We can now talk with each other, can't we?" he smiled broadly at her. "Mount your horse. We go to Tiberias," he said to Cos as he pulled Mary up behind him.

"I didn't understand any of that. What was that place you visited, and who were those men?" Tony said from behind Cos.

"Who did you think they were?"

"I have no idea, but I can tell you that I know the type. Both were killers and thieves. I was about to draw down on them when you came out of the house."

"Looking at them, my guess is that they would have acted more swiftly than you. Did you see that even Antonius was careful? Killers and thieves? Does it take one to know one, Tony?"

"Something like that. Say, Cos, you are from Rome, aren't you? Have any connections there?"

"You mean, do I know any Mafia, don't you?"

"Yeah. Know any of my extended family, something like that?"

"You are Mafia, Tony?"

"We don't use that term. It's The Organization, you know, and yes, I'm connected."

"My grandfather was a capo and died in an Italian prison. I don't have anything to do with them and don't want to. Tell me, Tony, why did they send a tough guy like you in here. What are you supposed to do? And don't tell me that you are here to protect us, because I saw you nearly killed at least twice so far."

"Can't do that. Ray's orders."

"Okay then, here are some of mine. You listen to what I say here, because here, I am connected. Get out of hand, and I won't lift a finger to help you. It would take a miracle for you to find your way back to the Portal without us."

"Look bud. I gotta do what I do. You are under orders to find Jesus. That's all you need to worry 'bout."

The horses plodded along a little faster than a walk, and much of the trail toward Tiberias was uphill. The Romans had constructed their famous roads only along the coast, up and down from Caesarea, but not inland at this time. The road they travelled went east and north toward the coast of the inland fresh water Lake of Galilee. In the interior of the land of Galilee, the lake was a source of food, harvested as fish by the collection of small and poor fishermen working from both the eastern and western shores.

Cos kicked his horse forward until they drew beside Antonius and Mary, who were chatting freely in Aramaic. "What do you two find to talk about with such intensity?" he asked Mary in English.

"Oh, Cos! He is a vast source of information that we could harvest forever and not get to the bottom. It's fascinating to talk with him. Did you have any idea how educated he really is? He can compete with any Roman history scholar, at least up until this time. And he has an incredible understanding of philosophy, as well. He has been all over

France, right up to the English Channel, and down into Spain. He has crossed the Med several times, visited Egypt and Syria, and knows Rome like the back of his hand. I believe that he has traveled more than both of us combined."

"Yes, yes, I know. Don't bother to get him going on mathematics or geometry or even celestial bodies. He easily knows more about those subjects than either one of us. But...can you please save a little regard for your partner who needs moral support, and perhaps give me the occasional smile to let me know that you still remember that I exist?"

"Are you jealous, Cos?" she laughed, and as she did so, Antonius twisted slightly to look over his shoulder at her, patting her on the hand which was around his waist. His action made Cos wonder if he understood what they had said.

"Yes, Mary. I'm jealous. It's easy to fall under his spell, I understand that. But you are the first woman I have met that..." He stopped talking as Antonius abruptly halted his horse. Blocking the road ahead was a group of men, some of whom had spears.

"Ready yourself, Cosimus. We may have need of your sword skills after all," Antonius warned. The two groups watched each other from a safe distance of twenty yards, each sizing up their adversary.

"Romans!" a voice called out in Aramaic. "We will have your purse of coins for use of this road."

"Are you willing to die for a few coins, bandits?" Antonius answered. The bandits remained silent but didn't move off of the path.

"What's happening?" asked Tony over Cos' shoulder.

"Bandits. They want our money."

"Let me handle this," Tony said. He slid off of the horse and walked in front of Antonius. "Tell them to leave, or I'll kill one of them," he said loud enough for Cos to hear.

"Antonius," Cos called, "Tell them to leave now or one dies."

"Leave or die," Antonius announced, then quietly said, "Are you kidding me? Him? He protects us?"

"This one will be the first to die, Roman," one bandit said as he held his spear over his head. Before any unnecessary translation, Tony pulled his pistol and shot the man in the chest, the sharp crack of a pistol echoing among the endlessly contested hills for the first time in history.

The man was hurtled backward, falling lifeless into the dirt. The others scrambled to get away, fleeing in several directions, leaving their fallen comrade where he lay. Tony shouldered his pistol and walked confidently back to the horse.

"A bolt of lightning from his hand. What manner of weapon was that?" Antonius asked.

"Ray said Tony was here to protect us, and I guess he just did. That was called a firearm. A small explosion sends forth a small piece of lead. Similar weapons won't be seen again for a very long time," Cos explained. The horses avoided stepping on the dead bandit as they continued on toward Tiberias, and even they did not mourn his passing.

"Antonius," Mary said. "Tell me about Tiberias. There isn't much left of it in our time other than ruins of a small amphitheater and remains of an aqueduct.

"Tiberias was recently constructed in the Roman style by one of the sons of Herod who is called Herod Antipas. He seeks favor from Tiberius and named his new city after the Emperor. Antipas spends most of his time there or in Jerusalem. Workmen were recruited from the province of Syria and even from Rome to build it. Few Romans inhabit this place even though it was built in a familiar manner. I have been instructed to insure that Antipas remembers that Rome still rules this land. Our posting is there for the next two months, when we may return to Caesarea or Jerusalem as ordered. There are public baths and shops as may be found in all Roman cities. You will be safer there than any other place, especially when the Yehudim understand that you are under my protection. Outside the walls of the city, you will never be safe from bandits or from those people who don't hold women in high regard."

"Do you hold women in high regard, Antonius?" she asked softly.

"Roman women are treated with respect by all Romans. Women who are not Roman, perhaps not. What are you, Mary?"

"You may think of me as Yehudim from the future that you saw. Does that make any difference to you?"

"I see you as a beautiful and desirable creature worthy of my protection. I care not what God you worship."

Mile after mile, the group plodded along the path, at times unsure that there was a path, but Antonius knew the hills by sight and was always confidant of their location.

"Three more hours and we will crest the Mountains of Naphtali and see Tiberias," Antonius announced. Their water bags were drained by midday, and the remainder of the trip grew more difficult by the mile. Somewhere near the crest of the trail, the air cooled, and Cos and Mary began to enjoy the scenery. More frequent trees were found at this modest elevation, mostly short evergreens, and also sparse grass for the horses. Antonius announced a stop for rest, and they all dismounted, the horses allowed to forage for themselves.

"If you look right there," he said, pointing, "you can see the walls of the city and beyond, the sea." The sheen of the white stone made the city seem to float, hovering at the edge of a large lake. "There are many hot baths and many springs. People come for their skin ailments, because the water is said to heal all things. Our camp is just outside the city, for it is narrow, crowded and close to the water." They mounted and continued mostly downhill as the last light of day turned the sky orange over the hills behind them to the west. They reached the Roman camp just as night had overtaken the heavens. Dismounting just outside of the well-marked grounds, they were greeted by several heavily armed men who led the horses away. Antonius engaged in conversation with two of his men, and Cos and Mary could see him occasionally pointing toward Tony.

Antonius, accompanied by two particularly large, formidable soldiers, approached Tony with a grim face. "You will give me your weapon," he ordered in Latin.

"He wants your gun, Tony," Cos called out. "Look, you have no choice here. If you don't believe it, look at his men." There was little doubt that Tony was outmatched, even with a gun.

"Am I gonna get it back?" he asked Cos.

"Tell him that he will get his weapon back when he leaves this camp. I will not have any of my men injured or killed by this man," Antonius said.

"Give it up, Tony. They mean it," Cos told him. Tony reluctantly handed Antonius the gun, who studied it carefully before handing it over to one of his men. He turned his back to Tony, ordering, "Go with these men and you will receive food and shelter."

"Better go with them," Cos advised. "We'll come and get you when we leave the camp."

Antonius motioned Cos and Mary to come with him, and they walked toward the center of camp where a large tent was softly fluttering in the night air. After entering, Antonius pulled up a chair for Mary, and they all sat down at a large table as food and wine was promptly served. "I am sorry about making you go to sleep dirty, my friends, but we'll go to the baths tomorrow. Tonight is about food and rest. Tomorrow will wait until tomorrow."

"Where will we sleep?" Mary asked. Antonius waved his hand absently toward the corner of the tent.

"Here. Tomorrow night, Mary, you will sleep comfortably in the palace of Herod Antipas. I will see that it happens. You, Cosimus, will sleep here until you accomplish your mission or until my centuriae leave the area. The matter is settled."

Chapter 12

Herod Antipas

As Mary emerged from the hot springs bath, an attendant unfolded a large towel and enveloped her in it, keeping her hands on Mary's shoulders as she led the way from the caldarium to the separate room of the frigidarium. There were several women bathing that morning, and all were pleasant and smiling. The hard cool tile felt good against her feet, and on the way through the small vaulted passageway, she was able to appreciate the incredible mosaic tile work on the walls and floor. Most images were in tones of blue and green, creating artistic representations of dolphins or of Neptune himself. Very high above the pools, enormous skylights opened to the blue sky, but at her distance from them, and under the glare of the sun, she couldn't determine the construction method. Niches circled the pools, housing exquisite white marble statues of Greek or Roman deities framed by oval openings. Mary was surprised to see this display of Roman tradition given that few Romans lived in this cosmopolitan city by the lake, but Romans built according to custom, and this bath house was likely very similar to many others around the Roman world. When at last they reached the polished and curved marble border of the crystal clear, cold final bath, the attendant removed her towel and indicated that she should enter the pool. The room was circular, built to display fluted Corinthian columns separated by stone walls of finely cut terra-cotta blocks. Between each column was a stone Gorgon's head fiercely looking down at the bathers. A shaft of yellow light pored into the room from above, striking the colored tiles of the mosaics, scattering a rainbow of light into every corner. The circular pool was several body lengths in diameter. Little ripples disturbed the surface of the water indicating fresh water supplied by a distant source. As she entered the cold water, her skin raised little goose bumps, and the attendant snickered behind her hands while watching from beside the pool.

"This water is very cold!" Mary said, her teeth clicking together.

"Feels good after the hot bath, does it not?" the girl answered. It did feel good, and the jolt of cold water was as good as caffeine to awaken a bather still drowsy from the hot water of the caldarium. Mary rolled over, floating on her back, gazing at the sparkling dome of light far above her. The echoed voices from other parts of the baths murmured and reflected around the chamber making a pleasant, nearly musical background. Her morning had started abruptly at dawn when an apologetic young Roman soldier entered and shook Antonius awake. As Mary watched, Antonius had sat up from his bedding, rubbed his face briefly and sprang to his feet, grabbing his new sword on the way out without even a glance in their direction. Cos was wrapped in layers of bedding a few feet from her spot, and he remained soundly asleep. Mary lay still, listening to the sounds of the awakening camp but didn't hear any unusual or threatening noises. She decided to arise and sat up, looking around at their enclosure. The dawn was beginning to light the upper part of the tent, soaking its dark corners in a linen-colored warm light. Beside her bedding, she found a small package, wrapped in white cloth and tied with a slender red silk ribbon. She touched it, realizing that it had been placed there while she slept and obviously meant for her to find when she awakened. Pulling the ribbon, the folds parted, revealing several carefully folded items of women's clothing. The two on the bottom were of dark silk interwoven with glinting gold thread. On the top was an undergarment of the finest linen, embroidered with small flowers and vines around the collar and sleeves. And between was a gossamer wrap of the purist white silk. Mary had trailed her father through Paris, browsed the finest shops along Avenue des Champs-Élysées, and never saw anything to compare to these garments. She felt herself tearing as she held them up to the light. They would fetch hundreds of thousands of any currency if sold in the twenty- first century. She almost didn't notice a smaller package bound in soft leather which had been hidden in the folds. Inside were several items of gold jewelry. A necklace, matching earrings, and a gold ring with facing snake heads reflected the soft light of the room. She recognized the necklace as Egyptian and had seen similar things displayed in the Cairo Museum. The ring was a perfect fit for her left third finger, and she slipped it on, holding her hand up to view it in the light.

"That looks good from here," Cos said, sitting up. "Where did that loot come from?" His hair was tousled, and he needed a shave.

"A package left beside me. The wardrobe is fit for the lady of a king, as is the jewelry. I have no idea where it came from, but I suspect Antonius will know."

Cos fell backward with a thump and exhaled air noisily. "That guy is after you, Mary, and I can't compete with him. He is simply a better man than I am in every way. He's even better looking, and it takes a lot for me to say that. It's working too, isn't it?"

"He's right out of a movie set and bigger than life, as they say. But he is real flesh and blood and not just an image. You like him also, don't you?" she asked.

"Of course. I've never met anyone like him. He's a man's man and watching him with you, the tender side is there also. Then there is the opposite side of him. The last place you would ever want to be is on the sharp side of his sword. I don't blame you, Mary, for swooning over Antonius, but it makes me feel like a pimply-faced teen with no date at the dance."

"If it makes you feel any better, Cos, I like you, and I think you are handsome. This whole life will end for us when we go back through the Portal, and it will seem like we dreamed it. So far, this experience has been wonderful, exciting, and more than I expected, and it just keeps getting better." She held up a shimmering silk dress for him to see.

"Yes, you'll look good in that one. You already look good in your homespun wool so I can just imagine your figure flowing under that thing."

The tent flap opened abruptly as Antonius and another officer came in. "Arise Cosimus, Roman soldiers get up with the light," Antonius commanded. "Good morning, Mary! I see you found my gift. Is it suitable to you?"

She stood up and pulled back her long hair. "This is the most wonderful gift that I have ever received. I am not worthy of such fine things." She looked up at Antonius with her soft dark eyes reflecting not even a hint of artificial emotion.

"I saved those things during my travels, knowing that someday a woman would come to me that would be beautiful enough to wear them. You are that woman, Mary. I long to see you adorned in this manner."

"These are not suitable for a military camp, Antonius. I would stand out like a zebra in a field filled with dark horses."

"You are to enter the palace of Antipas later this morning. He will be told that you are of royal blood and are from Egypt, and you are under Roman protection. He and his court will treat you with respect, because they have to, and also because of the way you will look in those clothes. It is a ruse, but one that they cannot refute. I want you there for safety and comfort for a few days, and during that time, my men will locate this Jesus you seek, and you can complete your mission. The palace was instructed to send a litter for you this morning." He turned to Cosimus who was now up on his feet. "This is Agrippa Sesemas, my optio. He will accompany you for food this morning. You are to continue your sword training today, starting with the next man in line. You are not to stop for the remaining hours of the day except as nature demands. This evening, Agrippa will take you to the Baths, and afterward, the fresh uniform of a tesserarius will be waiting for you."

"Does this mean that I am now in the Roman Army?" Cos asked.

"It does. You are under my command. Now get moving," he said and waved the back of his hand toward the grinning Agrippa.

Cos gave Mary a small feeble wave, grabbed his things and hurried to catch up with Agrippa, currently striding with determination toward a gathering of men around a fire.

"Do not fret, Cosimus," he said, when they were shoulder to shoulder. "Antonius likes you, and he is trying to have you trained as well as we are. Ready for food?"

"Yes, Agrippa, food first. I took a pounding last time I was in training with a wooden sword. Is this to be more of the same?" Cos asked.

"No, Cosimus," he laughed. "These men were told by Antonius this morning not to spare you any discomfort and to give you no quarter. I expect that it will be far harder than last time." He laughed again. When they arrived at the group, some of the men seemed glad to see Cosimus, and a couple of them playfully slapped him on the back. He could see that he was fully accepted as an equal and pride swelled up inside him, causing him to relax. He was from this time forward a Roman legionary with the rank of tesserarius.

As promised, a *lectica*, carried by four husky men, arrived mid-morning, and was also accompanied by two mounted guards from the palace in Tiberias. Mary was met outside the bath by Antonius and ten of his men, all fully armored, standing at rigid attention. Antonius helped seat her in the litter and rode beside it as the whole procession slowly made its way toward the palace.

"You are a sight to behold, Mary. The clothes are fit for a princess like you," he said, smiling and leaning toward her from his horse. She retrieved her small camera from her clothing to catch a photo of Antonius with his decorative helmet and armor, proudly and majestically sitting erect on his steed as the shining ivory buildings behind him slowly slipped past. "What is that you have in your hand," he asked.

"This is called a camera. It makes pictures. I wanted to remember how good you look just now. This is the most exciting thing that has ever happened to me. Thank you, Antonius, for this day."

"Your day may be unpleasant. You are to meet the Roman appointed ruler of Galilee and his wife, Herodias. I am told that she is a conniving and bitter woman. Are you aware of her?"

"Yes, she and her husband Antipas will be banished by Emperor Caligula in ten years. After that, history loses track of them."

"Tiberius...how much longer does he have?" Antonius whispered.

"Roughly nine more years," Mary answered.

"What kind of leader does Caligula make?" he persisted.

"Mary looked at him with her head tilted a little. "Antonius, this is the last question about this. You understand that you shouldn't know the future, don't you?"

"That is what Cos said. I don't agree, though. Tell me about Caligula."

"He will be considered insane before he is killed by the Praetorian Guard. He was one of the worst of all of them, but he will only last four years."

"Can I ask how much longer Rome has?"

"Many more lifetimes. You have nothing to fear about that in yours or your children's." He sat back up on his horse and looked ahead, thinking.

Looking at her again, he obviously yearned to ask another question about the future. She took a deep breath. Should she withhold any information from him, and what would be the point really, she thought?

"The man you seek, this Jesus. Why?" he asked pointedly.

"This one I can't answer for you, because what happens concerning him will happen just four or five years from now, and I wouldn't want to think that you would be involved because of something that I told you."

"That just makes me more curious than ever," he said.

The palace was just ahead, and she could see little clusters of people standing outside the columned entrance, waiting for her to arrive. She felt her pulse increase, and her palms started to moisten. This was, as they say, showtime. After bobbing along the remaining few feet, the bearers set the litter down carefully. As she stood up, she could see the women gasping at the sight of her in her shimmering gown of black silk, laced with gold threads. Her necklace alone would turn the head of any woman from any era, and it had the same effect on the gathered group in front of the palace. Antonius dismounted and quickly was by her side. He reached for her arm and gently guided her down to the stone-paved entrance. "You are the most beautiful woman to ever have lived," he whispered to her. "Remember to act just as you look, and remember what else I told you."

A woman came toward her who was also elegantly dressed but more in a local way. Her cloak was of very fine wool and edged with contrasting stitching. She gave a slight bow toward Mary, but her eyes were cunning and malevolent. "Greetings, I am Herodias Antipas, wife of Herod, ruler of Galilee, and I welcome your company. I understand that you are from Egypt," she asked in Hebrew.

"Mary Solomon, noble one," she said and gave a slight bow allowing her earrings to move and be noticed.

"You are very lovely, my dear Mary. How is it that your husband allows you to travel with these Romans?" she asked sweetly.

"They are my protectors; they serve me well."

"Where in Egypt is your home?"

"Thebes," Mary said and looked her in the eye without flinching.

"So these Romans have chased your Greeks away as they have ours. Is it not so?"

"It is for the better," Mary answered.

"Do you speak the common language of my land, also?" Herodias asked in Aramaic.

"Yes," Mary answered in Aramaic.

"And the language of Egypt?"

"Yes, that too," Mary answered in English.

"I assume from your answer that you said yes. Would you and your gladiator accompany me?" Herodias asked and turned toward the opening.

"Wait a moment, Herodias," Mary said in Hebrew. "This is Antonius, he is a Centurion. He is no gladiator," she stated and waited for a response.

Herodias was not used to being refuted, and she turned with harshness on her face. Antonius just stood there, backed by his troops, immobile, and seemingly waiting on an apology, even though Herodias suspected that he didn't understand Hebrew.

"Well, just a slip of the tongue, my dear. Pardon me please, Centurion. I do know better, and it won't happen again," she spoke directly to Antonius, ignoring Mary. She spun without another word and quickly disappeared into the darkened opening of the palace.

"Good work, Mary. That will throw her off balance," Antonius whispered.

Antonius spoke to his men, and they positioned themselves on either side of the door, their long spears held vertically. Taking Mary's arm, he led the way into the cavernous palace. Before entering, Mary had a glance down a short hill from the palace at the sparkling water of the lake. Inside was typical of Roman architectural grandeur of the type she expected to see, with expansive floors of fitted stone, long drapes of woven cloth depicting scenes of nature, matching and complementing colorful frescos on the walls. Statues and busts of ivory stone, some much larger than life, were scattered along the walls. Ahead, Herodias led the way without looking back, leading the procession alongside a lengthy pool of moving water, noisily emitting from a stone lion's head at one end. In spots, they encountered groups of young females who twittered as Mary came past, her gown sweeping behind her. Mary held her head regally high, looking forward as if she were the embodiment of the

Egyptian queen, Nefertiti. The path led into a large room set up for entertainment and eating, Roman style couches and chairs along the walls. At one end was a throne, and Herodias headed straight for it. The center chair was occupied by a round- faced fellow, bedecked with gold necklaces. Tetrarch Herod Antipas awaited her on his throne.

Antonius stopped in the middle of the room so that he could be seen and heard by everyone. "Pontius Pilatus sends his regards, Herod. He asks that you see to the needs of Mary Solomon while she is in Tiberias for a short time, and he grants me permission to voice his gratitude." He spoke with a deep commanding voice using the official Latin. Herod struggled to his feet showing his ample belly, visible under his loose clothing.

"I am the servant of any woman with your rare beauty, Mary Solomon. May I ask what brings you to Tiberias?" he said, giving her a large smile.

"My reason is personal, King. I am not at liberty to discuss it." Mary said and gave a small bow.

"Well, no matter. If Pilatus requests it, then it must be so. You are just in time for a meal, and you will dine with us, will you not?" he asked with a flourish of his hand, and the rattle of dinnerware came from just outside of the hall.

"It would give me pleasure, Tetrarch. I would ask that Centurion Antonius also be present. Will you permit it?" she asked politely.

"Are we to infer a close relationship, then?" he probed.

"This centurion and his men have been my companions and protectors since I disembarked in Caesarea. I have seen his courage and also his personal tenderness, and I am unashamed to think highly of him."

"Very well, my spectacular guest. He is invited as well. You are in luck, because my daughter, Salome, will entertain us as we dine."

After they were seated and the food served, several musicians filed into the room and started a musical number. They played well and with intensity but were ignored by Herod and his wife who were busy dining on the elevated throne area. The music stopped abruptly, and everyone looked up to see a young woman enter, trailing a long pink silk scarf made from fabric so thin that it was nearly transparent. She was barefoot with flowing long dark hair and moved like a professional dancer with grace and natural feminine beauty. As she quickly swept by Mary, their eyes locked for a brief moment, and hers radiated instant jealousy. Salome was used to being the most desirable woman in Galilee, but she was suddenly faced with a competitor who had more beauty and also dressed more lavishly than she had ever seen before. Mary could hear Antonius chuckle to himself, but he never changed his blank expression. The dance continued, but Salome held Mary in her eyes so frequently that it seemed that the dance was meant for her and not for her father. Suddenly, she held up her hand for the music to stop, and she headed toward Mary. "Here she comes," Antonius whispered. "Get ready."

Salome stood before Mary's table and looked her over carefully and defiantly before speaking. "Who is this stranger that eats in the home of my father?" she asked in blunt Aramaic.

"I am called Mary Solomon."

"Why have you come to my city?" she demanded.

"Why, it is because I was told of a young woman of timeless beauty who lives here and who dances as if taught by Venus herself. Are you that person?" The words had the desired effect and Salome's face softened.

"I must be. I am Salome, daughter of the King."

"You are of rare beauty, Salome, and your dancing, what I saw of it, is of the heavens. Can you not continue for me?"

Salome looked intently at her expecting to find some trace, some small hint of insincerity but could find none. "You are most handsome, Mary. And your jewelry is the most desirable that I have beheld. May I ask where it is from?"

"It was a gift from a close friend and admirer and someone whom I hold dear to my heart. It is from the tombs of Egypt and was worn by the wife of Pharaoh more than one thousand years ago." Mary watched Salome's eyes play over the necklace, then move to her dangling earrings.

"If we become friends, will you let me try those on?"

"I will. They will look especially wonderful on your slender, young neck." Smiling, Salome spun away from the table and, to enthusiastic applause from the Tetrarch, resumed dancing.

"I heard what you said," Antonius murmured. "It nearly made me weep, and it doesn't look manly for a Centurion of Rome to cry."

"I meant it. You are dear to me, Antonius. But you know that already."

"Ah, Mary. I long to hold you in my arms and taste your lips," he said as softly as possible, his mouth barely moving. She flicked her eyes briefly at him but didn't respond. This moment, sitting beside him and pretending to be something that she was not, was a most amazing out-of-body experience that no one would believe and no one could invent. She wanted so badly to take photos but understood that it would create problems and questions that should not be brought up. When the dance was over and the applause died, Herod waved, summoning Mary to his table. "It's all right," Antonius assured her. "He must be treated as a king even though he is only a puppet controlled by Pontius Pilatus. He is disliked by both Rome and his own people. Herod caters to Emperor Tiberius so you have nothing to fear from him." They both got up and slowly made their way across the room, giving the assembly a full view of the beautiful Mary. She walked regally, her hand loosely resting on the arm of Antonius.

"You two look charming together," Herodias said. "Are you free to notice your strong but elegant companion, Mary?"

"I am not attached, if that is your question," Mary responded.

"Is that the same as being available?"

"At the moment, I am not 'available.' "

"Pity," Herodias said, shaking her head.

"What service may I do for you, Mary Solomon. My kingdom is yours for the asking," Herod said, clearing his throat and trying to regain control of the conversation.

"I request that you provide shelter for her as your guest for several days, Tetrarch Herod. She should be protected and cared for as you would do for your own. Rome does not have facilities worthy of her in Tiberias at this time," Antonius said.

"She has already made a friend with Salome, Centurion. It will be an honor to have another beauty in these walls. You can be sure that she will be safe."

"Thank you, King Herod. I know that you won't mind if some of my men stay in sight of her at all times and also guard her quarters at night." At this suggestion of invasion, Herod's eyes widened. He realized that a refusal would be reported to Rome, and he decided to wisely acquiesce instead of protesting.

"If that makes you and her happy, Centurion, I will allow it."

"Thank you," Mary said and lowered her eyes.

Chapter 13

Birth of a Soldier

Once again, Cos was looking at the sky, holding his shoulder. At least they weren't hitting him in the face. "Get up, Cosimus," came the cry from the crowd of soldiers who had formed about two hours ago. This was the current camp amusement, and they seemed to have nothing better to do at the moment but watch their new Tesserarius get whacked until he could barely lift his arms. He rolled to his knees and looked at his smiling opponent, who was still waving his hard brown stick around.

"More, Tesserarius?" his opponent asked. Yes, there would be more, and Cos jumped to his feet and sprang at the man, bringing his wooden sword down beside the man's neck. The soldier dropped to the dirt, moaning. At last, he finally put this one away, the tenth today. How many more are left, he wondered. He looked up to see a much bigger man entering the ring as others pulled the last one away, still clutching his shoulder.

"You may not have such luck, Tesserarius, with me," the man growled, and looking him over, Cos believed him. He pointed his stick at Cos and smiled. "You will fall easily. I have been studying you for some time. I know what you will do." It was true. Cos didn't have many tricks, and by now they all knew them. Besides, he was dead tired and covered by dirt, which had been rubbed deeply into his skin from the many tumbles he had taken face down in the soil of Galilee. Cos lamely brushed the sweat and dirt from his face and studied the man. He was thickly made with a short neck indicating massive shoulder muscles. There were several big scars on his face, the kind that should have required suturing, the scars which resulted were wide and ragged. It gave his face a certain amount of appeal, much like a favorite old toy that had been dog chewed. There was experience in his eyes, accumulated from many years of brutal combat. Likely, he had killed many men in his day, and by comparison, Cos was a military idiot.

Cos slapped the end of the sword in his hand like he had seen the others do and crouched, waiting on the strike which would come soon. And it did. The man raised his sword over his head and rushed directly at him. Cos knew by now that this was meant to frighten, making him lose concentration from fear of getting hit. Unfortunately, Cos was too tired to be afraid and the rush happened too fast to raise his sword for defense. He did the only thing he could do and pointed the sword low, as far out as he could reach, allowing his opponent to spear himself right between the legs. The man dropped to the ground, both hands clutching his crotch. The other men erupted, shouting, picking up Cos in the air, where he saw Antonius heading their way still dressed in his glistening armor.

"I saw that. It was a lucky strike, Cosimus. You will have a chance again tomorrow to prove that you have that much skill. Recall that Aristotle said, 'We are what we repeatedly do. Excellence, therefore, is not an act, but a habit.' This play with wooden swords will someday save your life."

"If I don't die while playing," Cos said with effort.

Are you tired yet?"

"What do you think, Master?"

"You look like you need a bath. They will likely try to charge you more because of the dirt you bring in. Go get your things, and I will go with you."

"What about Mary? Where is she?" Cos asked.

"Mary has become a celebrated Egyptian princess. One renowned for her charm and wit and is at this moment at the palace of Herod where she is probably being worshiped for her beauty. She is also safe, because I left ten good men there to protect her."

"Egyptian? With the name of Solomon. Did they buy that?"

"They believe because not one of them has ever been to Thebes. Have you?"

"Sure. Luxor and the Temple of Karnak are across the Nile from Thebes. When I was there, it was mostly an old archeology site with only a small population of permanent inhabitants, and I'll bet that it's no different right now."

"They don't know that. If any one of them has even been to Alexandria, I would be surprised. She is speaking your English to them, and they think that it is some kind of Egyptian. Amusing, don't you think?"

"Hilarious, as long as they don't find out differently."

"Tomorrow I want you to continue your training, while I will send out scouts to find this Jesus for you. Mary will still be in the luxurious palace, holding all the males in the palm of her hand and watching the females squirm. Ready to get clean, Cosimus?"

The hot bath felt relaxing, and Cos floated on the surface, spreading his arms out while looking up at the darkening skylight, letting the hot water sooth his many bruises. There were several other male bathers, all speaking in Aramaic. Cos couldn't understand them, and Antonius pretended that he didn't either, but he had been listening to their conversations without being obvious. He discretely pulled Cos over to one side.

"They are talking about us, Cos. They don't like Romans and resent us being in here. I have no men here with me, so if there is trouble, it is you and I alone against several. They won't attack us in the pool, but from what I hear, they plan to wait outside in darkness and kill us when we come out."

"Who are they?" Cos asked quietly.

"This is a city of diverse groups. Herod recruited most of the population, and he was forced to use people who are not Yehudim. Only half the city worships the one God and few Romans are here. This bunch could be from anywhere. See the big one with his back to us? The scar is from a sword. He has been in combat previously."

"Our swords are in the changing area. I am going to try and get them while you stay here and listen," Cos said, casually easing out of the pool of hot water. He toweled off, strolled casually, ignoring the other men, heading toward the far end, and was able to pass without notice into the adjoining room. The swords were hanging just where they were left, and he quickly grabbed both and headed back to the pool. Antonius looked relieved to see him and extended his arm, the signal to toss a sword to him. Just as the sword was in the air, there was a shout from one of the men who attempted to get out of the pool. Cos drew his sword and planted his feet squarely as he had done all day. The four men realized that their conversation had been overheard, and now the two Romans had the advantage. Their hands went up in submission as Antonius waded toward them holding a razor sharp sword in one hand, its metal scabbard in the other.

"So, you would plot to kill a Roman, would you?" he said, still moving toward them with menace and determination on his face. "Still feeling brave?" he taunted, getting closer. One of the men started to tremble, and the rest backed up against the hard marble with Cos at their back.

"Wait!" one cried out. "Don't you remember that I was the one you talked with in Nazat?"

"Yes. You are the one who spied the purse of coins and sent his men to rob us on the trail. Did you hear that one of your men died by lightning that day?" Antonius asked, stopping within his sword's reach.

"We heard," another said.

"So you would rob us then and kill us now. You will die tonight, thief, and we will be rid of your plotting."

"I have more news of Jesus about whom you inquired," said the first man holding up his hand.

"You said that he is at the Jordan. We heard you."

"This Jesus becomes two...," the first man exclaimed, excitement in his voice, but as he spoke one of his men reached behind and grabbed Cos by the ankle, attempting to drag him forward into the pool. At the same time, the other two lunged toward Antonius, using a large splash of water meant to distract him. Cos shouted an alarm and tottered on one foot, attempting to pull back.

"Use your sword!" Antonius commanded. Cosimus swung the blade down toward the grasping hand and arm, striking it just past the elbow, severing it cleanly with one blow. He looked up to see Antonius swing at the first man's head, which came off easily, followed by a tremendous fountain of blood emitted by twin streams from his neck. The sword flashed again and another man went down with a scream of anguish. One suddenly lunged out of the pool toward Cos who instinctively and defensively pushed his blade deeply into the man's abdomen, pulling it away as the man fell backwards into the sword of Antonius. When it was over, two arms and a head were resting on the bottom as four bodies slowly submerged out of sight in the now pink frothing water of the bath. The odor of fresh blood filled the room as Antonius climbed out. They stood looking into the water now contaminated with violence and death. Where there were four men who lived and breathed and had hope and loves, there was now only ugliness and horror.

"Come with me," Antonius commanded. Cos followed him with his sword hanging limply at his side. They entered the room containing the cold water pool where Antonius grabbed Cos by the arm, jumping together into the pool, still clutching their swords. The cold water snapped Cos back alive, and he came up breathing rapidly.

"Your first combat, Cosimus, and you handled yourself with courage. I am proud to call you a Roman," Antonius said and slapped him on the back. They washed the blood from their hands and bodies as screams and shouts erupted from the other room. "There will be trouble about this, Cosimus. It isn't over yet." Cos nodded that he understood that even here, brutal murder in a public bath is outrageous.

"That man was trying to tell us something about Jesus. He started to say something about Jesus becoming two. Did you understand anything he said?" Antonius asked.

"I heard the word Jesus, but I don't understand that language. Becoming two? I have no idea what that could mean."

"Let us get back to camp while we can," Antonius suggested, and Cos readily agreed.

Chapter 14

Repercussions

Cos wakened facing the tent wall, trying to place where he was. The memory of last night flooded into his head. He had killed a man from the past. Had he changed the future by his action? Things felt the same, he thought the same and remembered the past clearly. But, he reasoned, if changes in the past changed the future, it wouldn't seem like change. You would never know it, never understand that things were different. The other path of reason is that he didn't change anything. He was destined to have done what he did. It was already part of history before he was born. That line of thought makes everything that happens destiny instead of free will. If only he could know what lay ahead. For the first time, he understood clearly how Antonius must feel. From now forward, he would tell Antonius anything he asked. Nothing would be held back, because it won't change anything that is already destined to happen. It is like being in a movie theater and watching action and words that were previously filmed. The movie doesn't change even if you don't like what is on the screen, because the ending was written long before you watched. He threw back the covers and looked around. Antonius was already up and gone, and the light of dawn was still only a suggestion in the sky. He got to his feet, and the first thing he looked for was his sword. Cos now understood the old phrase "live by the sword." In this land, you could never be without one for very long. He started pulling on his new clothing and his heavy chain mail armor as the tent opening was pulled back.

"Good. I see that you are up, Cosimus. Centurion is waiting to eat with us," Agrippa said and waited for Cos to finish dressing. Putting on real Roman armor for the first time filled him with a strange sensation. He had donned recreated armor previously, but this was the real thing, and he was now a real Roman soldier. He wasn't just viewing ancient history, he was part of it. This was his past, his present and his future. Agrippa smiled, "You look just like us now. Welcome, Cosimus. I heard of your bravery last night. You saved the life of our beloved Centurion, and his men won't forget and neither will I."

Antonius looked up as they approached. He was eating from a small metal dish heaped with steaming food. He pointed to the cauldron near the fire with the tip of his small knife. "Have all you can hold, Cosimus. You may need it today. We have been summoned to the palace for an explanation of last night." He studied Cos carefully over his bowl of grains. "We are not barbarians, Cosimus. Romans have to shave each morning. After breakfast, report to the barbers who await your presence."

"Yes, Centurion," Cos said. Antonius looked up and chuckled at the formality.

"You did what you had to do last night, Cos. Any regrets?"

"None. They chose to die, and they have become part of history. I am at peace with it."

"As you should be. In this world, if you don't or won't defend yourself or what you believe, there is always some evil fate which awaits you. Strength is very much like honor, you have to use it to keep it."

On the way into the palace, Antonius stopped to confer with one of the two Romans standing outside the entry. "What have you heard concerning last evening?" he asked.

"There was bloodshed at the Baths. There is much anger inside."

"Rested and fresh men will be here shortly to relieve you, until then keep your ears open." Antonius shrugged toward Cos. "As expected."

"Are we in danger, Antonius?" Cos asked.

"We will see. Be unafraid, Cosimus. Remember what Julius Caesar said, 'In the end, it is impossible not to become what others believe you are.' If we are attacked, many of them will die also, and my men will take revenge afterwards."

They were led by an armed guard into the royal chamber where Antipas waited, anger showing on his broad face. "Men of Tiberius were slain last night in the public bath. Do you, Centurion, have knowledge of this act?" he asked.

"This soldier and I were the ones who killed rather than be killed. I have no apologies but instead a question for you. Who were these men who were allowed to provoke conflict between allies?"

"Centurion, I will accept no accusation about my role in this matter. You and your lady are here by my grace alone. This can change," he scowled.

"Remember that Rome protects its own. You must think before you act in a rash manner, either with words or arms. Some acts cannot be undone," Antonius said and slowly turned to survey the room and its occupants, his hand on the grip of his sword. The threat implied.

"These men were not acting on my directions. I am informed that they were part of a lawless band residing near the mouth of the Jordan. You and your men would be advised to avoid this area. I can't afford to have a larger presence of Roman troops in this city. More killing would be inevitable."

"Has Mary Solomon been a burden to you, Tetrarch?"

"Only her memorable beauty. All eyes are on her when she walks or talks, and my daughter Salome is fixated by her charm. I can see in her eyes that she knows much of the world, but I cannot decipher what it may be. What do you know of her, Centurion?"

"Only that she is the living image of Aphrodite with the appeal of one of the Vestal Virgins. She rivals the Oracle of Delphi in knowledge of the future. She is to be protected with your life, Tetrarch, as I do when she is with me."

"You have reason to bring such a person into this lawless land?"

"What I was told, I now feel, was not the entire truth. I confess that I do not know the real reason she is here."

"Stand where you are, Centurion. No harm will come to you in my palace," Antipas said, then instructed his servant in a voice too quiet to be overheard. The man left hurriedly, which caused Cosimus and Antonius to glance at each other. Both were ready, muscles tensed, for anything coming through the door. Antonius promised himself that Antipas himself would be the first to die if armed men entered. After a few tense moments, a rustling sound was heard just before Mary, in regal splendor, swept into the room followed by several maids in attendance. She stopped, eyes widening, with the two men she cared about the most standing there smiling at her. She regained her composure rapidly, but Antipas saw her reaction.

"She loves one or both of you. I wondered about that, and now the fact is evident. Is it proper for a woman of high birth and so gifted by nature to be drawn to two lowly ranked Romans as yourselves?" he asked with sarcasm.

"It is not, Tetrarch, but speaking for myself, I can't help my feelings toward her. Hers toward me is also beyond my control," Antonius said, and as he spoke, he saw the glinting eye of emotion in Mary's face.

"Mary Solomon, I have just heard that you can foretell the future. To thank us for our hospitality, I ask you to tell us our fate," Antipas requested, then leaned back in his royal chair awaiting her response. Cos caught her eye and almost imperceptibly nodded that she could tell what she knows.

"Tetrarch Herod, you have been gracious to me, and I want to repay you, but before I tell you the future, you must be sure that you want to know it. Perhaps you won't like what you hear," Mary said, looking into his eyes.

"Speak, Mary. What is to befall me."

"You and your wife will be banished from Galilee. You have several years, though, before that happens."

"Impossible. I govern by order of Tiberias. He is my friend and ally."

"Tiberias will die. Then you will be banished forever."

"What is the fate of Salome?"

"She is to be married twice and bear three children, all sons."

Antipas was flustered and waved his hands in protest. "How do we know these things will come to pass?"

"You will have to wait and see, Tetrarch," she answered calmly.

"What else can you tell me?" he asked, impatient to have some good news.

"You are alive and in good health, Tetrarch. Enjoy each day. I have answered you in return for your shelter and protection, but I have no more to say."

"You must say more. I deserve to know more. Answer, I command it!" he said standing up.

"One last thing, then, and you are never to ask me again. Is this agreed?"

"Yes, I agree."

"You will do two things which will make your name known to the world for at least two thousand years and likely much longer. A time span that erases the memory and the name of nearly every other person alive today. Your name will be cursed and hated above any other person who now lives in Galilee."

"What are these things that I do? I will pay you any price to know the answers."

"No more, Tetrarch. I will not tell you more."

"I tell you that I must know!" he screamed.

"You agreed, Tetrarch. No more," Antonius said with force.

"Then I banish you from this palace. Take her with you today, Centurion. I will not look again into her face, however lovely it is."

"No!" a shriek came from outside the room, and suddenly Salome burst in and ran to Mary's side. "I heard the whole thing, Father. She only told the truth about the future. It is not her fault if it doesn't suit you, besides I heard you agree to her demand. If she goes, I go with her to the Roman camp. Is that what you want?"

"You will not enter the Roman camp."

"I will, Father, and you know I will."

"I will have you flogged, my daughter, will that suit you?"

"You know that I will run away and sleep with the Romans. I am a woman, and I have my own mind." Antipas chewed on his lower lip fixing his disobedient daughter in his gaze. He knew from experience that this headstrong girl would attempt to do what she threatened. She was most dear to him, and he gave into her every whim. He knew that it was a mistake, but he couldn't bear to have her unhappy.

"What would you have me do, Daughter?" he asked, knowing the answer she would give.

"You will let Mary Solomon stay until she desires to leave. I will keep her away from you, if that is still what you command."

"Agreed, Daughter. Mary may stay but only to please you. Remember that...only for you." Salome clapped her hands, jumped into the air with happiness and reached for Mary's hand to lead her away.

"I have a demand, also, Tetrarch," Antonius said loudly. Every face turned toward him and all could see him standing with feet apart, planted firmly on the stone floor, his armor sparkling with light, and his purple horsehair plums swaying slowly from his helmet. When the room was quiet he spoke, "If Mary Solomon is to remain here under your protection, she will do so with a doubling of my men in the palace."

"That amounts to a Roman invasion of the home and office of the Tetrarch of Galilee. You ask for too much, Centurion. I cannot allow it."

"Then Mary comes with me," Antonius said with finality.

"Please, Father," Salome pleaded, rolling her head toward her father in a flirtatious, suggestive way. They all waited, knowing that Antipas would give in, and he did.

"Of course, Salome. For you I accept humiliation. I agree, Centurion, but they have to stay out of the way." Herod rolled his eyes around hoping no one would notice his double embarrassment at the hands of his daughter.

Antonius came to Mary and removed his helmet, both smiling at the victory they had achieved, and the secrets they both shared. "I will find this Jesus soon, and you will be able to return with Cos to your world. Is there anything you need before we go?" he said lowly so that only she could hear.

"They treat me well. I am comfortable and safe. The only things I do miss are you and Cosimus. Thank you for everything, Antonius. You are in my thoughts each moment that I am awake. I heard what happened last night, and somehow I knew that you both were involved. My fear is that you are heading into a place of great danger. Do not risk your lives for this mission of ours. Promise me."

"I made a vow that I would help you, and I will. We will search with twenty of my second best men. The twenty best men will be here watching you, and you can be sure that all three of us will be safe."

Chapter 15

Mary and Salome

The entry to Mary's room was covered by an elaborate tapestry outlining the history of the Tribes of Israel and adorned with embroidered faces of Moses, Abraham and David. She would have loved to roll it up and take it back through the Portal. Such a treasure, she thought. Outside the entry, she could occasionally hear her four Roman guards shifting their weight or conversing in low voices. Her room, though small, was outfitted with a raised wooden bed, the stone floor covered by another, but lighter, woven wool tapestry. There was a small table with two chairs and cloths of various colors hung on the walls. An open window displayed a panoramic view of the Sea of Galilee. In the distance hovered the blue hills rising above the other side of the lake, the infamous Golan Heights. She remembered that malaria was a constant threat at this time, and being so close to the water meant that she too was at risk of infection from a mosquito bite, the open window causing her some concern. She took out her camera and reviewed the images she had taken so far. Someday, perhaps, they could be seen by people from her time. The Portal seemed far away, and she started to wonder if they would ever make it back. She raised the camera and photographed her room and the lake full of small sailing craft, their sails reflecting the rim of the rising sun, just visible over the small mountains to the east.

She heard a female voice conversing with one of her guards, and a slender hand started slowly to withdraw the drape. Salome's smiling face emerged from the cleft and behind her was the glint of armor worn by one of the large guards. "Greetings, Mary. May I enter?" she asked in a small voice. Without waiting for permission, she came fully into the room. Mary judged her age to be fifteen, perhaps sixteen. Enough for her to have the body of a young woman and old enough to understand how to make full use of her feminine charms. There was no doubt of her attractiveness, her perfect teeth and her long auburn hair matching her slender but curvaceous female body. She was wearing a sheer, nearly transparent, overlay of shimmering dark red silk exposing her bare left arm and shoulder, giving a rather clear view of her well developed breasts. On her feet were delicate sandals of stitched hide, adorned with small gold bells at the ankle tie. Mary understood that Salome was dressed to impress her alone this morning, and that this was the day they were to spend together, sharing, Salome hoped, girl talk.

"Welcome, Salome," Mary said. "You look splendid this morning."

"As do you, Mary. Of course, you always are beautiful."

"Is there anything you wish, Salome?"

"I only wish to be with you, Mary. You are the most interesting person who has been with us. Your beauty rivals mine, I am told, but I have no jealousy about it."

"Thank you, Salome. Nor should you. I have seen you dance, and you are far more accomplished than anything I can do. Your youth and nimbleness combine and compliment your already beautiful appearance." Salome smiled and fussed with her hair. Mary could tell that she wanted something specific and guessed what it was. "I remember that I promised you that you could wear my jewelry, do you recall?" Salome nodded enthusiastically. Yes, that was what she wanted. Mary found the small soft leather bag containing her precious possessions. She carefully spilled its contents onto the bed, the gold, faience, and glass necklace uncoiling before them, spreading its magic as it did at least a thousand years before Salome was born. Mary held it up to the light of the window letting the moving parts dangle in front of Salome's mesmerized face.

"Oh! It is more beautiful than I remembered. Where did you say this came from?"

"I'm sure that it was found in the Valley of the Kings in upper Egypt. Very long ago, the Pharaohs of Egypt were buried in secret vaults far below ground, and their treasures went with them to the afterlife. Tomb robbers plundered the graves over time, and some of the treasure was seen again. This was once worn by the Queen of Egypt, and it is at least one thousand years old. Its value is far beyond the simple weight of the gold used to make it. It is part of human history, our little glimpse into how they lived."

"I don't recall ever seeing anything so fine. Our things have no value today," Salome said, holding the necklace in both hands.

"Not true, Salome. Things, buildings and even people from this time will decay and disappear into the soil only to be uncovered as treasure once again. If people from the future could only see you as you are right now, that alone would be priceless."

"Can you tell my future, Mary?" she asked coyly.

"You heard me say that you will have two marriages and three male children."

"Yes. But whom will I marry? Do you know this?"

"I do, but it would spoil the excitement and fun if I tell you, don't you think?"

"Yes. I see that you are right. Too bad Father doesn't feel this way." Mary put the necklace on Salome and also the earrings and watched as she twirled around the room trying to see her neck. "Am I not as beautiful as you now?" she asked.

"More," Mary said.

"May I wear them to show Father?" she said with hooded eyes.

"I cannot allow them out of this room, Salome. Those were entrusted to me, and I am their caretaker."

"I am princess here," she said with flashing eyes. "I will take them if I want to." She suddenly turned to leave wearing the jewelry. Mary knew that it would be the last time she would see those pieces if Salome left wearing them.

"Guards!" Mary called and when Salome opened the curtain to leave, she found the exit blocked by a thick, husky Roman, armed with a long spear, behind him three more.

"I am sorry, Salome. I would give you these things if they were mine to give, but I am only the temporary holder of history. You have to take them off now." Salome's eyes showed hatred and rage. She wasn't accustomed to being denied, and especially of something she desired so intently. She unclasped the necklace and earrings and flung them on the bed.

"We are no longer friends, Mary," she said and pushed her way past the guards. The one closest to the door peered in after she left.

"Problems?" he asked in a throaty voice.

"Get your men assembled. I am leaving this place before there is trouble. You will escort me to the camp."

"You will have to walk. We have no litter or horse for you here."

"I have no problem walking. Be ready because I will be out soon," she said. The man pulled back and shouted at the other men, and Mary could hear the order being passed through the halls of the palace. As she put on the least showy of her garments and collected all her belongings, she heard the hall filling with voices. Twenty Roman soldiers awaited her outside the room, and she could hear the clank of metal against metal. They were fully armored and armed and were prepared to protect her at any cost.

Two men lead the procession with Mary following, her silken ivory garment fluttering and trailing behind her. The rest of the column noisily followed. The ruling family was not to be seen, but spaced along the walls were palace guards watching quietly but threateningly with spears at the ready. The Romans seemed to know that there was no real danger given their deserved reputation for ferocious combat at close quarters. The lead men, at least, ignored the palace guard, and the group proceeded quickly outside into the open. Once there, the formation changed into a box with Mary in the center, and they headed toward the city walls and the Roman encampment on the other side. Mary looked up to see Salome watching silently from an upstairs window. Her petulant face revealing her to be a spoiled child, not the woman who would be instrumental in the brutal death of John the Baptist in a short two years. He dared speak out against the marriage of her father to Herodias, because she had been the bride of Antipas's brother. Mary remembered clearly the words of the historian Josephus, who recorded that Herod Antipas had granted Salome any wish for having danced for him. He discovered that her wish was for the head of John the Baptist, and the wish had been granted. Would giving up my jewelry have bought enough influence to spare the life of John the Baptist and change the future of the world, Mary wondered with regret. The image of Salome grew smaller and smaller, fading into history. What was is what is to be.

Antonius looked down at Cosimus from his horse and smiled. "If you were an Optio, you would be riding. A Tesserarius walks. I should have told you. Hope you can handle the heavy armor and the spear. Got enough water?" he teased, amusement on his face. Cos looked up in mock anger. Because of the other men listening behind him, he was unable to joke back and was at the mercy of Antonius who was in a good mood. The sea spread out on their left, and the sounds of birds and the occasional splash of small waves made the journey south pleasant. It was only four miles to the marshes near the mouth of the Jordan, and along the way there were many groups of fishermen coming and going from the sea in their small craft.

"Don't you think we should stop and ask some of these fishermen if they know a Jesus?" asked Cos.

"Don't bother, none of them would talk to us, and if they did, you couldn't believe them."

Just as he finished speaking they heard a cry from a small hill rising from the sea. A man waved as he shouted, "Romans!" The column stopped when Antonius held up his hand, and they waited as the man descended the hill to stand in front of Antonius, holding up both hands to indicate that he was not armed. Antonius pointed right then left, and several men instantly dispersed into the brush, providing flank cover if needed. Antonius waited for the man to speak as his horse nervously pawed the ground, observing that the man was dressed similar to others they had seen in this area, for the most part in soiled dark rags hung around his neck, extending to the ground. He wore a short well-groomed military-styled beard and had visible skin instead of hair on the top of his head. His hood made it difficult to determine if it had been shaved. There was something athletic about the way he moved, a certain lightness on his feet. It was the eyes, though, that were troubling. They were narrowed and dark, deep enough to hold hatred, alert enough to act quickly. He looked intently at Cosimus and then back to Antonius.

"I am told that you look for Jesus of Nazat," he said, his voice powerful but low.

"How do you know this?" Antonius asked. Two Romans moved behind the man without being directed to do so.

The man looked over his shoulder, worried. "I know." He again looked hard at Cos, studying his soul and making him uncomfortable by his close proximity.

"Speak then, what have you to say?" Antonius demanded, his intolerance growing. The horse sensed the tension and began to shake his head, snorting, flank muscles quivering. The other men were also agitated and started intently looking around, perceiving an ominous but unseen threat.

"I know where this Jesus will be," the man said, becoming nervous, recognizing his peril.

"Do you not know where he is?"

"Tomorrow, he will be there tomorrow."

"There. Where is there?" Antonius shouted, now angry.

"A grove of trees near the water, not far from here. You will recognize it by a sunken boat which lies near. He will be there tomorrow."

"Where is Jesus right now?"

"I do not know, Centurion."

"Take this man captive. We will march to this spot he has told of, and if he has lied, we will slay him there," Antonius commanded. The two soldiers behind the man poked their spears into his back and marched him toward the rear of the column. Antonius turned his horse south toward the promised spot, followed by Cos and the column of men. The stranger's hands were tied behind him, and he was led by a noose pulled tightly around his neck.

Around the next bend, the prisoner at the rear started yelling, and the column stopped again. "This is the place," he shouted. A small discarded fishing boat lay near the water and was half-full of sand and mud. Nearby, on the right side of the road, stood the grove of trees, exactly as described. Several men fanned out from the ranks, scouting the area. At the moment, there were no other people in evidence, not even fishermen, the area deathly silent. At a wave from Antonius, the prisoner was brought forward.

"Do you know anything of this Jesus becoming two?" Antonius asked with narrowed eyes.

The man looked suddenly pale, and his eyes rolled around furtively as if someone or something was listening. "Yes," he finally said, swallowing hard.

"Do you need torture to free your tongue?"

"Both are called Jesus, both are near here. The one you seek will be in this spot tomorrow."

"How do you know this," Antonius demanded.

"He told me to find you and have you here tomorrow," the captive answered.

"Sounds like a trap. Revenge for the Baths," Cos said loud enough for Antonius to hear.

"I agree," Antonius frowned. He kicked his horse and headed around and above the trees, disappearing for a time. They could hear his horse moving away at first and then back toward them, the sounds seeming to echo off the still lake. He came through the trees and pulled up abruptly near Cos, his horse throwing up a cloud of red dust. "There is no threat in sight today. Tomorrow we will return in strength and trap the ones who seek to trap us. Bring the captive with us. We return to camp."

Cos started thinking over recent events and was quiet for a time as they marched back the way they had come. "You have been quoting Ovid! Now I remember where I heard some of those. I had no idea that your education was so broad," he said looking up at the mounted rider looming over him.

"I knew Ovid. We met when my legion was stationed briefly at Tomis in Scythia. It was about ten years ago, and he was an old man at the time, exiled there by Augustus, but I never understood why. I made acquaintance with him and read as many of his works as I could before we left. A great man, Ovid, Rome's greatest poet of all time, and there he wasted away, bereft of books and family. At least I can say that he and I were friends once."

"I, too, have read some of Ovid's works. His books and poems will survive for two thousand years. That tells you something about their lasting importance."

"Did your study inform you that Ovid was passionate about women? He couldn't get enough of them, even in his old age." Antonius laughed at the memory.

"A worthwhile way to live or die," Cos agreed.

Life and Death Among the Trees

At the Roman camp entrance, it was obvious that something was amiss. Antonius scanned the grounds, and he saw far more of his troops there than he expected. He dismounted and a decanus greeted him, taking his bridle.

"What is happening?" Antonius demanded.

"Much, Centurion. Your woman awaits in your quarters and has been there since shortly after you left this morning. We have seen a steady stream of armed men heading toward the palace, and we have misgivings about what it means. Also, a message delivered from Caesarea is awaiting your response."

"First, the message. Find the courier and bring him to my tent." The column of soldiers noisily filed by behind him, the men tired and ready for food.

Antonius waited for Cos outside the tent, and when he arrived, he took off his helmet and wiped his sweating face. "Mary's back, and there is an army gathering in Tiberias," Antonius said, placing his hand on Cosimus' shoulder. "I just saw another group go by."

"What caused such sudden hostility? Is it about the men you and I killed?" Cos asked.

Antonius paused momentarily collecting his thoughts. "The cause is hidden. The effect is visible to all," he quoted, wondering if Cos would remember the source. Antonius brushed the sweat droplets from his forehead with the leather guard strapped to his wrist and stared across toward the walls of Tiberias. "It's really about a man too small for his appointment. I don't think we should worry; Herod would not dare attack Romans. We are the only thing keeping his own people from killing him and his entire family. It's a bluster meant more to impress his wife and daughter than us. Nevertheless, we have to assume the worst and be prepared to defend ourselves." The courier came running toward them holding a scroll. Without a word, Antonius unrolled the letter from Ponticus Pilate. "Our commander directs us to proceed to Jerusalem to form part of a cohort he is assembling there. The order instructs us to proceed with haste." He put down the paper, then noticed the courier waiting for a reply. "I will comply, of course," he said and then waved his hand in dismissal.

"Cosimus, we can 'kill two birds with one stone' as Ovid said. Early, before dawn, we will break camp and proceed down to the lake and solve this Jesus problem of yours, then continue along the Jordan, south until Jericho. From there it is only a day's march to Jerusalem. Without unforeseen events, we should be there in five days or less. It will look as though we are fleeing Herod's men, but I will be relieved to return to Judea which is entirely controlled by Rome."

Cos looked worried. "That means that we won't be going anywhere near Nazat. We can't return to our time unless we travel alone back the way we came."

"Remember the bandits? Also, there is some reason Mary is waiting inside for us, and you can be sure that this means Herod and his brood are unhappy with her and therefore us. You can't go back that way alone, Cos, I won't allow it. Mary will come with us and so will you."

"What about Tony? What has happened to him?" Cos asked.

"Oh, Tony. He was imprisoned, but I will allow him to go also as long as he behaves. He may yet prove useful."

Antonius removed his helmet and entered the tent, followed closely by Cosimus. As their eyes adjusted to the darkened chamber, they saw Mary smiling at them. She was comfortably seated on several pillows, her cream-colored silken robes brightening the dark room.

"I hoped that you wouldn't stay away too long. It is a wonderful thing to see you both together and safe," she said, rising and walking gracefully toward them, right into the waiting arms of Antonius. She rested her head softly against his breast plate, looking toward Cos.

"Tell us what happened?" Cos said in a whisper, not wanting to spoil the moment for them.

"I chose to leave. My time there was over."

"There is a growing number of soldiers headed to the palace. Do you know of this?" Antonius asked, still holding her tenderly.

"Salome was angry that I would not let her steal the jewelry you gave me, but there is more going on. I saw men entering the palace who gave me a chill when I looked upon them. There is something evil happening, like we are all puppets playing a role in a big play." She arched her back and neck and looked up at Antonius. What Cos saw in her eyes and face was different that he had ever seen when she looked at him. Mary was beaming with love and so was Antonius. She was dressed in a flowing garment, pulled over one shoulder in the Roman style, and her beautiful neck, with its curves and shadows, flowed from her head into her chest in timeless majesty and continued unseen to emerge into the living flesh of a Greek goddess standing on her toes. The realization that Mary belonged to Antonius and he to her hit Cosimus with sudden pain. He had grown to love them both, but he couldn't help but to feel left out. He was the unwanted third party in the room.

Cos cleared his throat softly before speaking. "Antonius, Mary, I leave you to find Agrippa and help him carry out plans to leave early tomorrow. I'll see you both in the morning." He hesitated for a moment as he looked at the pair who had just realized the intensity of their love for one another. "Ovid comes again to my mind just now, and I leave you with a quote that I remember which seems appropriate, 'Hurry to your goal together. There is full bliss when man and woman lie equally conquered.' "

Cos muttered to himself as he walked away, "Ovid also said, 'There is a certain pleasure in weeping.' On that, he was wrong."

The men labored most of the night to break camp and be ready for travel by dawn, without making noise to disturb the sleep of their Centurion and his lover. At the first hint of diminishing darkness, they were ready to march, and the formation silently assembled in front of the command tent to wait for Antonius. The tent flap flew open with a slap, and he stepped through the entrance, fully dressed, as if for combat.

"As soon as Mary Solomon comes out, take this tent down and see that she is fed. Optio, start the men marching south along the lake as soon as you can, and we will catch you before the sun fully rises."

"Are you not going with us, Centurion?" he asked.

"Cosimus and I are going to ride around the palace. I want to see for myself what is being assembled and what we may shortly face."

"Is there not danger in going there, Centurion?" Agrippa said with concern.

"There is more danger in showing fear," Antonius said as a mount was brought forward for Cosimus to ride. They rode toward the walls of Tiberias and toward the approaching dawn without looking back.

The horses slowed to a walk as they steadily moved toward the palace. There were many groups of men sleeping on the ground, scattered about with no obvious organization. Several were leaning against the walls and looking toward the horses, spears in hand. A feeling of hostility mixed with the damp air, though no words were spoken. The sounds of hoofs in the gravelly soil caused several men to sit up from their slumber and defiantly watch. Out of the shadows, a man moved to block their way and they stopped. He was darkly dressed and carried a metallic circular shield. His pointed helmet shone in the predawn light.

"Romans. You are not welcome here any longer," he said in Aramaic. Cos watched Antonius' face, because he understood none of the man's words.

"You will either move, or you will quickly lose your head," Antonius said in a level tone. The man glared back, reluctant to give way. He looked around quickly, but no others were willing to assist him, and he sullenly made way for the horses.

On the way past, the man spat into the ground and said, "Your time here will not last the day. You are headed to the end of the world." He laughed with a menacing rumble as the horses and riders slid by.

Antonius, ignoring him, said in Latin, "Someone thinks that they have prepared a trap for us, but it is they who will not see another day." They continued slowly and defiantly around the palace as the night continued its inexorable slide around the globe of Earth, dawn not long away. At last, they reached the west gate and turned south, spurring their horses into a trot.

"I counted at least three hundred. We will be taking the road along the Jordan where water is on one side and hills the other. They will have to attack us in a narrow place, and if that happens, we are especially well-equipped and trained to counter them."

Cos said, "That will be no place for Mary. I couldn't bare to see her hurt."

"She will not be, I assure you," Antonius responded quickly. "Virgil said, 'They conquer who believe they can,' and I know this to be true. If I were plotting such an attack on a formation like ours, I would try to get my opponent squeezed between two forces. One from the front and one from the rear. In this area, there would be no place to go. My plan is, therefore, to defeat any force coming at us from the front, turn and destroy the rear before they can flee. A divided force is a weaker force, as Julius Caesar observed."

"Why would they attack a Roman column which has been peaceful and who belongs to an ally?" Cos asked.

"It will mean destruction of Galilee when our legions from Syria respond and move south against them. It is an act of a fool or is being directed by something evil. Mary is right. I can feel a strange presence here, and one which is watching us right now. There is some force here which seeks to cause chaos and death. Could it be the Jesus you seek?"

"No! Certainly not. He is a man of peace, not war," Cos said with conviction.

"You know that opposites attract, Cos. In every man there is both good and evil. As dark is to light and evil is to good. There are opposing forces in everything. That is the way ordained by the Gods because it keeps a balance among men. We were told that Jesus has become two. Now I understand what the man meant. One Jesus is good, but the other waits for us and has arranged our destiny so that we will convert to his side or die by the sword. We are going to encounter the evil Jesus and his followers today. That is who will be waiting for us. I wonder how he could know about you and your quest even before you started asking?"

"You think, then, that this meeting was always destined to happen? We are just pawns in a game larger than we can imagine?" Cos asked.

"Seems so, doesn't it? You came looking for Jesus, and he was waiting for you all along. Whatever happens, it is to happen today. I will take many of them with me before I fall, and I expect the same from my men and the same from you."

"I will do no less, Antonius, and I will be at your side no matter what comes at us," Cos said.

They reached the last few men trailing the column and among them were the captured informant and Tony, walking side by side. Both were in chains and walked with effort, hands fastened behind them. Tony looked up as the horses drew alongside.

"Well, aren't you a pretty boy in your little Roman costume, complete with a shiny fuzzy helmet. So you've become one of them while I am stuck in chains. If we ever get back, you can count on one hand the days you have left to live, you snake," Tony sneered and spat.

"Tony, I didn't know this is what happened to you. I feel bad about it, and if you promise to behave, I'll urge them to set you free. Is it a deal?"

"What's behave mean, Cos? I am suppose to protect you and Mary. I already did once, don't you remember the bandits? I don't have anything to prove."

Cos turned to Antonius who was expecting a translation, "You should free this man as you promised. He saved us previously, as we both remember." Antonius didn't look moved and, for a time, just looked at Tony without pity as he dragged himself along, occasionally prodded by a sharp spear to his back.

"Free this man," Antonius commanded. "If he tries to flee, kill him." With his last remark, he trotted his horse forward toward Mary's mount.

"Where's my gun, Cos?" Tony asked as soon as his hands were free.

"I have no idea, and besides, you don't need to worry about our protection any longer. As you can see, there are eighty very tough and experienced boys who will gladly do that for you. By the way, the Centurion just ordered his men to kill you if you try and flee, and trust me, they will do anything he says."

"Where are we going?

"We are trying to find Jesus this morning who, we are told, may be waiting for us. There is a possibility of three hundred armed men coming down this road behind us, so you would be wise to stay alert and keep quiet just now." Tony didn't seem threatened by warnings of danger, and his darting eyes said that he was already calculating his next move. Cos left him and rode forward alongside the marching men, heading toward the two horses near the front.

Cos arrived just as Mary was transferred from behind the smiling

Agrippa to the raucous approval from some of the men. She gave a little wave to Cos as he drew near and he could see, to his relief, that she was dressed in her black, humble, and therefore inconspicuous, clothing. She pulled the hood farther over her face in response to something Antonius said and extended her slender arms around his waist from behind, nestling closer to him. The footsteps of the men and the sound of gravel under the hoofs of the horses were the only sounds made by the column which bore steadily south along the lake. No fishermen were out this morning, and the lake was calm but grey, reflecting sheets of clouds hanging low overhead. Flickers of distant lightning punctuated the early morning, followed by deep, threatening rumbles of thunder. Cos felt a chill come over him and then he realized that there were no birds to be seen, not even the occasional call of a bird or even the buzz of an insect. The area seemed deserted and barren of life other than the men in the small troupe making their way slowly south as the sun's first rays split the night between the clouds and the distant hills. As the march continued, the wind freshened, coming off the lake from the east, bringing with it an ever increasing chop of troubled water breaking into waves against the shore. The wind turned suddenly cold, rapidly increasing in intensity, howling past the men's heads and chasing around like little demons inside of their helmets. Cos used his arm to shield his face from the intensity of the stinging wind to notice that they had arrived where they were stopped by the informant the previous day. He shouted at Antonius and pointed to the hill where the man had been standing. Antonius held up his hand, and the column stopped abruptly.

"Optio," Antonius shouted above the wind. "Take thirty men and head up the hill toward the left. In about three hundred *passus*, you will find a stand of trees. Go around silently and secure your men on the far side." Agrippa nodded that he understood and, with a few arm signals to his men, left in a hurry, disappearing into the blur of wind and leaves.

"Cosimus, you will take the same number and hide on this side of the wood. I will take the rest and come down the road. If they are waiting for us, as I expect they are, we will attack on three sides and push them into the sea. When fighting starts, spare no one. All of them are to die. You understand?" A closer sear of lightning punctuated his order.

"No!" Cos shouted holding his hand as a megaphone. What if this is the peaceful Jesus? We might be tricked into killing the wrong one. This could be a trap that we are springing on ourselves."

Antonius thought about it for a moment, then said, "We will bring your Tony to the front with me. I will send him in first. If he is slain, then we will know."

"And Mary?" Cos shouted, pointing to the object behind Antonius, completely covered by her cloak which was shaking in the strengthening wind.

"You must take her with you," Antonius said and drew close to Cos and his horse. Mary looked puzzled but transferred behind Cos without an argument. She pulled the hood away from her face and looked sorrowfully at Antonius as if she might never see him again. The wind continued to escalate, and they were getting spray from the ever more maniacal waters of the darkening sea. The meager light of the morning faded to a dull grey, robbing color from the world, threatening to darken even further as the storm approached rapidly from across the lake. Speech was no longer possible, except directly into an ear which Mary sought by pulling Cos toward her.

"What is happening?" she shouted. "I'm frightened."

"We are about to encounter Jesus, and it seems some God is angry with us about it. You and I are going to soon find shelter in the trees close to the road so we can watch what happens." He spurred his horse and motioned to the group behind him to follow. He looked back and saw that they were leaning forward into the wind, holding on to their helmets, but they were coming, nevertheless, and nothing would stop them, not even if Hell was waiting for them on the other side of the trees. He glanced backwards toward Antonius and saw him sitting erect on his horse, looking down the road toward whatever fate awaited them, determination carved crisply into his face, his red cloak extending away from him like a flag, cracking in the wind. Never had Cos seen a more majestic sight. Not even in the paintings of the old masters had this scene ever been matched. He realized that Mary was right to choose Antonius over him, because Antonius was the better man. Far better, Cos told himself regretfully. After they headed up the hill, the rain started, first in hard stinging drops, followed shortly by sheets of water, as if the lake itself was moving inland over them. Through the water, Cos caught sight of trees ahead and pointed the way for his men. He dismounted and tied his horse to a tree, then helped Mary down. Together they crept down toward the road staying just inside of the tree line. After stumbling and sliding over roots and brambles, they began to make out the road and the movement of men who walked back and forth as if waiting for something. He held up his hand to halt, and his men quietly took up their positions among the trees. The rain lessened slightly, and he began to see more clearly as the light grew brighter over the lake. Clearly, many men were waiting in the road, and the glint of sharpened metal from their weapons spoke the obvious. They were armed. A large man in the center stood apart, dressed in dark clothing, his face covered by a deep hood. It was evident he was in charge because of the commanding way he pointed and the way his men showed deference. He slowly turned his head to look in the direction of Cos and Mary, as if he knew they were there. Something radiated from him, some force that grabbed Cos by the throat and squeezed. He felt suddenly helpless to resist, as if he wanted to get up and walk down the hill into the road. Suddenly, they all turned to look up the road toward the north, a quick movement of heads, as if they were a gathering of birds. Cos sensed that Antonius and his men were approaching, drawing their attention. He waved for his men to follow, and they crept downhill, closing the distance while still hidden by trees. The group on the road fell behind their leader who stood out front like the point of a pyramid, obviously unafraid. He held up his hand to stop Antonius and his men from approaching any closer.

"Greetings to you, Roman. I offer you to join us rather than face certain destruction. You could command an army of immense size and have unlimited power. Does that not appeal to you?" His voice was harsh, riveting, and commanded attention. Through the trees, Cos could see Antonius remain seated on horseback, twenty men close behind him. His sword was drawn and was being held in his right hand, pointed straight downward.

"Mary, you are to stay here. I am leaving five men with you. Do not follow us. Do you understand?" Cos whispered.

"Yes, Cosimus. Be safe," she said, and huddled down behind the shelter of a large tree trunk. Cos took the rest of the men, and they silently drew swords as they crept closer to the road. The rain had nearly stopped, and the wind lessened as they stealthily closed the distance. Cos could clearly see the leader who stood in the middle of the road looking toward Antonius, who approached slowly, his men spreading out behind him.

"I am Jesus. You seek me, and I seek you. I offer you riches, wealth and power, or you can accept death, if you prefer."

"It is not I who seeks you," Antonius shouted. "It is him!"

Tony jumped down from behind Antonius and walked confidently toward Jesus and his group, who seemed to be expecting him. They showed no movement, either defensive or offensive as Tony closed the distance with a confidant stride. Tony was either the bravest or the dumbest man he had ever seen, Cos thought. The morning light had brightened enough to see silver shimmering from the gun in Tony's right hand. Cos watched helplessly as Tony drew closer to the group and their leader, who stood alone, silently watching Tony's approach as if drawing him, summoning him, through the one-way gate of doom. Cos felt a sickening intensity increasing as if a gigantic siren was triggered, as if unstoppable and opposing forces were focused on this very moment in time. This was a pivotal moment in human history, perhaps the pivotal moment, where everything in history that was to occur from this point forward might be at risk. Tony was preparing to shoot the evil being who called himself Jesus. Cos realized for the first time that the man standing in the center of the road could only be the Antichrist, whose coming was so feared by early Christians. They all watched, mesmerized, as the distance closed to twenty-five feet when Tony suddenly raised his pistol and fired three shots directly at the man he obviously believed was the real Jesus. It finally dawned on Cos that the plot all along had been to kill Jesus Christ. This moment was what The Commission wanted. The death of Jesus Christ was the reason they all had been sent back in time. The bullets hurled at Jesus seemed to have no immediate effect, but nearly simultaneously, there arose screams of rage from men swarming toward Tony with swords flashing in the air, their eyes wild with anger. Two more shots rang out, and Tony bolted across the road toward the trees, just as Antonius charged forward with sword raised, his arm cocked for a swing. Cos raised his sword, and he and his men, screaming in unison, rushed forward from the trees. The clamor and chaos of violent hand-to-hand combat rose from the sleeping woods with men slipping and sliding on the wet slope and blood flowing in the road and among the trees. Two men with swords raised came rushing at Cos from different angles, hate and rage in their faces. Instinctively, Cos pivoted toward the closest, deflecting the man's sword with his shield and driving his gladius through the man's chest in an instant almost too brief to remember. He spun around just in time to avoid a crushing sword blow skipping across the armor on his back. He brought his gladius around in a long sweeping arc, landing it at the base of the man's neck with a sickening dull thud. The man spread his arms out in agony and fell face first into the wet soil, instantly dead. The noise level fell abruptly as the Romans quickly gained control. The remaining enemy regrouped and prepared to flee south along the road but ran headlong into the fresh troops of Agrippa coming around the trees. They fell quickly to the more experienced Romans in a furious climax, followed by a deathly stillness. Cos cautiously stood erect and looked around at bodies strewn among the trees and in the road, frozen in the agony and terror of death. The rain started again, slowly at first, but this time without the ripping wind. It was as if the heavens had decided to cleanse the killing area, softly and gently. Cos could hear Antonius calling, and he continued down the road toward his voice.

"Assemble in formation," Antonius ordered, and the men obeyed, some limping from wounds. "Ahead," he shouted, and the column started moving north just as the sounds of an approaching group of men could be heard coming over the hill. As the approaching army crested, they caught sight of the Romans, who remained at full strength. A hand went up halting the men as their leaders realized that the Roman column was moving rapidly toward them, swords drawn and shields up. Antonius waved his men forward, and they started running toward the larger opposing force who collectively seemed to quiver, stop, and freeze with sudden panic. Before the Romans closed the distance, the army from the north turned and retreated in disarray, some of their men scattering up the hills and away from the road as fast as they could flee. The others turned and fled north along the lake with a great clamor.

"Stop," Antonius commanded, and his men halted to watch their would-be opponents flee for their lives back toward Tiberias. Cosimus remembered that he had left Mary in the woods, and he turned, running in that direction, scrambling over fallen bodies, heading relentlessly uphill. She was still where he left her, shivering under her wet cloak, surrounded by five soldiers who stood like stone statues, their faces hidden and anonymous in the shadows of their helmets.

"Mary! It's over," he said and gently pulled her to her feet. "They are all dead or fled, Mary. There is nothing left to fear." He enveloped her in his arms and felt her trembling. He pulled her hood back to look into her face, and once again was struck by her large eyes, full lips and tenderness which radiated from her face. Antonius was a fortunate man to have the love of this woman.

She looked up at Cosimus, wiping the rain from her face, "You are every bit a Roman officer. Seeing you in your blood splattered armor...well, I will never remember you any other way. This was your destiny, after all." She brushed wet hair away from her face and seemed lost in thought for a moment. "I saw Tony. He came running right by us, heading uphill. He flung his gun away as he ran, and shortly after he went by, there were three others chasing him. One of them looked right at me, and I felt a wave of dread come over me as if I could feel the very hand of death close by. The creature looked at me, and I saw a wild wolf's face, the face of a predator, crazed and violent. Good thing you ordered your men to stay with me, or they would have at least tried to kill this...whatever it was, and I don't think they would have survived."

"I saw Tony fire three shots directly at this man you just described, and I don't see how it was possible to miss from such a close distance. After the shots, there was utter confusion as the battle started in earnest, and I really didn't see much of anything else other than what I was doing."

"Is Antonius injured?" she asked.

"You can see for yourself, because he is headed this way." She turned to see Antonius, still mounted, his bloody sword clutched tightly in his hand, slowly working his way uphill toward them. "You love him, don't you?" Cos asked.

"Yes, Cos. I love him. I hope you aren't upset, but I can't help it."

"He is everything a man should be, and in my way, I love him also. I can't see how this love of yours could work out for either of you, because your destiny is to return to our time. His is to stay here. This," he said, sweeping his hand around at the battlefield, "this will be a memory of things long, long past and so will Antonius. For both of us." The last statement of obvious fact opened a steady stream of tears, and she was still sobbing when Antonius stopped, towering above both of them.

"You are not injured, my love?" he asked as he dismounted.

"No. Are you?" she responded. He opened his arms, and she sagged into them, feeling gratitude that he was not harmed but weakness from all the violence and savagery which had just taken place in front of her.

"This is my life, Mary. My past and my future. I will be a soldier for ten more years and travel and fight wherever they send me. I make a meager income, hardly enough to support a wife and not enough to buy a place for her to live. If I manage to stay alive until my discharge, I will have some money due me, but presently, I have nothing of value to give you. I love you, but while fighting this morning, I realized that you are too good for me and too precious to waste on me. It was wrong to allow you to love me in the belief that, somehow, we could work this out." He raised his bloody sword and held it in the air. "This is what I am. Simply a sword and nothing else."

"No!" she sobbed, clutching his arms, pulling his extended arm down. "You are not simply a weapon. You are everything that I ever dreamed of, and I won't let you leave me. I will work this out for us, just give me more time. Do not close yourself off from me in a wish to do the right thing. You and I, together, are the right thing. I don't want to lose you," Mary said, and her tears returned, mixing with the rain, running down her shining face.

"Don't worry, Mary. I am not strong enough to part from you. Only death will do that." They embraced as a gentle rain kept falling, washing away any doubts from their souls. Death. Only death would part them.

The River Jordan

Antonius and Cosimus rode amongst their men looking for those who were injured and needing assistance. One that Cosimus spotted had a bad leg gash and was being held up by two men. Cos dismounted and inspected the man's wound. He saw that it needed to be sutured and bound, or the man would continue to bleed heavily. He signaled to Agrippa, who came up quickly.

"This man needs treatment. Is there anyone who can repair his wound," Cos asked.

"I have some instruments in my bag. Would you care to assist?" Agrippa asked, while searching in his saddle bag.

"I will do my best, Optio," Cos answered. He directed the man to lie down beside the road and instructed the other men to hold him steady. Cos knew that he had little to no medical knowledge to offer other than what he had seen on television. He understood that no anesthesia was available, and there was no concept of bacteria in the first century. The soldier was uncomplaining and willingly and gratefully submitted to treatment.

"First, wash the dirt from his leg and wound with water," Agrippa said over his shoulder while still preparing his instruments. Cos accepted a canteen from one of the men and rinsed the wound thoroughly. There was no complaint or suggestion of pain from the man, who watched the process intently.

"Now, Cosimus, rinse the wound with wine," Agrippa said and handed Cos a goatskin of wine. This time, the irrigation caused the patient to gnash his teeth, but as before, he didn't make a sound. The wound oozed freely and was roughly as long as the span of a man's hand and well into the muscle of the right thigh. Agrippa spread out his cloth and sorted his instruments. There were two needles, one small and the other at least six inches in length. Both had eyelets and were strung with black thread. There were several cloth wads, tied in a roll by the same black thread. Two forceps, one quite long, were available for retrieval of foreign objects. A small knife, sharpened to a glistening tip, was lying threateningly at hand along the top. Agrippa indicated that they should hold the man tightly, and he proceeded to unhurriedly stitch the wound with neatly tied sutures. He picked up the long needle and looked his patient in the eye, "This is necessary, Ueima. You must hold still." He plunged the long sharp needle into normal skin at some distance from the cut and pushed the tip out on the other side. The same was performed slightly down from the first, and then he strung the cloth bundles with the suture and tied them down firmly, compressing the wound from either side. "Bind the leg tightly," he instructed Cosimus, then stood and began putting away his instruments. "The idea is to prevent excess fluids from accumulating. I will see him again tonight, and we will dress the wound again." His patient fell backwards, sweating profusely, but never uttered any sounds of pain or complaint during his treatment. The procedure wasn't much different than a modern approach, Cos realized, except for sterility and anesthesia.

"A suggestion, Optio," Cos said. Agrippa turned toward him, with some surprise in his face, waiting expectantly for Cos to explain. "There are agents of infection around us everywhere. Some are already on our skin before an injury. Some come in on the opponent's sword. The ones we can control are present on instruments used for treatment. My suggestion is to soak your tools in wine before and after they are used and to use a flame through which you pass your instruments prior to using them. It may help avoid spreading infection. All water used to rinse and clean the wound should be boiled first."

"How do you come by this knowledge, Cosimus?" he asked.

"TV. Before you doubt me, try it. I promise it will make some difference."

"TV?" Agrippa asked and furrowed his brow. Before he could ask the obvious questions, there was a call to assemble from the front of the column. The march was about to start again shortly. Cos quickly and tightly bound the wound and helped bring the man to his feet. Ueima expressed his gratitude by slapping Cosimus on the back and took his place in line. Cos remounted and headed forward where Antonius and Mary waited. As they slowly proceeded south, their horses stepped over the dead littering the dirt road, and the smell and vision of death rose to assault their senses. The carnage was appalling, with some bodies seeming to stare blankly at the victorious living, screaming at them with silent mouths.

"Do you see your Jesus among the dead, Cosimus?" Antonius asked while looking around.

"He isn't here. Mary saw him chasing Tony, and they both disappeared over the hill. Two other men were with Jesus. I think they were the only survivors," Cos said.

"It would seem that Tony couldn't kill this one with his lightning bolts. We are best rid of both of them. Where is our prisoner who tried to lead us to slaughter?"

"At the rear of the column, still bound."

"Bring him up front when we are past the fallen," Antonius commanded.

"What are you going to do to him?" Mary asked over his shoulder.

"He must die. It could have been us, and you, lying here in pieces. He will become an example for others who pass this way. This must be done, Mary, but you should look away when it happens."

"It's over, Antonius. We are safe. Can't you spare his life? It can't matter now, can it?"

"I understand your natural sympathy, Mary, but if we spare his life now, we will just have to kill him again in some other place. We can't change what he believes, and since his master has escaped, he will follow Jesus again, just as he did before." Mary was silent, thinking it over from Antonius' point of view, as they started to pass from the small forest out into the harsh light of day. Antonius halted his horse, and they waited for the man to be brought forward. Two large soldiers threw the man on the ground before Antonius, and he looked up with hate and contempt at his Roman victors.

"Look at what you accomplished today. Does the image of your fellows' sightless eyes weigh heavy upon you?" Antonius asked the man.

"I only wish that I could piss into your dead, open mouth, Centurion," the prisoner said and spat on the ground for emphasis.

"See what I mean, Mary?" Antonius said softly for her ears only. He returned his attention to the man on the ground. "I could spare your life if you will truthfully answer my questions," he said.

"I will tell you nothing. I fear Jesus more than you."

"We will see about that. You want to give up your life so easily as to provoke me now? Is it worth so little to you?"

"I obey Jesus only. He is my savior, my master, and I obey him without question."

"He has fled, leaving you in my hands. I am the master of your fate now. You will answer my questions or die badly." The man's face softened as he realized that Antonius was right. He was at the Roman's meager mercy, like it or not.

"What do you wish to ask?" the man said hesitantly, hoping he could not be heard by the forest of dead men behind them.

"Where did this Jesus you follow come from, and why do you follow him?"

"I do not know from where he sprang. Suddenly he was with us and among us, and his voice and his thoughts compel us to submit our free will to him. We heard of the other Jesus first, the one at the Jordan, and we heard that he was good and earnest and seeks to help other men understand that they need to help their fellows. I believed that there was only one Jesus, but there are two. One invites, one compels. I have been compelled to follow this one, and he pulls me toward him as a lodestone pulls a fragment of iron toward it."

"Will you still follow or are you free of him?" Antonius asked.

"I must follow, I must," he said and held his head low in resignation.

"Thank you for your honest answers. You will understand that I also am compelled to do what I have to do." Antonius turned and looked at his Optio who nodded that he understood what had to be done. Antonius moved slowly forward, Mary holding on but looking backward toward Cos, trying to understand what was about to happen.

"You, Cosimus, are with me," Agrippa said. He motioned for the men to pick up the prisoner, and they quickly pulled him out of the road and started to bind his legs and hands tightly as he struggled. Two groups of men fell to separate tasks without direction as if they had done this on many other occasions. One group started digging a large hole in the center of the road, and the other group could be heard cutting wood. Cos looked around trying to take in what was about to happen, but then it became clear. The prisoner was going to be crucified and left in the center of the road. Cos was horrified that he was to be party to it. He had not fully understood the conversation between Antonius and the prisoner, but he clearly understood the facial expressions and the contempt radiating from the prisoner toward Antonius and his men. This was going to become another source of local hatred for the Romans, this display of brutality, in an area which was otherwise peaceful. Cos sighed to himself at the tragedy of the whole thing, these bloody disputes which had occurred and will occur in this troubled land, seemingly forever, just as the bible predicted. Wars upon wars until the end of time.

The primitive cross was readied quickly, and the man was dragged toward it; knowing his fate, he kicked and screamed until he was silenced with a blow by the hilt of a sword to his head. While unconscious, the man was spread out and methodically nailed, hands first, onto the limbs. He revived just as they were holding his feet together and a long, ugly, forged nail was hovering above his feet about to be driven through them into the wood.

"No!" he shrieked. "I told you what I know. You said you would spare my life!" Agrippa indicated that they were to continue and they did, causing the prisoner to again collapse unconscious, as the last blow was struck on the spike through his feet.

"You were promised your life, and you are still alive. The birds will take the rest of you. Blame them if you will," Agrippa said and waved his arm skyward as the cross started on its journey into the prepared hole. The scene was an apparition from Hell, with the still alive prisoner hanging from his hands and feet, overlooking a battlefield of two hundred bodies scattered randomly before him. Evil presiding over evil.

It was late afternoon before there was any conversation at the front of the column. The afternoon sun had cleared the skies of clouds, and the birds and fishermen were again present. The horses and men clomped onward with an ancient soothing rhythm along the upper Jordan river. Across the river, the east bank was steep, with hills rising nearly from the water's edge, while the left bank was more level and, for the most part, had a well traveled primitive road. Reeds and rushes softened the water's edge and wildflowers sprinkled the landscape.

"Cosimus," Antonius spoke softly to get his attention. When Cos looked up at him he continued, "You conducted yourself with distinction today. I am proud to call you friend and fellow Roman."

"Thank you, Antonius. Coming from you, especially you, that swells my pride."

"Nevertheless, you don't look happy. You should take deeply the breath of life and look around at these men who fought so well and feel privileged to be serving among them."

"I do feel honored, Antonius, and unworthy. It's all the deaths that trouble me. So many deaths and what did it accomplish? Jesus got away and will only recruit more followers."

"We are alive and conversing, and Mary is safe. My men only suffered scratches, and most of all, we had no choice. It was kill or die. The Greeks say that Zeus has a plan for all of us, and if that is truth, we only do what he wants." Cos had no answer, and they continued their slow progress south.

"Cos," Mary called to him. "You remember that Jesus Christ was supposed to be in this area about this time. We should look for him while we are here."

"Yes, I remember. You understand now why we were really sent here, don't you?"

"No, I still don't understand. You know that I don't speak Latin, but you and Antonius usually speak to each other in that language, so I miss a lot."

"I don't understand Aramaic, and I don't know what you say to each other either. Good thing too."

"I know you are picking that language up quickly. You can't fool me, Cosimus. You understand most of it." Cos grinned at her because she was right, he was picking it up quickly. He spoke to Mary only in English, but he suspected the gifted Antonius was also absorbing this new language at a rapid pace. As they rode along, Cos couldn't help gazing at Mary who held on to Antonius tightly, as if she feared that she could fall off, but also to stay close to him, to feel his body against hers.

Mary finally noticed his stares and pulled away her hood, "What are you thinking, Cos. Are you bothered by my love for Antonius?"

"I'm in love with you, Mary. I can't help it anymore than you can help loving him. There is no jealousy in me, but I can't make my heart behave as well as I can my words. Virgil said 'No day shall erase you from the memory of time,' and I can add 'or from my heart.' " Mary looked at him with her pear-shaped eyes, her face impassive, unreadable.

Antonius turned slightly to look at Cosimus and said, "I count him braver who overcomes his desires than him who conquers his enemies, for the hardest victory is over self." Cos now knew that Antonius understood much of what had been said. The quote was from Aristotle and with that short but profound sentence, Antonius made it known that he expected Cos to bear his emotional wound in silence. Cos nodded respectfully that he understood and would comply.

"Mary, we were sent as translators just to assist Tony. His mission was to kill Jesus Christ, and that's what he thought he was doing. He couldn't have understood anything being spoken, but he picked up on that one word, 'Jesus,' and did what he was probably paid to do."

Mary rode in silence, thinking it through, then said, "I think that is the only explanation. But why would they want Jesus killed? It doesn't make sense."

"The Commission is a bunch of nerdy, intellectual historians. My guess is they wanted to prevent the regression of civilization which occurred after the Roman Empire collapsed in the fourth century. They obviously blame Christianity for the onset of the Dark Ages. This would have been a grand experiment in human history, but their efforts won't accomplish what they intended. I'm still of the opinion that what we do here is already history. We aren't changing anything by being here. We were here before we were born."

"I'm not sure about that, Cos. I still believe that I have a choice in what I do. I'm not a robot under some divine control as Antonius suggested earlier. Tony did change things by trying to shoot that man pretending to be Jesus, and I'll bet right now he is sorry he tried."

"Getting away from Jesus would be hard, even if you could speak the language. The chance of Tony getting away and finding his way back to the Portal again is slim to none. We can forget about Tony, whatever happens, happens, and likely, has already happened. But I wonder about the man, if he is a man, Tony tried to shoot. If he is some sort of opposite to Jesus Christ, that would mean he could be the Antichrist or the Devil. Perhaps he can't be killed. In that case, it isn't about us not being able to change the past. It's about us uncovering a demon who can't be stopped. His plans, whatever they were, were foiled. We should be prepared for retaliation by his fanatic followers. We may not be so lucky next time."

"If you had not made friends with Antonius your first time out, we would have found this demon on our own. I shiver to think what that could have meant."

"He seemed to know we were coming. I have yet to understand how he could have known. We didn't know. No one knew. He could not have known, yet he did."

Through the bushes and the scattered trees, they could see a group of people by the water ahead. Most were dressed in white clothes and stood out like beacons in the bright sunlight. As they got closer, the scene unfolded like a painting which had been rolled. As the scroll unrolled, they beheld a baptism, with one bearded man holding another younger man in his arms, gently lying him backward into the River Jordan. The crowd cheered each time it happened, and suddenly they became aware of Roman soldiers passing close by on the road. All heads turned toward the Romans, and Antonius gave the signal to halt. Both groups stood watching each other for a time, carefully, suspiciously. As the Romans appeared to be watching and not interfering, the group turned back to their activities. Cos and Mary studied the group carefully, looking over each person thoroughly and methodically.

"There," Mary pointed, "the one on the far right standing by himself." Cos followed her finger and spotted the individual. Yes, he was about the right age to be Jesus, and the way he carried himself, there was something special about him. The young man was aware of the attention and turned to look directly at them. The effect was vastly different than was seen radiating from the Antichrist. A feeling of peace and contentment, which was hard to explain, came over Mary and Cos. It was his turn for baptism next and as they watched, he waded into the water toward the older man who was smiling and clapping his hands, delighted by the opportunity.

The dipping occurred quickly, but just in time, Mary found her camera and started taking photos as Jesus emerged from the water, wiping his face. The older man helped him from the river as the crowd parted, and they both stood on the bank together, dripping, cautiously studying the Romans for any hostility. Mary and Cos waved, and Jesus waved back as the column again started slowly moving ahead and southward.

"Was that John the Baptist and Jesus Christ we just saw?" Mary asked.

"I don't know, but it seemed to me that it was. Didn't you think so?"

"Yes. I feel different after watching that scene. Different."

"Are you converting?" Cos teased.

"No, Cos. The Jewish people have long admitted that Jesus was a prophet but just never believed that he was the long awaited savior, the Son of God. He was, I'm sorry, is a holy man, and you can't dispute his message. I feel blessed to have seen him. It made this trip worthwhile."

"So, that was the real Jesus?" Antonius asked.

"We think so," Cos answered.

"The other one is something that crawled out of the river Styx. My hope is that we won't meet him again," he said.

Chapter 18

The Path to Jerusalem

At Mary's urging, Antonius had directed a search of the hills for a campsite away from the road, the river, and its mosquitoes, and his men found a small valley, safe and protected by hills. They were traveling light without the usual retinue of tents, blacksmiths, and servants. Everyone was expected to sleep directly on the ground, the only comfort being boughs and leaves that could be gathered. A fire was quickly started and water for cooking brought from the nearby river. Cosimus and Agrippa made their rounds together, tending wounds and injuries among the men and hearing their complaints.

Agrippa looked concerned, "We must find a spring nearby or be forced to drink the water from the Jordan. Most say that it will make you ill with the grip, but I find if the water boils first, it will not." He showed Cosimus his standard issue metal bowl. It was much like a Sierra Cup, so common with campers of the future, but larger. "I have an extra, take this one," he offered. To his relief, a scout announced that he had found clean water, and a line of men was assembled to bring the water into camp. Several men arrived carrying four goats hanging from poles, their heads dangling, and a cheer went up among the men.

"We have a safe site to rest, abundant water and food, and we are with friends. Does life offer more than this?" Antonius asked loudly. Everyone agreed that it didn't. Some answered that the only other thing that would have made it better was wine, lots of it.

"I'll send two men to the river and see if any fishermen will sell their wine," Agrippa suggested, thinking the same way.

"Better if no one knows that we are here. It would not be wise, Agrippa. Besides, I want to get an early start before dawn, and I don't want complaints of headache from anyone." They settled back to wait on the meat to cook, assembled in a large circle like a large collection of girl scouts.

"Now can you two tell me about Jesus, why you searched for him, who he is or what he is destined to become?" Antonius asked, resting on his elbow against the leaves.

Mary spoke first. "Our fear is that you will know something that might interfere with an important world event."

"Did not Cosimus just say that events which happen here happened before either of you were born?"

"Yes, and I said it in English," Cos noted.

"If you are right, then telling me will not change what is going to happen. It just might become the reason it happens. Can you see my point?" Antonius said, ignoring the comment about English.

Cos wrinkled his brow and nodded, "It is what I feel as well. I think you should tell him what we know, Mary." "Besides," he continued, "he will be so intently watching your face that he may not even hear what you say."

Antonius chuckled and shook his head as if to indicate that he not only understood but agreed.

"Jesus, the one we saw getting baptized this afternoon, will be worshiped by at least one third of the world's population by our time. He will be considered the Son of God, and more will know his name than any other person in history," Mary said.

"How can this be possible. What we saw was only a collection of poor fishermen, bathing in a muddy river. How can this man achieve such greatness?"

"Because people believe. That's the only answer. He will be crucified on the hills outside Jerusalem by your fellow Romans in less than four years. His followers will be called Christians, and in less than three hundred years, most of the Roman Empire will also be Christian."

Antonius lay back and looked at the stars in silence. "Then we are together at an auspicious time. Is that why you came? To kill Jesus?"

"We believe that Tony was instructed to kill Jesus. Cos and I are only interpreters and guides. The people who sent us wanted to change history."

"And what is wrong with history, that it should be changed?"

"Your Roman world is one of the high points of human development. You have ideas of government, science and order that we still try to copy two thousand years into the future. All of our important buildings still look just like yours. Most of our languages are derived from Latin. Even your ideas and traditions about marriage and the rights of women remain the basis of what we believe. All of it will disappear with the fall of Rome, and for more than a thousand years, the Western world will be smothered by what we are to call The Dark Ages with the church near the top of the pyramid of power and influence."

Antonius sat up and looked at each of them in turn. "And what do you believe should happen?"

"I don't think we can change anything," Cos said, still lying on his back and watching the stars. "It is still going to happen just as it did. Even if we could change history by killing Jesus, the result may not be better, just different. Men still have to have their gods, always have and always will. There are other reasons that the Roman Empire fell to barbarians. It grew too big to manage, and its enemies learned how to fight. Any human endeavor has a rise and a fall. It is a cycle built into what we are as humans. There is constant change, and it is the only thing about people that is constant."

"My people worship one God and will never believe in Jesus Christ as their Savior. They will be persecuted by every nation for all of time, but still I would not want to change what is to happen. We saw the dark side running up the hill after Tony. What would happen if he were to collect a vast following bent on evil. I can see that there would be no hope, no salvation, and it would end with a single last human, after slaying his one remaining opponent. We can't leave the world with only the bad. Evil must be balanced with good. That is why Jesus is important. He will preach a message of peace and love and will leave the world better than it was and better than it would become without him."

"I don't understand why Romans will kill Jesus. What will he do to cause this? Antonius asked.

"Romans only care about stability and money gathered from taxes. The Priests and Levites of the Temple will demand his death, because they will feel threatened by his presence. Romans will do their bidding to keep the peace, however temporary," Mary recalled.

"I have heard of these Temple Priests. They live as well as wealthy Romans and nearly as well as you observed when you visited the palace of Herod Antipas. They continue to collect a Temple tax from their people even though the Temple is long ago complete. We are aware of the unrest and expect an uprising, directed at their own leaders, someday."

Mary shook her head. "No, Antonius, they will uprise, but against Roman occupation. It will happen about forty years from now, and it will cause the deaths of many Romans and many more Yehudim. Titus, who will be the Roman general in charge, will order the absolute destruction of the Temple of Jerusalem and the expulsion of the Yehudim. Even that won't end it, because there will be two more, even more bloody, revolts early in the next century."

"Wars until the end of time," Antonius sighed and fell back onto his back. He reached across and took Mary's hand in his. "Ever read Plato?" he asked quietly.

"I know of him, but honestly, I don't think I ever read any of his works," she answered.

"Plato wrote, 'According to Greek mythology, humans were originally created with four arms, four legs and a head with two faces. Fearing their power, Zeus split them into two separate parts, condemning them to spend their lives in search of their other halves.' " He rolled his head to look into her face to be sure she heard the second part. "'...and when one of them meets the other half, the actual half of himself, the pair are lost in an amazement of love and friendship and intimacy and one will not be out of the other's sight, even for a moment.' "

"You big sweet man," she said, her eyes glistening in the firelight. "No, I don't want to be out of your sight either...even for a moment."

"I have found my other half. Who would guess that you had to come back in time to find me and for me to find you in this wilderness."

Cos slowly and silently got up and ambled over to where Agrippa was lying. "May I join you?" he asked.

"To be sure. Is there a problem over there?" Agrippa asked.

"To much love. Painful," Cos said unable to fully express what he felt.

"I see the way you look at her...so does Antonius. Did he take her from you?"

"No, she was never mine. I just hoped that she would be, someday."

"A love such as they share will never die, Cosimus. Give up any hope for her love and move on. She will belong to Antonius even after they both are dead. You remember the famous poem which says 'Every heart sings a song, incomplete, until another heart whispers back.'?"

"Yes, I remember. I didn't expect even you to throw all those quotations at me."

"Romans like Antonius and I are very educated. The past means a lot to us."

"And me also. I studied history, and now I am living it."

"Antonius has not told me where you came from. I always thought of you as a high-born Roman. Is there more I should know?"

"I was born in Rome. There is nothing more for you to know. My mission here is complete, and someday soon I will be able to return home."

"Don't count on Mary returning with you," Agrippa said and smiled. Cos could feel a sinking feeling, as if molten lead was being poured into his skin, weighting him into the soil of Galilee. He never considered that Mary would choose to stay here, but Agrippa was right.

The morning sky hinted purple with sunrise still an hour away, and already they were marching steadily southward. To his and those of his tent fellows unending gratitude, Cosimus insisted that Ueima ride his horse, because his leg had swollen greatly during the night. Cosimus took the man's place in line, shouldering his share of gear and water. He was learning Aramaic quickly but was only able to speak in simple terms to the men around him. They, in return, knew some Latin, and by mixing bits and pieces of the different languages, they managed to converse fairly well.

"Tesserarius," the one to his left said. "You have shown promise as a leader. Your bravery and kindness have not gone unnoticed by us."

"Bene facis!" Cos said. "That wasn't bravery. I was fighting for my life."

"You showed no hesitation, and you didn't even consider flight. We all are afraid in battle."

"I'll try to live up to your image of me. What is your name?"

"I am called Sagimus. I was born in Damascus, but now I am Roman."

"Do they agree that you are Roman, Sagimus?"

"Well, truthfully, only after my discharge in fifteen years. Then I will be a Roman and own land!"

"I hope you live to see the day, Sagimus."

"I wish that for you also, Tesserarius. You should continue your sword training to insure your survival. I will volunteer to spar with you, for I am considered a good swordsman."

"I will be honored to learn from you, Sagimus."

"Tonight, then, when we stop?"

True to his word, after the camp settled down, Sagimus appeared, grinning and beaconing to the troops to form a circle. He was carrying two wooden swords, which were little more than rounded sticks,

"Is this your idea, Cosimus?" Antonius called out from the sidelines.

"No, his."

"This could be a mistake, Cosimus, because even I would hesitate to engage Sagimus. *Fortunatos*, Cosimus."

Cos knew he had made a mistake as soon as Sagimus took off his armor and tunic. He was rippling with hard muscle, and he had a predatory stance and look. The easygoing soldier had been replaced by a hardened combatant.

"Parati estis?" Sagimus asked and slapped his hand with the end of his sword and started circling. The men forming the circle started to clap in unison, shouting encouragement to both of them.

"How many enemy have you slain, Sagimus?" someone called out. Sagimus shrugged without taking his eye from Cosimus as they circled, looking for an opening.

"Triginta duo," [thirty-two] another answered, provoking a round of loud guffaws. The remark made Cosimus start to sweat, which was probably the idea. They were all watching him for any sign of wavering or cowardliness, probably even Mary was watching. He forced himself to concentrate on his opponent. There must be an opening somewhere, he hoped. Sagimus yelled loudly and rushed Cosimus while thrashing his sword back and forth to ward off any defensive blows. The distance was close enough that Cos couldn't mount a reaction or defense, so he did the

only thing he knew to do. He flung himself forward toward the rushing Sagimus' feet, sliding like a batter coming into first base. Sagimus went over the top of Cosimus before he realized it, but it was too late to ward off the blow which came to his shins from Cosimus' hard wooden bat. Sagimus went face down in the soft soil, crying out in pain. The men erupted with a cheer and picked Cosimus up and carried him around camp three times in celebration. After they put him back down, he found Sagimus still sitting, holding his legs.

"May I look?" Cos asked.

"No need. Good work, Tesserarius," he said. "Only don't try that on the battlefield. The next enemy along will find you helpless on the ground and find it easy to place his sword or spear in you."

"I was desperate, Sagimus. I am no match for you, and I never will be. Could we try that again without everyone looking and start slow?"

"Yes, you are right. I wasn't thinking. Next time, neither one of us will be injured. My promise."

Sagimus got up without assistance, and he and Cosimus exchanged manly embraces to the cheers of the nearby soldiers.

Cosimus felt a new hand on his back and turned to see Antonius grinning at him. "It was not as I expected, but I am happy that once again you proved what you are capable of. You have had a long day, *amice*. Can you sit with us tonight, or is it still too painful for you?"

"I am getting used to the idea, Antonius. It will be my pleasure to be with both of you.

After they settled into place to watch the evening's fire, Antonius said, "By tomorrow night, we should be able to reach the fortress of Alexandrium. There is a small group of Roman soldiers stationed there, and we should be able to find better quarters for sleeping. I'm sure we can find enough wine there to make my boys happy."

"Have you ever been there?" Mary asked.

"No, but it has a well-known history, and it was restored not too long ago by Herod. History says that Aristobullus made his last stand there against the Legions of Pompey. After restoration, it has been mostly used as a prison and burial site for many of Herod's family who were executed there. A lonely outpost."

Mary said, "I have seen what remains in my time. It was completely destroyed by the Legions of Titus in the war of the first revolt. I'll be most anxious to see it as it is now and to explore every nook and cranny."

"There will not be enough time for that, Mary. I'm sorry, but my orders are to proceed quickly to Jerusalem, and we lost much time battling the hordes of Jesus."

"I recall that Herod The Great's wife, Mariamne, was executed and buried there. She was falsely accused by Herod's sister of plotting to kill her husband. Mariamne was reported to be a woman of infinite beauty," Cos remembered.

"I don't agree with calling Herod, The Great," Antonius said. "From what I have heard, he was a simple butcher. It was a mistake for the Roman Senate to appoint him as King. You probably know that Pompey took this land for Rome but allowed Hyrcanus to rule it in Rome's name. Antigonus Mattathias took Judea from Hyrcanus, and Herod, with our help, took it back from Mattathias. There has been a long string of battles over this impoverished land, and most of the fighting has been between factions of the Yehudim. From what you tell me, even Roman rule won't be enough to stop the fighting, and they will even turn on us."

Mary interrupted, "Even in our time, there is still a struggle for this land. It is easily the most contested part of the earth's surface."

"But why, Mary, why must they continue to fight for this mostly desert land?" Antonius asked.

"It comes back to religion every time, and what is written in the Holy Books," Mary said. The crux is the site of the Temple, which has been considered holy for at least a thousand years, and two thousand years from now, it will still be so."

Cos said, "We should talk about what is to happen when we get to Jerusalem. What are you two planning to do?"

Antonius sighed deeply and put his arm around Mary. "I think Cos is right. We have to discuss a subject which we have sought to avoid. When we reach Jerusalem, I will be a small part of a bigger force. We cannot live together in Jerusalem, no one would permit it. They could send me anywhere from there. Refusal would mean death for me, perhaps for you also, if they discover why I left. I don't have any place to keep you safe there. You'll have to depend on each other in Jerusalem."

"Is there any way you would consider returning to our time when Cos and I return?" Mary asked.

"I would be lost. I saw all the strange things happening there. What could I do, what would I be other than a freak from the past? How could I take care of you?"

"You would do well there, eventually. In the short term, I would take care of you."

"I would be a man hiding behind my woman's cloak. Is that what you want?"

"Yes. We would be together. You could easily earn money just because of what you know of the ancient world, your world. You would, in time, support me."

"Another problem, Antonius," Cos said. "It's me. I can't march into Jerusalem pretending to be a Tesserarius in the Roman Army. Even if I were accepted, they wouldn't let me leave either. Who would care for Mary?"

Antonius picked up a small stone and flung it away in frustration. "You are both a problem for me. I love both of you and don't want to let you go, but it does not seem possible to keep either one of you around me."

Cos said hesitantly, "Antonius, I have thought this through, and I feel that we have to part ways before we reach Jerusalem. Mary and I should head back north toward Nazat and the Portal."

"Nooo!" Mary cried and held her head in her hands. "There must be a way," she sobbed.

"Here is my way," Antonius announced. "I have to discover what the commander has planned for me and my men. Until that happens, you both stay together and find lodging in Jerusalem. We can only make plans if we have all the facts. After I know more, we will meet and talk this out."

Chapter 19

Trouble at the Fort

ate in the afternoon, the stone walls of Alexandrium could be seen high up on a rocky hill and some distance from the river. The climb up the steep road was arduous, and by the time the men reached the gate, most were irritable and sweating.

The fort loomed above them, hanging like a bird of prey in the yellow twilight, its gates locked tightly. Looking up the sloped walls, Cos had a chill come over him, like a child who fears a monster under his bed. No human was in sight, as if the entire structure was deserted long ago.

"Open the gate," Antonius demanded. "In the name of Rome, open the gate." One of his men beat on the door with the end of his spear, the thumping echo coming back from several directions. Two heads appeared on the walkway high above the gate, and both were armed with crossbows which they trained toward the unwanted guests. After a few moments, a loud scraping noise began, then slowly, very slowly, the heavy gate crept open, pushed by several men from the inside. When it banged fully open, a Roman officer, wearing a helmet similar to Antonius, came forward with several armed men behind him and raised his hand in salutation. He walked stiffly into position with shriveled and bandied legs and planted his long spear deliberately and defiantly, holding it askance for maximum effect.

"Greetings to you, fellow Romans!" he announced, then just stood there motionless.

"He is a retired Centurion and old, it appears. Guarding this small fort for continuing pay," Antonius whispered loud enough to be heard by those near the front.

"I am Centurion Antonius Severius Maximus, under the command of

Pontius Pilatus, commander of Idumea. You are required to give us food and shelter."

"I am Gadus Rancius Tullia, commander of Alexandrium, formerly of the Ninth Legion. You may enter, Centurion, if you dare," he said and stepped aside. On the way past, Antonius and Gadus had a good look at each other, like a pair of fighting chickens circling with wary eyes. Antonius led the long line into the small fort, and each of the men, in turn, looked over their host and his ragtag group standing behind him. The squeak of leather and the soft jangle of armor from the column was more noticeable inside the walls of the fort. Antonius dismounted near a water trough and surveyed the interior of the fort. He signaled Agrippa to come closer and put his hand near Agrippa's ear.

"There is something troubling here; I feel a threat because of the strange formality and frank hostility we just saw at the gate. Assemble some men, at least twenty, and instruct them to be prepared for possible action. They are not to remove their armor. Be discrete, and let no one suspect." Agrippa nodded and left to carry out his instructions.

"Something wrong?" Cos asked.

"Perhaps," Antonius said with a frown. "We'll see in a few moments. Don't let down your guard. Walk around and get a feel for the place and see how many soldiers are here, while I talk to them." Antonius walked alone back toward Gadus and his men, who were still standing by the gate as it swung slowly closed. He glanced around at the walls surrounding the small fort and spotted at least ten men, all armed.

"Thank you, Gadus Rancius, for giving us shelter. I would like to know how many men you command here," Antonius asked.

"I don't discuss my security with anyone, Centurion," Gadus said. Antonius saw an older but still formidable man in Gadus, and one who obviously had seen his share of combat. His eyes said that he was unafraid.

"We are in need of food, water and wine as well as sleeping quarters. Can you provide this?" Antonius asked bluntly.

"No, Centurion, my provisions are meager. I will supply you nothing."

"You will comply or you will answer to Pontius Pilatus after I report you."

"You have to get back to report me, Centurion. You may never make it back."

"What makes you think so, Gadus? Who will stop us?" Antonius asked.

Gadus' eyes wandered, sizing up his adversary. "You passed down the road by the Jordan?" he asked.

"Yes, we came south from Tiberias. Why do you ask?"

"Did you encounter any hostility?" Gadus smiled a tight smile as if only he knew something, some critical fact.

"No, it was peaceful. Only fishermen plying their trade. Is there something that I should know, Gadus?"

"There is a new master in Judea, Centurion. I expected him to meet you." He smiled that all knowing smile again.

"Who is this master, Gadus? Has Pontius Pilatus been replaced in my absence?"

"I am talking of a new master, who exceeds the authority of Rome. He commands us to do his bidding as he will command you when you meet him."

"You are his only subject in Alexandrium, his only army, Gadus?"

"No, there are others here who do his bidding."

Antonius slowly looked around for threats, and when he did, he saw that Agrippa was ready with his men and also looking for any sign of hostility while waiting for Antonius' signal.

"Gadus, you have given a lifetime of noble service to Rome. Perhaps your mind was taken from you by this new master and you no longer think like a true Centurion. I would not like to see a man such as yourself harmed in the service of something evil."

"He is not evil, Centurion. He is master of all he surveys, and he commands lesser people such as you and I to do his bidding."

"What if I told you that this man is evil?"

"I would dispute that with my sword," Gadus said.

"Think about this, Gadus. You are in the service of Rome as you have always been and just as I am. What does this man mean to you that is larger than Rome?"

"He is God, Centurion. Can even the Emperor say that?"

"Some say that Julius Caesar was God."

"True, but men declared him God. This man needs no such

declaration. He simply is God."

"Has this God a name, Gadus?"

"He is called Jesus."

"I have seen two such men, Gadus. One is evil, and one is good. Yours is the evil one, and you are under his spell. Clear your thoughts and think of your responsibility to Rome and to your men who follow you." Antonius glanced up to see Cosimus flashing his open hands three times. Thirty men answer to Gadus and will do his bidding without question. Antonius turned to face Gadus again.

"Gadus. Once more I appeal to you as a fellow officer. You need not provoke violence here. All we require is food and shelter. We don't want to be involved with your beliefs...you can keep them if you like. My men outnumber yours by more than double, and they are experienced and have been tested in battle. I don't want to be responsible for killing fellow Romans."

"It doesn't matter, Centurion. If you didn't meet Jesus on the road from Tiberias, then he is sure to have followed you and should appear shortly. His men outnumber yours. You are trapped here. Your choice is to believe in Jesus and do what he instructs or to die."

"We did meet him, Gadus. We slew all of his men and watched as he fled the battlefield leaving them lifeless in the road and in the wood. So much for him being a God. One last time, Gadus, I will ask. You are to surrender your sword to me right now, I will accept no other answer." Gadus stepped backward and looked at the walls, evidently the signal for his men to ready themselves for a surprise attack. He turned his focus back to the motionless Antonius, and slowly drew his sword. Antonius raised his hand, palm up, and Agrippa and his men moved to the center of the courtyard with crossbows cocked, aiming at the men positioned on the high wall. At the same time, there was a scuffling sound as ladders were being rapidly ascended by men heading up to the high walkway. Gadus looked around with wild eyes, and a scowl enveloped his face. He rushed toward Antonius, his sword pointed directly in front of him. At the last possible second, Antonius stepped aside and as Gadus rushed past, a big hand caught his throat, slamming him to the ground, gasping for air like a fish out of water.

Antonius stood over him, one foot on Gadus' right hand, preventing him from raising his sword. "Consider yourself fortunate, Gadus, that you can still feel your neck at all." He looked around and saw all of Gadus' men standing with their arms raised in surrender. "You men!" Antonius shouted to them, "Come down from there." He pointed to a spot just in front of him and waited, his hands on his hips, while they assembled.

"Soldiers of Rome," he began, "who among you are followers of Jesus?" Three tentatively raised their hands looking nervously over their shoulder. Antonius motioned them to move away from the others. "Would anyone volunteer to point out the followers of Jesus? I swear that no harm will come to you if you step forward." Two men stepped forward. Antonius motioned for them to come to him.

He place his hand on one man's shoulder and said, "You don't believe that Jesus is God?"

"No, Centurion."

"Why do they believe and not you.?"

"I came to this post after Jesus left. I know of him but never saw him."

"Very well," Antonius said. "Point out all who follow Jesus for me." Both men went into the group and pulled several out by force. Antonius motioned for them to join the other believers, then summoned Cosimus from the sidelines.

"Cosimus, have you ever seen this sort of madness before?"

"We call it brainwashing. Some will get over it in time. Some will not."

"I like that term, brainwashing. It fits. Suggestions?"

"You have to lock them up, because they can't be trusted."

"My thoughts also. I don't want to kill men who are in the service of Rome." He turned toward the remaining, uncontaminated, men and said, "We have to lock up your fellows, because they are led by an evil force. From now forward, you are not to hear their voices, no matter what they say. Do you understand?"

The men shouted, "Yes, Centurion," in unison.

"Cosimus, take these men captive and find a prison for them." Cosimus motioned to some of his men who drew their swords and surrounded the believers. He conferred briefly with one of the trusted men who went with them to the locked cells. In the caverns below the fort were several natural caves which had been closed off with metal bars and a metal door. The group of twelve men were herded in, but not without protest.

"Our God, Jesus, will come to save us and destroy you. Wait and see," one said. "I will eat your flesh raw, Tesserarius. No cell will confine me," said another, as Cosimus and his men withdrew. After returning to the courtyard, Cos could see Antonius still addressing the new men.

"Were any of you present when Jesus was here?" he asked loudly. Four hands went up. "Did any of you see him." The men shook their heads no. "Is there a man here who saw Jesus?" Antonius asked. No man raised his hand. Antonius paced back and forth in front of them. "Did any man leave this camp who had seen Jesus?" he asked. For a moment, there was no response, then a man stepped forward.

"You should know, Centurion, that ten men did leave here before we came to relieve them. By now, they have returned to Jerusalem."

"And so, contamination spreads like the wilt disease of grapes. One batch infects another until the entire crop fails," Antonius said. "I have to ask the remaining men of Alexandrium to willingly be confined tonight. We will set you free before we leave, but you have to understand that we cannot trust any of you fully. To sleep among you would be folly." There were shouts of anger from the remaining men who protested that they had done nothing wrong and didn't want to spend a night in the caves. The order was given, however, and Cosimus led them away to be confined for the night. When he returned, the tension in the courtyard had broken, and most of the men had removed their armor and stacked their weapons. A few patrolled the walkways around the top of the walls. Antonius was seated in a shady area, accompanied by Mary, and he beckoned Cosimus to join them.

"Agrippa found some wine. Come sit with us and have a well-deserved drink, Cosimus," Antonius said.

"What happens in the morning?" Cos asked.

"We leave the second group in charge of the first and hold our breath. I'll report this and dump it in the lap of Pontius Pilatus. Let him sort it out."

"What if Jesus is in Jerusalem? Have you contemplated that?" Cos asked.

"If that has happened, then we are all doomed. We can only hope that he is still chasing your Tony around in the wilderness."

"Jesus has to be stopped," Mary offered. "Perhaps we should try to find him and kill him or at least lock him away."

Cos shook his head, "Three bullets didn't seem to do anything. Perhaps he can't be killed if he is the Antichrist."

"Explain please, what is an Antichrist?" asked Antonius.

Mary looked surprised, "Why he is the equivalent of Pluto who comes to the surface to be among men."

"Not exactly," Cos said. "Pluto presides over Hades, but there is no evil intent. He is simply the God of the Underworld and is in charge of everything below ground, just as Neptune is in charge of the sea. This is different. The Antichrist has been called 'The Deceiver,' 'The Beast with Ten Horns,' or simply a force of concentrated evil. Romans of this age don't have a clear parallel with our Devil. Our understanding is something like the opposite of God. We have seen with our eyes what this evil Jesus can do, and I don't think additional description will add to Antonius' understanding."

"Thank you, Cos, but I get it. I really do. The main idea is that he converts everyone who gets close enough to see and hear him into followers, and they do anything he says after that. There is a great danger to Rome from this man. I am not convinced that he cannot be stopped or killed. He seems to be just a man to me, and I have seen other bad men fall in battle. You both have told me that Romans will kill the other Jesus, the good one, who will be considered the Son of God. What is the difference?"

"You know, Cos, he could be right. We both know of orators and politicians in our time who could convert people to their beliefs, and who died like other men after all," Mary said.

"We all saw Tony shoot him from close range. He didn't even seem to feel it."

"Perhaps Tony missed," she suggested.

"Well, I hope you both are right. Hitler versus Satan. We'll find out, I'm afraid." Cos stood up suddenly and walked away, as if something just occurred to him.

"Did we say something to offend him?" Mary asked.

"No. Perhaps he is still bothered by our closeness. He is in love with you, as I am. You know this, don't you."

"Yes, I knew nearly from the first moment we met," Mary said.

"Do you feel love for Cosimus?" Antonius asked.

"It's you I love, Antonius. Only you. Forever you."

"Thank you, Mary. It is how I hoped you feel but hearing it from your lips is especially sweet." They exchanged a brief kiss and sat for awhile looking into each other's face. Antonius reluctantly said, "I need to find some food for us and talk with Cos." He kissed Mary softly again, then got to his feet and walked toward the fire, burning in the center of the court. He looked around for Cosimus as he walked. His men had received a wine ration and felt at home in the small fort, and as a result, the place was alive with conversation and laughter. Cos was not in sight, but he found Agrippa who was already eating his dinner.

"Have you seen Cosimus? He walked this way only moments ago."

Agrippa shrugged, "He did not come this way, Antonius. Want me to search for him?"

"No. He can't have gone far with the gates closed and men on watch. He will turn up." He picked up a loaf of bread and a large platter of food and slung a wine flask over his shoulder. "If you see him, tell him to come find me," Antonius said, heading back toward the waiting Mary.

After Antonius sat down beside Mary, he said, "You know that I am the luckiest man I ever knew, yet I'm not to be favored by the fates. My insides churn."

"Whatever are you talking about?" Mary asked.

"You. I have you, which is all I ever wanted but didn't know it until you came into my life, or I came into yours. But, I am fated to lose you. The thought has removed my will to live; I can think of nothing else, and I am being driven mad." Mary took his arm and snuggled close, looking up at his sincere face.

"You must consider my offer of coming back with me. It's the only way, Antonius, the only way. Don't be afraid of the future. It is just like this in most ways. People are really the same, the only difference is the things we have."

Antonius looked at her while he thought, his eyes caressing her face and neck. Her long dark hair hung over her shoulder, shining along its curves and reflecting little rainbow spots of the evening sun. Mary was delicate but strong, both in body and mind. He had never thought about women like this before, that they had the strength of a man but measured in a different way. Mary captivated him and took his soul into hers, and they merged leaving two people with one mind. He sighed, "Ovid said, 'Thus I am not able to exist either with you or without you; and I seem not to know my own wishes.' I never knew what he meant until now." He paused for a second, then continued, "I am afraid of your time. I know nothing that would be of value there. At least here I am a Roman citizen, and I help protect the Empire from its many enemies. Besides, I have a duty, a sworn duty, to Rome."

"Didn't you just say that we were not going to decide anything until Jerusalem? Don't think about it right now. Just look into my face so that my eyes can tell you how much I care for you," Mary said and pulled his head downward so that she could kiss his cheek. "I don't quote as often as you do, but I remember one from Plato that seems to fit. 'Love is the pursuit of the whole.' I feel whole with you beside me, and I will stay here in this time and wait for you if that is what you decide."

"I can't live without you, Mary. If I searched the entire world, I could not find another you. I promise that we will stay together until life takes one of us. As if you were Eurydice, I will travel to the underworld to bring you back if you die before me." He leaned over her as he spoke, and she pushed her lips into his as the world with all of its cares spun silently below them.

"Ahem!" Agrippa said, turning his face from the sight of their kiss.

"Yes, Agrippa," Antonius said with some irritation.

"Cosimus can't be found. We have covered every inch of the fort, and he is not here. The gates have not been opened, and the guards on the walls never saw him. I have no explanation, he simply is not here."

"It is clearly impossible. Look again, and this time check the prisons. Don't come back to me unless he is found."

"Yes, Centurion, we will do it again. What do we do if he still cannot be found?"

"He can be found, and I order you to find him!" Antonius shouted, his eyes bulging from the effort. Agrippa shrugged and trotted away calling out to his men.

"Is there any way your people could have snatched him back to the future?" he asked Mary, after Agrippa left.

"As far as I know, we have to pass through the Portal first and that is a long way from here. He must be here someplace."

"Meeting you and Cos and then Jesus tells me that there is a lot I don't know. My head is spinning with new ideas that I never before thought possible. The disappearance of Cos has meaning, but I don't know if I can deal with any more surprises."

"There is always an explanation, Antonius. In time, we will understand."

"Then explain God to me."

"I can't explain God anymore than you can explain Zeus. It's just something you believe. It helps us explain what we are and our role in life. It helps us understand what happens when we die, and it gives us a code of behavior while we live. Every human society has worshipped Gods. In our time, there was an effort made to get rid of religious beliefs, but it didn't work. Humans have to have God. It's the way we are made."

"You, Mary, are my God. I worship you."

"No, Antonius. You love me. There is a difference. If you look at me long enough you will understand God. He put me here and made your mind see His image in me. You think me perfect because He created you to think that way, and He created me to fulfill your life. If we have children, you will see that they are in God's image too, and you will love them as you do me."

"In one way you are right. I thank God that I can be here with you, touch your skin and hair and hear your lovely voice and feel the warmth of your body next to mine. It is enough to make me believe in something that I can't see or touch but something that is truly real."

"We have the rest of our lives to discuss this and hold each other tight. Right now, I also worry about Cos. Could you search for him yourself? I don't want anything to happen to him either."

"I will," he said and got to his feet. "Agrippa, what have you found?" he shouted and headed out toward him in the darkening night.

"Nothing yet, Centurion, we search still," Agrippa answered. The grounds of the fort were in darkness and the shadows impenetrable. Here and there, men moved, silhouetted by fires or torches.

Conversations came from every corner and echoes from others. Antonius let his eyes become accustomed to the dark and started his search by the front gate, reassuring himself that it remained impassable. He decided to walk the four corners, looking into every crevice. "Cosimus!" he called uselessly, hearing his voice bounce from the hard stone walls. After he nearly completed his circle, his shout was answered.

"Here!" Cosimus called out from black shadows near the gate. "I am here, Antonius." Antonius turned to see Cosimus stumbling out of the dark.

"Are you injured?" Antonius asked and held the weakened Cosimus up by the shoulders.

"No, I don't feel injured."

"Where have you been?"

"Here. I never left here. But..."

"We searched every crack. You were not here, Cos. Don't you remember anything?"

"I seem to, but it is more like a dream. Little bits of things that make no sense. The last thing I remember is the feel of my sword in my hand and being afraid. I was very afraid, sick afraid."

"In your dream, where did you go," Antonius asked.

"I remember you, and I remember Mary. We seemed happy, then things changed...." Cosimus fell to his knees clutching his stomach and vomited on the pavement stones. Antonius waited patiently for him to finish, then helped him to his feet.

"Wine and good company will settle your stomach, my good friend. Come with me and get something to eat." He led Cosimus away, motioning to Agrippa to bring food and drink for him. Mary was waiting with open arms which she threw around Cos.

"Thank all the Gods that you are safe, Cos. I was afraid to the pit of my soul that something had happened," she said.

"No. Same old Cos. I'm feeling better now that I'm back with the both of you," he said and sat down heavily against the wall.

"Anything you care to tell us, Cos?" she asked.

"If I can make sense of it, perhaps. Not now. I would rather not think about it," he said.

The morning dawned in shades of pink and yellow, ignored by most of the men who went to sleep pleasantly intoxicated from the evening's wine. "Arouse yourselves!" Antonius commanded from the center of the courtyard. He was fully dressed, including helmet, and the first rays of the sun bounced from his polished armor. "This is what I get for giving you men a little present, is it? It well may be the last time then." At that the rustling grew louder as the men got up and started the morning rituals.

"Cosimus, Agrippa!" he ordered. "Come with me." Without waiting for his junior officers to comply, he started in forceful strides toward the entrance to the prison complex. Behind him, Agrippa and Cos hurried to catch up.

"You intend to turn them loose?" Agrippa asked.

"I intend to decide momentarily," Antonius said over his shoulder as he continued briskly down the stairs. They came upon two of the guards that Agrippa had posted the previous evening. Both looked drained and expended.

"You men. Are you injured?" Antonius asked looking closely into one of the men's eyes. "Have either one of you had wine?" he demanded.

"No, Centurion. We are exhausted from lack of sleep. It was a bad night."

"Well? What happened?" Antonius asked sharply.

"Most of the night they screamed insults and threats at us. They demanded release, all of them...many times. They shook the bars, frothed at the mouth. I lost count of how many times I heard the name 'Jesus.' These people are mad. I pray that you do not set them free. Even the naked barbarians in Gaul now seem reasonable to us." Antonius didn't respond but walked toward the metal door enclosing the imprisoned Roman soldiers. As soon as he got close enough, there was a collective moan and a scramble of feet as they rushed toward him, extending their arms in an effort to grab him and pull him in.

"We will get you, Centurion. Some day we will get you, and we will get those two also. We will pull you apart and eat your hearts while they beat," several seemed to say in unison. Their faces were contorted, and they drooled spittle with eyes bulging wild with hatred.

"Gadus! Come forward," Antonius commanded. The captured men

slowly parted, and an elderly man came between them and stood before Antonius and held onto the bars. The old eyes looked over them one by one and seemed to stop on Cosimus.

"You, Tesserarius, have seen him," Gadus said and smiled, showing his yellow teeth. Antonius turned and looked questionably at Cosimus. "He has seen the Master, our God. I can see it in his face," Gadus shrieked. "You have to help us, Tesserarius, for now we are brothers."

"You are right, old Centurion," Cosimus answered. "He was in the clearing before the battle started. I did see him. Unlike you, I am not under his spell. I could feel his evil, and I would have killed him if I could." His comments caused a new outburst of animal intensity inside the cage. It was as if boiling water had been thrown through the bars. Except for Gadus, who didn't move and continued to hold Cosimus in his gaze.

"No. There is more, Tesserarius. I smell the master on you. You have been close. Do you not remember his eyes?" Gadus said, murmuring, coaxing, trying to evoke a buried memory in Cosimus. His words had an effect and suddenly before his eyes, Cos could see the creature called Jesus standing in front of him...the penetrating yellow eyes and the flaring nostrils. He stepped backwards and held his hands over his eyes to block out the vision. "Yes! You have seen him! He is part of you now, and he will grow inside like a maggot." Gadus cackled an old coughing laugh, expelling all the corrupt air within him one wheeze at a time. Antonius stepped between them blocking Gadus' view of Cosimus.

"You will be silent now or forever, Gadus. Not another word if you value your head," Antonius said between his teeth, his hand on the hilt of his sword. Gadus backed slowly away out of sword reach.

"We all are ready to die for our Master. To kill one of us won't make a difference. We are like the angry bees. Together we will swarm over you and suck the life from your body," a man shouted from within the group.

"I have seen enough," Antonius said and motioned that they were to leave.

Before they were able to get out of sight, Gadus called out, "I hope you will meet our brothers when you get to Jericho. I send my regards." The laughing rose up like an echo from the caverns, bouncing around the walls until the last word, "regards", came at them from all sides like a living creature.

They stood looking back into the caves from the safety of the outside, each breathing rapidly. The experience had been unsettling. The men in the cave had become something other than human. They had lost all ability to converse or to think, and it would clearly be dangerous to set them free.

"That was like a dream I had as a child," Agrippa said, his upper lip beaded in sweat. "In the dream, I descended into the underworld, and things came at me from the shadows. I had trouble getting to sleep for months after that."

"Cosimus. Something happened to you last night. Can you remember anything?" Antonius said holding Cos by the shoulder.

"You are right, Antonius. Something did happen, because I remember snatches of it. You were there, as was Mary. I felt happy, then something happened. Gadus just pulled the memory of a monster out of me. I must have seen his face and heard his growl, but I am not his subject, and I am not under his spell. There is something I can't remember which keeps coming back but is just out of reach. Some part of me doesn't want to remember whatever it was, I am afraid to."

"We have to get away from this place," Antonius said. "Agrippa, take ten...no, twenty men and release the other soldiers one at a time. If there is even a small hint of what we just saw in any of them, then pull them aside and lock them back up. Be ready for a sudden and unexpected attack. Take no chances. When you are done, we will feed the men who had to spend a night in the caves. It's the least we can do."

"I understand, Centurion. It will be done," Agrippa said and grasped his sword by the hilt.

Chapter 20

Entering Hostile Territory

Alexandrium receded into the distance, step by step, as they went down toward the Jordan and the path south. Cos was riding alongside Agrippa, and both rode behind Antonius and Mary. She held on to Antonius tightly as their horse picked his way among the stones and loose rock. Cos could tell that they were carrying on constant conversation but couldn't really hear them or really want to hear them. During the night he had gone over and over scattered thoughts regarding his mysterious disappearance, trying to piece them together into something intelligible. He did remember Mary's smiling, happy face and saw Antonius with her, but it wasn't the same Antonius. He was relaxed, casual, and wasn't wearing armor. Cos seemed to remember seeing the Portal but it was out of sequence with other events. He remembered intense fear, and the loneliness of standing and waiting for something to happen. His hand started to sweat as he remembered the feel of a gladius in it. Waiting. The last memory was of a sound, deep, guttural, angry, the voice of a big jungle cat protecting its kill. It gave him a chill to remember, and he quickly forced his mind elsewhere. He tried to remember that they were headed toward Jericho. Antonius had said that Jericho was only a half-day's march. Legendary Jericho. Cos forced his consciousness to remember history, ordering himself to forget the nightmarish growl still searing his brain.

Cos looked at Agrippa, swaying back and forth in his saddle, obviously comfortable. He must have spent much of his life in a saddle, in the service of Rome. "Been to Jericho previously?" Cos asked.

"No. This is the first time. It's a famous city, as you probably know. Or do you?" he asked smiling at Cos.

"They say that it is one of the oldest cities in the world. There were people living there at least eight thousand years ago. I understand that it has a good climate in the winter, and plants grow easily there."

"Yes. You do know something of it. There have been several palaces built there for the rulers of these lands. Herod build three palaces, and one still stands. I hope we can see it, but after the threats that Gadus threw at us, I don't see how we can stop."

"How far is Jerusalem from Jericho?" Cos asked.

"It's a full, and very hard, day's march, most of it uphill and without water. A difficult day even if we stop for a rest tonight. I would guess it is *viginti quinque milia* [twenty-five miles] and no place to stop and rest until Jerusalem."

"What happened when you let the other men out?" Cos asked.

"We killed two. It couldn't be helped. The rest seemed to be normal. We hope so since they are now responsible for keeping the fanatics locked away until relief can be sent back to them."

"What will happen then?" Cos asked.

"I don't want to think about it," Agrippa answered and turned away. He was clearly upset at being forced to kill fellow Romans. Cos couldn't blame him and was sorry that he forced Agrippa to tell the story. He looked up and noticed that Antonius was waving for him to come forward. Cos spurred his horse forward and drew alongside.

"Mary seeks to talk with you. I would like you to take her on your horse for now, because Jericho is not far from us. I don't want to meet any of Gadus' friends while she is behind me. You understand?" he said and gave a knowing and long look at Cos. He hadn't told Mary of the possible danger which lies ahead.

Cos reached for her, and she transferred quickly and held on to him. Her arms were now around his waist, and her hands were pressing into his abdomen. The effect was immediate, and he tried to push the image away, without success.

"Hi, stranger," she cooed from behind his shoulder as she pulled tighter to elicit a response from him.

"Hi, yourself. I am glad to have you back there for conversation. Want to talk to me?" he asked.

"Yes, I know something is up. I can read his mind by now. There is something he is keeping from me. What is it, Cos?"

"Nothing. We are coming into Jericho shortly, and you know how he is. He is always prepared for the unexpected. I imagine that is what has kept him and his men alive. He wants you with someone he knows will protect you...and who will keep his hands off of you. That's me!"

"I trust you, Cos, in every way. You are my best friend. The best that I ever had. With both of you in sight, I feel that nothing could ever happen to me."

"As long as I am alive, nothing will." He felt her arms tighten around him in response. She was the best way to forget the memories tugging at him from the previous evening. The warmth of her body that he could never hold and the aroma of her skin that he would never caress came to him and invaded a part of his mind that he thought he had repressed. The mystery of attraction was opaque for him, as it always has been for men, but...the pull of attraction toward this woman whom he loved was nearly irresistible. There was never a moment when they were together that he took her presence for granted, but for some reason, she obviously never felt the same strong attraction for him. A part of him felt happy that she had chosen Antonius, because he was indeed a fine man. So am I, another part thought.

Cos could feel that something undefined had changed. Things connected now in a way different than before with both urgency and inevitability at play. Was it something to do with what happened to him, or perhaps, is it what will happen? Cos, Mary, Antonius, the Portal, and, of course, the demon Jesus were all connected and were swirling around in a haze of confusion just outside his comprehension.

Mary interrupted his thoughts. "Say, I thought you wanted to talk to me. Are you upset or injured or something else I don't know about?"

"I'm mentally ill. Don't you know?" he said. She was silent for awhile, and then he felt her head lying against his back and the pat of her hand. She understood a lot of what he was going through. There was no need to tell her how he felt.

"Cos," she said. "No matter what happens, I want to stay friends with you for the rest of my life. I want to be near so that I can see you and hear your voice forever."

"You and I have had quite the adventure, haven't we? That sort of thing...danger and excitement, always brings people closer. You already know how I feel about you, but what you don't understand is how much it will always hurt to just be a friend to you. What you want is not possible for that reason, but there is something else bothering me. There is a growing feeling inside my head that my destiny leads in a different direction. Still, I believe that you and Antonius have a future together and will become that whole being that you both seek. I am happy for you, and I don't want to see anything get in your way."

Just as he finished speaking, he saw one of the men pointing. Between the mountain slopes was a fertile plain with the tops of structures showing above the trees. Jericho was just ahead. Antonius held up his hand to stop the formation. He rode back down the line repeating the same instructions so that they all could hear it.

"We have reason to feel that more fanatics of Jesus are here and may be waiting for us. Do not respond to anything they may say to us...even threats or jeers. We will only respond to protect ourselves from harm and only on my order." Back at the front, he waved them forward again, and now, all idle conversation between the men stopped as they focused their attention on what was waiting for them.

As they marched forward, there were some watching in the distance, their faces hidden deep in their hoods. Nearing the city, small groups observed their passing in silence. They stopped what they were doing and watched, as if waiting for a signal, glaring defiance at the unwelcome troops of a foreign empire. Hatred hung in the air, crackling like static before a storm, and then it happened.

Antonius' fist came up, signaling a halt. A group of men were blocking the road as others waited in small bands just off the path.

"Romans are not welcome in Jericho. You must leave!" the man yelled.

"Swords!" called Antonius, and the ring of eighty swords sounded in the air as they cleared their scabbards. Light reflected from the polished blades and danced around like the many souls who had perished on them. Everybody held their positions with the tension of the moment building rapidly. One by one, the men from Jericho seemed to focus on Cosimus, pointing him out to each other.

"Him! Your Tesserarius has met our Lord!" they shouted as Cosimus tried to shield his face from them.

"Forward," Antonius said, pointing with his gleaming sword at the group blocking the way. The column moved forward like a human train, unstoppable and irresistible. At the last moment, the men on the road moved aside, bristling with undisguised anger as the Romans filed by. With the threat of confrontation all around them, the column inched toward the outside wall of Jericho, turning at the last moment with an abrupt change of direction, and moved toward the Jordan river, bypassing the city.

"Where do you think he is leading us?" Mary asked.

"He's trying to avoid the city. You saw what was waiting outside for us. Just imagine what is inside the walls. It would be a trap, and we would have to fight our way out," Cos answered.

"But we can't go all the way to Jerusalem today. There isn't time," she said.

"What's on the other side of the city? You know this place, don't you?"

"Yes and no. In our time, Jericho is in Palestinian hands. They allow tourists in but give the Israelis less access. We haven't dug here in years. As I remember, there are remains of a large temple complex just southwest of the city. In this time period, the palace of Herod the Great still stands, and I'll bet that's where we are going."

"Who would be occupying the palace now?" Cos asked.

Mary thought about it for a moment, then said, "Likely, the family of Herod's children. Rome was favorably disposed toward them, and Emperor Claudius installed Herod Agrippa as King of Judea in 41, or about twelve years from now. It only lasted three or four years, then Rome took it back, but eventually appointed Agrippa's son, Marcus Julius, to be King. Right now, Herod Agrippa lives in Rome under the protection of Tiberius. I believe his relatives live in the palace, but which ones would only be a guess."

"Seems like we are about to find out," Cos said and pointed to a long row of white stone columns. "There is a large structure ahead, complete with moat. That's got to be it." As they made their way forward, the size and splendor of the decidedly Roman palace became apparent, the buildings looming in both directions.

"Wow," Mary exclaimed. This place is larger in real life than I expected. The Romans destroyed it at the end of the first revolt, between 69 or 70, so in our time there isn't anything left but foundations." She kept looking over Cos' shoulder as they approached the first bridge. "Wow!" she said with even more emphasis. Antonius dismounted to meet with several guards who came out of the palace fortress. After a long conference, he mounted again and led the way into the complex. As they passed over the deep trench just outside of the walls, it was apparent that an approaching army would be at a disadvantage trying to cross the moat and then scale the wall. This was a very secure palace indeed, but, unfortunately, its fortifications would not stop Roman Legions who would come this way in just forty years.

The procession filed into a courtyard, and Mary and Cos were instructed to dismount. Cos helped Mary down by holding her under her arms and slowly easing her to her feet as if she was a fragile and delicate piece of glass. Their eyes met only briefly on her way down, but it was enough to set off a small, simultaneous electric jolt in their brains. She looked up at him trying to express something, a thought that was forcing its way to the surface, but couldn't find the right words. Cos saw love in her eyes in that brief, lingering look, and it was all he ever could expect from her, that one look, but it reassured him that in some measure, she shared the feeling he had for her. She loved him. Not in the same way that she loved Antonius, of course, but more a tender, kind and compassionate kind of love. It would have to suffice, Cos knew, because the physical part of love, the touching, the kissing and the embrace of love could never happen. Even if Antonius were to be out of her life, she will love him forever and would never allow another lover to inhabit that spot in her soul.

Antonius called out, waving them forward, and together they moved through the lavish palace with its fountains, baths and gilded finish, leading them down a short flight of stairs which opened onto a bridge to the other side of a deep ravine. "This is Wadi Qilt," Mary said. "Look down! There is water moving through the gorge below us. I expected it to be dry!" The bridge was narrow, but substantial, and led to the South Palace and a wall of rock rising vertically on the far side. Cos could see the strategy of coming here. Any assault would have to first gain entry to the palace, by itself a difficult challenge. Passing over this narrow bridge and through the Roman soldiers guarding it would be nearly impossible.

After ascending a short staircase, they came upon a large courtyard surrounded by pools and exotic plants. It was cool and shady and instantly felt pleasant and comfortable. At the west end, another, steeper, set of stairs ascended a mound topped by an elaborate circular stone structure which shimmered and hung, guardian-like, above the palace and the plain of Jericho.

"Agrippa!" Antonius called. "Send ten men to protect the bridge. Another four to the lookout tower. The rest can relax and await food and wine." A small cheer went up from the men who rapidly took off their armor and jumped into the pools.

"Tomorrow, Jerusalem," Antonius said as he walked toward them. "This is the last night for us to be together as we have been. It grieves me that it has to end."

Chapter 21

Our Little Palace In The Sky

ome with me, Mary," Antonius said, gently taking her hand in his. "I have arranged for you and I to share a private meal and count stars in the heavens." He pointed to the striking circular temple hovering above the rest of the palace. "I have sent food, wine and bedding up there. It is ours, our little palace, at least for the night." Mary blushed and looked around to see who was listening to his plan of a dalliance that everyone could see. He hesitated for a moment, waiting for her to collect her thoughts, then gently tugged her in that direction. They went up the long flight of stairs, arm in arm, ascending far above the frivolity in the courtyard and the pools. At the last step, the whole of the temple complex, the vast wadi beneath them, the city of Jericho and its famous walls, the Jordan river and the valley beyond, extended to the limit of sight in a vast panorama. The circular temple was about four meters in diameter and obviously built for just this sort of occasion. She could picture Herod the Great with one of his beautiful wives holding on to the curved railing of stone and looking over all they owned, smug with pride. The wind, chasing the contours of the land, flowed up the hill and held Mary's hair in its shaking grasp, extending it out from her face and fluttering it softly as though it was of black silk. She turned toward Antonius and pulled his face to hers, and they kissed long and passionately, letting history come to rest for a moment, as the world stopped turning and all noise and distraction ceased, allowing the entire universe to become their lips.

"Thank you for taking me up here. I stood in this spot years ago, and there was nothing here but dirt and some traces of broken stone. To see it like it was, and to be in your arms...it is as if...well... it was all meant to be. I have found so much here that I always dreamed of seeing, and now that it is a reality, it feels like being complete, as if all the fragments of my life are restored, all my dreams fulfilled. Finally, I understand history. The time between us seems so short now, so continuous. I can almost see all the lives of the people who lived between us, I can feel the presence of their lives, hear the murmur of their voices. I understand. For the first time, I understand."

"And I understand," Antonius said. "I know that you are the one meant for me. The sight of you, the sound of your voice, is nourishment to my soul, filling me with energy and hope for the future. A soldier always assumes that he is to die and that way does not fear death. Now, I fear death for the first time, because I would be separated from you and you from me."

"Your bravery is deeply locked inside of you, dear Antonius. Love takes nothing away while it adds richness and meaning to life. I can enjoy my life more fully in your presence, and now I understand why I was born and why I live. Our meeting was always meant to be, as was our love for each other." Antonius looked into the distance, one elbow on the railing and the other arm around Mary, feeling her softness, her suppleness. He looked down at the courtyard, at first not realizing what his eyes fixed on. Cosimus was sitting on the bottom stair of their steep stairs, his back to them, a long spear in one hand.

"Look below, Mary," Antonius said and pointed out Cosimus.

"That's Cos!" she remarked. "What is he doing?"

"He protects us and gives us privacy from himself and others. Likely, he will spend the night on that step. A better friend for either of us could not be found." In spite of herself, Mary welled up with tears.

"I feel so sorry for him, Antonius. He has been left out."

"Do you love him, Mary?"

"Yes. I love him. But I love you in a different way, Antonius. I love Cos like I would love my brother, my best friend, a soul mate.

"I love him just as you do. We must protect him as he protects us. We owe that debt to him." He wiped his face with his hand and turned toward her. "Life is funny, Mary. You two came into my life from out of nowhere, and suddenly you are the most important people in my life. I don't believe that I could return to the man I was before we met. The thought of losing both or either of you takes something out of me. Things would never again be the same."

They watched the night slowly settling into the Jordan Valley toward the east, the distant hills disappearing first as the horizon blended into the wave of advancing blackness. Behind them, the setting sun dipped below the last peak of rock, shutting off the light like a switch, allowing the flickering stars to emerge in purple twilight and show their bright faces. Far away, a dog barked, and just below in the courtyard, there was an occasional laugher rising in the night air from one of the men.

"I'm not ready for the day to end, Antonius. Tomorrow is filling me with anxiety because there are too many unknowns."

"If you choose to worry about things to come, you lose the moment. This time and place will never come again into our lives, but it is here for us right now. You are in my arms, and you belong to me. This night and this small room at the top of the world is mine, and I give them all to you." He pulled her toward him and felt her hair cascade over his hand on her back as her face came up to meet his.

The aroma from cooking bread and meat drifted, bound with the smoke from the fires, and found its way to their nose at the moment the first shadows from the rising sun threw hard lines across their sleeping faces. Antonius opened his eyes, and Mary's face filled his view, her eyes still closed, her head partially covered by his crimson cape. This was the latest he had slept in years, and he could already hear his men below organizing for the coming march. He studied Mary as she slept, his eyes lingering on every part of her face, becoming overwhelmed by its perfection. She was a gift from the Gods, either his or hers. It didn't matter that she was two millennia younger than him and was from a people that believed that they were a separate race. He loved her. He wondered, smiling to himself, what was this thing called love? He recalled that Plato had devoted a lot of effort to describe love. After admitting that love was a "serious mental disease," he had also said that "the madness of love is the greatest of heaven's blessings." Indeed, as he studied her face, her eyes narrowly opened, letting his image in as the realization that her love was still beside her caused her eyes to open more fully.

"This is the first time I have awakened to find you still with me." She smiled as she spoke, her voice slightly crackled and low. She placed her hand on his cheek and slowly withdrew it, sending a shower of sparks out of her lingering fingertips into his skin.

"On this morning, I do not wish to rise. The joy of being with you is so strong that nothing else matters."

"We have every day for the rest of our lives to behold each other, and in the coming years we will become even closer than we are at this instant."

"I cannot believe that I can feel any more drawn to you than I am at this moment."

"You will. I am still new to you, still exciting. The real love comes later."

"Centurion!" Agrippa called from below. The day was starting, and no force could contain it.

"Coming!" Antonius said and groaned as he pulled back the coverlet. He leaned forward and kissed her on her nose, very delicately, very softly. Their eyes locked and both understood how much they both wanted to linger but couldn't. He stood and looked over the railing and was rewarded by both Cosimus and Agrippa smiling up at them and holding food trays. He waved them up then alerted Mary, "Food comes, the day starts for us, my love." Mary quickly pulled on her cloak and stood up just as Cosimus made the last step and entered their sanctuary.

"Good morning to you both," he said and placed the food tray on the stone floor. He looked out at the rising sun, now fully parted from the hills of Jordan, its yellow light pouring over the parched landscape. "Magnificent view from up here!" Cos said. Mary adjusted her cloak over her head and turned the spotlight of her eyes on him.

"Did you remain at the bottom of the stairs all night, Cos?"

"I slept fine and feel rested. Hope you both did as well. Since this is the first time I have been up before Antonius, I feel proud of myself this morning."

"And you should," Antonius said. "Are the men ready to move out?"

"Nearly. By the time you eat, we will be ready. Eat slowly and enjoy. The march uphill is ahead, and the day will prove long," Agrippa interjected.

"Any trouble from the city last night?" Antonius asked.

"All quiet as far as we know. The earlier we leave the better, though," Agrippa answered.

Antonius looked down at the still sleeping Jericho. "Something about the place feels less evil this morning. Even last evening, the fanatics were there but...perhaps less fanatic than I expected. Do you not agree, Agrippa?"

"Yes, Antonius, I feel it too. On the battlefield when the leader flees or is taken, the men lose their zest. Perhaps the fleeing Tony has led Jesus far from here."

"Or perhaps, for some reason, he is losing his hold over them. Nevertheless, when we depart, tell the men to be especially alert. We will be vulnerable until we get deeply into the mountains and closer to the Roman Cohort being assembled in Jerusalem."

As they were leaving, Antonius laid his hand on Cos's shoulder. "Thank you, Cos. You are a man above most other men, and I have known many fine ones. There is no way that I can repay you except to tell you how much I value your friendship." Antonius caught a hint of moisture in Cos' eyes before he turned his head away.

"It means a lot to me that you are both happy. I do what I should do, what I am compelled to do, to see that you both have as much time together as possible. Life is short and our future uncertain. Moments which fulfill us are fleeting but can be recalled with joy for years and years afterward. That is what will happen with you and Mary. I believe that my destiny will be revealed to me shortly, but your destiny, Mary's destiny, is to be together in your mutual love. You both have earned at least that." Cos and Agrippa descended out of sight leaving Mary and Antonius alone, floating above the cares of the world and its eternal struggles.

"Our Cosimus rises to the level of a Centurion and beyond," Antonius said, looking down into the courtyard. "That is exactly what they expect of us...to rise above your own needs and wants and sacrifice yourself for a more important cause."

"Are we more important than Cosimus?" Mary asked.

"No, but the love we share is, at least in his view."

"Did you ever discover what happened to him when he disappeared?" she asked.

"I am convinced that he met your Antichrist that night. Others see it also. He changed after he returned. There is no more joy in him, and he is as if he is afloat on a large river of water, being swept along without a struggle to an inevitable destination. At this moment, I don't think he knows what happened, but he will, in time, remember."

Chapter 22

At Last, Jerusalem

Agrippa was right. The trail quickly became steep, and the horses drew deeper and deeper breaths and more frequently missed steps causing a breathtaking lurch of the saddle toward the steep edge of the gravel-strewn path. The clanking behind them grew louder as the men made the required effort to ascend the mountain, bearing their load of gear and water. Beside the trail was a steep drop off of the mountain slope, at times approaching the vertical. In the ravine far below ran a trickle of water boring its inexorable path down to the Jordan and ultimately beyond to the Dead Sea. High overhead soared vultures, hanging from the sky with bent wings and heads down, scouring the earth's surface for rotted flesh.

Mary turned to look back at Cos, behind and downhill of her, and he caught sight of her lovely dark eyes and knowing smile just before she turned again and resumed her embrace of her lover from behind. Cos understood that she was sending a message that she had not forgotten him, that some part of her still cared deeply for him, but in some ways, the message also said that she rather liked where she was presently. He hadn't changed his mind or opinion about Mary. Not at all. She remained an outstanding female companion, both lovely and intelligent but...seeing her now was like passing a store window with an expensive item some part of you might desire. You know that you could never acquire a thing so far beyond your reach so you reach an agreement with your brain not to dwell on it, not to give in to desire. You simply can't have it, and you go on with your life. That doesn't mean that the love he felt for Mary was over. It wasn't over, he had just placed it lower in his list of priorities. He resolved to remember what had happened to him when he went missing.

His first priority.

Each time he summoned his memory, he saw the same visions, repeated as in a loop. There was always the smiling and happy Mary, accompanied by Antonius. They were in a familiar place. Was it near the Portal? They must have been inside the Portal, because he didn't remember any rock or red soil there. Why were they there and when was it? As he concentrated, the same thing happened again. The demon face was in front of his, the flaring nostrils, the yellow eyes, the hate, the scream. He forced it from his mind like he always did, forced himself to think about the present, the precarious cliff and the carrion eaters hovering overhead. No matter what he did, the visions kept returning, over and over. Stop! He screamed in his mind. He put his hands to his temporal areas and squeezed, trying to push his thoughts out, just as his horse misstepped and dropped his right shoulder sending Cos over the side head first toward the steep ravine. His slide was arrested by his cape which became entangled in the larger rocks. His feet dangled in the air with nothing below them but distance as he grappled with nearby rocks to prevent his body from sliding into oblivion. Two sets of strong arms grasped his and lifted him up and to his feet. He looked around to see that everyone was watching him, wondering how and why he could be so inept. He suddenly felt weak and sat down, leaning forward into the dirt of the trail. That is when his mind focused enough to remember what he had been trying to clarify. He realized that he was remembering the future. An event which has not yet happened, but yet, he clearly remembered it. He saw Mary and Antonius together and happy in the future and on the other side of the Portal. The rest, the meeting with the monster, could not be summoned. He was still repressing it, because it was too horrible to remember.

A warm tender hand stroked his head, and he remembered her scent before she spoke, "Cos, what happened? Are you ill?" Mary murmured softly.

He looked up into her smiling, gentle face and felt a peacefulness settle over him. At least he knew that she will be safe, she and Antonius, and they will be together. "I seem to have had an accident. That's all. I feel well enough now. Thanks for your concern." She and others helped him to his feet, and someone placed a wine flask in his hands, and he took a long deep drink of sweet red wine. He looked up and saw Antonius still mounted and looking down at him with a stern expression. Cos didn't understand his look which could mean disapproval or recognition of his weakness.

"You didn't sleep last night, did you Cosimus?" Antonius asked.

"No."

"You find that your day suffers because of your nighttime vigilance. I should not have let you do that, Cosimus. I feel responsible that you were almost lost over the edge."

"I'm fine now. I just had a moment of inattention and almost paid the price for it. It won't happen again," Cos said and stood erect. He motioned for one of the soldiers to mount his horse and ride in his place and assumed the man's place in the line.

"You have become a superb example of a Roman soldier, Cosimus. An example to follow," Antonius said. He paused momentarily to look again at Cosimus, then pulled Mary up behind him and resumed the march.

Cos fell in line and started to feel better after his muscles were under load and sweat started in earnest under his layers of protection. After a mile, mostly uphill, he began to question his judgment of walking. Each time he glanced in the direction of his horse, its rider grinned back at him, both happy to be mounted but also delighted that at least one of the officers could experience the difficult trail for himself. At midday, they seemed to reach the crest, and afterwards the road became mostly downhill. At a rest stop for food and water, they were allowed to briefly remove their armor and helmets to their great relief.

"Two more hours, Cosimus, and we will reach the outskirts where we may meet other Roman troops. I want you back on the horse when we resume the march. It is not according to our custom for officers to walk instead of ride, however highly the men think of you for doing it," Antonius said.

"Sorry. I had to sort myself out, and the effort did clear my thinking," Cos replied.

"Still bothered by your dreams?"

"I have not seen the end of it yet, but some facts I do recall more clearly. At the moment, I am trying to avoid any more memories."

"I feel as I know how you feel, that we cannot change what is to be.

Some things you don't want to know in advance."

Cos did feel better, in fact, a lot better. His mind cleared and returned to the present and the expected difficulties ahead. Somehow, he, Mary and Antonius were to return to the Portal, and all three were to go back into the future. That much he knew was to happen. How it was going to work out was still a problem. There were too many unknowns ahead to envision how it could happen, or when it would happen. The trail led decidedly downhill, and they started to encounter others using the primitive road.

To their relief, the column of soldiers was given a wide berth, and there were no insulting remarks or obvious hostility from those they passed. They were all worried about encountering the cult of Jesus around Jerusalem, but at least that danger seemingly had dissipated.

In the distance, a cloud of dust billowed behind a group of riders heading rapidly toward them, and as they came closer, it was apparent that the group consisted of mounted Romans, their shields shimmering in the strong light. "As I expected," Antonius said. "An escort has arrived. In the days of the Republic, they would be *Ordo Equester*, but this group will be locals. Nevertheless, they are here to guide us safely into Jerusalem, as a token of respect from our commander, Pontius Pilatus, who obviously knows where we are."

The riders pulled up sharply and dramatically in front of Antonius and his men, allowing the cloud of dust to catch up and drift down silently between the groups as they looked each other over. There were ten of them, all fresh and crisply uniformed, resplendent in the sun. "Greetings Romans, Pontius Pilatus awaits your arrival," one called out.

"Greetings from Antonius Severius Maximus and his men," Antonius called back.

"We are directed to assume your duties and allow you to ride into Jerusalem. You are to proceed directly to the palace," the man called out. Antonius looked at Agrippa and Cosimus. The order was meant for them also.

"What about Mary?" Cos asked. "Does she go with us?"

"I am not about to leave her here. She goes," he answered, then rode forward and received his written orders from the equestrian officer. He unrolled the directive and confirmed the order, then rode along the long line of his men and said, "Your officers are directed to leave you under the charge of these men. You will proceed to the camp without us, but we will rejoin you after you arrive. You have all proven yourselves many times since we left Caesarea, and it has been a privilege and honor to command you. I hope that we are not separated, but if we are, I shall always remember that the finest men in the Roman Army are standing here today in front of me." A general shout emerged, and most of the men drew their swords and shook them in the air in an enthusiastic tribute to Antonius. He settled back on his horse, enjoying the moment, Mary peeking around his shoulder.

Five of the mounted soldiers led the way and were followed by the three mounts of Antonius, Agrippa and Cosimus. The pace was fast, and Mary held on tightly, pressing hard against Antonius' back. Cos worried about her ability to hold on, and he kept a careful watch over her. In the distance, the Temple was the first thing spotted, and it loomed above the city walls, dominating it, surrounded by the three towers also built by Herod. Mary pulled her camera out of some fold and took several photos, anxious to record this view which was destined to permanently and forever change in less than one lifetime. The group pulled up to rest the horses and to dismount for water, and they all stood together for conversation.

"Who is the woman?" one asked curtly.

"Mine. That is all you need to know," Antonius answered.

"You can't take her in to see Pilatus," he said.

"This I know," Antonius said. The man shrugged and inspected Agrippa and Cosimus closely as if he alone could decide who could meet with Pilatus.

"Have you heard of a man called Jesus?" Antonius inquired casually.

"I was told that a group arrived from the east who were infected. That name seems familiar."

"What was done with them?" Antonius pressed.

"They remain confined. Their spies are to be executed tomorrow."

"Why?"

"*Barbarus* seek to undermine the authority of Rome," he said with surprise. Antonius looked at Cosimus and raised his eyebrows. This was what happened to any threatening newcomers. The message he sent to

Cos was clear. If the truth was discovered, or even suspected, Mary and Cos would meet the same fate.

"Have you personally seen the *Barbarus*?" Antonius inquired.

"Yes, briefly," the officer bristled.

"How are they different?"

The man looked taken aback that Antonius would care. "They speak in an unknown foreign tongue. They both have small chin beards, like a little goat. The sight of them makes my skin crawl. They beg like dogs and have no courage or dignity. Is that enough for you?"

"Yes. Thank you for your description," Antonius said. He huddled discreetly with Agrippa and Cos. "There is something familiar in what he says, isn't there?" Agrippa looked blank, but Cos said, "Could be. I should go and take a look at them when we arrive."

"I don't understand," Agrippa said.

"I want to know if they speak any language that I understand. We might find out more about this Jesus and what happened to him if I can converse with them," Cos said.

"Better wait until after we meet with Pilatus," Antonius suggested.

Chapter 23

Pontius Pilatus

On the way into the palace, Antonius, Agrippa and Cosimus walked side by side, escorted by several guards. "He is a fair-minded but very tough commander. Don't let him get under your skin, especially if he yells at you," Antonius said under his breath. Agrippa and Cosimus nodded that they understood. All three were thinking about Mary, who had to be left alone outside the palace. Even their horses were led away by the tenders, leaving her without anything familiar. The last they saw of her, she was across the paved street, hiding in the shadows of a vertical wall, trying to be inconspicuous.

The double door was flung open, and the guards stopped at the threshold. Across the spacious room, a large ornate desk of ivory and ebony stood apart from the wall and behind that was the partially bald head of the commander of Judea, Pontius Pilatus. He looked up as their hobnails clicked on the polished marble floor.

"Well, Antonius Severius, I have been getting reports on you, and complaints. Seems that you have taken on the duly appointed Tetrarch of Galilee. Comments?"

"No comments, Prefect. Likely, your reports are accurate," Antonius said.

"Then it is true that your centuriae, with your leadership, fought and killed two hundred men?"

"It is true, Prefect."

"How many casualties?"

"None, Prefect."

"How did you manage that?" Pilatus said as he leaned back in his chair, frowning.

"My men are superb fighters; they give no quarter."

"That, and their leadership is excellent. Was there more you want to tell me?"

"We re-formed and turned as a unit, after the first battle, and met a second force coming toward us to our rear. We caused them to flee back to wherever they came from."

"How large was the second force?"

"Duo vel tres centum." [Two to three hundred.]

"So your force of eighty-three men prevailed from a surprise attack of nearly five hundred men?"

"Those are the facts, Prefect," Antonius said.

"And, who are these two?" Pilatus said, looking over Cosimus and Agrippa.

"My Optio, Agrippa, and my Tesserarius, Cosimus," Antonius answered.

"How did they conduct themselves?"

"With honor, they are among the best I have ever fought beside."

Pilatus got up and walked around the desk and wordlessly embraced each of them in turn. He put his arms on the shoulders of Antonius and said, "You are to be promoted, Antonius. All three of you are being promoted. You, Cosimus will become Optio. You, Agrippa, are now a Centurion." He walked around to his seat but remained standing, smiling, saving the best part for last. "Welcome, Pilus Prior. You are now First Centurion of Legio Tertia Cyrenaica. Your legion is presently in Syria but is being moved to Gaul shortly. The Legate wrote to me asking about you, but now, with what you have just accomplished, the promotion is certain. Congratulations."

"I am deeply honored, Prefect," Antonius said haltingly but did not smile.

"Is there any difficulty with your promotion?" Pilatus asked, some tension in his voice.

"I can only respond with honesty, Prefect, even though you might become angry."

"Hold your tongue for a moment. There is the issue of a complaint against you. Actually two complaints," Pilatus said and hunted through his scrolls. He held the document up and waved it in the air. "This states that you and one of your men killed four men in the public baths in Tiberias. Is this true?"

"Yes, it is. My Tesserarius and I were defending ourselves."

"The second part is about some woman that you had stay in the palace by invoking my name. The report states that she is very beautiful and highborn. Is this also true?"

"Yes, Pilatus, on both counts."

"You still have this woman with you?" Pilatus asked.

"She is waiting outside, Prefect."

"You let a woman like that wait in the street?"

"Yes, I had no men with me that I could leave."

"Go and get her, Centurion. I wish to see this beauty for myself. Your men will remain with me," Pilatus said and pointed to the door. Antonius spun and sprinted away. Pilatus watched him leave and then focused on Agrippa and Cosimus. "Agrippa, you are to assume command of your present centuriae. You may leave now and await further orders. By the way, do you have any comments or requests?"

"Prefect, there is a matter of the fort at Alexandrium. We had to imprison more than half the men there, because they had become followers of a fanatic cult. The men guarding them should be relieved as soon as possible," Agrippa said.

"Your first assignment, Agrippa. First, rest here for a week then return with your centuriae and take command of the fort. If your prisoners remain as you say, you have my authority to execute them on the spot. Remain there until relieved by a permanent force. Understood?"

"Yes, Prefect. Thank you for my promotion. I will not fail you," Agrippa said, then slapped Cosimus on the back and headed for the door.

"Now to you, my fresh Optio. I don't remember you. Tell me how you came to be with Antonius. You were not present when his centuriae left Caesarea." Pilatus sat down and folded his hands, studying Cosimus like he was a bug in a jar. Cosimus swallowed hard. This could be a defining moment, even a life or death moment. He could feel a small row of sweat beads clinging to his upper lip.

"You are correct, Prefect. I met with his unit south of Nazat."

"How did you come to be there?" Pilatus pressed.

"I was attempting to be a historian, Prefect. Now I am a Roman soldier, and I am very proud of it."

"So you should be. Where were you born?"

"Rome, Prefect."

"So, you were pressed into service by Antonius and distinguished yourself in combat. Is that about it?"

"Exactly correct, Prefect."

"Welcome to the Roman Army, Cosimus. But we have a problem. You will not have the correct record of enlistment on file. No record, no pay, no retirement. Understand?"

"Yes, Prefect."

"You are to go with Antonius to Caesarea where he will embark, along with his cohort, for Ostia. You will formally enlist at our headquarters in Caesarea and be assigned from there. Understood?"

"Yes, Prefect."

"Now about Antonius and that woman. Do you know this woman?"

"Yes, Prefect. She is called Mary Solomon. I was traveling with her."

"Solomon is the name carried by members of one the Tribes of Israel. She is of the Yehudim?"

"Yes, Prefect."

"So she is not highborn?"

"No, Prefect." A grin started to appear on the face of Pontius Pilatus. He threw back his head and laughed out loud, becoming red in the face.

"You mean that you pulled one over on old Herod Antipas. He thought she was something extraordinary. I love that. Congratulations to you both."

"She is extraordinary, Prefect," Cosimus said.

"Tell me, Optio, is Antonius in love with this woman?"

"Very much, Prefect."

"It's a problem because she cannot be with him after he leaves with his men. You know her as well. Are you also in love with this woman?" Pilatus asked, studying him carefully.

"I am in love with her, Prefect, but she loves Antonius only."

"You seem to be in luck, Optio. He will leave Judea soon, and you will remain. You will end up with the woman after all." He felt happy that he had resolved their dilemma for them and smiled with satisfaction. The double doors opened abruptly, and Antonius and Mary stood together at the threshold. She was still dressed in her simple dark woolen cape, the hood obscuring her beautiful face.

"Come forward, Antonius, Mary," Pilatus boomed, waving them in with his beckoning hand. He watched intently as they came forward, trying to see what he could of this reported beauty. "Please, Mary, could you remove your cape so that I can see for myself what I have read about you?" She nodded and slowly removed her outer garment. Underneath, she was still wearing the thin white silk toga, which caught the late afternoon sun, sending thousands of gold shafts spinning about the chamber. Delicately, and with consummate grace, she held the edge of the garment between her fingers and gave a slight bow to Pilatus.

"Yes, I could take you for royalty myself," Pilatus said and rose to his feet. "She is a remarkable beauty, Antonius. Remarkable indeed." He walked around the desk and then around behind Mary, looking at her with unabashed interest. "Yes, I would want this one for myself. And I would have her too, if she didn't belong to this fearsome warrior beside her. I would guess that any man who touches her will meet with instant death. True, Antonius?"

"True, Prefect," Antonius answered calmly in a deep voice which seemed to resonate off the stone walls.

"Well, you have earned something, Antonius, after all you have been through recently. You may keep company with her as long as it lasts. You have two days here in Jerusalem, and then I expect both of you to return to Caesarea. These are your orders. Now here is a small bonus for each of you," he said and tossed two leather bags of coins to them.

"Thank you, Prefect. I have one more request, if you will permit," Antonius said. Pilatus looked irritated and frowned, somehow knowing he wouldn't like the request. He waited expectantly without giving verbal permission to continue.

"May we visit the two spies who are to be executed in the morning?"

"What for?" he responded.

"The force we fought at the mouth of the Jordan, the Roman soldiers in Alexandrium as well as some men near Jericho were all followers of a cult. The leader escaped us during the battle. I wish to know if these two men you hold are connected to him in any way. If they are, we may be able to learn why we were attacked near the Jordan. They seemed to know we were coming before we did."

"By all means, Antonius, do so. Thank you for being so responsible. Let me know what you find. Be warned, however, that my order for execution of those two will not be rescinded, even if they are not infected."

"Did they do something other than being suspected spies?" Antonius inquired.

"Two Roman soldiers were killed, and I believe that those two were the ones responsible. Enough of your questions, Centurion. I have one of my own. The letter of complaint from Herod Antipas said that Mary is able to tell the future. Is this so, Mary?"

She looked at Pontius Pilatus, deciding if she should tell him anything or even if he would believe what she said. He wasn't appointed to run this wayward province because he could be easily duped. She could tell, at a glance, that Pontius Pilatus was smart and tough, and she knew that he was a good judge of people, the kind of man who will likely sense a lie. Even though he will allow Jesus to be crucified four years from now, history records that he will not be convinced that Jesus Christ was guilty of anything and, at first, will refuse to take part in his punishment.

"Of course not, Prefect. That is clearly impossible, is it not?" Mary answered.

"It was always thought the Oracle at Delphi could tell the future. Perhaps it is possible. Tell me Mary, where will I die?"

"How will it serve you to know that?" she asked quietly.

"So you do know. Is there anything I can give you, or do for you, in return for your answer?" Pilatus asked, his voice nearly pleading.

"I want nothing from you, Pilatus. My knowledge is free to you, but I caution you that I don't know very much about your future."

Pilatus could tell that Mary was nearly willing to speak about what she knew but needed more incentive. "I will be in your debt, Mary. I beg you."

Mary took a deep breath and looked steadily at him, "Pontius Pilatus, you will serve in Judea for another nine years and then die in the mountains of Gaul."

"How do I die?" he asked impatiently. All of his instincts told him that Mary was telling the truth. He wanted to know all that she knew if he could just convince her to tell him.

"Truly, I do not know that. I don't know how or why or at what age. I am sorry."

"Is there anything good you can tell me about my life to come?"

"In general, you will be well-regarded as a man who did his duty, but one who could at times be brutal and harsh. You are destined to be exceptionally famous in history."

"What will I do to deserve that honor?"

"It will happen without you knowing the answer to your question. Don't worry, it is part of your fate," she said. Her expression told Pilatus that she would say no more.

"How famous will I be, Mary?" he continued.

"Your name will be known to billions of people. Many times more than all people alive today. Please ask me no more, Prefect."

"As I promised, Mary, I am in your debt. Anything in Judea is yours for the asking."

Mary turned away, then slowly turned back to face Pilatus as if she remembered something she wanted. "All I want is for you to do your job with honesty, kindness and fairness. Be the best that you can be, Pilatus." She took Antonius' arm, and they left Pilatus standing there, thinking, watching them leave as he mulled over her words.

Pilatus thought about what Mary had told him, rolling it over and over in his mind. Was he a stern and harsh governor of Judea like she suggested? Truthfully, he was, he admitted, though there were reasons, clear reasons, for his methods that history would not record. He had made an effort to discover the history of Judea, and had studied it carefully even before being appointed by Tiberius. Because of Judea's location between Egypt and Syria and, of course, Babylon and the damned Parthians still farther east, there have been armed clashes and wars here from the beginning of time. And there were the various and competing groups of the Yehudim. Pilatus tried to recall them as he ticked each off on his fingers. "The Pharisees, the Sadducees, the Essenes, and, of course, the Herodians, the crazy Zealots." He paused trying to remember the rest, keeping his fingers in the air. "Oh yes, the Levites, the Scribes and the Elders," he said with satisfaction. He had grown to hate all of them. What they all wanted was to have power over the rest. Tiberius had personally cautioned him not to let the groups fight openly among themselves, lest one come to power, unite the Yehudim, and then take on their Roman masters as a unified force. Of course his methods were harsh, there could be no other way to rule a land so nearly ungovernable. From what Mary said, he still had a long time to go as master of this place. There was, perhaps, still time for him to bring peace to Judea. He sighed at the load on his shoulders and sat back down behind his elaborate desk, wishing he was back in Rome.

Once outside, Antonius looked at his friends and said, "Looks like we are to be together after all. We have two days in Jerusalem and a sack of money to spend."

"First, we must see the two prisoners," Cos reminded him.

"Yes, I have not forgotten. They will be kept under the Tower of Miriamne. Follow me." Antonius led the way down the narrow streets and around the carts of food, produce and other items for sale in the crowded city. The Western Gate was protected by three tall towers of stone which could be seen from every part of Jerusalem. The shorter one was named after Herod The Great's wife, Miriamne, who was executed by her husband for imaginary transgressions. They stopped at the gate to the prison, which was guarded by soldiers.

"We are here to see the spies," Antonius said to one of the guards. The man looked over them carefully before responding.

"You have orders?" the man inquired.

"Verbal permission from the mouth of Pontius Pilatus, just now," Antonius responded. The man looked at them again, deciding if he should comply. He clearly wanted a reason to deny access to the prisoners.

"They are to die on the morrow. You know this?" the guard asked.

"Yes. Nothing changes that order. We want to talk with them."

"You will not be able to do that. They speak in a foreign tongue," the guard said.

"Open the door right now. I will play no more games with you," Antonius said forcefully. The guard reluctantly opened the steel door and led the way to the cell in the darkest corner of the prison. Groans from the imprisoned men floated in the fetid air, and the stone floor was wet with some slimy substance of questionable origin. They caught sight of men's faces on the way past other cells and saw the hopelessness and filth that was their fate. Some were chained, others huddled in dark corners, their red eyes shouting in pain. At the end, the guard stopped and pointed to the spies. Their faces were pressed against the narrow metal bars, their pleading eyes trying to look toward the approach of new feet. The party stopped just in front of the cage.

"You are dismissed, Guard. We can find our way out," Antonius commanded. Knowing that no simple guard is a match for a Centurion, the guard shrugged and left silently. They turned back to the eyes behind the bars who watched intently and with apprehension at their new captors.

"Either one of you speak Latin?" Antonius asked.

"*Dico aliqua,*" one answered.

"Greek then?" Antonius asked. They shook their heads no.

"The local language?" Mary asked hopefully, using Aramaic. Again they shook their heads.

"What about English?" Cosimus asked from behind. They saw the men's eyes widen in disbelief, and they looked at each other.

"God has answered our prayers! Thank you, Lord, for our deliverance!" they shouted, trying to reach out and touch their new saviors. "Who are you people?" they asked with jubilance.

Cosimus stepped forward and asked, "The question is: who are you and how and why are you here?"

"First, I want to introduce ourselves. I am Jasper Cruze and Tom Simon is standing beside me. I'm betting that we got here just the way you did, only we got here sooner."

"No, my friend, that won't do. How exactly did you get here?" Cos asked.

"We went through the Portal at the Tevatron."

"Why?" asked Cos.

"We found out what you people were up to. The murder of Jesus Christ. We were trying to stop you. There is a grad student at Fermilab named Stridor. He helped us get in first."

"How, exactly, were you going to stop us?" Cos persisted.

"Simple, we were going to find Jesus and warn him," Jasper said.

"You mean you were going in without a knowledge of Aramaic and minimal Latin skills?" Cos asked incredulously.

"There was no time to prepare adequately. We did what we had to do," Tom offered.

"Okay. You got in ahead of us. Did you find Jesus?"

"We got lost. The maps we brought along were of no use. We stumbled around, nearly dying of thirst, and found a small village where we started asking if anyone knew about Jesus of Nazareth. The people we encountered were mostly hostile to us, and some even threw rocks our way, but then we found someone who listened. This man led us along for a couple of days, heading into the mountains. We thought that he was going to kill us for awhile but then we were shown a cave guarded by several tough-looking men. One of them could speak some Latin, and he pointed out a man in the cave that he said was Jesus. We couldn't see Jesus clearly, but given all his men, he had to be the one we were looking for. We told our story, that someone was seeking to murder him, and the killers would likely show up in Nazareth first. We don't even know if he got our message. We saw him talking to his men and then they led us away." He paused to catch his breath and to moisten his parched lips.

"You found the wrong Jesus," Mary said. "Who sent you into the past with such poor preparedness?"

"You, too, are from the future?" Tom asked her.

"Obviously. Now answer my question. Who sent you?"

"The Our Faith group. They said it was an emergency. I am a high school Latin teacher," Jasper admitted. "Tom is an office worker who agreed to go with me."

"You poor dumb idiots," Mary said. "You set in motion a very bad thing, boys. The Jesus you found is something very evil. He was waiting for us with two hundred armed men. By the way, he got away in the battle and is still out there someplace."

"That wasn't Jesus?" Jasper asked.

"The Antichrist, perhaps, but certainly not Jesus Christ," she said.

"Can you let us out of here?" Tom pleaded. Mary looked at Antonius who was silent up until now.

"Pontius Pilatus has passed judgment. It cannot be undone," he said.

"I understood that!" Jasper said. "I didn't know that was Pontius Pilatus. Can you tell him that we were here to save lives, not for any nefarious reason?"

"You killed Romans?" Antonius asked.

"No, we didn't. We were framed. They made it look like we killed those men. They were dead when we arrived, then the Roman soldiers came out of nowhere and took us prisoner." Tom said with panic in his voice.

"You will be executed tomorrow. There is nothing we can do." Antonius said.

"Can you tell us how we are to die?" Jasper said, tears streaming down his face.

"Crucifixionis."

"What did he say?" Tom asked.

"Crucifixion, like Jesus." Jasper told him. The true horror of what was about to happen struck both men dumb, and they backed into the stone wall and slid slowly down to a sitting position, holding on to each other.

"Explains a lot," Cos said. "Too bad about them. They thought they were doing what was right, now look at them."

"Nothing we can do for them. It does show how evil this Jesus is, doesn't it? Come, we will try to forget what we saw here," Antonius said and gently pushed them toward the outside and the fresh air.

"I wonder if Jesus will be nearby tomorrow to see the men he framed squirming on the cross?" Cos thought out loud.

"You don't want to be there Cos," Mary said.

"You wouldn't recognize him," Antonius said. "None of us really saw what he looked like."

"I would feel his presence," Cos said. "What if we could stop him here before his influence spreads. Wouldn't that be worth it?"

Antonius paused for a moment, then said, "All right, we will do this, we will look for the Antichrist, but I warn you both that seeing the crucifixion of those two men will trouble you for the rest of your lives. I don't want Mary to be there."

Mary put her hand on Cosimus' arm, "I will visit the Temple tomorrow morning. Cos, take the camera with you. Someday I want to show the pictures of this crucifixion to the people who sent Jasper and Tom to their deaths. They should see what their haste and panic brought."

"Is it allowed that you visit the Temple without male accompaniment?"

Antonius asked.

"Some areas will be restricted to me, but I can still see it and get the flavor of it. For a Jewish person, this is a very important moment in time. It is what we dream about and talk endlessly about. All the people who have prayed at the Wailing Wall mourn the loss of the Temple. I have a chance to see it first hand, to touch it, and feel the past come alive."

"You should take the camera with you, Mary. Don't you want pictures of the Temple instead of the horror awaiting those pitiable wretches?"

"Yes, I would, Cos. But if I'm seen with a camera, I will end up on the cross myself. Nothing will happen to two Roman officers, no one will question anything you do."

"Mary is right, Cos. We can't let any suspicions fall on her. She speaks the languages they do and knows everything about their history and their future. I believe that she will be safe in the Temple, and we can meet her at the gate at noon," Antonius said.

"There are thirteen gates," Mary said. "Only one is open to women, the *Shaar HaNashim*, on the north side. I will be on the stairs at noon."

"Anyone hungry?" Cos asked. "And has anyone considered where we will sleep for the next three nights?"

"The solution to both questions is simple, Cosimus," Antonius said. "We are still in the Roman Army. We will dine and sleep with our men until we leave. I have permission from Pontius Pilatus to keep company with Mary while I am in Judea, so there will be no questions, and our men will feed us well."

"Where are our men?" Cosimus asked.

"There is a small grove of olives, just to the east of the city wall. I am certain they will be encamped there. Night is falling soon. I suggest that we find the East Gate and the olive grove." Mary and Cos exchanged glances. They knew that the olive grove was the same place mentioned in the New Testament. The place that Jesus Christ was arrested the night before he died. The famous Mount of Olives.

Antonius caught their exchanged glances, "Something wrong?" he asked.

"No, Antonius. That is a place mentioned in history, but, at the moment, it has no special significance," Cos answered.

The East Gate, south of the Temple, was crowded with people moving in both directions. After they passed through, Antonius pointed to the northeast, and they saw a hill taller than the ancient city. There was smoke curling slowly up from several fires, indicating that Antonius was correct. There was a rather stiff climb up the hill, and by the time they reached the camp, the stars were aloft with the North Star hanging just over the rise of the earth.

"Centurion!" the guard called out. "We thought you had abandoned us for better posting," the man rushed forward to greet each of them.

"Agrippa keeping you men well?" Antonius asked.

"Yes, we have fresh supplies. You are just in time for dinner. We heard that you are now Pilus Prior. It is an honor which you deserve, Centurion." The guard yelled for others to join him in welcoming their own back, and they dropped whatever they were doing and gathered around in a circle.

Agrippa came out of the crowd and wrapped his arms around Antonius. "Welcome back, Centurion. I thought that you would be too good for us now." He extended his hand to Cosimus and bowed to Mary. "All of you, welcome back."

After dinner, Agrippa asked what they all wondered. "When are you leaving, Antonius, and are Cosimus and Mary also going?"

"We were given two days here. We will leave for Caesarea together."

Agrippa thought this over while studying their faces. "I understand that you will be going to Gaul. Have you thought about what will happen to Mary?" he asked.

"You have hit the spike through my heart," Antonius said. "We have not dared talk about this issue."

"I must remind you that Caesarea may not be the ideal place for Mary. She might be better off here with her people."

"Are you offering to take her off of my hands, Agrippa?" Antonius asked. He had stopped eating and was staring at Agrippa.

"Don't pull your sword, Antonius. You know that either Cosimus or I would take care of her if you asked. We would guard her with our lives, even if you were to never return. You know this, do you not?"

"I am sorry, old friend. Of course I know that. I trust you both more than any other. It's just that I don't want to part from her."

"Stop right there, both of you. I am going to Caesarea with you,

Antonius, but I can take care of myself when you leave for Gaul. I don't want anyone to sacrifice their life for mine. That's final," Mary said.

Antonius held up both palms, "No more talk of separation. I refuse to think about it now. We are here together, and that is what is important. Savor the small moments someone should have said."

"By the way, Antonius, the command tent is yours tonight and for as long as you need it. Cosimus and I will sleep elsewhere," Agrippa said.

After Antonius and Mary had left for their tent, Agrippa motioned to Cosimus, "What do you expect them to do?" he asked.

"You brought up the same issues as I did and as Pontius Pilatus did. What they both want is impossible for either of them. Perhaps on our travel to Caesarea, the reality will hit them, and they will be able to face the facts. As you said, Agrippa, you and I will always watch out for her."

"You, Cosimus, are you really going to enlist in the Army?"

"Yes, Agrippa. I feel that this is what I always wanted. To serve under you would be an honor."

"Tell them at headquarters that is what you want. I'm sure I'll be seeing you back here."

"I have had recurrent thoughts about the night I disappeared. Somehow, I know what will happen, but my brain isn't able to part with its secrets yet. I remember a gladius in my hand, so I have begun to accept the fact that I will never go home again. This is my place now."

Chapter 24

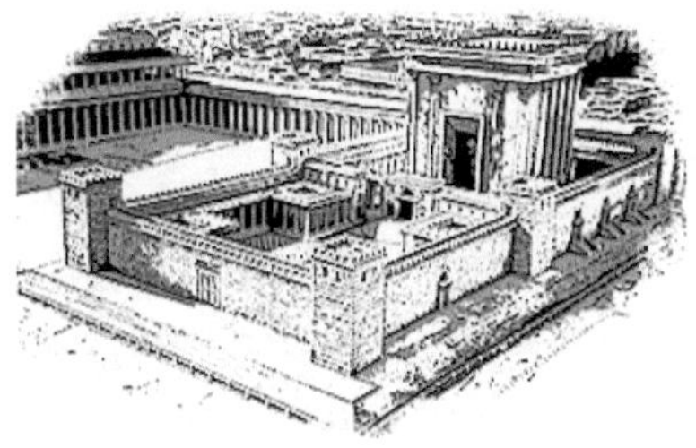

Herod's Temple

Mary awakened feeling fright or apprehension, she couldn't tell
which it was. As she lay there listening to Antonius' breathing, she
thought about coming events. She didn't want to part with Antonius,
because she felt that he and she were meant for each other. She wasn't
sure what he would decide to do, even now. She was sure that he loved
her, but she realized that he had been given an important advancement,
and one that he badly wanted. If he accepted the position, he would leave
the Levant, probably for good. She would have to remain here and either
wait for him to send for her or wait for ten years until he retired. In either
case, she knew that the chance of him being killed in combat was high.
Centurions had the highest rate of casualty in the Roman army. She held
her stomach trying to calm down. She wondered if she could convince
him to return with her and Cos to the future, that is if the Portal was still
functioning. He was frightened, that was all. Afraid of the unknown, of
being useless, of losing his manhood. Then there was Cos, poor
beautiful, wonderful Cos. Something had changed in him. He was quieter
and joked less. He had a hunted look, lean and watchful, tense. She wasn't
even sure that he wanted to go back. She knew that part of his problem
was her, that he was in love with her, loved her just as much as Antonius
did, perhaps more. She saw it in his eyes or when he avoided looking at
her for long. It was painful for him to look at her, painful to watch
Antonius put his arm around her and especially painful for him to see the

love for Antonius in her eyes. Each caring touch she gave Antonius, every murmured softness, seared Cos with pain. He was right when he said that they could never be together as a group, they had to separate. It dawned on her that Cos had decided to stay in this time. If she also remained and Antonius left for Gaul, it would be Cosimus she would rely on, and he would be there for her. If Antonius agreed to return with her to the future, Cos would stay here so that he would not have to watch the woman that he loved be possessed by another man.

In the far distance, a rooster crowed as the first rays of light inevitably entered the dark world, lighting the top of the Temple and spreading a warm glow over sleeping Jerusalem. Mary opened her eyes, realizing that the day had finally arrived. She remembered the gaunt faces of the condemned men who are to die on this day by the most horrible method ever created by humans. She started to cry, softly at first, then the flood of tears opened, and she wept with shaking sobs, folded against the back of Antonius. He rolled over and took her in his arms, pulling her to his chest, stroking her head softly as she tried to fight the reality of life.

"My love," he said softly, "We have each other, does any other thing matter?" After a time, she shook her head. At first he couldn't tell if she meant yes or no. "What is troubling you, Mary?" he asked.

"Everything," she sniffed.

"Does that include this man who loves you above all things?"

"Yes," she murmured.

"It's not possible that I could love you more than I do. Then tell me what else you need from me."

"I don't want to part from you."

"We are not going to part."

"You are going to Gaul, I am not."

"I am going with you through the Portal."

The sobbing slowly stopped, and she raised her head to his. Her lips were puffy and her eyes red, but she was the most beautiful thing he had ever beheld. They kissed the passionate salty kiss of forgiveness and acceptance, separating just enough to again breathe.

"You will give up your career to be with me?" she asked with her face touching his as she spoke, her breath embracing his lips.

"I would die if we separate. I must go with you, even though it frightens me."

"There is nothing for you to fear, and there is much you can do there to be happy and successful. I get to take care of you there," she said and moved her arm up to embrace his neck and allowed herself a small smile.

"Could we return to Rome someday?" he asked.

"It's the first thing we should do. I'd like that." She remembered that Cos might not be there and the thought was painful. "Cos is the one to show you Rome. Together, you would be able to better understand the evolution of the city."

"Has it changed much?" Antonius asked.

"There is a lot still there of what you remember, but of course, it has changed in two thousand years."

"Cos and I will walk with you to the Temple this morning," he offered.

"We don't know a lot about what it was like or even for sure what it looked like. I'm very excited to see it. There will be a historian called Josephus who will write about this era, and it is nearly our only source of information."

"Are you sure you will be allowed in the Temple?"

"I'm not sure of anything. For me, just to be there will be enough."

Antonius cleared his throat and said, "You may be upset to see how women are treated in Judea. We Romans may have a lot to learn, but I do know that Roman women are held in higher regard in Rome than women in Judea."

"Don't worry, Antonius. If I get in trouble, I can always threaten them with you," she giggled.

"Be inconspicuous, Mary. Think small and invisible. I won't be there with you."

The three walked together back to the East Gate, just south of the Temple Mount, with the huge edifice looming above them. Both men were dressed in full battle gear and carried spears, and for the first time, Cosimus wore a plumed helmet. Mary was sandwiched between the two large men, detecting hostile stares from the descendants of Solomon who scrutinized the trio as they made their way around the Temple. It made her feel uncomfortable and apprehensive about what would be said to her after her Roman guards left. They reached the southwest corner and the stairs which climbed toward the vast side of the Temple Mount.

"I need to go in alone," Mary said looking up at the gate high above them. "I will wait for you by the Women's Gate on the north side of the Temple. If we get separated or if there is any problem, I will be here instead." She looked nervous and clutched her cape. "Oh, I almost forgot. Cos, please take the camera and record the deaths of Jasper and Tom for me." Cosimus took the camera from her without words, his face grim with remorse. With so many hostile eyes looking on, they dared not part with kisses or gestures, and Mary turned and started climbing the long flight of stairs, occasionally stealing a glance below. She saw that both men waited, looking up at her until she disappeared into the cavernous spaces of the Temple complex.

A young man was ahead, directing people entering the Temple. He was dressed in a glowing white robe and a full beard dangled against his chest as he talked. After he spoke to each of the male visitors, he pointed the direction they should take. Finally, it was Mary's turn.

The young priest looked her up and down in a contemptuous way. "‏?האם אתה כאן לבד‏" [Are you here unaccompanied?] he asked.

"Yes," she answered in Hebrew. He paused again considering her answer.

"Have you touched a corpse," he asked.

"No."

"Have you bleeding?"

"No," she answered, feeling more uncomfortable.

"You are born of the Tribes of Israel?"

"Yes."

"Where is your *Korban?*" he asked, looking her over again.

"I have no *Korban* with me," she responded.

"You must take *Mikveh* before you may enter. Go that way," he said, pointing down a darkened corridor. The path would lead her to a water immersion bath. Mary hoped that other females were present when the time came. As directed, she proceeded down the hallway and down several sets of stone stairs. She could smell the water before she arrived. Another young priest wordlessly directed her down a smaller set of steps, where she suddenly encountered a large female attendant, glowering at her from under a black robe.

"You are here to take *Mikveh?*" the woman asked. Mary nodded that she was, and the woman pointed to a short set of steps leading to a two-layered narrow pool. "Take off your clothes and take your *Mikveh.* Make sure your entire head is covered, or you risk impurity. Understand?"

Mary looked around nervously but saw no one else other than the burly bath attendant, who was watching her with narrowed eyes. Mary started to ask the woman to turn away but realized the futility of such a request. She noticed that there was no bath towel to dry herself after the immersion.

"Get with it," the woman growled. Mary slipped off her robe and underneath was still the shimmering gold and white silk toga, pinned at the shoulder by an elaborate disk. Before she could take it off, she felt a heavy hand on her shoulder. "That is no proper clothing for a true believer of God. Are you a harlot?" she asked with authority.

"No," Mary said nervously. "I am not a harlot."

"Are you married?" the woman demanded.

"No."

"Do you have sexual intercourse with men?" There was the question. An admission would likely result in stoning rather than an innocent visit to the Temple. Mary didn't need to think about her answer very long.

"Of course not," she answered, faking indignity.

"So, you are a virgin?" the woman continued. Mary hoped that an affirmative answer would not result in a physical examination.

"Most assuredly," Mary answered calmly and quickly. The big woman hesitated and watched Mary's face for any sign of deception.

"Then get on with it. I don't have all day for you," she said and turned her broad back to Mary.

The water was cold and slowly moving. A quick dip over her head, and she came up sputtering, wiping her eyes. Thankfully, the large woman's back was still in view. Mary decided to engage the woman in conversation. "How do I dry myself?" she asked.

"You should have been prepared. Either stand there until you dry or put your clothing on wet. Your choice." She turned her head and appraised the nude Mary from over her shoulder. "You are very attractive. Are you sure there have been no men in your life?" Another suspiciously leading question.

"What are you called?" Mary asked, ignoring her trap.

"I am called Bayla, if you want to know. What is yours?"

"Mary Solomon. I was born in Jerusalem, but it is my first time here."

"What part?" Bayla asked.

"Upper," Mary said, knowing that in this time that was where the wealthy lived. The answer brightened the stone face of Bayla.

"That explains the beautiful clothing. Why have you never been here before?"

"You know that girls are not allowed much freedom where I live, don't you?"

"It's true. So you want to see the Temple now that you are growing up?"

"Yes. Can I see the Temple?"

"Are you going to kill your *Korban*?" she asked.

"I don't want to kill any animal," Mary answered.

"I feel the same. Do this. After you get to the Gentile Court, purchase a small foul and when you enter the Women's Court and have your look around, just let it fly away. Make it look unintentional."

"That is most helpful, Bayla. For your help, may I give you a coin?"

"I would not refuse," she answered, holding out her hand. Mary complied with a copper coin. "For one more, I can get a towel for you," Bayla said. Mary quickly gave up another coin, and just as quickly, a large bath towel was presented to her.

"Since you have not been allowed out on your own, I will give you some free advice, Mary." Bayla looked at her for some sign of interest in what she was about to be told.

"Please. I am hungry for knowledge," Mary said.

"Don't dare talk to any man or boy anywhere near the Temple, and be careful any other place or they will think you are a loose woman. Always cover your hair, everywhere except your home. Don't expect to be welcome at any religious service, here or elsewhere. Being a woman, you will never give your opinion about anything to a man, and in public, you are to walk six paces behind your man." Mary thought about how she looked this morning, walking between her two men instead of behind them. Of course, neither one would have tolerated it. She waited for Bayla to finish her discourse on female social behavior.

Bayla helped Mary on with her clothing as she continued talking. "During the times of your menstrual bleeding, you may not be touched by a man on any part of your body lest he become unclean. You are discouraged about learning to read and write or handle money. Your job is to make your man happy and raise his children. The last and most important thing...don't associate with or talk to Romans. It would not be tolerated."

Mary nodded that she understood, and after she pulled her hood back over her hair, she gave Bayla a much larger coin. "For you, Bayla. May your life be long and happy." Bayla smiled back at her, showing her missing front teeth.

"And you, Mary Solomon."

Mary found her way up the winding stairs and emerged into the bright spaciousness of the Court of the Gentiles. It was paved with large multicolored rectangular stones, and in the center was the Temple, containing, according to legend, the holiest of holies. She remembered previously seeing fragments of the stone pavers in her other life. Along the walls and under the columned porches, there was a cacophony of noise, where trading was taking place, purchases of various animals for sacrifice, money changers trading Roman coins for any other currency, and souvenir purveyors. She saw no other women among the supposed worshipers. She stood in front of the Temple with its white marble Roman columns rising to support a gilded and ornamented roof. In the center, and visible through the open door, was the inner Temple entrance, the one few could enter. Around the perimeter rose a low wall, interposed with short stone columns. All the columns were engraved in four languages to inform readers that all outsiders were excluded. No exceptions. She walked over to a stall selling pigeons and watched as a man paid two copper denarius for a bird.

"Yes?" the vendor inquired, looking her over as if she were a side of lamb.

"I have decided on a pigeon for my *Korban*," she said and offered him two denarius.

"Four denarius for you," he said, looking at her in a hard way.

"I just saw that man give two, and that is what I am willing to pay."

"I could always say that you offered your body to me. It would go badly for you," he sneered.

"If I call the two men who came with me over here, I assure you that it is you who will suffer," Mary said and extended her hand with two coins. The vendor looked furtively from side to side with wide eyes, fearing to see the men who would gladly harm him. He quickly decided to relent and handed her a pigeon imprisoned in a small net bag.

Armed with her sacrifice, she went around to the north side of the Temple, looking for the Women's Gate which lead to the Court of Women in the forward part of the Temple. She could feel male eyes on her as she carefully avoided the many men walking around, finally making her way to the small door. Just as she was about to enter, another priest stepped into the door opening, blocking her entry. This one was not young and not friendly.

"You are about to enter a holy place. Are you pure and clean?" he asked.

"Yes, I have had my *Mikveh* just now."

"This is your *Korban*?" he asked reaching for her bird. She pulled it back close to her chest.

"Am I not to be permitted to perform the sacrifice myself?" she asked.

"Have you your husband with you?" he asked.

"I have no husband."

"A single woman may not have *Korban*. You are ritually unclean. I must perform the *Korban* for you," he said and reached for the bird again.

"Am I not permitted to enter the Court of Women?" she asked.

"Only to wait on the *Korban*," he said with irritation.

"Let me enter, and then I will give you my *Korban*." He stood blocking her way, trying to think of another reason that he couldn't let her in. She stood impassively, defiantly waiting for his decision, but finally he stood aside, and she found herself standing in the front court of the Temple which soared above her, gleaming in the sunlight. The bronze Nicanor Gate was closed, blocking her view of the Temple. She wondered if the so-called Beautiful Gate was the one on the front of the Temple, for the moment out of sight. She saw the priest approaching, expecting her to relinquish her offering of sacrifice so she tore at the small net enclosing the live bird, sending it speeding into the blue sky, escaping death for now.

"Well, you are done here, are you not?" he said with disdain, pointing at the Women's Gate. She lingered for a moment, looking around, wishing she had a hidden camera. Reluctantly and slowly, she exited the Court of Women and left the Temple, going back down the stairs. She sat down on the lowest step, intending on waiting for Cos and Antonius.

"You can't loiter there," shouted the senior priest standing in the Gate and waving his hand for her to move away. She got up and walked around the Temple, determined to soak up as much of the atmosphere as she could. Standing in the center of the court, she studied the structures and the people. It was grand, better than she could imagine...yet...she resisted feeling negative, but there it was inside of her. Disappointment. Disillusionment. This circus of animal slaughter, profiteers, and artificial rules and customs finally came clearly to her. Jesus will be right, the entire system is corrupt. There was nothing wrong with their strong belief in a single god, and it was also right to honor their troubled and celebrated past, but like nearly every other human endeavor, the elite get rich at the expense of the poor, and they make rules to keep themselves elite. Seeing them use an ancient religion to do it was disgusting. A racket based on religion is like no other, because devotion is used to hide the truth of corruption and special privilege. She knew it will also happen to the Catholics and many other religious groups. There was no difference, really, between any of them.

She became aware of being noticed. Being the only woman in sight and standing in plain view, many were looking at her as she remembered Antonius' advice about being inconspicuous. She wasn't. Slowly, she walked away from the center of the court, but as she neared the congested sides, she gained proximity to the men watching her. The experience of the Temple was rapidly turning sour, and she decided to leave by the closest exit gate available. There were no signs, no obvious path leading to the outside. She would have to mingle with the men and stumble into one. Her pulse and breathing were accelerating with the stress she felt, and her temporal vessels were pounding. Suddenly, she became afraid, as if she could hear the thoughts and intentions of all the bearded men in sight, even though not a word had been spoken to her.

"You!" a commanding voice called, causing everyone to turn and look. "You, woman!" he called, singling her out. She saw the priest coming toward her using a fast pace, his walking stick thumping on the hard stone. The scowl on his face told her that she had done something wrong, whatever it was she couldn't imagine.

"Why are you here?" he demanded, hovering over her in his raven black garments.

"To worship God, isn't that why everyone comes to the Temple?" she asked.

"Have you been cleansed, are you pure?" he asked and thumped his stick. She was aware that a hundred male faces were listening and watching.

"Yes."

"Did you perform your *Korbanot?*" Again the stick thumped for emphasis.

"Yes, as best I could," she answered, trying not to sound flippant.

"The answer is either a 'yes' or 'no.' You have not answered." The stick thumped loudly.

"My *Korban* flew away and is grateful to still be alive." She couldn't resist tweaking him just a little. It was a mistake, however, because his face darkened.

"Are you unaccompanied?" he demanded with a thump.

"I am waiting for my men. They will be here shortly," Mary answered. The priest paused, looking hard at her as if deciding her fate, while from somewhere above, a sheep or goat's bleat was cut short by a sharp knife to its throat, causing the live ones to answer with an excited chorus. That same moment, she became aware of a thousand pigeons' soft coos, coming in little waves like crickets of the night. Along with her, they, too, awaited their fate.

"Remove yourself from the Temple and this court at once. You will not be warned again." The stick thumped twice, signaling the end of the conversation. He waited, hovering like a bird of death, as she silently turned and headed toward the outside wall, spotting the gate as men silently parted for her.

Outside, the air was fresh, and the sunlight streamed over her upturned face, cleansing it and restoring her mind. The smell of animals and people inside had become claustrophobic, unbearable, especially when she knew that every animal in there was slated to die in sacrifice. The platform above the steep staircase provided an excellent view of Jerusalem, and she paused for a moment to burn it into her mind. To the left was the low lying area of slums that the poor inhabited. The rise of the earth toward the right was topped by the expansive settlement of the Heights, the home of the privileged and wealthy. Just ahead was the spire of the Tomb of David and beyond rose the three towers standing guard over the West Wall. The shorter one was the Tower of Miriamne where Jasper and Tom had been held the previous night. She could just make out smaller walls enclosing Herod's Palace. She looked down, hoping her two brave Roman soldiers were waiting for her. They were not, but several darkly robed and bearded men below were pointing up at her. It looked as though her peril was just beginning.

Chapter 25

Zealots

"Move along," a deep voice commanded from behind Mary. She turned to see two large hooded men standing just behind her. Rather than risk their wrath, she immediately started moving down the long staircase toward the men waiting for her at the bottom. Footsteps behind followed her as they descended the stairs. After reaching the rough stone and gravel of the street, she looked anxiously around in hope of seeing either Cos or Antonius but instead saw several men advancing toward her. She felt her mouth go dry and her heart accelerating. Her mind raced, trying to discover what had caused her dilemma. In her mind, she saw herself arm in arm with two Roman soldiers who were obviously being solicitous of her. Antonius had warned that her people hated the Roman occupiers. She expected to encounter a volley of stones at any time and looked around desperate to find a way out.

"My dear child," she said in a motherly tone, wrapping her robe-draped arm over Mary's shoulder. "You come with me, my dear. It looks like you need a friend just now." Mary jumped with surprise at the woman's touch but then felt comforted by her soothing voice and her protective arm. Her face was older and wrinkled, but her eyes were soft and loving. "Now, what is your name, my child?" she asked.

"Mary Solomon. Are you to be in danger from helping me?"

"No!" she laughed. "I have two strong sons who protect me. They are watching out for us right now. We have nothing to fear." She started urging Mary to move forward by the pressure of her arm, and they walked slowly away from men gathering in the street. Mary looked around for the woman's two sons and had no problem identifying them. Two muscular men, bare from the waist up except for a wide goatskin belt over one shoulder, walked parallel to them, defying the other men with their body language. Both had long curved daggers at their waist, a loosely tied cloth around their heads. Mary saw that they were feared by the crowd who backed away. She heard the word, "*Sicarii*," murmured several times. She tried to remember the word, a powerful one, which struck a chord somewhere in her head.

They turned onto a small side street, and Mary heard two men walking behind them, making little noise. "I am Beth, Mary," the woman said and stopped walking suddenly. Her sons came to them, towering over Mary, making her catch her breath. There was something about their faces that seemed familiar, then abruptly, she remembered the word, *Sicarii*. It meant killer or dagger men. Their faces were like some of the hardened Roman soldiers she had been traveling with. Men who had been in combat many times and had killed often, their faces reflecting their past and their future.

"This is Benjamin and David," she said, pointing to each of them. They both smiled at her and seemed to relax when she smiled back. "Did you just come from the Temple?" Beth asked, likely knowing the answer.

"Yes, my first trip inside."

"And tell me about your experience. Did it challenge your faith even a little?" Beth asked. Mary was unsure of the purpose of the question, feeling trapped by what she wanted to say, her real thoughts. "Now, don't be afraid," Beth said and patted her shoulder. "I'm sure I have the same feelings as you do. Just to put you at ease, we are part of a group who dislike what is going on in the Temple."

Mary studied their faces but couldn't detect any trace of insincerity. They appeared to be secure in their views and straightforward in their manner. "I enjoyed seeing it. The spectacle of it...but I wasn't treated fairly, because I am only a woman. The killing of animals to worship God seems wrong to me. The priests, I have heard, live well, yet they demand tribute from all who enter. My faith in God is unshaken, but I was disheartened to see how our faith has become a business."

"You are one of us, Mary," Ben said. "We want to rid the land of the parasites who prey on us, both the Roman occupiers and corrupt priests. There is no other solution but to kill them one at a time." Mary felt her eyes widen, and she suddenly became afraid. Had they seen her with

Romans and were playing her along. This would be a good spot to kill her if they wanted to.

"How does your group view women?" Mary asked, looking between Ben and his brother.

"Anyone who thinks or says that our mother is not any man's equal will find his throat cut," David said and grasped the hilt of his knife.

"As you can see, they both can be violent; unfortunately, that is what is required to make change," Beth said.

"Thank you for rescuing me. I thought my life was in danger," Mary said.

"It was. And it still is. You can't go back there without an escort," David said.

"My child, what did you do to provoke them?" Beth asked.

"I didn't do anything. I only spoke to the priests and to one vendor to purchase my *Korban*...a small pigeon."

"Did you kill your *Korban?*" Ben asked, surprised.

"No, I let it go in the Women's Court. It was the only way I could get inside to see the Temple." The three laughed at her story, and she was relieved to see that they apparently felt just as she did.

"Then, perhaps they all saw that you were insincere. Intentionally letting your bird go was an insult to God, the way they would view it," Beth explained.

"Do your people hate the Romans?" Mary asked

"Most of all," they all said. A problem, she realized. How was she to make contact with Cos and Antonius?

"You do know that if you kill a Roman, more will come. They have a vast army, three Legions, in Syria. They would flood Judea with men bent on vengeance," Mary said.

"No matter. We would rather die than remain occupied," David said.

Mary thought about the consequences of telling them the truth, but she had little alternative except to be frank. "Listen carefully, my new friends, because I have to tell you some truths about me." They watched her carefully, somewhat taken aback by some new revelation yet to come.

"I was trying to wait for my two friends when you saved me. They will arrive shortly and will wonder what happened to me."

"Then one of my boys will meet them and bring them to us," Beth said and patted Mary's shoulder.

"You don't understand. They are Roman officers," she blurted.

"We mean you no harm, Mary, but you have to explain to us why you know the enemy, our enemy," David said, no longer smiling.

"I promise you that these men are not your enemy and especially not mine. They both would protect me with their lives, and they are the finest men I have ever known," she said, then continued. "Look, they dislike the powerful priests just as much as you do. They mean you no harm. They are just soldiers and do as they are commanded to do. You must believe me. I think you would have much in common, even grow to like each other, if you give them a chance."

The looks between the three said a lot. They didn't like what Mary was telling them. To consort with Romans was an unforgivable travesty, especially for a woman to do so. Mary began to wonder if she had traded the frying pan for the fire.

"How do you know these men?" Beth asked.

"I was hired as a translator, because I speak Aramaic, the common language that you use, and Hebrew. We were sent to find someone. The Romans, I spoke of, speak other languages as well."

"So you have been traveling with them?" Ben asked.

"Yes, I have. They treat me with the upmost respect, as do their men."

"Their men? You mean you have been with a whole Roman troop?" David asked.

"Yes, eighty men. They all treat me with respect. Far more than I received in the Temple of my own faith."

The three withdrew from her and huddled together in conversation. When they returned, Beth said, "I have convinced my sons to do as you ask. If your men are as you say, then no harm will come to any of you. We shall see. Now tell David their names, and he will wait for them beside the Temple."

Mary wasn't sure if she was being duped into forming a trap for Cos and Antonius but decided to trust them. "Cosimus and Antonius. They both are officers and wear the tufted helmet. Be warned that they will be suspicious. Make no gestures of ill will toward them, because they will be quick to respond."

"It will be done," Beth said, "Now come with us." She put her arm around Mary and guided her forward, following the road as it went uphill.

They walked in silence for a while, seeming to head toward the area of wealthy homes. "Are your people called Zealots?" Mary asked. Beth shook her head and smiled.

"So you have heard that word. Some do, I must admit. There are many of us, scattered about from here to the sea. Most often they whisper *Sicarii* because of the long knives the men carry and the kills we make in the night. We are people who fight from inside and call ourselves the Fourth Sect. We seek to overthrow those in power, but we also don't like the Roman occupation. Someday, we will lead Israel to revolt and kick the Romans out of the country. Someday."

"What if your revolt leads to the destruction of the country that you love, the deaths of most of its people, and even destruction of the Temple of Solomon?" Mary asked.

"That will never happen," said Ben. "The might of our God is with us. We cannot fail. God rode with Joshua, and he will ride with us."

"My impression is that the Romans don't care much about religion or your beliefs, as long as there is no conflict. They will react harshly if attacked. What if you could make peace with them as has the Herodians? Make them help you toss out the wicked by being their friends."

"We want to restore Israel to its former glory. There is no room for Romans in our plan," David said.

"Do you have knowledge, Mary, that we do not?" Beth asked.

"I know that the Romans are too powerful to resist by arms. They view this area as critical and will never let it go. Resistance will bring destruction of everything you love."

"Are you on their side or ours?" Ben asked.

"I am Israeli, born in Jerusalem, and I resent the question," Mary said.

"You would agree that our people are oppressed? she asked.

"You mean as I was oppressed in the Temple by the Levite guards?"

"That and more," Beth answered. "You understand that the Sadducees control the Temple and are the ones who advocate the cult of sacrifice that you abhor. They are powerful and wealthy, and it is they who collect the Temple tax from the people. We Zealots seek to depose them and distribute their ill-gained wealth back to the people. We despise the Romans just as much, and they need to be driven from our land. Don't think that it cannot be done. Remember the Maccabees who won against the Seleucids."

"Yes, I remember that history. The Maccabees would not have won except for Roman attacks on the Seleucids at the same time. It was in Rome's interest to let us win so that later they could install Herod as their puppet. This time, they cannot be driven from what they now call Ludaea."

Beth could see that her new young friend had an impressive knowledge, far beyond what she would have expected. "Mary dear, are you literate? Do you read as well as write?"

"Yes, Beth. I can read and write in several languages, including Hebrew."

"How came you by this knowledge? Most women are never schooled, and yet, here you are seeming to know as much as any man, and more than my two brave, but backward, boys."

"My father saw to my education," Mary answered, not wanting to elaborate. The walk ended at the gate of an impressive private residence where Mary and Ben waited while Beth disappeared inside. They looked at each other with interest but were silent, having no commonality for conversation. Mary remembered that it will be the Zealots who initiate rebellion against Rome and are generally held responsible for the complete destruction of Jerusalem and the Temple by the armies of Titus. Later, they made their last stand at Masada, where they committed mass suicide. She was always taught that the Zealots and the *Sicarii* were criminals and savage killers, both groups having killed many of her people. Her brow wrinkled as she imagined her two Roman officers meeting David, wishing that she could get away before there was the inevitable violence between them. At last, Beth came out alone and walked calmly toward the gate. She made eye contact with Ben, and he acknowledged her with a nod. Without a word, Ben headed into the dwelling as Beth urged Mary to walk away with her, back down the hill.

"What is happening? Why did Ben go in there?" Mary asked.

"There is much you don't need to know, dear Mary. Keep walking, and we may find David and your two men," she smiled, giving Mary her motherly and loving smile. Mary knew that something bad was happening back in the home, but there was nothing she could do. If there was a crime being committed, there was no one to tell, and even if she did, she might implicate herself. She didn't want a close examination of who she was, it would go badly for her and likely for both Cos and Antonius.

After they were nearly back to the Temple area, Mary saw two Romans in armor heading toward her with David leading. At last they were back and were unharmed. She breathed a sigh of relief, and her eyes clouded with tears.

"Ah, this must be your men now!" Beth said and put her arm over Mary. "Is something wrong, child? I see no need for tears; you are safe now."

"I must know, Beth. What did Ben do back there?"

"You won't like what you hear. Better not to know, my dear." She smiled her warm smile again, almost making Mary believe that things were not as bad as she feared. David held his fist in the air as the groups closed the distance. None of the men were smiling, and Mary could feel the tenseness hovering in the air like a cloud that moved with them.

"Mary, we were worried about you," Antonius said and took her hand in his.

"I can see that there is more than friendship here, Mary," Beth observed. David moved to the rear of his mother, watching the two Romans with narrowed eyes.

"Who are these people to you, Mary," Cosimus asked.

"They saved me from harm and have treated me kindly. This one is Beth and that is her son, David. Without their intervention, I'm very sure I wouldn't be here right now. I was hoping that we could all end up on friendly terms."

"Why Mary," Beth said in her motherly way. "We cannot possibly be friends with Roman soldiers. A word of advice for you, my child. You are committing the worst offense possible as far as your people are concerned. Some would harm you because of what I see before me."

Antonius pulled Mary slowly behind him and squared off. "I thank you deeply for keeping her safe. It is a debt I owe you, and I will honor any request that you make of me. I do not want to be your enemy, here or at any other time. My name is Antonius, and this man beside me is Cosimus. We are leaving Judea shortly, and we bear you no ill will. A friend of Mary's is a friend of ours."

David gently pushed his mother aside and stepped forward. "You Romans have no business in Jerusalem or Judea. You oppress our people, and you appoint your own puppets to govern. We want our homeland back. Can you grant that request?"

"No, David, I cannot. I have served with the Roman army in Gaulia and Hispania. I saw Rome build cities there and improve the lot of poor people. They have laws, roads, baths, and trade; they are happy now and part of the Roman people. The same can be done here. Remember all the conquests that have been made of this land by various groups from the east or west? As long as Rome rules here, that will never again happen. Things will get better. Fix your own house before you want to tear down ours."

"We are fixing our own house," said Ben, who appeared behind his brother. There was no need for additional conversation between the groups, no possibility of good will or reconciliation, no hope of peace.

Cosimus attempted to shake hands with Ben, offering his hand, but Antonius pushed his arm downward and said, "We are done here, Cosimus." They slowly backed away keeping the two *Sicarii* men in sight.

"Better keep a close eye on your woman, Roman," David said, laughing as he watched them turn away without comment.

After they were out of sight, Cosimus asked Mary, "Who were those people?"

"*Sicarii*," said Antonius, answering for her. "Good thing for them that they rescued Mary, or I would have killed all three. They are the scum of Judea, killers, thugs and terrorists."

"You knew?" Mary asked. "That's just what they told me, and I think that Ben may have killed someone up the hill from here."

"That explains why they rescued you," Antonius said. "They are smart enough to use you to buy favor from us. We just happened to be there like a tool you find in the road. That last comment was meant to give us warning, Mary. They will kill you if they get the chance. Their technique is usually to stab their victim in a crowd and then disappear quickly."

"Mary, if you have seen enough of Jerusalem, we should consider leaving here as soon as possible," Cos said, looking very tired.

"Did you witness the executions, Cos?" she asked, looking at him with concern.

"Horrible, very horrible. They are both still alive up there, hanging from the cross, waiting and hoping to die." He choked on his words, and his lip trembled softly.

"He didn't see Jesus, or sense his presence, nor did we meet any of his fanatics. Jesus seems to have vanished, taking his influence with him," Antonius said.

Chapter 26

Leaving Jerusalem

Antonius realized that he didn't have to get up at dawn any longer. The men belonged to Agrippa now, and Antonius could hear him shouting orders, somewhere in the camp. He lay there with Mary beside him, feeling for the first time a sense of peace enveloping him. Responsibility was removed from his shoulders, and he could look forward to a better future than he could have ever imagined before. He realized that he was happy, satisfied, his mind clear.

The tent flap opened and Agrippa motioned to him to get up. He rose carefully, letting Mary sleep in peace, gathered his clothing and quietly left the tent.

"Problem, Antonius," Agrippa said with a grim look. Antonius continued to fasten his armor in place without answering. "There was a killing yesterday of a high priest of the Temple. They are looking for a woman who was seen in the area about that time and who left with three known *Sicarii*. They are asking us to take part in the hunt. Sounds like Mary to me."

"I know it does, because it is Mary. She was there and met the *Sicarii* as did Cosimus and I. They used her. She committed no crime. They staged the whole thing, knowing she would be sought."

"What do you want to do?" Agrippa asked.

"I am certainly not willing to turn her over to the Temple guards. We were leaving soon anyway."

"You will need a mounted guard to ride with you, especially now."

"Yes, for many reasons. The distance to Caesarea means that we will need to camp along the way. We'll need some pack horses and equipment as well. Under no circumstances are we to admit that Mary was involved, and I ask that you forbid anyone from the Temple to visit this camp."

"Of course. Will you be leaving today?"

"As soon as possible," Antonius said. "How is Cosimus this morning?"

"He is already sparring with the men, but something about him is different. Brutal would be the right word for how he acts, as if he is fighting for his life."

"Something wrong?" Mary asked from behind them. The both turned to see her and were met by her radiant smile.

"You are sought in connection with the death of a Temple priest," Agrippa said.

Mary looked stunned and held her hand to her mouth. "It was Ben. I thought he might have killed someone," she said.

"Yes, you said so at the time," Antonius remarked.

"Agrippa, I could not even kill my little pigeon yesterday. Surely they couldn't think that I killed a man?"

"We all know that you didn't kill anyone, Mary, but the Temple guards want to get their hands on you. They seem to think that you did," Agrippa said.

"Gather your things, Mary. I will find Cosimus and tell him what is happening," Antonius said. He walked slowly through the camp, looking at life from a different perspective. To his left was Jerusalem, surrounded by its stone walls, a barrier to the many armies who had come this way and will come again. So much killing, he thought, and for what? There was little of actual value here except as a trade route connecting Egypt to Syria and beyond. The whole area seethes with religion, boils with it, and from what Cos and Mary had told him, will continue to boil and simmer far into the future. The soft dirt under his feet was a rest from the hard stone pavement in the city, a grove of olive trees ascending the hill to his right softened the air with fragrance. This was a nice place to camp, he thought, away from the city, its noise, stench, and religious fervor.

"Centurion!" the soldier shouted, running toward him holding up a small scroll. Antonius stopped, waiting for the man to come to him. "I have an order for you from the Prefect," he said, handing Antonius the scroll. The document bore the seal of the Prefect but was written by his scribe. It directed Antonius to come to the Palace immediately. After dismissing the messenger, Antonius continued to search for Cosimus by simply following the hollow sound of wood striking wood. In a clearing, Cosimus was in the center of a circle of men who were chanting and calling out his name. He was in armor and faced a burly opponent as they circled each other waiting for an opening. This was not the same Cosimus whom they found hiding behind a rock. He was confident, strong and wily, eager for the chance at combat. In a split second, the two men closed the distance, and suddenly Cosimus was the only one standing. It happened too fast to tell where the blows fell. Impressive, thought Antonius. This victory was by no trick or accident. The men in the circle rushed in and lifted Cosimus above their heads, carrying him around in a victory celebration. He spotted Antonius approaching and instructed the men to let him down.

"Good work, Cosimus. You have become the warrior I knew resided in you," Antonius said and rested his hand on his shoulder. Someone threw Cosimus a towel, and he took off his helmet and wiped his face.

"Some problem, I surmise, Antonius?" he asked. Antonius led him away from the men before speaking.

"We have to leave soon. Can you be ready to travel shortly?"

"I can, but why?"

"Mary is accused of murder. So far, I don't believe that they know whom they seek, but sooner or later they will find her. I have just been summoned by Pontius Pilatus, so I assume that he suspects her. If she is to be arrested, I will get word to you so that you both can get away from here as fast as possible. Head north, and I will find you when I am free."

"Count on this—no one will take her while I am alive." There was no doubt that he meant what he said. Antonius paused to look at this Roman whom he had created. He was no longer a frightened, inexperienced historian, but a man who would conduct himself with honor and courage, no matter what came at him. Mary may have chosen the wrong man to love, he reflected, but he was grateful that she had chosen him. Antonius knew that if something happened to him, Mary would be in good hands. They embraced in a manly way, without words, and none were needed.

Antonius' hobnails clicked on the polished marble as he made his way to the office of Pontius Pilatus. Two guards snapped open the doors as he arrived, and he could see that the Prefect was waiting for him.

"Centurion, are you aware that there was a murder of a priest in his home yesterday?"

"I heard just this morning, Prefect."

"The city is like a hornet's nest. They search for a small woman who was seen at the Temple just before the killing."

"I noticed the clamor as I came in, Prefect."

"You know why you are here. Your woman…is she whom they seek?"

"Yes, Prefect, I believe that she is. She has committed no crime; I give my word to you."

"Of course she didn't," Pilatus said. "This was clearly the work of the *Sicarii*, very typical of how they kill. Our problem is that there is no reason or deliberation coming from the Temple. There never is. They make demands on me and to keep the peace, I often have to give in to them." He looked at Antonius while rubbing his chin, deciding on the fate of not only Mary but his finest officer. He understood that the two could not easily be separated, even by force.

Antonius spoke up, sensing the Prefect's dilemma, "I saw the *Sicarii*. There are three of them, two young toughs and a mellow older woman. They pretended to save Mary from a mob after she came from the Temple Mount. At the time, I spared their lives to thank them for helping Mary, but I had no idea that they had murdered."

"I know you speak the truth, you always do. The facts and truth don't matter here. Not a bit. They will take your beautiful love apart if they can find her, and short of starting a war, we won't be able to stop them. You must take her away from here, far away, and quickly."

"Yes, Prefect, it is the only way."

"You must make haste to Caesarea. You will be safe there." He clapped his hands together, and the door burst open instantly, admitting two capable soldiers holding long spears. "Take my Centurion to the stables. He is to be supplied three fresh mounts and ten of our best men who will accompany him on horseback. Requisition all the supplies the party will need for an extended ride. This will happen very quickly, or you will answer to me. Is that clear?" The two men nodded enthusiastically that they understood and seemed anxious to carry out the order. Pilatus got up and embraced Antonius. "We will never again meet in this life,

Centurion. I hope the Gods treat you well in Gaul or wherever they send you next."

"And you, Prefect. A soldier could never have a better commander."

"Tell Mary for me that I am trying to live up to her expectations," Pilatus said and smiled.

Cos stood with Mary beside the command tent, their possessions tied in tight bundles behind them. They squinted in the morning sunlight, trying to watch the three visible gates of Jerusalem in case there was any movement toward the camp.

"Mary, you had a bad experience at the Temple, didn't you?" Cos asked.

"Don't think that, Cos. Being Jewish, it was one of the most meaningful things that ever happened to me. The Temple is important to our culture and religion. This is the site of the first Temple built by King David's son, Solomon. The first is thought to have been of wood and was lost during an invasion by Babylonian king, Nebuchadnezzar. The Temple had been raided and plundered many times before that by Egyptians and about every other regional power. It was rebuilt and plundered again throughout history. The one we see today was built by Herod, and it is the one which will be destroyed by Romans at the end of the revolt. In our time, Jews only have a small bit of the western retaining wall of the Temple Mount to worship at, because the Temple was totally lost. All Jews dream of the day that the Temple will be rebuilt."

"It is a beautiful, imposing structure," Cos said while looking toward the east wall of the Temple Mount.

"The rest of what you said is correct. They don't treat women very well right now and seemed to resent my being there, especially without a male escort. Ritual killing of animals, especially on the scale practiced in there, appalls me. Nothing I have experienced, however, shakes my faith or my belief in my Jewish heritage. I am Israeli, every bit of me."

Through the gate, just north of the Temple, came a group of horsemen riding fast. They were clearly Roman and wearing armor which glinted in the sunlight.

"I hope they are not coming for us, because we could never get away. Just stand still, and let's see what happens," Cos said calmly. Mary experienced a profound fear of what might happen and edged closer to Cos. He felt her trembling and looked down at her, the old repressed feeling coming back strongly.

"I have seen the future, Mary. Nothing but good is going to happen to you or Antonius. You need not be afraid."

"And you, Cos?"

"That is not so clear."

"You saw this in your dreams?"

"Not dreams. Something else I don't completely understand yet."

The riders grew closer as they came up the hill, dust billowing behind them, the lead rider wearing the plumed helmet of a Centurion.

"It's Antonius, Mary," Cos said. The riders pulled to an abrupt halt, and Antonius jumped off and rushed toward Mary and Cos.

"The whole town is being turned upside down searching for you, Mary. Pilatus has granted us an escort, and we must leave now." Antonius picked her up and twirled her around, relieved that the decision had been made so quickly and with no other options.

"Where are we going?" Cos asked.

"To your Portal!" Antonius answered and put Mary down. "Aren't you anxious to return to your time?"

"I have grown to like it here. There is not much back there for me. I have no family left to return to, and no one will miss me," Cos answered.

"That can't be the reason. It's the visions you had; they still tear at you."

"Partly. I have a destiny, but I can't grasp it yet."

In the distance, there was a faint sound of human voices rising in anger, which made them turn and look toward the gates. A mob was headed their way out of the Golden Gate at the base of the Temple. It kept pouring out in a continuous stream, like a gigantic snake, heading toward the olive groves.

"Mount up," Antonius shouted. He pulled Mary up behind him as Cos tied their belongings to the spare horse. The party eased out of camp, heading west, with a last wave at Agrippa, who was busily deploying his men toward the oncoming mass.

Chapter 27

Search For The Portal

The trail led due north, into the mountains and the wilderness of Samaria, a path chosen by few other than bandits and rarely by Romans. This was the shortest route to Nazat but not, by far, the easiest. Water was in short supply, and the journey required that they stop frequently to rest and seek sources of fresh water. In the distance rose the famed Mt. Gerizim, hovering low on the horizon to the right.

"Do you know this place, Mary?" Antonius asked.

"Yes, rather well, and I know the history. There is much ill will between my people and the Samaritans. Their holy place at the foot of Mt. Gerizim was destroyed by my ancestors about two hundred years ago, and a schism was created which will never be bridged. There is a source of fresh water at the base of the mountain, so we must go there. There are both Samaritans and remnants of other tribes of Samaria around us and, I suspect, many bandits."

"We are in what is called the West Bank in our time, is that right?" asked Cos.

"Yes, controlled by the Palestinians. They are not fond of Israeli archeologists. I have previously traveled in this area with the same apprehension that I feel right now."

"You have nothing to fear," Antonius said. "These men with us are superb fighters. None but true fanatics will take us on."

Cos looked around at the men with them who rode in silence and without complaint. "Antonius, have you considered what to do with these men if we enter the Portal? We have to tell them something."

"First, we have to find the Portal and see if it opens. It has been a long time since we were there, much could have changed," Mary answered instead.

"They promised us six months," Cos recalled. He realized at the time the promise was made there was always the chance of not returning. Mary was right, many things could have happened. There was his vision, though. He was certain that they would see the Portal again. They had to.

The first sight of settlements and people came as night was falling, the trail becoming harder to see. There was no expression of welcome, and likely most of these people had not seen Roman soldiers previously. The group was given a wide birth, most of the watchers seeming harmless enough, until everything came to a sudden stop. Mary could hear swords being withdrawn all around her, the scrape of hard metal and the low ring of hardened steel. Ahead in the path stood a large group of men dressed in dark cloth.

Both groups watched each other warily, for any sudden movement would likely set off a frenzy of bloodshed. Finally, one of the men stepped forward and put his hand up.

"What do you want in this holy place?" the man asked.

"Nothing but water. We are passing through and will be gone at first light," Antonius responded.

At first there was silence, then the murmur of discussion, then deathly quiet.

"We have no quarrel with Romans. You may continue through without harm. Follow this man who will show you where to find water and a place suitable to sleep."

"One question before we leave," Antonius said. "Have you heard the name Jesus?"

"Truly, I have heard of men called Jesus. Is he a person whom you seek?"

"No, we do not seek him. Thank you for your kindness," Antonius said. "May we do anything for you?"

"Be gone at first light."

They were shown a small grove of trees nestled against the base of the mountain, sustained by a constant source of water nearby. It was an excellent place to camp, and soon the men had a bright fire burning and their tents standing in a neat row. To the rear of camp was the ascending mountain, a small stream of water flowed on the left, rippling over rocks. The smell of roasting bread filled the camp, and the men settled in to eat.

"Sto!" one of the guards called, and the men stopped eating and listened. "Centurion!" he shouted, and Antonius grabbed his sword and ran toward his voice. There was a man, barely perceptible in the dark, standing close to the guard whose armor reflected the firelight. The guard had his long spear pointed toward the stranger's chest.

"What is it that you wish?" Antonius asked.

"A word, Roman."

"Speak, I am listening," Antonius said and tried to look beyond the man for any threats. He could hear his men gathering their weapons and the snort of agitated horses behind them.

"We saw a woman with you. Do you admit this?"

"We don't allow anyone to ask what we do, it doesn't concern you."

"I have need of a woman. My wife is in childbirth, and there is no woman to help. Will you permit your woman to help?"

Antonius was taken aback for a moment, then said, "Wait here, do not move." He hurried back to the tent where Mary was waiting for him. "Have you ever assisted with a birth?" he asked, breathless.

"No, but I have an idea of what happens. Who is having a baby, causing you to ask that?"

"A man came to the camp asking for a woman to help his wife."

Mary got up quickly and then looked around. "We have no tools, no clean cloths, no light. Agrippa would know what to do." She moaned in distress looking around anxiously. "I might need some help," she said.

"They will never let a strange man close to this woman. You are all she has. Can you help?"

"I will try. Will you be close by?"

"I will be as near as possible. Anything you need?"

"I need some twine or string and a small sharp knife. Clean cloths, if there are any. Is there any wine in camp?"

"You can tear a piece of my cape off for string and use the rest of it for your cloth. Here is a small sharp knife, but we have no wine," he said. "Cosimus!" he shouted. "Have one of the men make a torch and hurry."

Mary took his cape, tore off a long strand of fabric, and put his knife into her waist band. "Let's go," she said.

Antonius called for three men to accompany them, and each carried a torch. The stranger led the way, moving quickly forward down a dark, wooded path, eventually leading to a small mud brick hut where a small candlelight shone from inside. The husband stood outside and pointed into the hut, his lip trembling slightly as he did so. The Romans held their torches high to look around for threats but saw only a few goats tethered to a post.

"Give me a torch, and ask him to find some wine," Mary said.

Antonius relayed the message to the husband, and they conversed for a moment. "He wants to know if you are going to drink the wine before you help her?" Antonius said loud enough for Mary to hear.

"No! It is to cleanse my hands. Get the wine!" she barked. Antonius relayed what she said, and the man shrugged and trotted away into the night. They could hear the woman moaning, and her cries seemed to come in waves. "Someone bring water, please, lots of it," she said, stress in her voice. The cry of pain came back again, this time stronger and more demanding. The men outside the hut shifted position, becoming distressed by her cries, unable to do anything to help.

The cry became a chilling shriek, but during lulls they could hear Mary's soft, comforting voice. The men looked at each other trying to determine if their comrades felt the same unmasculine sympathy that they did. At last, the husband returned with a goat-skinned wine flask and tossed it to Antonius.

"Your wine and water have arrived, Mary," he called. Momentarily, she rushed out, grabbed the wine and water and disappeared back inside, just in time for another penetrating cry of anguish from the woman in labor. The cries became nearly continuous, then abruptly stopped. All the men looked at each other for some signal to do something, but since no instructions were given, they remained helpless, feeling not much different or useful than the goats. The crickets chirped their continuous, uncaring song as if nothing in the world ever changed.

A baby's voice rang out, and the men erupted in cheers. The new father was cornered and received vigorous backslapping and congratulations. When the shouting died down, they could hear two women's voices coming from inside the hut. Antonius invited the father to enter his hut, giving him one last pat on the shoulder.

Mary emerged, wiping her bloody hands on what was left of Antonius' red cape. "Sorry about your cape, but it is being put to good use." She smiled wanly up at him and then leaned into his chest as he folded his arms around her.

"Thank you, Mary, for helping this woman. This is something that no one else could do."

"I thank God that He let me be here to help. What a wonderful thing to do, help bring a new life into this world. It was the most wonderful experience for me. Something you should know, Antonius, that occurred to me while it was happening. Someday, if my turn comes, you have to be there with me. You must do what I just did."

"I am no physician. I could do nothing for you," he stammered.

"You could comfort me and see your child born. It is something I would expect of you."

"If that is what you desire, then I will be there," he said. He decided to poke his head into the hut to see if there was anything else they could do. The woman lay on soiled rags which scantly covered the packed dirt floor holding her baby, wrapped in a bright red blanket, to her chest. A tiny candle burned dimly by her side illuminating the fact that they owned almost no possessions, not even a chair to sit in. Some clay pots were scattered by the open fireplace which was not burning, and there was no obvious fuel nearby. The husband was squatting, but seeing Antonius, stood up, giving a slight bow.

"Thank you, Roman, for your help in our time of need. It won't be forgotten," he said.

"It was Mary who helped, not I," Antonius said. He felt for his money purse given to him by Pilatus, the money he was to spend however he wanted in Jerusalem. He weighed it in his hand for a moment, then tossed it to the husband. "A gift from me to you. Use it for your child."

The husband opened the purse and poured out the bright coins into his open hand, looking at Antonius with a gaped mouth. "So much!" He started to cry, then showed his wife the treasure, causing her to cry with him. "How can we thank you, Roman?"

"You have need of it, and I don't. There is no reason to thank me. I wish your family a long and happy life." He left as the two embraced each other, crying into their shoulders.

When he emerged from the hut, Mary was also crying. "That was the nicest thing I've ever seen anyone do!" she said and embraced him. He signaled to the three soldiers that they were leaving and allowed them to lead the way. For a time, he and Mary walked in silence, but close enough that their hips touched, her arm entwined with his.

"You saw how they live?" she asked.

"Yes, pitiable."

"If there is anything I learned from being in this time, it would be how difficult is the lot of women. Many of them die in childbirth or soon afterward. Most of the deaths are from infection, something which can nearly be prevented by cleanliness. They are used by men as possessions, treated no better than farm animals, if as good. They are not educated nor are they treated with respect, and for nearly any reason, they can be turned out or stoned to death."

"I don't feel that way, and I hope you don't think that I act that way, Mary. To me, a woman is the most important thing a man can have in his life. She is to be protected, honored, loved and cared for. Her every wish should be granted if it is in the man's power to do so. Women are the most beautiful thing the Gods ever created, and they did it just for men."

"That's why I love you. You are different."

"So is Cos," he said.

"Yes, so he is."

Ahead, they could see fires burning in their camp and shadows of men moving in the flickering light, while above were the stars of the heavens amid the smear of the milky way.

"A lovely night," Antonius said.

"I never realized how nice this area is. For some reason, there is more growth here and less heat. There is a peacefulness about it, a simplicity."

"We will leave the mountains tomorrow, and it is another long day until Nazat. I will have to let our guard go on to Caesarea about midday. The risk to us is low, because the population between here and Nazat is scant," Antonius said.

"They were ordered to protect us. You really think they will abandon us?" she asked.

"I am not their direct superior. Frankly, I'm not sure."

Mary put her arm around his waist and looked up at him. "Can I ask a question that I have never asked?"

"Of course you can," he said.

"Do you believe in God?"

"I have thought much about this since I met you. You understand that Romans have many gods, even some that are dead or living emperors. We enjoy talking about them, writing and reading about them, but we don't really take them seriously. It's just a way of giving a face to what life brings us. Jupiter is our God of Gods, but I don't think any Roman feels about Jupiter as you do about your God."

"Well…what then, do you believe?" she persisted.

"I think that, deep down, I believe just what you do. God is all around us. He is in the trees, the wind and the sky. I know He is in you. Let me be clear though, I would never ever go to your Temple and kill an animal because of my beliefs, or drop coins into their baskets to further enrich a rich priest. When I hold you in my arms, I believe in God, and I thank him for His gift." He felt her squeeze harder, and they continued toward their tent in silence.

There was commotion in camp, and men started running toward the sound. "Centurion!" they called. Antonius grabbed his sword as he ran. Above, dawn was just starting to grow in intensity, and the faint pink sky was framed by darker ragged hills. Some of the men were struggling to don armor as others faced the perimeter, weapons in hand. As he approached the entryway of the camp, he saw several donkeys being led by men in dark clothing, heading toward them. None of the men bore weapons, and some of them waved in a friendly manner.

"Put down your weapons," he told his men. "These men mean us no harm." The camp seemed to relax, and they all watched the little caravan grow closer.

"Hail, Romans!" one said. "We bring you gifts of food." He pointed to the loads on the back of the donkeys. Antonius directed that his men assist in receiving the food, and they quickly helped unload the animals. There were freshly cut sections of meat, olives and fruits, and several large skins of wine.

"This a welcome honor, friends. May we pay you for this food?"

Antonius asked.

"You have already paid enough. We seek to balance your favors with ours. We wish that you leave Gerizim, but with a full stomach and a peaceful mind. May God bless all of you." They gathered their sacks and animals and made a friendly departure.

"Would it be that every village treated us so well!" one soldier said, holding up a skin of wine.

"Perhaps there is a lesson for all of us," Antonius said. "They will respond as they are treated." He turned and noticed Cosimus standing by himself. "You missed the excitement last night," he said. "We…I mean Mary…helped a woman birth her baby. It was a grand thing to be there."

"I heard from the men who went with you. This food is in repayment for our help?" Cosimus asked.

"That, and I also gave the couple some coins. At least we didn't have to fight our way in or out of this place. How does this day find you, Cosimus?"

"I am well, Antonius, and anxious to get on with the day. I have been trying to recall the location where the Portal will open. It may not be easy to find after so much time."

"Try not to concern yourself until we get closer, Cos. This time there are three minds here to remember where it is. Have you decided if you are going to go back or stay here?"

"My vision implied that I will go back. I saw that you and Mary will be happy and safe."

"And you?" Antonius asked. Cosimus shrugged and seemed to be somewhere distant in his thoughts. Close by, the aroma of cooking meat was accompanied by the sizzling sound of fat dripping into flame.

The sun was nearly overhead, and the blue hills of Gerizim were behind them as the land ahead spread out into a long and vast valley. Just to the left were the hills of Mt. Carmel running diagonally toward the coast, the path splitting with one thread heading to the north of the hills, one south toward Caesarea. This was the time of decision, Antonius realized. He called a halt and ordered everyone to dismount.

When he had their attention he cleared his throat. "The path leads in two directions. To the left is Caesarea, about a half day's ride. The other leads north, around the mountains. I give my permission to you men to head to Caesarea without us. We are to continue north to try to find something called a Portal."

One of the senior men stepped forward, "Centurion, what happens if you find this Portal?"

"I am not positive that we can find it," Antonius said.

"Then, explain what the Portal is," he asked.

"Fair enough. It is an opening to another world. You can enter and leave without harm."

"You have seen this Portal?"

"Yes. I went in once and came back."

"Our instructions were directly from the Prefect. We are to accompany you to Caesarea. Where you go, we go, on that there can be no discussion."

Another man said, "The ships embarking for Ostia leave in two weeks. There is time for all of us to go and see this Portal."

"All of you agree?" Antonius asked, looking at their faces. "Yes!" came the shout.

"Will you let us enter the Portal?" one man asked.

"If we find it, yes, that will be your choice. One other thing that you have to know, the Portal only opens twice a day for a brief time, then disappears. We hope that it still opens, but there is no way to know until the location is found."

"The Portal is an opening to Hades?" another asked.

"This is not the underworld of Pluto. Have no fear of that," Mary said.

The men seemed to be interested, above all they loved new adventure, and so the small group assembled, continuing on the path toward the north and Nazat, their horses cantering into the setting sun.

In early afternoon, the party slowed as Cosimus and Antonius watched the landscape carefully, nervously trying to find the rocks where Cosimus had hidden.

"It has to be here, right here," Cosimus said with exasperation. "Soon we will see Nazareth, we must be close."

"We found it once, we will find it again," Antonius said, an idea crystalizing in his head. "We were dumb not to mark it on your map the last time we were here. I have an idea which may help. You and I will ride north until we know we are past it and then ride back. The terrain will seem more familiar from that direction. The others will stay here."

"You mean to leave Mary alone?" Cosimus wrinkled his brow, thinking of unpleasant probabilities.

"She will be safer with ten warriors than with us. It also will give assurance to the men that we are not leaving without them," Antonius said.

"Are you certain of this?"

"These men may look longingly at her but not one of them will touch her. I am certain of it."

"Don't worry, Cosimus," Mary said. "I am comfortable with that plan, and I have nothing to fear from these men."

Antonius called a halt, and after they gathered in a group, he said, "The Portal is near, but Cosimus and I have to search for it from the other direction. Make camp near here and post a guard. The last time we were near Nazat, we ran into fanatic bandits. Allow no one near Mary."

The men looked relieved to dismount, and they were already busy making camp as Antonius and Cosimus rode away.

"What if we can't find the opening?" Antonius asked.

"Or what if it doesn't open?" Cosimus answered. "I have been thinking about that for several days. There is a time element at play. You have to either enter the Portal or keep your scheduled embarkation for Ostia. I would expect the Roman Legions to come looking for you if you don't show at all."

"It is a death sentence to abandon your post. They will come for certain."

"Then if you have to leave with your men, I will take care of Mary. Don't fear that I would ever try to become her lover. She will be safe with me and treated as though she is my sister."

"I know that, my old friend. You are truly a man who will keep his honor and his word."

"Antonius, I tell you again that you and Mary will enter the Portal. I have seen it. I know it will happen," Cosimus said.

"Let's just hope that your vision was not just wishful thinking."

They rode until the buildings of Nazat were first visible on the horizon. Daylight was starting to fade as they turned their horses south and began the search in earnest. Cos remembered that they had been able to spot where the horses had stood, where there was a slight bend in the trail to the left. They both sat up straight, intently watching the terrain, slowly moving forward as the last ray of sunlight extinguished behind the hills.

"This place seems familiar," Cos said. "I want to have a close look on the left, because my intuition tells me that we are close." He dismounted and while Antonius waited with the horses, he scrambled over the rocks, pausing to study the endless and similar terrain. Recognition just wouldn't snap into place for him, and after a while, he became confused and disorientated. He sat on a large flat rock and tried to remember the first time he came out of the Portal. In the distance, a horse snorted and pawed the ground, similar to the time he was hiding behind the rock. The memory came flooding back to him, his fear that they would even hear him breathing. He heard feet on the loose stones crunch behind him just as he had heard before a spear point was poked into his back.

"Find anything?" Antonius asked, placing his hand on Cos' shoulder. Startled, he jerked upright, but suddenly he did remember. It was right here, the same rock, he clearly recalled.

"We found it! Right there," he said and pointed to a nearby stone.

"Yes, it seems right to me also," Antonius said. "We sat on this very stone waiting for the Portal to open. The truth is that I never believed you until it actually appeared before my own eyes."

"What time does your watch say?" Cos asked.

"Six and half," Antonius said with satisfaction. "When is it supposed to open?"

"Thirty minutes. Better sit and get comfortable," Cos said. Antonius decided to bring the two horses closer and headed in that direction, leaving Cosimus alone on the rock.

Cos stretched out on the warm flat rock to gaze at the purple sky. The big and little dipper winked back at him, and a small wisp of a cloud scurried past, heading toward the advancing black of the sky. No moon gleamed its ivory light for him, the ensuing blackness more total than usual. Back to where I started, Cos thought. He knew more about the past now than he could have ever hoped. In some ways, it was pleasant to be in a time when you knew what was going to happen, at least in general. The past always seems so inevitable and the future so in doubt. For Cos, the future was the past, for at least two thousand years. Living here would not be so bad, he thought. With a little money as a starter, he could become wealthy almost overnight. There were so many inventions he could reinvent and start manufacturing them for profit. Just think of how the printing press, a simple thing, could take off and be profitable. Or just an assembly line of interchangeable parts, making almost anything. Yes, he thought, the future is what I can make of it. He smiled to himself and then remembered that he was from the future. None of his ideas will actually occur for centuries. It was not going to happen, this dream of riches. Wasn't it he who kept saying that they could not change the past? He also remembered that he saw himself with Mary and Antonius in the future, on the other side of the Portal. He was fated to return to the future, not live in the past.

"Fifteen more moments," Antonius said.

"Minutes, not moments."

"Yes. The time draws near. Are we to enter if it opens?"

"Sure. We have to let them know what is going to happen. Ray won't like it when we let ten soldiers come in with us."

"Do you care what this Ray thinks?"

Cos laughed. "We accomplished the mission and a lot more. At least we did what we were instructed to do. We were not told that the real mission was to kill Jesus. I don't care what the lying Ray thinks."

"We have to talk, man to man, about Mary," Antonius said seriously.

"I already know that she loves you and not me. There is no going back; I have accepted it. There is nothing to discuss."

"Is this the reason that you have withdrawn into a shell? Why there is so little humor about you?"

"At first. Not now. You have a future with Mary, an endless progression of happy days lie ahead, wrapped in each other's arms until you grow old and grey. My future is not so clear, but I cannot see any happiness in it, only duty."

"Are we to part ways?" Antonius asked.

"We will always be friends, no matter what happens. I want you to be happy, both of you, because I love you both. As far as being close, I think that our paths have to diverge either here or back there." There was silence as each thought about what could happen, and what could have been. Cosimus sat up and watched the area intently, as if wishing the Portal to open, creating it with his willpower alone. All their hopes and expectations depended on the Portal opening. "Check your watch again," Cosimus asked.

"Five minutes after. It did not open," Antonius said, observing the obvious. "Is there any doubt that we are in the right place?"

"No doubt," Cos said. They looked at each other for a moment and got up. "There is another opening scheduled in eight hours. Let's mark this place clearly and return before dawn," he suggested. Together, they built a small cairn just beside the trail and headed, despondently, back toward camp.

Chapter 28

An Interminable Wait

The entire camp awaited some word about the Portal as Antonius dismounted, their eyes and thoughts creating a breathless pause. Even without words, defeat hung over Cosimus and Antonius as they turned to face their comrades.

Mary was the first to speak, "Did you find the Portal?" She asked what everyone expected her to ask, while already knowing the answer.

"We found the location. It's about three miles from here. The Portal didn't open while we were there, but I'm going back before dawn and wait for the next cycle," Cosimus said.

"What if it doesn't open then?" Mary asked, her face showing her worry. Cos shrugged and turned away from her, wanting to disguise his own fears. The other men watched and listened, intent but silent.

"Time for food, a good fire and some conversation among friends," Antonius announced and smiled, putting the camp at ease with a few words. The food had been prepared and was scooped into metal bowls, even before Antonius and Mary sat down. "All we need is some wine!" he joked.

"Here is some we saved in spite of our haste to depart, Centurion," one of the men said and handed him a skin of wine. They formed a circle around the fire, the yellow light flickered on their faces and reflected from their eyes as the warmth from their hearts mingled with the heat of burning, snapping wood. It was as if no other humans existed, as if this small camp in the wilderness contained all in creation who ever mattered.

"You all heard that the Portal didn't open as expected," Antonius announced. The group fell silent waiting on his words. "I assure everyone here that I have personally seen this thing and met the people who control it. I believe that it will open again, and we are going to stay here and keep a watch on the spot until it does. We have to stick together while we wait. It's uncomfortable here in the heat of the day, and we are certain to run low on supplies if too many days go by. Nazat is not far from here, and we can buy food as we need. As I said, there are bandits in the area, so don't let down your guard. If trouble comes, we are ready to defend ourselves. We are Romans!" A shout went up, and the men raised their fists and shook them in the air.

"Nicely done, Antonius," Cos said quietly. "After they get to sleep, I will go watch the Portal and be back before dawn. Perhaps tomorrow, if tomorrow comes, we can move the camp closer to the Portal."

"Take two men with you," Antonius advised. His raised eyebrows indicated his misgivings about being alone in this area.

They easily found the small pyramidal stack of rocks, helped by the moonlight now brightly illuminating the barren landscape. The horses snorted their disapproval with being left alone, tied to a small bush. Cosimus took down a wine flask from his horse and showed the men where to sit.

"If it happens, it will be right there," he said, pointing to the spot.

"What does it look like?" one man asked.

"It will suddenly appear as the shape of an egg, slightly shorter than a man's height. It's like a window or opening."

"Is this the work of the gods?" the other one asked.

"No, just the work of some really smart men. There are no gods, evil or good here, just men."

"How did you discover this…Portal?" he asked.

Cos was at a loss to answer the man's question. He could see that the truth would be more confusing to them, and more threatening. "An accident," he said. "The column was going past this spot, and it was found by chance."

"The dawn approaches," one said pointing to the rim of purple in the distant east. An outline of the hills was dimly apparent. Cos let out a sigh. The Portal should have opened by now.

"We will wait for the first rays of sunlight," Cos said. They did wait, impatiently, until a shaft of bright light broke over the largest hill, and the sky glowed with pink hues. Cosimus stood up looking tired, his nervous energy expended staring at dark rocks in hope that some crazy opening into the distant future would snap into focus. The whole idea seemed preposterous as the daylight changed what was mysterious into just another pile of red rocks. The two men with him looked disappointed but didn't voice any opinion on the trip back to camp as they rode in silence, enjoying the cool early morning.

Cosimus glanced at Antonius and Mary as he made his way back into camp. They knew by that look that the expected opening had not occurred and felt their hearts sink lower. There was absolutely nothing that they could do and nowhere left to hide. The opening had to occur and occur soon. Cos walked to where they were standing and accepted an offer of food, then they all looked into the distant hills, having nothing to offer which would be encouraging.

"What is Caesarea like," Mary asked, breaking the silence.

"Very much like a real Roman city. There are ports and docks, even larger ones than at Ostia. A small theater and baths are found only a short walk from the harbor. There is a small arena for chariot racing and many public buildings and temples. A pleasant and surprising city and a tribute to Herod who built it."

"Do you think that I can find a place to live there?" she asked.

"Are we giving up so soon?" Antonius asked her.

"We have to face the future. If the Portal doesn't open, we have to make a plan. All of us."

"What if they are opening it but at a different time for some reason?" Cos ventured. "Susan said that it took a lot of power and cost a pile of money to run the machines. Perhaps they have decided to open it only on occasion."

"Or perhaps they told us a lie, and it will never open again," Mary said.

"We have a week, no more," Antonius said. "After that I have to report, or they will search for me. There is no running or hiding from the Roman Army."

"Will these men wait in this desert for another week?" Cos asked, noticing that the other men were in a huddle probably discussing the Portal site and the fact that nothing was seen last night.

"Every day will become harder. I don't know," Antonius admitted.

It did get harder by the day, as Antonius feared. The camp was moved closer to the expected location of the Portal, but the effect was that most of the men spent their time watching it, growing their frustration, disappointment and, increasingly, disbelief.

When the food was nearly exhausted, Antonius reluctantly agreed to allow four men to travel to the city of Nazat in an attempt to buy food. They were supplied with coins by Cosimus and had strict instructions not to reveal the location of the camp nor how many soldiers were there. After they rode north, Mary pulled Cos to the side, obviously wishing to discuss things privately.

"What are we going to do, Cos?" she said desperately, not wanting to be overheard. "These men will not last much longer out here. They have lost faith that there is a Portal or ever was one."

"I know. There isn't much time left anyway. Two or three more days, and it's all over for us. We have to resign ourselves that we are trapped here and make the best of it."

"Could we leave a message before we leave just in case they ever do open the Portal? At least we can show and tell them what it was like for us."

"You mean a video or something like that?" Cos asked, thinking it over.

"We can't do a video with my camera, but we can do an audio tape on top of the pictures we have taken. Several from each of us, for history if nothing else."

Cos and Mary used the morning to record their messages, leaving the small memory chip in full view where the Portal was expected to open. That afternoon and throughout the next day, one of them would occasionally look to see if the chip was still present, but to their disappointment, it remained undisturbed. After the last possible step had been taken, and the last hope the Portal would open was gone, they began to think actively about the immediate future.

"Tomorrow is the last day," Antonius announced. They all knew it was coming, but now it was official. The three looked at each other, knowing that the future was not to be as rosy as they had hoped. Antonius pointed with his thumb toward the other men who had begun to lose discipline and even respect for Antonius as a superior officer, and it was obvious that they were nearing revolt. "We should leave by noon tomorrow," he continued. He reached out and held Mary's hand, knowing what she was thinking. His life would continue as it always had, but hers… Mary was the one who would bear the brunt of being abandoned in time, and she was to be left alone in this strange land without money or a protector. Cos would do his best, but he was also subject to the whims of the Roman Army and could be sent anywhere fate chose.

Antonius called his men to him and looked at their faces before speaking. "I know what you are all thinking. This was a foolish waste of time for all of us. You are probably doubting my sanity or veracity by now, and I don't blame you. I wish there was some way to prove what I have been telling you, but there isn't. The first time I was told about the Portal, I didn't believe it either. We are going to leave tomorrow and start back by midday. You have been loyal and brave, and I salute you for staying with us."

"Why not leave right now, Centurion?" one asked. Antonius always suspected this one would be a problem.

"And why not, one last night?" Antonius countered.

"Because we are sick of this talk of a magic window. We don't believe it and are ready to be gone from here. We will go without you, if needed."

"I would have let you all go days ago if you wanted. Now we must stick together as a unit, and I order you to stay here for this last night."

"And what will you do if we just ride away?" the soldier asked defiantly.

"You will be the first one I cut in half. They can tie the pieces of your body to the horse for the trip to Caesarea…tomorrow." His demeanor and his reputation spoke clearly that this was no idle threat. A moment of silence hung in the air briefly as they sized Antonius up. Cosimus got up and stood behind his Centurion, one hand on the hilt of his sword. The men broke eye contact and found busy work to do, the crisis passing as quickly as a puff of dry air.

A guard had been posted to watch the Portal area since they moved camp. The one currently on watch suddenly voiced an alarm.

"Centurion!" he shouted and ran into camp trying to point to the Portal area. "I saw something move!" The men gathered around him and looked where he was pointing but saw nothing amiss and nothing moving. "It was there, something shiny, metal, it moved!" he persisted, pointing to the Portal area. The entire group moved toward the Portal and bent over, seeing nothing but rock and sand. Mary pushed her way past the men and knelt down and pushed the sand aside carefully.

"They took the chip," she said. "They are still there, after all." She stood up looking at Antonius with tears in her eyes; there was still hope, after all.

"Chip? What does she mean?" one of the men demanded.

Cosimus pushed forward and held his arm over Mary's shoulder. "The chip is a small black square we put there two days ago. It was a message for the other side. What you saw was a metal tool they stuck through the Portal after which they must have turned it off again. I'm sure we will see it open tonight. Our wait has been worth it."

Chapter 29

Grand Entrance

Inside the Tevatron, Batavia, Illinois

McMurphy sat down to wait, nervously looking at his watch. Fifteen more minutes. The HAZMAT team was busy setting up just down the hall, putting up their enormous plastic barriers and running back and forth in their white puffy suits. He glanced at Susan and could see the apprehension on her face, the dread of admitting another demon from the past, but at the same time, he knew that she wanted their translators to return to the present. The images from the past had made an impression on McMurphy as well. Hell of an adventure, he mused to himself, secretly wondering if he had ever been man enough to go back in time like they had done. Probably not, he admitted to himself. He stole another nervous glance at his watch.

"Susan? Are you ready on your end?" he asked, just to have something to say to her. He motioned to the two shotgun carrying patrolmen to move back against the wall. It was bad enough, the anxiety of opening the Portal again, but to have the threat of violence right in Susan's face was too much.

"Ready as I can be," she answered, not looking up from the computer screen.

"This Roman you mentioned. Think we will see him again?"

"The one called Antonius. He and Cos seemed very comfortable with each other. I wouldn't be surprised. You remember that I felt that he was dangerous, don't you? Tell your men not to make any sudden moves toward him, he could react quickly if threatened."

"Can you…talk to him?" McMurphy asked.

"Sure, if you spoke fluent Latin you probably could. You remember that English didn't exist two thousand years ago?"

"Are we going to let him stay here or send him back?" he asked.

"I have no idea. As far as I am concerned, I am here to open and shut the Portal. You get to make all the other decisions," she said, pointedly looking at him to be sure he heard her.

"Two more minutes," McMurphy said to the air. The hum and whine of energy surging in the tube caused the hair on the back of his neck to vibrate just before a loud clunk echoed through the tunnel. The whine grew louder, causing the other men to start looking around apprehensively, waiting for some imminent threat to appear.

"Any time now," Susan shouted, pointing to the expected location. They all turned to watch, unable to breathe or move. "There!" she exclaimed. The Portal snapped open in an instant and ominously hung just above the concrete floor, a black hole to the past.

McMurphy got as close as he dared and shouted into the hole, "Anyone there?" In a moment he got his answer. "We are here and coming in shortly, be patient," a female voice answered. They could hear conversations taking place and some shouting, but the language was unfamiliar. The policemen leveled their guns at the opening, tense and alert. They saw a female hand, then a slender arm, gracefully appear followed by the rest of her. Mary. She came all the way in but continued to look back toward the opening, waiting for something. A loose fitting dark robe hung on her, flowing over her form, timelessly and intensely beautiful. She pulled back her cape allowing her long hair to spill over her shoulders. The contrast of course dark wool against her pure white skin was as if Rubens had somehow painted her on the air itself. It was a powerful, biblical image, making the men in the room catch their breath. A metal helmet appeared and a muscular, armored Roman followed it. He wore a polished anatomical breast plate above thick leather straps which extended to his knees. After entering the tunnel, he looked around slowly, his head held high, defiant.

"Thank God!" Susan said, holding her hands over her mouth. She didn't want to leave the computer terminal in case she needed to shut down quickly and could only watch as they came through. "Is that

Cosimo?" she asked, blurting it out even though she realized that this man could not be the boy whom she saw last.

"I am Cosimo. Hello, Susan," he said calmly. She looked again and realized that only his face was the same. The rest of him, his body language, his confidence, his hard eyes, said that he was someone else, someone she had never met. As they watched, another man came in. This one had a plumed helmet, but the plumes were across instead of front to back. He was thicker, darker, and more threatening, looking over the two nervous policemen like they were two insignificant bugs. His presence was unsettling to McMurphy who hadn't expected anything like him to emerge.

McMurphy stepped forward, intent on introducing himself but was halted by Antonius who held up his hand, palm facing out. "Stop. There are others waiting to enter. Do not be alarmed, but make no gestures."

"For the love of Pete!" McMurphy exclaimed. "Am I hearing things or did he just speak to me using English?" McMurphy backed up as five heavily armored soldiers came in, nervously looking around. Antonius partly reentered the Portal, pausing for a moment as if waiting for more. They could hear shouts and horses whinnying, then the distant sound of galloping, fading into the past.

Antonius looked at Cosimus and Mary and said, "The rest have fled and have taken all the horses with them."

"May I shut the Portal, Captain?" Susan called.

Cosimo took off his helmet and said, "Please, we are all in that want to come in. Shut it down forever."

At a signal from Antonius, the men slowly took off their helmets but remained standing in a small group, unsure of what they had just done. An ominous slamming noise occurred, making the men jump as the opening to the first century winked out.

Susan Harmes rushed from her terminal and embraced Mary. "I'm sorry, dear Mary, that you had to wait for the opening. We are so happy to see you and Cos again."

"Hi, folks! I am Captain McMurphy from the Chicago Police Department. Welcome to the twenty-first century." He stuck out his hand for a shake but was ignored.

"Captain, my name is Cosimo, but you can call me Cos. These people never shake hands, no offense."

McMurphy took his hand down and wiped it off on his pants, aware that they were probably correct to refuse a handshake. "Cos, do they intend to stay here permanently?"

"I do," said Antonius as he took off his armor and his sword, lying them aside. He put his arm tenderly around Mary's waist, making it apparent why.

Cosimo took off his armor and indicated to the men that they should do the same. "Captain McMurphy," he said. "It would really be helpful if you could find some clothes for these men. A shower would be nice as well."

"Do you people have an expense account we can use?" McMurphy asked Susan.

"Sure do. We'll charge it all to Ray's account. Whatever they want, they get," she said, smiling.

"What about food?" McMurphy asked.

"Send someone for fast food. Lots of everything. Wine, don't forget the wine," Mary suggested.

McMurphy shrugged. "You men put down the shotguns. One of you go buy a big pile of food, the other one goes to Walmart for clothes for six men. Guess at the sizes for now. Get moving."

McMurphy was aware that the HAZMAT team was waiting for instructions. "Can you give these people a shower in that thing?" he shouted at them.

"That and a lot more. Is that all you need?" the team leader asked, irritation in his voice.

"Well go ahead and do what you think is best," he answered. "Lady first." He motioned to Mary that she was to go through first. In response she smiled, dropping her course cloak to her feet, revealing the soft, shimmering silk toga underneath. All the men watched transfixed as she gracefully made her entrance into the plastic fortress, her moving hips just visible beneath the semi transparent garment.

"That's a lot of woman you have there, Antonius," McMurphy noted.

"I know," he answered in perfect English.

Food, beverages and clothing arrived just as the last Roman soldier exited from the plastic enclosure. They all were wearing temporary, paper gowns and it was obvious that the men were very self-conscious about it. McMurphy had all the new clothing put in a room and showed the men where to change. When they were done, happy with their new casual attire, they were all shown into a larger conference room where the table overflowed with hamburgers, fries and fried chicken. Two five-liter jeroboams of wine stood by paper cups in the center.

"Sit. Eat," Antonius instructed, and they all dug in with delight.

"What in the world are we going to do with these men? None of them even speak a useful language," McMurphy fretted aloud, watching them wolf down the food.

Susan took his arm softly and said," Didn't you just talk to the Catholic Bishop? I'll bet he knows Latin, and I'll bet he will take these men under his wing and teach them English."

"Damn good idea, Susan!" he said and looked at his phone. "Too late tonight. Any place around here they can sleep until tomorrow?

"I'll work it out. Don't worry about it."

"Okay. Next is our debriefing. Round up Cos, Antonius and Mary, and let's find a room to talk," he said. "And see if this Raymone Chauncy Servierlo can be reached for a video link. He will want to know what happened to these kids."

The last in were Mary and Antonius, linked by their arms and the smiles on their faces. Mary was wearing the same elegant black shift that she had worn the last time she and Cos had dined together. She was radiant and exceptionally lovely, and the sight of her tore at his heart. This was the part of his vision that he kept remembering. It was so familiar, watching them sit down together, looking like teen-age lovers who can't get enough of each other. He had seen this scene a thousand times before in his head. It was a glimpse of the future after all. Cos was reminded of his other vision, the one that brought back the intense fear, the one that he couldn't think through.

"Are you all right, Cos? Glad to be back and safe?" Antonius asked in English.

Cos looked up in surprise, catching their smiling faces. How wonderful to see them happy, safe and together, where they belonged and fulfilling his vision. He had no jealousy left. Destiny was deciding for itself what was going to happen. The distant past was over, for two thousand years it was over, an idea that impacted him with force. Everything that had just happened to them was ancient history, never to be seen and relived again. The people they had met and saw and walked with were long ago reduced to dust as was almost every other thing from that time. The whole experience was more like a dream, or a memory floating back in his head, a dream which will only dim with time.

"We are here to listen to your experience and to update you on things that happened after you left on your trip," McMurphy said. Behind him, the image of Raymone Chauncy Servierlo appeared on the large monitor. Ray waved as if he were actually sitting there in the room with them.

"Ah, my famous Roman Centurion, Antonius, as I remember. I thought we would meet again. Hello and welcome back, Cosimo and Mary. It is a delight to see you both in one piece. I can't wait to hear this adventure story of yours."

Cos frowned, two vertical slits appearing above the bridge of his nose. "Ray. You surmise, don't you, that we discovered the real reason we were sent back."

"Yes, Cos. Stupid, wasn't it? Not my idea, I assure you. Fortunately Christ was not harmed, and you both had the adventure of a lifetime. Can there be any real complaint?"

"Good thing for you, Ray, that you are here only as a video image," Cos told him.

"Yes, looking at you, I'm sure that what you threaten is real enough. You look more like a Marine than the boy we sent back in time. The experience has obviously been good for you."

"Wish you had gone back with us to find out, Ray," Cos said.

"No! That physical life is not my forte. I am more comfortable in a dark room, with a good book and a carafe of wine to keep me company," he laughed.

"Your hit man, Tony, tried to kill a man calling himself Jesus. The last time we saw him, he was running for his life with three men giving chase close behind. We assume that you will hear no more from him, ever."

"Not completely true, Cosimo. He is alive and well and not twenty meters from where I am sitting. He made it back. This tells me that you don't know the rest of the story, the bad part."

They looked at each other, then at Susan and McMurphy. It was obvious that there was more, a lot more, to the story. "How did Tony get back when we nearly didn't," Mary asked.

"I can't answer that. It doesn't make any sense the way he relates it. He tells a story of a long flight for his life across unfamiliar terrain, unable to converse with people, and with no map or communication. Even given the seemingly insurmountable obstacles, he made it back and crossed through the Portal."

"I don't believe it," Cos said. It would have been not only unlikely but clearly impossible."

"Yes, impossible. Yet here he sits. We have begun to believe that he was guided, herded may be a better term, by a being other than human."

"The Antichrist!" Mary said in alarm. "That was what was chasing him, or perhaps it was leading him. Tell us what happened," she demanded.

"Appropriate word, Antichrist. That is what the well-informed are calling him here, except his devoted and maniacal followers. They are calling him God."

"Did he come through the Portal also?" Mary asked.

"He did…in hot pursuit of Tony. Call it the revenge of Jesus, if you will. Unfortunately, it seems that he is going to take his revenge out on the whole world. He seems unstoppable."

"What does he want?" Cos asked.

"Power, all of it," McMurphy answered.

"What about Tony, is he safe now?" Cos asked.

"They will get Tony, me and everyone connected with our group. It's only a question of time. If they find out that you came back, they will get you also. We are seeing a dramatic change in our world, and we are about to watch the old one disappear as did the Roman world so long ago," Ray said.

Angrily, Cos spoke first, "You really messed things up, Ray,"

"Yes. No argument there. I deserve my fate, but the rest of the world doesn't. Pity about that."

"Why don't you kill this Jesus," Antonius asked in English.

"Why surprise, surprise. Our muscle bound boy has learned English. Your work, Mary?"

"Yes, my work. Answer his question, Ray," Mary snapped.

"From what I hear from Tony, he can't be killed. Besides, there are his fervent followers who grow in number by logarithmic progression. What would they do if we killed him?" Ray asked rhetorically.

"Everything that lives can die," Antonius stated. "He can and will die also."

"I leave that task to you, my Roman friend. This is not what I am paid to do."

Susan spoke up for the first time, "I feel partially responsible because I enabled all this to happen. I sent these folks back, and I opened the door through which Jesus entered. But I have an idea that could bear fruit, although I have to run some tests first. Ray, I will need your money to do it."

"Well, I'm waiting to hear your plan," Ray said.

"Nothing doing. I have to experiment before I get anyone's hopes up. It involves using the Tevatron, and I want you to back me up with the money I need for testing."

Ray sighed loudly. "In for a penny, in for a pound. Go ahead, Susan. What's money if you are dead, and I am sure to be dead if we don't fix this mess, and soon."

"Another item, Ray," she continued. "I want to keep Mary and Cos on the payroll for a little longer. You might as well add Antonius, since he is here to stay."

"What do you mean, payroll? There isn't any payroll, Susan," Ray laughed.

"Okay, Ray. What I mean is that I want you to pay their expenses so I can keep them around in case I need them. Knowing what they do about this may help."

"You got it. Any more surprises, Susan?"

"There's bound to be others before this is over. I'll let you know when I know, Ray."

"I hear the chopper landing on the deck right now. It was delayed because of a storm out here on the lake. I'll be there to see everyone in person tomorrow, and we can talk some more. Congratulations to everyone there, and truly, I am grateful to see that everyone made it back." The monitor went dark as Ray ended the call.

"That Tony!" Mary said. "The little creep made it back. What did he say happened from his point of view?"

"Tony wasn't that helpful," McMurphy answered. "He was debriefed yesterday by my team of interrogators, but he really doesn't know much and what he says you have to only half believe. What do you folks make of this Jesus? Know anything about him?"

"We all saw him," Cos responded. "We had a terrific battle with his followers one day resulting in two hundred dead. We ran into others later who seemed crazed, nearly animal like. Now that I know that Jesus went into your time, leaving ours, it explains the diminished effect we observed after he left. Like the phrase 'out of sight, out of mind,' once he was gone his effect was gone. It makes me think that Antonius is right, kill him and his followers will have no master. The other side of the coin is that we saw Tony shoot at him point blank. Even I would have hit him at that range, but there was no effect that we could see. This creature is not a man, he is a monster of some kind who gives the illusion of being a man. He can hypnotize and convert nearly everyone he comes in contact with."

"Believe me, son, we know that all too well," McMurphy said. "Now, what about you three. Any plans?"

"Captain, my plan is to make this man happy. That's all I want right now," Mary said and gave Antonius a quick kiss on the cheek.

"My plan is to try to fit into this new world," Antonius said.

McMurphy looked for a response from Cosimo, but he was quiet and appeared to be lost in thought. "Cos?" he probed.

"I don't know, Captain. There is something I have to do, but I don't know yet what it is."

"I have a plan. Want to hear mine?" Susan asked.

"Sure. Thought you didn't want to discuss it yet," McMurphy quipped.

"Not that, not yet. My idea will take some time to work out. In the meantime, you three need to get out of here and enjoy yourselves. You heard Ray agree to pay your expenses, didn't you? To me that means that you can go anywhere or buy anything you want. All I ask is that you will come back when I need you. Stay together please, and come back here as soon as possible after I call you. Agreed?" Susan asked.

"Tell Ray that we need a passport for Antonius. We can't leave until we get one," Mary said.

"I'm sure he can do that. Then it's settled?"

"No." Cos said. "I'm not going with them. I have to stay here and work on this problem with you. There is a solution in my head, but just out of reach at the moment. If I keep trying, I'll see it clearly."

"I would like to see Rome as it is now," Antonius said. "Would you be willing to show it to me. You are the only one who could. Please?" Cos sat up straight and looked at his friend. Without his armor, helmet and sword, he was a different person but still the best friend that Cos had ever had. From the first day they met, both had considered the other to be his brother. You couldn't let down a brother who was this close to you. And, this was the first favor that Antonius had ever asked of him.

"Of course, my brother, I would never disappoint either one of you, you know that."

"This is so exciting!" Mary giggled. I can have my father and mother meet us in Rome!"

"Mary, there is something I have been meaning to ask you," Antonius said, taking her hand in his. She turned toward him, her big eyes swimming in tears, her face flushed with emotion and anticipation. "Will you have me as your husband, Mary? Please say yes, Mary dear." She collapsed against his chest unable to do anything but nod her head yes.

Across the table, Susan was swept up with emotion and turned to Fred McMurphy, wrapping him in her arms as she wept in sympathetic happiness, burrowing her face into his big chest. He looked down at her head against him and, for a moment, didn't know what to do. He finally reached around her and drew her to him, stroking her hair and patting her on the shoulder. "Aw, that's just wonderful, kids. I'm so happy for you. What a story! What a story! Going back in time to find your perfect mate. Wow, what a story!" He stuck out his hand to shake with Antonius but remembered what Cos had said and quickly withdrew it.

Susan straightened up, wiping her face with her sleeve, "You could get married in Rome! Your parents will be there. Your best man will be there!" Then she broke down in happy sobs again and went back into McMurphy's chest.

Cos slowly got up from his chair and knelt down beside them. "I am so happy for both of you. The two best people I have ever known will be joined. It's the perfect marriage, and I predict, a long one. Congratulations." He leaned forward and kissed each one on the cheek, then put his forehead against theirs, holding it there for a long time before getting up. Mary managed to look up at him with one eye. Out of that eye came a message of love for him, the purest of love, everlasting love, and thanks.

"My men?" Antonius asked. "Who will care for my men?"

"They are no longer your men, Antonius," McMurphy said. "I am going to hand them over to the Bishop. They will become his men. He will see to their needs and their souls, you can be sure, and they will be in good hands. One more thing," he said. "You are going to need a ring. You can't ask a girl to marry you without giving her a ring."

"I have no ring to give her," Antonius said sheepishly.

McMurphy pulled out his wallet and methodically dug into it, eventually pulling out a ladies diamond ring with a nice sized stone. "Here, use this. My wife gave it back when she left me. I would love you to have it if you will." He extended the ring across the table to them. Antonius looked at Mary who smiled, indicating that she would accept it. She held out her hand and Antonius slipped the ring on for her. A perfect fit.

"Thank you, Captain. I shall always think of you when I look at this ring." She held up her hand so that all could see it on her finger.

"Well, it's time to look for a place to sleep. You two are not sleeping in the lab tonight. I'm calling a cab, and I'll book a room for you in the best hotel in Chicago. Don't even bother coming back tomorrow, you hear me?" Susan said, standing up.

"Truly, I am the happiest and luckiest man who ever lived. Such friends as you come only in dreams. And to have Mary with me the rest of my life? What could be better?" Antonius said, the moisture in his eyes reflecting the utter depth of his feelings.

Chapter 29

Chapter 30

Bliss

ntonius heard her musical, sweet voice coming from the other room. The occasional laugh, the murmured softness, her essence, washed over him like a warm wave, touching every part of him. This is what it's like to be truly happy, he thought. He wanted to get out of bed and stand and look at her while she talked, watching her dimples appear when she smiled, the little short hairs at the back of her neck wave and move when she did. He simply couldn't get enough of her, and their closeness grew by the minute. Reaching for the black box she had called the control box, he watched the screen on the other side of the room change as he pushed the buttons. Magic, he thought. He was already addicted to this modern world, especially the flushing toilet. Such a marvel. Outside the large window was the panoramic of Chicago, most of it below him. Blue sparkles came off the big lake, sifting between the big buildings and shimmering off the metal covered windows. He still did not have a clear idea of where they were, but it really didn't matter any more, he had Mary.

The bedroom door opened a crack, and he saw a sliver of her face. Her teeth gleamed at him when she realized that he was awake and looking at her. "Hi! Thought you were still asleep," she said and eased in beside him.

"Your parents well?" Antonius asked.

"Sure. Anxious to meet you. Full of questions. I had no way of telling them the truth about any of this, not sure I ever will. We discussed marriage…well, my mother discussed marriage. The fact that you are not a Jew hit both of them very hard. 'What is he then?' they asked. 'Not much of anything,' I answered."

"Wait a moment. I am something. I have to be something. You can do better than that. No wonder they were upset."

"Okay, smartypants. What are you?"

Antonius rolled over on his shoulder and looked into her beautiful eyes. "I am yours."

"Oh, you big wonderful man! You always know what to say to get into my head, don't you? Thank you for clearing that up for me. I am yours also, in case you had any doubts."

"None," he said, and kissed her nose.

"About the wedding. They are willing, and my father will take care of finding a Rabbi in Rome. About that, they are very excited, because they can always scheme to convert you. Since you are nothing, it gives them something to work on."

"Yes, I'm glad of that," he laughed.

"I talked with Susan earlier. Ray is already working on getting you a passport. Illegal, of course, but that doesn't matter to him."

"I'm not sure what this passport is exactly," he said.

"Just a paper which allows you to travel between countries. It's a must before we can go to Rome."

"What did you have in mind to do today rather than lay here and look at each other?" he said and stretched out.

"Clothes, shoes! Some for me and a lot for you. We need travel bags and personal things like cosmetics and razors. Stuff. It will be fun, you'll enjoy it."

"Do we get to hold hands and act like lovers while buying these things," he asked and chuckled.

"You'll see."

"How about this one?" Mary asked. She twirled her finger, and he spun in place. "Nice!" she said. "Looks perfect on you, don't you think?"

"I feel silly, and this necktie is killing me. What is this for?" Antonius asked again.

"Look, Antonius, try to calm down. You look incredible in that. It is called a tuxedo, and it is for evening wear or getting married." She turn to the clerk and said, "Isn't this a perfect fit for him?"

"Why, yes, Miss. You have good taste. I can see that. He could pose for pictures and get paid handsomely."

"Not the man, the suit," Mary said.

"Oh my, it looks good on him! Say, aren't you going to get the matching shoes, belt and topcoat as well?"

"Of course we are!" Mary said, mocking surprise. "You know the quote, 'Spare no expense.' Well that's me!"

"Should I ring this up, Miss, or can I interest you in a luxurious Italian camel hair sport coat? And you would certainly want the matching reversed pleated pants, also Italian."

"Well, most certainly!" Mary said, flipping her hand up and rolling her eyes. After the clerk scurried excitedly off, she laughed so hard she had to lean into Antonius who was no longer smiling.

"Mary, please. We have bought so many clothes that we won't be able to carry them. Stop. Enough. I don't want any more things."

"As you wish, my handsome man. Have you noticed how much attention you are getting? It gives me an idea about how you can earn a lot of money when we settle down."

"You mean the attention from all of the overly affectionate male clerks? Please…I don't want that kind of attention."

"These men have good taste, they have to. They know what looks good and what appeals to people. It's not your clothes, Antonius, it's you. There is such a thing as a male model in this world. They have to look a certain way, you understand, a look appealing to both men and women. That's you, my boy. I'll bet we can get a high salary for you, not to mention an easy life."

"Yes, and they haven't even seen me holding a gladius and wearing a breast plate."

"Don't get snappy. I'm thinking about your future, and mine. Someone has to."

"So am I. When I see the right opportunity, I will know it."

"Here he comes again. You behave now, because we are almost done. The photographer will be at the hotel in an hour for your passport photos. We have just enough time for your hair styling session, and I saw just the place for it."

"No. I like my hair just the way it is right now. Anyway, I usually cut my own."

The clerk looked at the charge ticket, his eyes widening briefly before he looked up at them, clearly hesitant to tell them the amount. "Ahemm….let's see….the total, with taxes, comes to $17,450.75. Sounds like a good deal to me, but I'm only a clerk. With that you get a discount of 25% on your next purchase. Credit, charge or cash?" He stood waiting patiently with a thin smile. Mary handed him a glossy black credit card without comment. She saw his eyes widen further as he looked it over.

"Well, this is certainly adequate. Yes, adequate indeed. We'll have to call on this one. ID please?"

Mary handed him a plastic card with her ID and photo under the heading Fermilab. His eyes widened further. "No need for the call, Miss. This will do nicely."

"Fine. Thank you for your excellent service and your valued opinions. Send the packages to our suite at The Peninsula, if you will," she said and tugged at Antonius' sleeve, herding him along to the next store on her list.

The photographer was efficient and businesslike, and the shoot was quickly over. After he left, Antonius threw himself on the bed and groaned. "This was a hard day. I'm exhausted. Battle with barbarians was never so difficult as this has been. Can we just rest now?"

"No dear. We are meeting Cos for dinner, remember? Go put on your new tux, but shave first. There isn't much time." From the bedroom came another loud groan, followed by a heavy sigh.

The uniformed driver held the door for them as they entered the limousine. "Where to sir?" he asked after they were seated.

"Alinea Restaurant. Know where it is?" Mary asked.

"Certainly, I do," he answered. "May I say that you both look splendid tonight. Is there a special occasion you are celebrating?"

"You might say that we have just been reborn," Antonius answered.

"How delightful. Just as I have been. Then you also are followers of our new Jesus?"

His question stopped them cold. The old feeling returned quickly, draining their fanciful bubble of high living apart from world cares. They exchanged knowing glances. The worst thing would be to make this man suspicious of them. No telling where they would be taken.

"Yes, we are following Jesus, very closely in fact. We have probably known him longer than even you," Antonius said.

"Then you must be his devoted servants, as we all are."

"We are very devoted. More than I could describe to you," Antonius assured him.

"Your accent. It isn't common. May I ask your origin?" the chauffeur said.

"Rome."

"Interesting. You know, of course, that our master often speaks of Rome."

"I'm not surprised. All roads lead to Rome, you know."

"Say, driver. We have an appointment for dinner. Could you just take us there please?" Mary asked. She felt a squeeze on her thigh from Antonius. His signal was meant to remind her not to treat this man with any disrespect.

"Of course, Miss. Right away," the chauffeur said as he closed the car door. The large car got underway and was ultra-quiet with nearly no road or motor noise. They kept the microphone to the front off and, by unspoken agreement, talked about anything other than Jesus or the first century during the short trip.

"Should I wait?" the chauffeur asked, holding the door open after they arrived.

"Not necessary," Antonius said smiling. He handed the man a folded bill just given to him by the ever resourceful Mary. "I think we will be traveling with another group. Thank you and God bless you."

"You will be at the meeting tomorrow, won't you?" he asked.

"Both of us. Count on it," Antonius said and patted the man on his shoulder.

They were quickly whisked to a table in a dark corner of the large dining room. There, by himself, was Cos, waiting on them. He stood as they arrived and whistled, looking them up and down.

"Man! You both are stunning. A million bucks worth of stunning!" he said and reached out his hand. "You might as well get used to a handshake. Everyone here does it." Antonius hesitated at first then vigorously shook Cos' hand.

"Not a million. Closer to $18,000," Mary quipped. She leaned out and kissed him on both cheeks. He started to pull her chair out for her but was beaten to it by a quick moving waiter.

"Was it only yesterday that we were sweating in the desert, wondering what was going to happen to us?" Cos observed. "Seems like I have already forgotten. How do you like your new world, Antonius?"

"She made me shop all day. I think I walked *quinque milia passuum* just inside one store, and there were many more after that. Exhausting. However, also exciting. I am getting to like this life."

"Run into any…you know…followers?" Cos asked quietly.

"Our driver was one. Does that mean that you did too?" Mary asked.

"You remember when we passed through Jericho, they could tell from looking at me that something was different? They all seemed to know, just by one glance. The same is true here. I have two watching me now. Don't look, but they are at a table to my left. They have continued to stare at me since I sat down."

"You may be in danger, Cos," Antonius observed. "We may all be in danger. I think we have to leave this city soon, before interest in us becomes a chase or a battle for survival."

"I have my passport in my jacket. Where are yours?" Cos asked.

"Mine is in my purse. They promised that Antonius' would be delivered tomorrow to our room," Mary said.

"That settles it. After his passport arrives, get your luggage together and head to O'Hare Airport. I'll be there waiting for you, and we will catch the first flight to New York. From there we'll go to Europe and on to Rome. Get out of Dodge, like they say," Cos said.

"The expression Get out of Dodge. What does it mean?" Antonius inquired.

"It's just a slang expression that Americans like. From a TV western."

"I saw TV!" Antonius blurted. "It is in our room!"

During dinner, Antonius and Cos couldn't take their eyes off of Mary. Neither could the waiters or guests at other tables. Not only was she radiantly beautiful but, because she was dressed in a simple long red gown, adorned with the necklace of the wife of Pharaoh, she was beyond remarkable.

"I don't think they see a lot of attractive women dining here," Cos remarked sarcastically.

"You can't really blame them, can you, Cos. Is there any woman who could match her beauty?" Antonius asked.

"Not that I have ever seen."

"Enough, you two. I am sitting right here and listening, you know," Mary said. A shadow approached their table, and they looked up to see a small round man, dressed elegantly and sporting a trim mustache.

"Greetings, valued guests. Allow me to introduce myself. I am the Maître d of this fine establishment, Gerod Jasmoush. I have the honor of asking you what everyone is asking me. You three appear to be famous, but no one has placed your names. Would it be permissible to tell me who dines with us tonight?"

"No, my friend. We prefer to dine anonymously. You understand, no? I will give you a hint, however. Three hints perhaps. Think Hollywood, Broadway and The Met. There, that will be enough to set their minds churning. Will that be all?" Cos said in heavily accented English, dismissing him with the back of his hand.

"Thank you, Monsieur! It will be quite enough. Pleasant dining, and your drinks are complementary." He left, backing up and giving repeated short bows.

"I have no idea what you just told him, Cos, but it did have a dramatic effect," Antonius chuckled to himself.

"The point was to throw my shadows off. I want them to think that they have seen us perform someplace."

The ruse simply didn't work, because they could feel the eyes that never left. Trying to ignore anyone but themselves, they enjoyed a grand meal, in impressive surroundings with attentive waiters who were ever present.

"That music," Antonius asked. "Where does it come from, and who is performing it?"

Cos listened for a moment and said, "That's what we call Jazz. It's a recording coming over the speakers."

Antonius frowned. "I didn't understand a word you said, Cos. Perhaps I have a lot more English to learn."

"The style is Jazz, but the players are not here. The music was captured previously, and we can hear it anytime we want. Do you like it?" Mary asked.

"Yes, absolutely yes!" he said. "This is a great place, your world. Even the food is better than the Emperor would have eaten."

"Wait until they bring the dessert, Antonius. You haven't seen anything yet!" Mary said.

"They are still watching. I can feel it," Cos said under his breath.

Antonius stood up and tossed his napkin on the table, "Enough. Let me find out why." They could tell that he was angry and saw his muscles bulging under his trim tuxedo. He walked purposefully to the offending table and towered above the two men. Both sat up, surprised at his presence and his obvious anger.

"You two men. You are staring at my table and offending my lady. Your reason for bothering us?"

"We aren't looking at you at all. You must be mistaken," one said huffily.

"Your front teeth would look good lying on your dinner plate. No more warnings for you." The sarcastic looks disappeared as they realized that the man hovering over them would not hesitate, even in this posh restaurant, to mutilate their faces. "We will be careful not to look over there, is that enough to satisfy you?"

"No. You will leave right now or face the consequences."

"But we have not finished eating," the man protested.

Antonius leaned closer and said, "Ten more moments. Leave while you can." It was clear what was about to happen, and they quickly arose from their chairs, looking around for any possible assistance.

A nearby waiter came quickly to the table. "Is there anything wrong? Is the food or service not to your satisfaction?"

"They are leaving. Bring their bill to our table, and we will take care of it." He turned to the two men and said, "I don't want to see any trace of you when we leave this place, or I'll make sure you have a face that your own mother won't know." They scurried off without looking behind them. The other patrons watched Antonius nervously until he sat down again, his back to the room.

"Thanks, Antonius. By the way, if you crush their faces, you will likely have to go downtown with a police escort. Try to have no witnesses if it happens," Cos explained calmly.

"There is no need to actually touch them. Fear is enough to send them running, and they have that now. We won't be troubled by those two again."

"Still the Centurion. Be careful, Antonius. You can do almost anything in self-defense but…well, I hope they took your advice," Mary said.

As Mary imagined, the dessert menu was long and exotic. She selected a thick chocolate dish for Antonius, and when it came with a flourish, she clapped excitedly, watching his face.

"What is this dark thing? Do I eat it?" he asked.

"Chocolate. The most wonderful food ever found. It didn't exist back then. Try it, won't you?" she pleaded. He did, carefully, a small nibble at a time, then quickly consumed the rest, smacking his lips and his fingers.

"Wonderful, marvelous! I could eat more!"

"No, my dear. You have to save room for snacks and drinks after we go dancing. Cos, you will come with us, won't you?"

"Will you dance with me if I do?" he asked.

"She will," Antonius said.

"I guarantee that you three will be the best dressed of anyone in there," the cabbie said when he held the door open for them. The sign read Club Royale, and there was a well-dressed bouncer guarding the door.

"Are you sure there is dancing inside?" Mary asked again.

"It's a real hot spot. The way you look, Miss, you will be the center of attention."

The bouncer stopped them at the door. "We usually don't allow unaccompanied males in. You three should become four, then try again."

"Listen, Buddy," Cos hissed. "This lady takes two to make her happy. We don't need another skirt. Take this C-note and look the other way." He stood really close to the man, making him obviously uncomfortable. The man nodded agreement, took the offered money, then held the door for them.

"Cos!" Mary said. "You sounded like an old Chicago gangster. Where did you learn to talk like that?"

"Old movies on TV," he said casually. "And some of my relatives are in the Mafia."

"I watched TV," said Antonius. "I didn't learn to talk like that."

"You don't need to. They can see your muscles," Cos remarked.

Chapter 31

Eternal City

A sudden drop in altitude and a gut wrenching bump rattled through the massive airplane, shaking luggage in the overheads and causing even the stewardesses to hold on. Cos opened his eyes just enough the see light coming in the side windows and hear the grumblings of the other passengers. He became aware of Mary's arm and shoulder touching his, and he could feel her moving slightly through their clothing. She was whispering nearly inaudibly, "It's just a bump, Antonius. You'll get used to it…no, the plane isn't coming down, not at all, dear."

Cos grinned to himself, and let his eyes close again. Two more hours to Rome, the Eternal City, so named by the ancients themselves. No parasitic followers of Jesus there, other than the ones worshiping the true Jesus. Chicago was far behind them, and he was nearly back on his own turf. He let out a big sigh, letting go all the tension of the past several weeks. He snuggled down in the seat, trying to relieve pressure on his hip, then remembered why it was still sore. A glimpse of a wooden sword, wielded by his muscular sparring partner came to his memory, just before it struck his hip, knocking him to the ground. In fact he was sore in several spots as well as having overall muscular fatigue. The adventure of it all, the drama, the fear. Nothing like it could be imagined by someone who had never been there, and he had actually been there. He couldn't help recalling Mary. Not the woman touching his shoulder. The other Mary, before she gave her love to Antonius. Her delicate, beautiful face so in contrast with her surroundings. Her soft comforting voice, her big dark eyes, her presence, came rushing to him in a flood of partial memories and remembered images. There had never been anything in his life he wanted more than her. He ached to be able to kiss her neck and feel her arms around him, her perfume intoxicating him. Being near her required incredible discipline. His eyes avoided lingering too long on hers, fearful of projecting his desires, making her want to avoid him. When she talked to him, he strained to concentrate on anything but her, while still trying to converse and answer her questions. It was both pleasure and torture at the same time. Good and evil, yin and yang. He learned that he could be two people at once, one yearning for her touch, the other recoiling from it. And there was Antonius. Cos dearly loved the man. A better friend could never be found, and he couldn't deny his friend from wanting the same woman that he also desired. Clearly the choice was Mary's, and she had made it. The subject was officially closed…forever. But neither time nor distance would ever erase the desire he had for her. That part of his mind was never going to let go of her.

The fasten seat belt sign came on at the same moment as a series of soft dings rang through the air. The plane's engines diminished in intensity, and there was a subtle change in level. Cos sat up and looked around, trying to see something familiar from the plane's windows.

"Have a nice sleep?" she asked softly, her voice seeping into the fortress of his mind, creating the usual weakening effects. He turned to see her smiling face and, just beyond, Antonius' worried face as he anxiously looked out the window.

"Yes. I drifted off a bit. Get any rest yourself?" he answered, looking into the innocent soul of her eyes.

"Not a trace. Antonius is fighting the experience a bit, not that I blame him. Are you looking forward to getting home?"

"There is no one here for me any longer. Rome is as familiar as the back of my hand, and there are lots of memories there, but it isn't really home unless someone waits for you."

"You'll find someone, Cos. Don't think that way," she said and patted his wrist with her electric hand. He wanted to blurt that he had found someone, it was her, and it would always be her.

"You could be right, Mary," he said, wanting instead to say what was true, that he never would find any woman to replace her in his heart.

"When do we get to see Rome? All I see is white," Antonius asked.

"As soon as we break through the clouds. The plane is still descending," Mary answered.

"Sir, could I check your seat belt," the pretty stewardess asked, leaning over Cos. He moved his arms away from his waist and looked up at her, realizing that what she wanted was to get his attention. Her long blond hair hung over her back, becoming visible again under her arm.

"Looks like you came from Italy," she said, smiling radiantly.

"What do you mean?" he asked.

"The suit. I mean it screams Italian. Expensive. You know!"

"You have a discerning eye," Cos remarked.

"Not so hard. I watched you board the plane. Are you a model or something? The suit just suits you!" she laughed a bewitching laugh, showing her perfect teeth.

"Lately, I've been traveling in the past. Where are you from?" he asked.

"The past?" she looked puzzled, wrinkling her nose but quickly recovered her smile. "I'm from Stuttgart, but I have an apartment in Rome. Will you be in Rome long?"

"I'm really not sure. I may be recalled to Chicago, but I don't know when."

"While you are here, I would love to show you the town if you want," she said.

"How can I get in touch with you?" he asked.

"I've written my number and address on this paper. Put it where you can find it. I'll be around most of this week." Cos accepted the paper and looked at it briefly.

He stuck out his hand and said, "Hi Bess, my name is Cosimo. I'll give you a ring when I get settled. Thanks for the invitation, but I'll be showing you Rome. I grew up there, and I know places to take you that you would never find on your own." Something made him glance at Mary, whose attentive face was somewhere in his peripheral vision. He caught a flicker of emotion in her eyes, quick in passing, but there, clearly there. A spark of jealousy and an instant of resentment for the woman pushing her way into his life came briefly to the surface. It was soul satisfying for him to realize that somewhere deeply buried under her mountain of affection for Antonius was at least a grain owned by him.

"That girl on the plane was right, Cos. You are handsome in that suit, and she didn't even see the white one," Mary said. The warm morning light was hitting the ancient tan-colored stone behind her, and the reflected light lit up her hair in a glowing crescent above her brow. She was wearing a low cut ivory dress, dramatically complementing her dark hair. The ancient glass ornament around her neck twisted in slow arcs, forcing all eyes toward her deep cleavage. She took a sip of her cappuccino, holding the small cup with the tips of her fingers. "This is grand, isn't it," she remarked, looking down the long sidewalk mostly filled with tourists laden with heavy purses or cameras. In the distance were several stately stone columns reaching into the sky but no longer supporting anything but a few birds.

Antonius looked at his coffee with suspicion, sniffing it from a safe distance. "I don't really like the smell of this…foul black liquid. You really have developed some strange tastes in this time."

"Try putting a little bit of cream and sugar in it," Cos suggested. "Truth is, it's an acquired taste, but once acquired, you will find that you can never do without it for very long."

"You managed, as I remember, to not drink any for many days," Antonius retorted.

"Yes, but I suffered. You don't know how much."

Antonius grimaced and finally put the cup to his lips, giving out a sucking sound as he pulled air over the hot liquid. "It tastes better than it smells, I will admit, but I can still do without it," he said as he put the cup forcibly down. He looked around slowly and methodically before speaking. "This is not the Rome I remember. Where is the Forum?"

"We are a few blocks from there. Do you have a clear memory of it, Antonius?" Mary asked.

"I was there many times. I know every inch of it. Standing in the Forum where Caesar once stood always gave me a thrill. Great men walked at the very heart of the Empire there."

Cos looked at Antonius with affection but concern. "Remember that it's been a very long time since you were here. In that long span there have been earthquakes, wars and destruction by ignorant necessity. After the Empire fell apart, a thousand years went by before people started to learn about the glory of Rome. A thousand years. During that time, education and access to books was limited to very few individuals. Even most rulers were not as knowledgeable as you and your fellow Romans. We call it The Dark Ages. The cities you built, the roads, the aqueducts and the baths fell apart in time and were never replaced. Rule by law and by representation was given over to rule by the strong. Even the modern world has been troubled by wars and poor government. We call your time the first century. Italy did not become a united country again until the nineteenth century. Mary and I, and similarly educated scholars, view your time as the high point of human civilization. The grandeur of Rome has never been duplicated. You are in for a shock, I'm afraid, at the change you will see."

Mary put her hand over Antonius' hand and said tenderly, "You are the only person in the world who has ever seen what Rome really looked like. The rest of us just guess. Look around at all the people who have traveled here just to see the little of what remains. Most of them, including us, would give almost anything to have seen what you have seen with your own eyes. Remember that you are here now, and you must accept that the world that we just came from only remains as fragments and dust. It is physically gone but not from our minds or our hearts."

Cos paid the breakfast bill and put on his sunglasses with a flare. His nightmares and visions had stopped, and he was becoming comfortable once more in the city of his youth. While Mary didn't quite have his Italian flair for formfitting suits, the kind of casual elegance that suited men his age so well, she managed to outfit Antonius with stylish, masculine clothing. He was wearing thin pleated wool slacks over soft black slippers. A dark red silk polo shirt was topped by a soft, light brown calfskin jacket. The resultant package was both elegant and comfortably timeless. They started walking along the Via di San Marco, Mary between the two men who adored her. Their casual conversation was brought to an abrupt halt as the street opened into the *Piazza Venezia* and the huge *Altare della Patria* loomed above them.

"I don't remember that temple," Antonius said, looking up the imposing stairs topped by a huge columned building.

"No, you shouldn't. That is relatively new…about one hundred thirty years or so. The Roman Forum is on the back side of it," Cos explained.

"Then it is facing the wrong way."

"It faces north, across the river; I'm sure the builders did not mean it as an insult," Cos said. They turned the corner and headed up the *Via del Fori Imperiali,* and in the distance, the Coliseum loomed into view.

Antonius put his arms out bringing them to a halt. He took off his sunglasses and squinted, pointing. "That's old. Funny, I don't remember that one either," he said.

"Easily the most famous structure in the world. That is the Flavian Amphitheater. It was built by Titus in the late first century with money his army took from Jerusalem and the Temple after the first uprising. To me it is a symbol of many evils. I have never seen the inside of it," Mary said.

"What was it used for?" Antonius asked, still inspecting it from a distance.

"Gladiator fights, mostly," Cos said. "The entry to the Forum and other ruins is just ahead to the right. I'll take you to the Coliseum later if you are interested."

"Thanks, Cos, but I'm not interested if she is not interested," he said and affectionately laid his hand on Mary's back. They continued to stroll slowly forward, allowing Antonius to take in the sights. After a couple of more turns, Cos intimated that they should stop. Around them was a nearly open area with the rubble of former buildings rising rectangularly in rows, punctuated by the occasional marble column still proudly resisting the centuries. The shortness between antiquity and the present unveiled itself before them in a panorama of broken stone as their minds saw the original structures around them, gleaming a noble white and rising into the blue sky. Only one blink of the eye of time. For the first moment in their lives, Cos and Mary saw the Forum as it was, understood the passage of time in a way they never could have before.

"Antonius, do you know where you are?" Cos asked.

"This place is unfamiliar," he said and studied the grounds carefully. He started to walk, looking mostly at the pavement below his feet, then suddenly stopped and looked up surprised. He pointed to a large rectangular area on the right. "That was where the *Basilica Julia* rose into the sky," he paused for a moment putting everything in place, "and that," pointing to another rectangular area, "that was the *Basilica Aemilia*. As a child, we came here to buy food. I was inducted into the Army in that building."

"You remembered. This is the Forum, isn't it, Antonius?" Cos asked, watching him carefully. Antonius didn't seem to hear and kept walking and thinking. He stepped into the large rectangle most experts have identified as the site of the Temple of Vesta, hesitated, looking around as if seeing it in his mind.

"This was where the Vestal Virgins kept the sacred fire burning. I was never in here before. This is the most important site in Rome, the most sacred, and it's gone as is my city and all of its people." He squatted down, holding his face in his hands and started sobbing. "Gone forever," he mumbled through his hands. Both Mary and Cos respectfully held their distance, letting Antonius vent his sorrow. After a long while he slowly stood and looked around one last time, intense sadness creating harsh lines in his face. Without saying anything more, Antonius, his blood brother and his future wife walked slowly away from the ruins of a past civilization and from all the lives of long ago, taking with them only traces of ancient dust clinging to their shoes.

Chapter 32

Experimenting with Time

Captain McMurphy adjusted his belt and walked slowly up the stairs toward the main door at Fermilab. His image reflected in the glass door for a brief moment before pulling it open. Old, fat, and tired it yelled. The years have gone by too quickly, and he hadn't used them well. Lots of regrets, too many to consider.

"May I help you Captain?" the receptionist cooed at him, her voice warm, but her eyes thinking ahead before he could answer. "Here to see Dr. Harmes again?"

"Yes. Know where she is this morning?" he asked. He was irritated that she had guessed correctly. And why shouldn't she? This was the third time he was out here this week, each time to see Susan. Sure it was business, serious business, but he had grown more fond of her each time they met, and he secretly hoped that she felt the same.

"She is in the Tevatron again. Do you need help finding her?" she asked, knowing that he knew the way by now. McMurphy shook his head that he didn't and started toward the same door again. He wouldn't mind so much, but the stairs into the tunnel were steep and long. Even harder going back up.

Back in the semi-dark tunnel, he wiped the sweat from his brow and slowly made his way to her lab. Rounding the corner to her office, he found her where he always found her, bending over her computer, hard at work.

"Susan!" he called, watching her come out of her trance and look up.

"Well, hi, Fred! I hoped that you would come by again. The break will do me good."

"Are you making any progress?"

"At last, I can say that I'm getting closer to a solution. This is a lot harder than targeting the original opening where we only had to shoot for an approximate time and location. This one has to be nearly perfect. We have been running tests around the clock, each time we make the slightest change in parameters. I discovered by accident that one particular parameter was the most critical and that has made a big difference. Soon, Fred. But I must be absolutely sure before we go with it. There will only be one chance to get it right."

"If it works, or rather when it works, Susan, you will earn the respect of everyone on the planet."

"No, Fred. If it works, no one will ever know, not even me." Her words stuck in his mind, but he couldn't sort out the meaning. How could even she not know?

"And how are things on your end?" she asked, changing the subject before he could ask any questions.

"I do a lot of sweating over this stuff, but it's mostly worry and tension. We estimate that at least one third of the city of Chicago and the surrounding communities' populations are devout, fanatic, mindless, followers of Jesus. He'll sooner or later turn them all, maybe even us. I still don't understand it, and the Bishop and I have spent hours discussing it. We even brought in psychologists from the University of Chicago and explored their views. The plain, ugly truth is that most people want to be led, be told what to do instead of making the effort to think for themselves. Perhaps that trait is hardwired in us, left over from our tribal roots. There can only be one leader in a tribe, the rest follow. The lies they are told pass in and out like a weightless feather, making no difference to their strongly held views. In Illinois, we have seen plenty of slick politicians do the same thing. It doesn't seem to matter if they openly commit crimes or fail to follow the law. People, most people, still slavishly follow where they are led. In the case of Jesus though, it is going to lead to another world war. The Muslims in particular will never convert, and they will be forced to resist. Jesus is calling for the destruction of Islam and all of its adherents. He intends to dominate the entire world no matter what the cost in human life. Bishop Malveccio said that he believes that Jesus has his sights set on taking over the

Vatican soon. If he manages to be declared Pope, it will give him an ever bigger platform and stage. He will be the first Pope who declares that he is God, not just His messenger."

"I try not to watch the news, Fred, and that's why. I am already working at my limit, and that kind of information just doesn't help. No more discussion of Jesus, agreed?" she asked.

"I'm sorry, Susan. Your point is well taken, and my lips are sealed, at least for today."

"Have you been in contact with our young heroes?" she asked.

"A couple of times. The three of them are over there living the good life on Ray's dollar. I hope he doesn't pull the plug on them."

Susan laughed, "Heavens no, he won't. All they would have to do is start talking. Ray already has to keep a low profile. Their story would make everybody insanely angry if it gets out. They can buy or do anything they want, and he won't complain even a little."

"In that case, we should envy them. They have each other and have had an adventure that no one could ever match. They deserve to be happy, given the risks they were asked to take."

"I'm not sure all of them are happy," Susan said. "Before they entered the Portal, I noticed the looks exchanged between Mary and Cos. I expected to see two lovers when they returned, but that's not what happened. Antonius has Mary's love, not Cos. Unfortunately for Cos, he is in love with Mary. I could see it clearly just the short time I was around them. He calls Antonius his blood brother, and they seem to have a deep friendship, so it adds up to a lot of pain for Cos. I don't think he wanted to go to Rome with them, but he is such a loyal guy that he did go in spite of what it will do to him each time Antonius touches Mary in his presence."

"What's going to happen when you find your solution?" Fred asked.

"They will have to come back."

"Do they know what you are going to expect of them?"

"Not a clue."

Chapter 33

He Comes

"I was offered a job this morning," Antonius said. He drained his coffee cup, wiped his lips and smiled with a twinkle in his eye. Mary and Cos looked up from their breakfast, surprised.

"We're waiting to hear, go on with it!" Mary exclaimed.

"I was just finishing my workout in the hotel gym. A well-dressed man and woman approached me, and after a few compliments, said they wanted to employ me as a personal trainer. They were very persistent about it."

"Just for them?" Cos asked, eyebrows up.

"No. They mentioned making a video, whatever that is."

"Interesting," Cos said, furrowing his brow. "What did you say?"

"I said that I had to talk to my counsel. That's you, Cos."

"Thank you. Are they coming back?"

"Hotel Lobby, after breakfast. I told them to wait for us."

"Do you want a job, Antonius?" Mary asked.

"It's been a month since we came out. I feel like being of some use to someone."

"Aren't you having fun in this wonderful city. We haven't even seen it all yet," Mary asked.

"We are to be married in ten days, Mary. I have to tell your parents that I can support you. More importantly, I have to feel for myself that I can support you." He folded his linen napkin carefully and laid it on his empty plate.

"I think it's a good idea," Cos said. "They saw something about you out of the ordinary… more unconventional. That's your appeal to them and to a bigger audience. This could be very interesting."

"Weren't you supposed to play tennis with Bess again this morning?" Mary asked, letting the word Bess have a subtle emphasis. She squinted in the morning sun at him, making it difficult to discern displeasure or sarcasm in her face.

"She can wait," Cos said with an Italian one-shoulder shrug. She would too, everyone knew. It was obvious by now that Bess would do anything he asked, whenever he asked. Perhaps it was the clothes that gave him so much confidence and power, or perhaps it was maturity alone. Cos was suave, debonair and picture perfect. He had a way of grinning slyly at women, a sensual message from a devilish boy inside an experienced man, hinting at adventure with just a glance. Mary watched the magic hypnotize one after another, young and old. He moved slowly but with purpose and elegance, the drape of his fine wool garments hitting just the right angles in their minds. His looks convinced women and men alike that he was wealthy, well-known, and outstandingly desirable. And it would only take seconds to form the concept of him in their heads, as their eyes looked over him again to be sure what they were seeing.

"You've become an Italian playboy, Cos. I close my eyes, and I see you in bloody armor, a sword in one hand. I open them to find a gigolo. Which, I wonder, is the real Cos?" Mary said.

Cos didn't answer, because the truth couldn't be spoken out loud. He was trying to make her jealous, and it was working. Fortunately, he had the good luck to be born handsome; Ray had provided the rest. A little experimentation perfected the formula to bring women to him. He could have any or all of them, except the one he really wanted. This was an outlet for him, a release, and a source of slight satisfaction when she protested. He didn't want to break up Mary and Antonius, because he loved them both, wanted to protect them from harm. What did he want then? He wasn't sure, but down deep he knew that his time was running out, and this was, for now, the only way he had of expressing himself, of proving that he was still alive.

Cos casually glanced at the newspaper, folded neatly on the side of the metal table. Usually he paid it no mind. The world and its petty problems no longer mattered to him. After comprehending the collapse of the Roman Empire, he realized that nothing really mattered, especially not politics. History and time would grind everything into rubble sooner or later. Humans and their petty struggles. Would it matter centuries from now what any one of them thought or did? The newspaper caught his eye again, and he looked at it with his conscious mind, picking it up and slowly unfolding it. The headlines were ten centimeters tall… "He Comes!" they screamed.

"What's so interesting, Cos?" Mary asked, puzzled at the change in his expression.

For a moment he didn't answer, absorbed in reading. "Bad news, I'm afraid," he said and looked up, color gone from his face. "Jesus is arriving in Rome this morning. Thousands are to meet him at the airport and along the route into the city. The paper gushes with excitement over it."

Mary reached out and tugged the paper from his hands and bent over it, flipping pages as she absorbed the print, then as quickly put it down. She looked back and forth between Cos and Antonius, realizing that an earthquake was about to shake the world apart. She wanted to scream or start running but instead was weak, too helpless to protest.

"It was too good to last," Antonius said. "Fair weather is followed by storms. Good by evil. We always knew that we would have to face him again, and now he comes to us."

"The smart thing to do is to run away, not face him," Cos said. "We can do nothing to him, and even if we could, he would die a martyr, and his orders will still be carried out by his devoted followers."

"Have you been in contact with Chicago?" Antonius asked.

"I talk with Captain McMurphy on occasion. He told me that there was some speculation that Jesus was coming this way, but he expected a conquest of New York first. I thought there was going to be more time before he came here."

"What are we going to do?" Mary worried aloud.

"We are going to meet with the business people, then I am going to play tennis with my favorite Barbie Doll. What are your plans for this morning?"

"All my plans flew away. I suddenly feel sick," Mary responded.

Antonius pulled her close and kissed her cheek. "Remember when we were in Chicago? Recall that you and I had no problem. It was Cosimus they noticed. He should be afraid, but you can see that he isn't. Relax and see what develops before you worry."

And he didn't seem worried, not at all, when he introduced himself to the well-dressed couple patiently waiting in the lobby.

Cos, in his most persuasive style and manner, approached them with his hand extended, "Saluti. Prime introduzioni sono in ordine. Io sono Cosimo Petronie. Io rappresento Antonius come amico e il suo avvocato. Dovrei rivelare che io rappresento anche un consorzio di stilisti di abbigliamento che sono internazionali e che ha anche cercare una nuova stella della moda maschile." [Greetings. First introductions are in order. I am Cosimo Petronie. I represent Antonius as a friend and his legal counsel. I should disclose that I also represent a consortium of clothing stylists who are international and who also seek a new star of men's fashion.] The couple stood hesitantly, overwhelmed by his elegant introduction. The woman was attractive and well-dressed. Mary watched as Cos took her in as if he were a snake hypnotizing a mouse before striking. One glance at Cos, and she was already willing to run away with him. The man was more sure of himself, but Cos disarmed him by his arrogant confidence and his impeccable good looks.

"May we speak English?" the man stammered. His accent said that he was neither American nor British, yet not Italian.

"Of course!" Cos said and slapped him on his shoulder playfully, winking at the woman as if he agreed just for her.

"You see, we are from Amsterdam, just visiting here, and we saw your friend working out. He is unforgettable, we felt, and just the man we were looking for to star in a new series of television programs about personal fitness. We have had enormous success so far but him…well, I can see clearly that women would watch just to see him move. This exposure will lead to other offers, we are sure. Can we make a deal?" he pleaded.

"We can at least talk about it. Can you give me your names first?" Cos asked in a conspiratorial voice, then smiled his winning smile. The woman almost buckled at the knees.

"Sure, sure. My name is Blevins. Hoosker Blevins. This is my associate and partner, Sarah Giacosa," he stammered. "Our company is Adonis. We are well-known in Europe, ask anyone."

Cos turned his attention to Sarah, "Giacosa? Does that mean an *Italiano* origin for you, my dear?"

"My father. My mother is Dutch," she beamed, loving the chance to look into his eyes.

Cos took her hand in his, holding it carefully, lightly massaging her fingers with his thumb. "No doubt we can have an agreement and be friends at the same time. It is the Italian way. And you are not yet married, I see." He turned and looked at poor Hoosker like he was just an intervener, an encumbrance. "And what do you offer my client?" he said, turning his attention back to Sarah before the man could answer.

"Well, your man is an unknown you realize. Until we find out if the public accepts him, we would be foolish to start high," Hoosker said.

"Then what? You must have a starting place in mind," Cos said, his eyes fixed on Sarah's.

Hoosker broke out in a fine sweat and looked nervously around. He had never been afraid of dealing in money, but this time the ground was being pulled out from under his feet. "Top figure...no higher...fifty," he blurted, glad to get it out.

"Surely you meant to say Fifty Thousand, isn't this the figure? And, of course, that is per episode, and only for the first six. Isn't that what you had in mind," Cos said.

"Do it, Hoosker," Sarah said. "Agree. You know it will work out." She smiled at Cos, considering it their victory, a win for the winning side.

"Make sure before you speak that we are talking about Euros, Hoosker," Cos said quietly, not looking away from Sarah. His eyes scanned her face as if taking measurements, memorizing every detail.

"Yes. I mean that is what I had in mind all along. Is it settled then?" he asked politely.

Cos stood erect, letting his arms fall by his sides and turned his attention back to Hoosker. "Send the papers to me at this hotel. Tomorrow, no later. We will get back to you."

He put his arms around Mary and Antonius and led them away, chatting aimlessly about the weather and the prospects for lunch. They could feel Sarah's eyes tracking his every motion, each lovely turn of his head.

"I taught you to use a sword, but your words are more powerful than any weapon. Such skill at manipulation I have never seen nor knew was possible. Thank you on behalf of both of us," Antonius said sincerely.

"Not just his words, Antonius. It's his power over women that you just saw in action. *Magnifico*, Cosimo. You are a bit frightening to watch. Be careful with that, my boy. It can turn on you. Remember the old saw about a woman scorned."

"Didn't Virgil say 'A shifty, fickle object is woman, always.' Except for you, Mary. He never met you, or he would not have said that," Cos laughed.

"I once quoted Caesar to you, Cosimus, and I'll repeat it in case you've forgotten. 'In the end, it is impossible not to become what others believe you are.' " Antonius said.

"Trust me when I tell you both that you know the true Cos or Cosimo or Cosimus. What you saw was an act. It's what was needed. You don't need to scold me, because I am truly humbled being around both of you. You are the noblest of the entire human race, the best that it can produce. I, Cosimo, am your servant." He stopped walking and gave each a slight bow, causing them to laugh and cry at the same time.

Mary and Antonius were alone for lunch, an unusual occurrence, the three being nearly inseparable during the daytime. They ordered, but kept looking around, hoping that he would change his mind and suddenly appear.

"Did he call you?" Mary asked. She tried not to be obviously anxious about missing Cos, but her voice betrayed her.

"I got a note written in Latin he left with the waiter. He excused his absence and requests that we meet for dinner," Antonius said as he tried in vain to read the menu written in Italian.

"Is he bringing that girl?" she asked.

"He didn't specify, but what if he does? She is most pleasant and decidedly lovely to look at."

"I don't like her, that's all," Mary said too quickly.

"Green eyes?"

It took a moment for her to focus on his meaning. "Are you asking if I am jealous?"

"No. Stating a fact. I watch you, you know. I know your moods, your thoughts, your wishes, secret and otherwise. You are jealous of her. You have me, body and soul, forever, if you want me. You can't have both of us. I shouldn't have to explain that to you."

Mary started to well up with tears, at first wiping her eyes with her napkin, but then it poured out of her like a summer rainstorm. She put her face down on his hand, sobbing helplessly. Antonius saw the waiter coming toward them and waved him off.

"Cos loves you with everything in him. I have always known that, and I find no fault in it. There is no wrong done for loving you, and I know exactly how he feels. He acts the perfect gentleman around both of us. He never utters a word, telling either of us how much he cares, how his heart hurts knowing that he can never have you in his arms. We know what is in his mind, because we know him. I love him, just as you do, so I know how you feel also. Next time you see him, tell him that you love him, it's what he wants to hear more than anything. Tell him so that both of you can get past it, and we can go on with our lives." When he finished, Mary began crying even harder and collapsed against him, putting her wet face against his neck.

"I'm so sorry, Antonius. I love you more than I love anything or anybody, including myself. I don't want to replace you with Cos, but I do love him, I admit it. It tears me apart watching him with all those other women."

"Yes, I knew that. Makes you realize what he is going through, which is exactly why he lets you see it. I knew all this before, and I still asked, nearly begged, him to come with us to Rome. I'm glad that I did, because we needed to get this out in the open and deal with it in person."

"What are we going to do?" she murmured in his ear, her tears running down his neck and wetting his white collar.

"You know that he had a terrible vision that night in Alexandrium. Since then he keeps having it. He believes that it is a vision of the future. He keeps saying that he knew we would make it back here, because he actually saw it. The horrible vision is the same. He knows that it is going to happen, and he feels that he is going to die at the hands of whatever he saw and that time is running out on him. I won't feel threatened or become angry if you tell him that you love him. It's true anyway, and I know that neither of you would ever act on it. I trust both of you with my life as well as my heart."

"Can you be sure that it won't make it harder for him if I say that?" she asked.

"I think that it will give him peace. Later, you will be glad that you said it."

"You are such an understanding and fine man, Antonius. I'll never let you go."

"I know, Mary. Cosimus is a fine man too. The finest man I have ever known. He would give his life for our happiness and may yet do so."

Chapter 34

Pursuit

"NEITHER CAN THE WAVE THAT HAS PASSED BY BE RECALLED, NOR THE HOUR WHICH HAS PASSED RETURN AGAIN."

Ovid

The motorcade crossed the Tiber using *Ponte Sublicio* and headed onto the broad *Via Marmorata* before turning northwest on *Viale Aventino* toward its destination: the grounds of the ancient Circus Maximus. The advance party representing Jesus had at first demanded use of the Coliseum but approval was swiftly denied by the authorities. Crowds of people were already assembling on the ancient site of chariot racing, so popular with early Romans. Packed along the roads were lines and layers of excited people, waving and shouting as the long black limousine and motorcycle guards swept past. *"Gesù, Gesù, Gesù,"* they chanted in unison, the sound echoing off stone raised by craftsmen two millennia ago. The city of Rome was alive with anticipation and excitement.

"Exciting, isn't it, to witness the return of our God, Jesus!" a man shouted into Cos' ear. Cos ignored him and pressed into the crowd, dragging Mary, who dragged Antonius, deeper and deeper into the throng.

Mary tugged at Cos, and he leaned close to hear her. "Isn't this illegal? I mean this is a preservation area. The police couldn't have allowed them to use this place, could they?" Cos shook his head no. The question was how could the authorities stop them. No possible way they could be stopped, not this many of them. The place has often been used for large gatherings, even as many as 500,000, Cos remembered. This crowd was even larger, spilling over and into the surrounding roads. They were close to the hastily constructed stage at the east end, near a preserved rise in the earth, the ancient entrance to the racetrack. When the motorcade was spotted, the throng started yelling, the sound traveling as a wave from those closest to the other end, echoing from the surrounding buildings in the distance. Hands went up, further obstructing their view, the noise swelling to a deafening monotone, blending every sound together, emerging as a primitive unintelligible gurgle. A glimpse of white robes on the stage surged the crowd to even higher levels of ecstasy and the chant of "*Gesù, Gesù, Gesù*" continued for some minutes. Seemingly without cue, the crowd hushed abruptly, listening collectively for any message from their master.

The message came, relayed by speakers positioned in rows along the swelling dirt walls ringing the old racetrack, "I am Jesus," the deep voice said. "I am your God, come as promised in your scriptures." The ground shook with the eruption of human voices, collectively making more noise than any man-made thing other than a bomb. There were people jumping or spinning in place as others fell to the earth in a swoon of religious fervor. It took fifteen minutes for the mass to again become quiet.

"Are there any here who do not believe the message I have given you?" the deep voiced asked. "Raise your hands if you do not believe," he commanded. Cos looked around. If there were any nonbelievers other than the three of them, they were smart enough to stay quiet. Then the message changed.

"Raise your hands if you believe in me!" he commanded, the voice sending a chill through their bodies. Cos, Mary and Antonius shot their hands high into the air and looked around to see if everyone had done so. Their vision was limited, but they saw no hands down. Jesus waited, looking with narrowed eyes at the crowd, then said, "No! There are nonbelievers among us. Cast out those who have not merged their hearts with ours." This time there were some muffled screams in differing areas of the crowd. Close by, an older man was seized by several youths who fell to beating him until he collapsed to the ground. Not satisfied, they started kicking him, others joining them until the man stopped moving and was dragged away toward the periphery.

Jesus spoke again, "Others are hiding among us. They are nonbelievers. Find them and repel them from us!" he demanded again, pointing at the crowd. Several of the fanatics looked harshly at Cos but were hesitant because of his obvious lack of fear and also because the muscular Antonius stood close by. Instead, a nearby woman was selected. There was no apparent reason for her to be singled out, other than she was small and unprotected. Again, she was rapidly reduced to an unmoving bloody rag by everyone close to her. Men and women, even children, joined in the beating, and after it was done, others stripped off her clothing before she was dragged away, lifeless and broken.

"I've seen enough," Mary whispered to Antonius. "I want to leave." He slowly put his hand to her mouth and shook his had no. Cos silently agreed. If they tried to leave they would be quickly killed. They were stuck here until the event was over.

"My coming does not signal the end of the world. I bring a new beginning, a new light to the old world. We must overturn the old world. We will destroy the nonbelievers, before they plot to destroy us." A continuous chant of *"Gesù"* started again, blocking out any other sound. The crowd exhausted after thirty minutes, and the chant slowly dwindled. Cos caught a glimpse of Jesus eyeing the crowd as if looking for something or more likely, someone. Him. Being this close to Jesus brought on a kind of bone pain in his body, a deep generalized pain grabbing him, beads of sweat appearing on his forehead. He could feel that Jesus was looking for him, but he dared not turn away. He slid behind Antonius who blocked any trace of him from the podium.

"Go now to the Vatican, the Holy City. I demand entrance. I demand to lead from there. We will march as an unstoppable force and take what we are not given," he screamed, causing the hair on Cos' neck to stand up, to vibrate in synchrony with the evil emanating from the stage. The crowd turned toward *Ponti Palatino,* the first bridge on the nearly direct path toward the Vatican, a journey of only three miles. Given the size of the crowd, it would take some time for all of them to cross the river and work their way west toward the Catholic stronghold. The Vatican had been unmolested since 1870 when Italian troops invaded to unify Rome into the greater Italian State. Cos knew that the Vatican would resist and resist violently, hopefully assisted by troops from the city and central government. It was their chance to slip away, hopefully unnoticed. At a signal from Antonius, they started to give way, allowing others anxious to proceed to go around. Mary feigned a foot injury and made a big show of hopping, assisted by her two men. Soon, the crowd largely passed away and congregated at the bridge, waiting to cross. They sat down to wait on the stragglers to leave and then saw the pile of bodies. Those who had been mutilated and stomped to death were discarded in a large pile. Most of the female victims were nude, and all were piled in a big heap, one on top of others, a stack nearly ten feet high, at least fifty in number.

"I wonder if it occurred to any of them that this was not what Jesus Christ taught," Mary said under her breath. She became pale and started to throw up between her spread legs, her men holding her up as she heaved.

"You people will miss the chance to help Jesus," a man said. They looked up to see a group of a dozen rough men gathered around them, glaring and predatory. Antonius slowly stood, facing them.

"We will come when we are ready. You are the ones missing it. Be gone or I will summon the crowd that you have avoided your duty to your God," he said, making his fist hard so that they could see it. Sullenly and slowly and with many backward glances, the group departed, joining the rest of the crowd pouring over the Tiber.

Cos looked around before speaking. "Looks like we and the dead are the last. Let's leave now while we can." They got up and headed up the small embankment on the east entrance and started slowly moving north toward the Coliseum and beyond, to their hotel. Mary slowly came to life, and they started moving more quickly.

"Don't look now, Antonius, but we are being followed," Cos said. "Four men, big men, are about a block behind. I know they are after us; I can feel it."

"Wait a bit before we act, be patient," Antonius advised.

"When we get to the Coliseum, I have a plan," Cos whispered. "The Coliseum has three outer walls with two walkways separating them. When we disappear around the west side, we can duck into one of the openings and wait for them in the deepest walkway. The openings are blocked by a fence, but I know ones which will open if you know how. And I do. Whatever we do to our pursuers won't be witnessed."

"What do you propose to do for weapons?" Antonius said.

"They have clubs. Those will be our weapons."

"I like it."

The plan wasn't perfect and relied not only on chance but on the aggressors following them to be ill-trained and unprepared. After Cos found a barrier which he could open, they picked Mary up and rushed into the darken passageways. The ancient, massive stone structure around them had been in constant use for a thousand years before earthquake and plunder had finally mutilated it into becoming just a symbol of an ancient way of life. It was an ideal place for an ambush, the heavy stone columns easily hiding them from view.

"Make no sound, Mary, no matter what happens," Antonius whispered to her. They heard the footsteps go by, and then one of the men said, "I don't see them. They must have hidden. Search in there." He must have pointed into the ancient site of gladiatorial battle, because the footsteps grew closer and more cautious as the men entered the darkened hallways. Antonius pointed to the other side of the broad column they were hiding behind. He started around on one side, Cos on the other.

"You men looking for someone?" Antonius asked, stepping into the light in front of them.

"You. We are looking for you. Where are the others?" they demanded.

"You mean so that you can beat and strip another defenseless woman?" he asked, moving closer. They readied their clubs, short pieces of stout pipe, slapping them into their hands just as Roman combatants used to do in this very place. Antonius slowly walked toward them, drawing their attention. Cos came around from the other side, behind and unseen, closing the distance silently. He chose the one on his right and focused on the man's right arm which held his club. Cos reached under the arm, seizing him by the wrist, and violently pulled his arm straight back, causing him to drop the pipe, which fell clattering against the stone floor. Cos swung his right foot in an arc under the man's arm, connecting heavily with his exposed waist, sending him crashing into the others beside him. He picked up the pipe and, in one smooth maneuver, tossed it to Antonius. The men in front of him had never considered that someday they would meet an armed, experienced, angry Centurion. But that was what was standing there now, and he didn't hesitate, not even for the blink of an eye. Three fatal blows fell in less than two seconds, and three men died before their bodies had fallen to earth. He tossed the pipe back to Cos who stood over the first man who was on the floor holding his broken arm.

"No," he screamed, but pleas would not be enough to stop the pipe whistling toward his head, and he joined his dead comrades on the floor of a structure unremorseful of death or pain.

Chapter 35

The Call From Susan

Have you seen the news?" Mary asked from the bedroom. Morning light was seeping past the closed curtains, giving the room a warm mellow glow. They had been up the previous night until early morning watching the struggle for the Vatican on live television. Every station was covering the action, and the reporting was frenetic. She realized that Antonius must not have heard her. She threw the covers back, sat up and listened, finally getting up and reaching for her robe. When she came into the main room, she saw that the balcony door was open, and Antonius was against the railing looking out.

"Hi," she said, putting her arm around him. "Did you get any sleep?"

"Listen, you can hear it from here," he said pointing to the column of rising smoke toward the west. She heard it, a rumble like distant thunder, punctuated by sharp reports from automatic weapons. The battle for the Vatican was still in play.

"It's like the end of the world," she said. "It can never go back to the way it was. This is the result of trying to tamper with the past."

Antonius turned toward her, studying her face. "And yet it brought us together and for that I am grateful. This struggle is just another example of humans, how they fight for an idea that's often wrong or even evil. How they are easily led astray, helpless to resist or to even recognize that they are only being used by others for their own ends. The fault is not with those who opened the Portal to the past but lies with those who so willingly believe what they are told. As a man of the past, I can see that nothing has changed about people. They remain exactly the same. You have found ways of doing things which add comfort to your lives since the ancient times, but you haven't found a way to make people better."

"Do you see any way out of this madness?"

"There is none. This struggle becomes part of human history as did your Jewish uprising against the Romans. Horrible at the time, but now just another page of history."

"Then it doesn't matter what happens?"

"It matters a great deal to those swept up in it, but the earth still turns and still goes around the sun. Winter still comes and is replaced by spring."

"But how do you feel, Antonius?"

"I love you. Holding your hand, looking into your eyes, hearing your voice and the warmth of your face against mine is what is most important to me. I once thought that Rome was eternal and would never end, but now you can only find traces of it buried like the bones of a long dead creature. The only thing eternal is the love two humans can have for each other. You and I came together, even though separated by an immense gulf of time, finding the miracle of true love. Nothing that is happening over there is as important as our love. It was bestowed on us by God, and it is the most important gift He could have given, and the only one that really matters."

They turned as they heard a knock on the door. Antonius opened the door cautiously at first, then swung it wide open to admit Cos. He came in holding an envelope and looked less well-groomed than usual.

"Mary, can you call for coffee to be brought up?" he asked, then sat down and opened the envelope. "Here are the papers for the job offer. I know the world is in chaos, but we still have to plan for the future. Antonius, I want your signature on these contracts before they change their minds. At the very least, they are obligated to pay you over half a million Euros even if you don't make a film for them. I can use this contract to start your other endeavor, men's clothing. Both will grow together, and in five years, everybody in Europe will know your name and face."

"Cos, why are you doing all this. Where is your part in it?" Mary asked.

When Cos looked up, they could see that his eyes were redden, his face strained. He had been up all night working this out. "My part is to be sure that you both are taken care of. It makes me happy to know that I won't have to worry about you. Except for helping get it started, there is no place for me, no role that I play."

"Do you know what is going on at the Vatican?" Antonius asked.

"No. War, it sounds like. When it's over, they will come looking for me, I can feel it. That's why I am preparing your future while I can.

"You will come to the wedding next week?" Mary asked.

Cos stood up and put his hands on her shoulders, looking into her eyes, "If I am still in this world, I will be there. If I am not, my spirit will be there, my hopes and wishes will be there, and they will always be with you as long as you both live."

"I love you, Cosimo," Mary said, her eyes welling up with emotion. He started to pull her closer but glanced at Antonius, hesitating.

"It's okay, Cos. I love you too," he said. The three fell into a group hug, none of them wanted it to end, and they separated slowly and with tenderness.

"I feel like my life is nearly fulfilled," Cos said. "and this is the high point of it. There is only one thing that I have left to do."

"It concerns your vision of the future, doesn't it?" Antonius asked.

"I know what it means now. Jesus is the monster in my vision. It is my destiny to face him."

"How is this possible, Cos? You will never be allowed to get close to him."

"I don't know, but it will happen, and soon."

The coffee at last arrived; the cart, complete with an assortment of breakfast buns and sweets, was pushed in by a crisply uniformed young woman.

"Signori, signora, il caffè, se non vi dispiace." [Sirs, Madam, your coffee, if you please.]

Cos bowed slightly and offered her a folded bill, *"Grazie mia cara. La prego di accettare questo piccolo segno."* [Thank you, my dear. Please accept this small token.]

"Grazie signore. Avete sentito il mondo possa finire? Sono così spaventata." ["Thank you sir. Have you heard the world may end? I am so frightened."]

Cos gracefully put his arm over her, affectionately walking her toward the door. *"Vi assicuro che il mondo non finirà. Io personalmente vedere che non è così."* [I assure you that the world will not end. I will personally see that it doesn't.] She flashed her eyes up at him, seemingly cheered by his assurance.

"I have to leave you for some unfinished business this morning," Cos said, after draining his second cup of coffee. There was something final about the way he spoke and looked, as if he were tying the last string around a package, the last gift to someone.

"Saying goodbye to Bess also?" Mary wondered.

"That too."

"Are you telling us goodbye?"

"Never goodbye to you. I might have to go to Brussels to complete this deal of yours, and I have to travel out of Rome to catch a flight, because the city is being so badly torn apart. If I disappear for a couple of days, don't worry about me, please."

"Of course we will worry about you," Antonius said. "Is this really necessary amid all the turmoil out there?"

"It might be our last chance to nail this down. Remember, you taught me well. I can take care of myself."

"Not if a multitude come after you."

"That is less likely almost anywhere but here. Besides, the followers are busy right now attacking the Catholics. When, and if, they win, we can worry." He stood up to leave, looking back and forth between Mary and Antonius, studying them, memorizing them. "I should leave now. Please don't go anywhere near the west side of the Tiber. Promise me."

"We won't, Cos. I promise," Antonius said.

"The other thing is that if Jesus and his bunch win and take over the Vatican, you should get away, far away from Rome. Go to Israel, you will be safe for the short-term, but I would guess that he will go there next. His origins are there, and he will take that also."

"This will become a world at war with no safe havens," Mary said. "The Antichrist has come, just as scripture warned."

Cos stood in the open door still looking at his best friends, torn between his love of them and his duty to protect them. He leaned down and kissed Mary on her forehead and slid his hand briefly over her shoulder, a contact and a caress, his last touch of something he so loved. He stuck out his hand for Antonius but was pulled into his chest for a last hug goodbye. He turned and closed the door behind him, tears in his eyes and in theirs.

"Good morning," he addressed the Concierge at the front desk. "I am checking out, and I need to find an airline out of Rome as soon as possible."

"The Army has closed them, sir. Radicals were coming in by the planeload. There are no flights in or out of Rome at this time."

"Are there no secondary airports, private ones?" Cos asked.

"Where are you going, sir, if I may ask?"

"New York. I need a shuttle to a city with an operative international airport."

"It may prove expensive. Should I still try?"

"Cost is secondary. Try," Cos said. While he was talking, he licked the seal on the envelope containing the contract and dropped it in a nearby postal box. He waited patiently while the Concierge made his calls. On the wall was a television screen with live coverage of the battle across town. The camera panned a field with a large number of fallen bodies, and then back to the close horizon and a spire of fire and smoke rising from large shadowy buildings in the background.

"We have a report that the Italian Army has evacuated most of Vatican City, but we have substantiated that the Holy Father still refuses to leave. There is more to this story, but we have been denied access by both parties to the conflict. Switching to our eye in the sky… as you can see there are still firefights in the *Piazza San Pietro*, and something new, a tank is parked near the ancient Egyptian obelisk. …Our pilot just informed us that he has been ordered away from the area by the military."

The view switched to the face of a very tired newscaster who seemed to be at a loss to report anything new and shuffled his papers.

"Sir, I have a flight for you," the Concierge said, bringing Cos' focus back to his problem. "If you make haste to Urbe Airport, I have a small plane waiting to take you to Pisa, and I am assured that the airport has not been closed there. From Pisa, you will find connections to Paris."

"Fine, I'll take it. Can you get me transportation to Urbe?"

"How soon can you leave, sir?"

"Right now."

"All I have is the bellboy and his private car, but I assure you that he can get you there safely."

Cos gave the man a hundred Euro note for his trouble and went to the curb to await transportation. In the distance he could hear deep and powerful explosions of a sort that indicated military action near the Vatican. At least they were trying, but it was a sad day for Italy and sadder still for Rome. While he waited, he thought about Susan's call yesterday. She seemed unsure of herself, jittery. At first she seemed to want to know about the attacks happening in Rome, but Cos could tell her nothing that already wasn't being reported by the American news people. She might even know more than him. He wanted to ask her if she felt personally guilty about what was happening, but he didn't. Of course, she did, he knew. She created the Portal, supervised it and even watched helplessly as the demon came in right past her. She would feel guilty, but Ray never would. He was cut from a different cloth entirely. Susan finally got around to what he knew she wanted, the reason she had called. They were to return. All three of them. For what purpose, exactly, was not discussed, just that they were to hurry back to Chicago. He wanted to ask why, his mind screamed it, but he didn't. Part of him didn't want to know, wanted to postpone learning whatever it was, because he knew that it wouldn't be what he wanted to do or hear. He had agreed that they would come back as soon as possible given the present chaos. At least on the phone he agreed. In his heart, he didn't agree. He would choose not to tell Mary or Antonius anything about it, and he would lie to them to prevent them from discovering that he was returning. There wasn't anything they could do that he couldn't, and he would rather take any risk by himself and leave them out of it. The visions had returned last night in his sleep. The face of a monster right in front of his, a growl in his head that woke him each time he closed his eyes. Whatever Susan wanted, it had to involve the monster. It was his destiny.

Chapter 36

"You Won't Like It..."

Chicago, CPD Police Headquarters

re they coming?" McMurphy asked into the telephone.

"Cos called me from Paris. They should arrive in Chicago tonight. Can you go pick them up and bring them here?" Susan asked.

"Better than that. I'm going to have a Swat Team pick them up. No sense in taking chances when we are this close. You are close, aren't you?"

"Testing only goes so far. I'm as ready as I'm going to get. My stress level can't take too much more of this. I could agonize forever and still not be positive, but I can say with confidence that it is the best I can do," Susan said.

"You keeping up with what is going on in Rome?"

"It's bad and keeps getting worse. They are saying now that the Pope has been killed. Is that true?"

"We at the CPD only watch the same news that you do. There is so much happening and so much confusion that I'm not sure what to believe. There is another twist that you might not have realized. Some of the reporting is tainted. Some of the newspeople are converts, and they are giving out biased news. You know, like they do here for political issues. They have taken sides. It makes me want to give up on the entire human race."

"That is why I am so nervous, Fred. The whole world is resting on the shoulders of four people. Me and those kids. And they don't even know yet what will be expected of them. What if they refuse?" She worried aloud.

"Not that bunch. From what I've learned about what happened back there, I know that you can count on them to do the right thing."

"Even if it means dying, Fred? Can we ask them to do that?"

"Come on, Susan. You don't know that is what will happen." McMurphy said. "Tell them the score. They know more than us what the risks will be."

"You are going to be here when they arrive, aren't you Fred?"

"Soon as you hear from them, call me, and I'll zip right over."

O'Hare International Airport, Chicago, 11:20 CST

"Hi, Susan. Cos here. Just arrived. You said something about transportation, didn't you?"

"Greetings Cosimo. Good trip?"

"It would have been better if everyone on the plane weren't talking about religion and the battle in Rome."

"I just need to let Captain McMurphy know. His boys are already there at the terminal. Be prepared, because he sent a Swat Team to pick you up. Mary and Antonius with you?" she asked.

"There is only me, Susan. I didn't want to tell you sooner, because I knew you would try to get in touch with them. I don't want them involved," Cos said.

"This is something we discussed before you all left. This is why Ray was paying for everything. You all agreed to come back, and now you are telling me that only you came and that you are the one who made that decision?" Her voice rose as she became angry, realizing that her plans were in jeopardy.

"I'm here, Susan. That's all you get. If you don't want me, I can always return to Rome. It is my home, after all."

She was silent for a long moment as the heat left her face, and she was able to think more clearly. "Cos, the five Romans who came in with you. Do you think they will be willing to take part in what we might do?"

"Really, Susan, what a ridiculous question. First of all, I don't even know what you have in mind. Do you actually have a plan?" he said, this time becoming angry himself and letting it show.

"We'll talk when you get here, Cos. Welcome back to Chicago." She pressed the off button and immediately dialed Fred McMurphy.

"Fred? Susan here. Only Cos came back. He's obviously protecting the others. He didn't even tell them he was coming, I'm sure. Have your team bring him over. I was also thinking about the five soldiers that you gave to the Bishop for safe keeping. Can you find out if they will help us? You can tell them that it is a chance to return to their former life? We don't have a lot of time left, I'm afraid, so you need to hurry."

After she hung up, the simple facts hit, making her want to run away, hiding from the pressure, perhaps finding a lover to be with. Being responsible for saving the entire world was too big a job for her. She was just a simple scientist who wanted to discover subatomic particles, someday retiring to Wisconsin to raise her dogs. She tried to make coffee and filled the machine as she had done thousands of times. Her hand was shaking and her concentration was inadequate to complete the task. It was fear, she realized, a surge of epinephrine from her adrenal gland, a simple panic attack, nothing more. She sat down and tried to breathe deeply, slowly, rhythmically and think. Think, Susan. Think what you are going to tell him in a half hour when he gets here. Think about the precision timing needed for this operation. Stay calm and think it out. It didn't work. The old adrenal kept pumping out its simple solution to fear; excitement, blood pressure and heart rate increase, dilation of the pupils, and, oh yes, diarrhea. She ran toward the toilet to empty both ends nearly at once.

"Susan!" Cos called out as he started down the long metal stairs into the tunnel. The Swat Team waited outside for additional instructions, and he had decided to enter alone. He reached the bottom and looked both ways in the dark but familiar tunnel. The place was dead quiet. He remembered where her office was located, and he started toward it in a jog, still wearing his custom Italian suit and shoes. Just as he rounded the last corner, he almost ran into her as she came out of the women's toilet area.

"Oh!" she startled and backed up, her hand in a defensive position. Her eyes widened, and she rushed toward him and enveloped him in a big hug. "Cosimo! I have never been so glad to see anyone." Cos didn't return her hug but stood there motionless, waiting for her to regain her usual diffident manner.

"Wow, Susan. I didn't expect that kind of greeting. Has the little electrons you live with finally cooked something in there," he tapped on her forehead playfully.

"I hope you didn't get the wrong idea, Cosimo, but I have not nearly been getting enough sleep since you left, trying to solve our problem. Looking at you, you were doing very well in Rome."

"Just kidding, Susan. Glad to see you also. If it wasn't for you, I would still be back in the dirt of Judea with a sword in my hand."

"And that is what we have to discuss. We won't go into the reasons you chose to deceive everybody by not including Mary and Antonius. There isn't much time left, and you of all people know we can't change what has already happened."

"Before we start, Susan. Is it possible to get something to eat around here?"

"Really no, but I have an idea. Are the Swat Team people still up there?"

"I think that they were waiting on instructions so I assume that they are."

Susan found a wall phone nearby and dialed Fred again. "On your way?" she asked. "Could you send one of your boys waiting upstairs for some food? Thanks." She hung up with a slight smile. She could just see the fast food restaurant when the Swat Team rolled in.

"Fred McMurphy and your food will arrive shortly. Let's go to my office and talk, Cos. There is a lot to go over. She took his arm and led the way down the long corridor, finally arriving into the brightly lit room. Cos sat down across from her and crossed his legs, leaning back in the chair, one arm casually draped over the back.

"I never realized how handsome you are, Cos. It just struck me."

"It's the clothes, Susan. Clothes make the man, remember?"

"Too bad Ray couldn't see you. I think he would be proud."

"Why can't he. Isn't he coming also?"

"No. The fanatics figured out a way to board the ferry The Commission was using as their headquarters while it was on Lake Michigan. They killed everyone on board including Ray, Gargan and their entire staff."

"When did that happen?" Cos said, a frown appearing on his brow.

"I think it was the last day Jesus was in Chicago, before he flew to Rome. A going away present, if you will."

"Didn't we hear that Tony was on that boat?" Cos asked.

"Got him too. That only leaves you, Mary and me. We are the only ones left for his revenge. The Government protects this place with the National Guard, but I have to leave someday. They will get me then, I'm sure."

"How are you running this place without Ray's money?"

"Two more Portal openings. That's all we get, then the money is gone. There is also a time element. The money is allotted by the month, and we are nearing the end of the month."

Footsteps and voices were coming toward them from somewhere deep in the sleeping building. Cos tensed and got up, waiting for his worse fear to appear in the doorway.

"Here, give me the food and go back upstairs. You guys wait there until I come out. No one comes in. Got it?" The man answered, somewhat sarcastically, that he got it, his footsteps receding down the echoing hall. McMurphy rounded the corner carrying a large white paper sack.

"Well, hello, Cosimo! I have been waiting to say that! Back from the Eternal City I see. Doesn't look so eternal at the moment. Both sides are tearing the place apart." He handed a grateful Cos the bag of food and watched as he pawed inside for a hot sandwich. They all sat down together on the long couch in the corner.

"What about what I asked you concerning the other men?" Susan asked, looking at McMurphy.

He sighed. "Talked to the Bishop just before I got here. He said that two had lady friends, two had jobs that had something to do with horses and one has decided to become a priest. They are here to stay, Susan. Sorry."

"Enough of all this mystery," Cos said with his mouth full. "Get on with it. It's time to tell me."

"Indeed it is, Cosimo," Susan said. "You are not going to like what I am about to ask of you."

"Perhaps I have guessed it. I had a strange vision when we were back in Judea. They said that I disappeared for a couple of hours. I don't remember all of it, but I do remember seeing Mary and Antonius clearly. They had returned to the future and were happy. I recently witnessed the same moment, exactly like I saw it in my vision. It was a memory of the future. There was another part that I only figured out two days ago. I saw a monster coming at me. An inhuman monster with a wolf's face, a crazed wild wolf out of a nightmare. He was coming for me, and I kept hearing his scream in my head. I think that it is Jesus that I see, and I expect that I will meet him soon. It was not a vision but a glimpse into the future. That's what I assume you want of me, and that is why Mary and Antonius have no part of it."

"What we will ask is too big for one man alone," Susan said.

"No more discussion, Susan. Tell me your plan right now," Cos said, putting his half-eaten sandwich back in the bag.

Susan cleared her throat and looked at him, trying to organize her thoughts. "When you were sent back in time, the scheme was to alter the past and therefore the future. Correct?

"We were selected so that Tony could murder Jesus Christ; yes, that was the plan."

"Do you have an opinion that anything you did while you were there altered our present?"

"We all talked about it constantly. None of us seems to have made any difference other than enabling the Antichrist to come through the Portal. We, at least I, killed several people. I don't know that it made any detectable difference. My opinion is that the past cannot be altered, whatever you do is already history."

"I hope you are wrong, Cos, because the future of our world is at stake. You have seen the creature that calls himself Jesus. Do you believe that he can be stopped?"

"I saw Tony shoot at him, right at him, and nothing happened. That's one problem, but the other is his followers. Killing him would make him a martyr, make his so-called subjects wild with anger. It would likely make no difference."

"That's what I thought. There is only one solution, Cos. We have to prevent him from coming into the future by going back in time again. Keep him away from the Portal until it closes."

Cos thought about it, looking up at the acoustical tiles above them. "You are proposing to open another Portal, but back in time to just before he came through. That way, you can prevent what is happening right now. Is that it?"

"More or less. The opening will not be in the same exact spot. That was always the problem we had. Each time the parameters of the Tevatron are changed, we get unpredictable results. We have to create an opening which is very close and occurs at a precise moment."

"Well," Cos asked, "can it be done?"

"That's why I called you back. I think I've done it. But when we open a Portal to before the creature came in, we take the chance that he is right there, ready to come in. It frightens me. You may as well know the whole truth. I don't know exactly where the new Portal is opening. Someone has to go in and see if it actually is close to the old one. Only you three would be able to find the location of the original Portal opening. You understand the risks, don't you?"

"I think I see what you mean. Someone— me— has to go back in time, locate the original Portal, keep the monster from going through it and somehow make it back to the new Portal in order to return to this time? Is that what you mean?" Cos asked.

"Yes. It's what I planned."

"It won't work, Susan," he said. "I couldn't guard two Portal openings from him. You remember that you were there on that day he came through. How are you going to know to close the Portal? How are we going to go back in time to tell the earlier you to close it? And if it is closed, how do you prevent yourself from opening it on schedule twice a night waiting for me, Mary and Antonius to come back? The logic is crazy. If you prevent us from coming back, how am I here now to do what you are asking."

"I don't want to stop this discussion, folks, but I am totally lost. Actually, I feel dizzy thinking about it," McMurphy said, interrupting.

"Look, Susan, I realize that your solution is out of desperation to undo the damage you feel that you have done to the world. Remember our previous discussion. My feeling is that you can't change history. Changing the future history or actually the most recent history is exactly the same thing as changing ancient history. You can't undo the past. It won't work," Cos said.

"Cos, it simply has to work. It is the only solution possible," Susan said desperately.

"If I may," McMurphy said. "You two are far above my comprehension, but I have a thought, nevertheless. What if you are wrong, Cos. What if the people you killed or the other things you did back then weren't important enough to change the world. In other words, perhaps you can change the past if you change the right things. Perhaps there are unimportant things which happen all the time which are not events which change history. Take out Adolph Hitler…big change. Take out some private in the German Army of the time…no change. He was going to be killed anyhow. He wasn't important. At least, that is my contribution to the subject."

Cos spoke first, "He might have a point, Susan. You can take bricks out of an arch and as long as they aren't the keystone, it will still stand. Perhaps we did change things, but we can't see enough detail of the past to notice them. Assuming I try this for you, my other points still apply. If I kill Jesus, then he won't come though any opening. If he kills me, he is coming in and you won't be able to stop him."

"I can't think this out, Cos. There are too many unknowns, too many ways this can go wrong," Susan said, then got up and started pacing, trying to reason it out.

"Let me suggest something, Susan," Cos said. "I will go in through your new Portal and locate where the first one is to open. I can find it, because I found it twice before. If your new location isn't very far away, that is. I have to calculate how much time it will take me to get there. When I go in the second time, you need to close the Portal behind me as soon as I am in to prevent the monster from using it. I'll have to get back in the original Portal and tell the old you to close it."

"That messes with what happened. You and Mary and Antonius came in later. How are we to prevent the monster from coming in with you then?" Susan asked.

"The problem is like a Mobius strip, an endless loop. The problem is impossible to solve. I don't know what is going to happen," Cos admitted.

McMurphy spoke again, "One question, Susan, and a very important one. When you opened the Portal on the day the monster came through, how long was it open before he appeared? How many minutes or seconds?"

"The opening into the past is only open for five minutes at a time. I remember that it was open for a while before Tony came in. He was followed by Jesus, and I closed it right after that. I don't know the exact time that happened. I think three minutes went by after I opened it, perhaps less."

"In other words, we don't know how much time we have," Cos said.

"Not exactly," Susan admitted.

"To sum it up," Cos said, ticking off his points on his fingers, "we have to first be sure that your new opening is close enough to get there in under two or three minutes," he held one finger up. "Next, we have to take the chance that Jesus is not waiting for us out there," he unfolded another finger. "Third, we have to quickly close the new Portal behind me," another finger went up. "Last, we have to somehow close the original Portal before he goes in." Susan and Fred shook their heads in agreement. "Plus," Cos continued, "we are not sure that we can even change the past, or if we change it, what will happen."

"Susan is sure that it is our only chance to prevent world destruction, Cos. I can't think of any other solution, can you?"

"No. And I have known for a long time that I would eventually have to face a monster. I agree we have to try. My life, the lives of any of us are unimportant. Our loss won't change the world."

"Does this mean that you are willing?" Susan asked.

"I am, because we have no choice. Can you open the Portal where you want and at any specific time now?"

"We have fixed on the where. That can't be changed without extensive testing. The time can vary."

"So we can open it, say…before any of us went in or even after we came back?" Cos asked.

"Yes, I'm sure we can," she said.

"If you will find the clothing and armor I was wearing when we came in, I'm ready right now to go in and look around." Cos said.

"They are still in a pile where you left them. Are you really ready right now?" She said, part of her hoping that he would say no.

Cosimus stood at attention, his helmet and breast plate in place, his gladius on his side. He waited patiently while Susan typed her instructions into the system. In a brief moment, the familiar hum started, growing louder by the second, followed by deep clanking echoing through the tunnels, a sound that always reminded Cos of an old movie showing King Kong banging on the huge gate keeping him enclosed.

"Soon," Susan shouted, pointing to the expected location of the Portal. Cos had designated the time for the Portal to open to just after they had returned from the past. He should be able to easily find their camp, because the campfire should still be burning, and there would be no Jesus or Tony to worry about.

"Now!" she said, and the oval popped open, pitch black and hovering just off the floor.

"You sure about the time and location?" he asked.

"Pretty sure," she answered.

"You have a time limit for this opening?" Cos asked.

"Five minutes. Just five minutes, and we only have enough money for one more opening so make the best of it."

"Good luck, son," McMurphy said and slapped him on his back.

Cos took a deep breath, bent down, stepping back into the first century. One of the flashlights he carried was placed near the opening on a high rock, lighting the spot to which he had to return shortly. He look carefully around, but recognized no landmarks, his pulse rising as time ticked away. After clambering onto a nearby rock, nervously scanning the surrounding terrain, he saw it. A soft glow emitted between two ancient rocks… a fire lowly burning. With one last look at his marker and then his watch, he started toward the fire. After a few paces, it was clear that this place was their abandoned Roman camp. The tents were still up and the iron pot over the fire still simmered on its hanger. He entered the clearing, trying to remember the orientation and location of the original Portal. It came back to him suddenly, finding it only a few feet from where he stood. He discovered his own footprints intermingled with Mary's and the others who had entered the Portal earlier this same night. In some ways, it seemed like a long time had passed, but it was actually only minutes ago that they all had left. He took off his helmet and listened, detecting the sound of galloping horses receding in the distance. What was left of their cavalry were still fleeing, taking all the horses with them. He looked at his watch and started pacing toward the new Portal, counting the steps. Arriving back at the spot where the flashlight beaconed from the sentinel rock, he had a last look around and realized that he missed the life that they had here. He loved being part of the Roman army, and he missed the adventure of it all. Antonius was right when he said that all a man should want in life was the love of a woman and a small piece of land to live on, but he was only talking about himself at the time. Not for Cos.

Susan watched nervously as Cos entered, helmet first, back into the twenty-first century. He was smiling, his demeanor more relaxed. "I'm back, and you are right on target. No more than twenty yards between the openings. It will only take one minute to cross the distance."

Chapter 37

The Demon Awaits

on't you think you should at least discuss it with Mary and Antonius before you take this task on by yourself?" Susan asked as he took off his armor. "If they leave Rome soon, there is still time for them to come back."

"No. I want them to marry, have children and be happy. Their lives are precious to me, mine isn't," Cos said.

"But what if you fail because you are too stubborn to ask for help?"

"I alone will face this demon Jesus, Susan. I have seen it happen over and over in my glimpse of the future."

"What happens? Do you see that too?"

"No, I don't know what is to happen, but I can guess."

Susan waited for the rest, unable to bring herself to ask him to describe his own death. Instead, she put her head on his chest and wrapped her arms around him. "Why does this horrible thing have to happen to you? You left the first time still a joyous boy, and now you have the weight of the world on your shoulders. You act as though you have no longer even a wish for happiness."

"Susan, listen carefully to me, and I'll try to explain it. One afternoon when we were back in time, I disappeared. The whole camp searched for me, and I simply wasn't there. During that time, I know that I was in the future, and I saw things which had not yet happened. It has been a long-held theory that you can't exist in two places at the same time. I think that I died in that future, then reappeared in camp and was found by Antonius. The events have been in my head since, and now it is apparent that I will die soon, probably at the hands of the monster who awaits me on the other side of the Portal. I have been half-dead since I was found, living in a short loop of history from which there is no escape. Being already dead has its advantages. You live for the moment, knowing the future doesn't exist. All the things you thought you wanted, you will never have, and you realize that you don't need them anyway. I finally understood that the only thing I ever wanted was right there in front of me and would never be mine, even if I were to live forever."

"Mary?" Susan asked.

"Yes. Mary is the one. I've known since we were introduced in Ray's office, but what I want most is for her to be happy, and she is. That's why I cannot put her or the one she loves at risk, she means too much to me. Neither one of them would let me do this alone if they knew. I didn't tell them, and I don't want you to. Please, Susan."

"I understand, Cos. What pulls at me is the sacrifice of your life carrying out a plan which may prove futile."

"If there is even a remote chance that I can stop Jesus from entering the future, then many lives will be saved. What's one life compared to that?"

Susan felt uneasy, unsettled. Something about the plan was flawed. She searched her mind looking for the thing that troubled her, going over and over what was about to happen. What would she have done if Cos came unexpectedly through the Portal screaming at her to shut it down? Would she have reacted swiftly, or would she have hesitated long enough to let Jesus in? She tried over and over to recreate her feelings of surprise, of doubt, of hesitancy about locking the others out. Assuming that she would have shut the machine down in time, what about the next opening? Would she not stay on the schedule, opening the Portal twice a day until the group came back? Jesus would eventually come in, she realized. She had to figure out some way to let herself know what to do. How could she go back and change the past?

Footsteps coming down the long tunnel made her stop thinking for a moment and turn her head toward the sounds. It was Fred returning after an excused absence while Cos entered the Portal.

"How did it go?" he asked, looking back and forth between them.

"He found the location. One minute away from the new opening. We are right on target," Susan said.

Fred glanced at Cos who seemed to be far away, lost in his own thoughts. "Are you okay, kid?" Fred asked. Cos nodded his head without looking at him. "Think you can pull this off?" he asked. Cos shrugged without answering.

Susan's thoughts suddenly became clear. Recalling Cos' theory that a person cannot be two places at the same time, she had a vision of herself entering the portal from the past into the present. Already knowing what to do because she remembered both the past and the future, she would shut the machine down quickly. She had to go back with him, it was the only way, and the thought gripped her with the most intense fear she had ever experienced. The demon was waiting on the other side for both of them. Looking at Cos differently now, she saw him more as a partner. He didn't know it, but they were going to go back together, back in time to rescue the world, and if it worked, or even if it didn't work, no one would ever know that it happened at all.

Fred McMurphy cleared his throat in a signal that he had something to say, something difficult and unpleasant. Susan and Cos looked and waited for him to continue.

"I made a telephone call while you completed your test."

"Don't tell me that, McMurphy," Cos said threateningly. "Don't tell me that you called Rome."

"Yes, Cos. Someone had to. They had to know what you were doing. You three were partners once, and as far as they are concerned, you still are. I needed to have their input, because they are the only ones other than you who might know what to do."

"Damn you, McMurphy!" Cos shouted. "I should drag your fat ass in there with me when I go. You deserve what would happen to you."

Susan raised her hands calmly and moved in between them. "What did you tell them, Fred?"

"I told them that Cos was determined to go back and face Jesus by himself. That you were testing it right then and would soon be ready, that the other Roman men refused to go back."

"What did they say?" Susan prodded.

Fred looked at Cos nervously, fearing a physical reprisal from him. "They were very upset and surprised, even hurt. Mary started crying, but Antonius was very calm and deliberate. They want you to wait until they get here, Cos. I told them that you would call when you came back from the test. They are waiting for you."

Cos paced ever faster, back and forth, muttering to himself. He couldn't face them again, the goodbyes had already been said, and there wasn't any reason to have remorse added to the fear building in him. He was prepared to go through now, as much as he was able to be, and he couldn't wait much longer lest Mary and Antonius try to return from Rome. The one thing he would not do was to allow either of them to go back in time again.

"No. I will not call them, and I will not wait for them to come from Rome. We need to do this thing, and waiting just allows more people to die in the struggle going on in Rome right now," Cos said, glaring at the Captain.

"Come with me, Fred. I need to teach you something," Susan said and tugged at his sleeve, pulling him away from the angry Cos. "I want to instruct you how to shut the machine down in case I can't. You will do this for me, won't you?" she said trying to get his attention.

"Sure, Susan. Anything I can do to help," Fred said. She led him to the computer terminal she used to start and stop the Tevatron.

"It's simple, Fred. Once the parameters are set and the machine is running, the display shows a red, rectangular button near the lower right corner which says 'Abort?' I can't show it to you now because it is already off, but when the program runs again, I'll point it out. All you have to do is move the mouse over that box and click. Another box will appear and ask 'Are You Sure? Y/N' Click the 'y' key, and the machine will shut down. Got it?"

"I think so. But why would you not be here to shut it down?" he asked. She could see Cosimo listening and watching them.

"We don't know what is about to happen, Fred. Call it contingency plans, but I want to make sure you will do this for me." She left Fred studying the terminal and approached Cos who looked sullen and angry. "I don't blame you for feeling the way you do, Cos. He meant well, but didn't know what all is going on. We can't let them just stand by waiting for you to call, can we?" Cos didn't answer, his face dark with anger, fear and regret. "If you permit me, Cos. I will call them and try to explain." He didn't respond and started to pace again, lost in thought.

Hotel de Russie, Rome

At the first ring, Mary snatched up the phone, "Cos? It that you Cos?" she asked.

"No, Mary. This is Susan Harmes. Cos is standing just down the hall from here."

"Captain McMurphy called and said that you are opening the Portal again and that Cos is going back alone. Was that right?"

"It's what he wants. He doesn't want to put either of you in harm's way."

"He can't do this alone, Susan. Don't you understand what he is about to face?"

"I don't, Mary, but he does. He knows that he is going to die. He is resigned to it. If he were here to talk to you, he would tell you that he doesn't want either of you to die with him."

"Can you hold this up until we get there, Susan? We might be able to persuade him, if we can talk face to face."

"No, dear. He wants to get it over with, and he won't discuss it. Believe me when I tell you that this is his final gift of love for both of you, but he could never say that to you himself. There is one thing that I can do, if you have the courage. I can set up a video link from the computer terminal. You can watch as he goes in, your last chance to see him, but be warned, it will be very painful for you to witness it."

"Please, Susan, set it up. Perhaps we can still talk him out of it," Mary said.

"I'm sorry. There will be no audio link. You can watch, but he won't be able to hear your voices. I have to go and get ready, kids. Be brave, be hopeful, and most of all, be thankful that you have had the privilege to know a brave man called Cosimo."

Mary and Antonius hurried downstairs to the business room where computer terminals were arrayed in little cubicles for the use of the hotel guests. Mary quickly typed in the link she just received by email, and the scene flicked on showing in black and white the area by now so familiar, the location of the Portal in the Tevatron tunnel. They caught glimpses of Captain McMurphy and Susan moving back and forth, busy in preparation. An occasional movement in the corner of the screen caught their eyes as they strained to see around the limits of the camera lens. Cos must be in the room, but just out of their vision.

"Are you sure you want to see this?" Antonius asked. "Wouldn't it be better to remember him as you last saw him, the dashing, handsome man who attracted every woman who had the misfortune to look his way?"

"I couldn't live with myself if I abandoned him now, could you?" she responded.

"No, Mary, I can't either. You know that I want to go in with him. My sword might make the difference."

"Hold me tight, Antonius. I am shaking with fear, even at this distance." He did. He held her against him, head to head, merging into one being with four eyes, all riveted to the low resolution image being sent from outside Chicago. Cos walked into the center of the screen, pulling on his chain mail armor. He didn't seem to be aware that anyone was watching, especially the two he loved the most. They felt like shouting at him, pounding on the screen to get his attention, but instead, just sat there holding on to each other. Cos methodically put on his breast plate and then his gladius which was given him by Antonius two thousand years ago. They watched as he pulled the sword from its scabbard, testing its sharpness with his thumb. When he seemed ready, he stiffened, sword still held in his right hand and nodded to Susan to begin. Susan whispered in Fred's ear, obviously not wanting Cos to hear what she said. Fred nodded that he understood, and they walked toward the terminal together, and for a moment, the screen was filled with a blurry close up of their chests as they stood in front of the camera. Several seconds went by, and then Susan moved away, pointing to an area on the floor. She quickly pulled off her lab coat and threw it aside, looking back at the camera, knowing that Mary and Antonius were watching but not understanding what was about to happen, when a black oval popped into view and hung just off the concrete floor. The window to the past was open, making Mary take a deep breath, her hands in front of her mouth in anguish of what they were about to witness. Cos wasted no time, putting one leg into the past, then hesitating for one last look back at the terminal and at Mary and Antonius. He did know they were watching. He raised his sword as he had been taught so long ago. A salute from a warrior. One last act of defiance and bravery before the contest begins. He disappeared back in time, the last bit of his shoe swallowed up by the black hole. Susan rushed to the opening and pointed her finger at Fred, mouthing a last order. She turned and went into the hole behind Cos, and in a moment, the oval flickered out. As they looked on, the link to the past was severed forever. They continued to stare at the screen, hoping that somehow the opening would reappear letting them return. All they saw was Fred walking back and forth, looking down, his hands behind him. The link ended, and the screen went dark.

South of Nazareth, The Portal Area, 27 AD

Cos heard a noise and spun around, his sword held high, ready to strike at anything moving. "What in the hell?" he said quietly, realizing that Susan had followed him in. The Portal had vanished behind her, now the only way back was the old Portal, soon to open. He waved for her to follow him, and his finger to his lips indicated that she was to be quiet about it. They crept stealthily, moving quickly in a straight line toward a destination only known to Cos. She looked around, fearful of what she might see coming their way, but the place seemed to be devoid of other life. They went over rock after rock, hunched down, looking in all directions. Cos stood looking at his watch, holding up his fingers counting down the seconds. He pointed to an area by a large rock, and Susan understood that he meant to show her where the Portal would open.

A deep guttural sound, panting, huffing, was coming toward them, accompanied by faint footsteps from someone running. Then there was the sound that they had been fearing, close and closing. A growl from a large predator, angry, hunting and close. He was coming. The demon was at hand. Cos stepped up on a larger rock facing the direction of the sounds. He was no longer afraid, and the hand that held the sword was steady and strong. He seemed to spot the source of the noise and turned to say something to Susan, just as the Portal opened. "Get in there, and shut it down!" he screamed, then bolted forward to meet whatever was coming at him. Susan dived into the hole just as the screaming behind her started intensifying, flooding her brain with fear. She heard Cos bellow in defiance one last time as she made it to the terminal, turning the Portal off with a click of the mouse. The room went silent. The link to the past existing only as a memory as she sagged to the floor, exhausted and in tears.

Where are we going, Mama?" he asked, looking up at her. He couldn't tug on her clothing as he usually did, because both hands were occupied, one held by his father and one by her. They would occasionally pick him up, dangling his feet as they passed over a curb.

"You'll see. Not much farther," she said.

"At least you could tell me where we are going Mary," Antonius complained.

"A surprise," she said, wrinkling her eyes with a partial smile. She knew something that she was keeping to herself. He would just have to wait. She wanted to see his face when they got there.

"Papa?" the boy asked, twisting to keep his eye on the billboard.

"Yes?" Antonius answered.

"It's you, Papa!" he said, pointing to the picture of a man curling his biceps and smiling at the viewer. The poster was ten feet tall and advertised a line of equipment dedicated to fitness.

"That's your dad, all right," Mary said and patted him on the head. "See any more pictures of your dad?"

The boy looked around, silently studying their surroundings. The street they traveled was one of Rome's widest and busiest, *Via del Teatro Marcello.* The boy waited, watching for what he knew he would find.

"There! Papa!" he shouted in joy as a bus went past, and he continued to point at the well-dressed man on the advertisement, this time outfitted in a tuxedo, his polished shoe poised just so on a chair.

"Yes, that's me, son," Antonius said. "I'm proud of how quick you are, Cosimo. Papa is very proud of his son."

"I'm proud of both of you," Mary said. Occasionally, a passing horn sounded, and Antonius acknowledged the wave and excited shout of his name.

"It does get old, doesn't it?" he asked Mary, worried that she was bothered by his fame.

"I like it. I especially like the money that goes with all that celebrity. It does remind me of someone though."

"You mean Cos, don't you?" he asked.

"Sure. He got all this started for you, and he knew what was going to happen. In my book, he gets a lot of credit," she said.

"Oh, and in mine also. Do you ever think about him?" Antonius asked.

"Just after we lost him, nearly every day, in fact, several times a day. Now, not as often. You?"

"The same. He comes back to me at odd times, like when I see a picture of an ancient Roman soldier with a sword. I've pictured him using his sword on the evil Jesus so many times I sometimes think I actually saw it happen. Other times it's just another well-appointed Italian gentleman in an expensive, fitted suit that I'm sure is him. My, he looked good in a suit."

"I've been thinking a lot about him more recently. I had a dream one night that I remembered when I awaked. In the dream, it struck me that the past is not really past. I went back and found you, and it was just like being here. And you! You went from being dead for two thousand years to being here with me and our son. Plus, just about everybody in Italy knows your name and face. Too bad we can't ever tell them the truth," she laughed at the thought.

"Careful," he said pointing down at the curly headed boy between them.

Mary laughed again, "Maybe he'll know someday! He has a right, you know."

"If Cos would have lived, we could dream about going back and finding him someday. We would have to be sure that he wasn't younger that us. I wouldn't want to compete for you with a Cos younger than me."

She reached over and playful slapped his shoulder. "Not to worry. I got you, and I'm keeping you. No younger men for me."

"Can't you tell me where we are going?" Antonius pleaded.

"Just ahead. Be patient, your son is."

Antonius looked around and squinted ahead of them. "Don't tell me we are headed to the museum again," he groaned. "You know it depresses me to see ancient Roman anything. Do we have to do this again?"

"This is the last time. I promise. There is something new on display that I heard about, and I am sure you will want to see it." Ahead, as they got closer, the *Musei Capitolini* rose above them. Antonius let out a big sigh, but he knew when his beautiful wife had her mind set on something, he had little choice except to humor her. They walked in the entrance together, then Antonius picked little Cosimo up to keep him away from mischief. They wandered slowly through the exhibits as Mary sought what she wanted. "Down this way, boys," she commanded, leading them toward an exhibit of bronze statues. She went down the line, studying the signs and the faces of the ancients, finally stopping, looking up at one and smiling. Antonius strolled slowly up beside her while talking to Cosimo about a dish of gelato at the museum bar.

"Is this what you wanted me to see?" he asked, stopping beside her.

"Yes, this is my surprise."

Antonius looked at the casting casually. It was the typical bronze of a Roman warrior with sword, shield and armor. The Roman artists were always careful to make very lifelike copies of their subjects. This one was no exception. It was as though a living man was coated in bronze, the eyes stared defiantly out at at any adversary unlucky enough to be in his way. Antonius had a sudden feeling that this bronze man was familiar. He had seen that face before. He looked down at the name set in a rectangular depression and cast in Roman letters, Cosimus Fabius Persicus. On the second line was one word, *Legatus*.

"Cosimus!" Antonius said. "It's Cosimus! He didn't die after all! Look, he even became a Legate." Antonius stood back, taking it in, wiping his face with his sleeve.

"Who is that Mama? Why is Papa crying?" Cosimo asked.

"That man," Mary said, "was your uncle. He was your father's brother, and he was my friend, my very best friend."

The End